Texas John Slaughter

THE EDGE OF HELL

Look for these exciting Western series from bestselling authors

WILLIAM W. JOHNSTONE
and **J. A. JOHNSTONE**

The Mountain Man

Preacher: The First Mountain Man

Luke Jensen, Bounty Hunter

Those Jensen Boys!

The Jensen Brand

MacCallister

Flintlock

Perley Gates

The Kerrigans: A Texas Dynasty

Sixkiller, U.S. Marshal

Texas John Slaughter

Will Tanner, U.S. Deputy Marshal

The Frontiersman

Savage Texas

The Trail West

The Chuckwagon Trail

Rattlesnake Wells, Wyoming

AVAILABLE FROM PINNACLE BOOKS

Texas John Slaughter
THE EDGE OF HELL

William W. Johnstone
with J. A. Johnstone

PINNACLE BOOKS
Kensington Publishing Corp.
www.kensingtonbooks.com

PINNACLE BOOKS are published by

Kensington Publishing Corp.
119 West 40th Street
New York, NY 10018

PUBLISHER'S NOTE
Following the death of William W. Johnstone, the Johnstone family is working with a carefully selected writer to organize and complete Mr. Johnstone's outlines and many unfinished manuscripts to create additional novels in all of his series like The Last Gunfighter, Mountain Man, and Eagles, among others. This novel was inspired by Mr. Johnstone's superb storytelling.

ISBN-13: 978-0-7860-4280-7
ISBN-10: 0-7860-4280-X

First printing: October 2014

10 9 8 7 6 5 4 3

Printed in the United States of America

First electronic edition: August 2018

ISBN-13: 978-0-7860-3371-3
ISBN-10: 0-7860-3371-1

AUTHORS' NOTE

This novel is loosely based on the life and times of legendary Old West lawman, rancher, and gambler John Horton "Texas John" Slaughter. The plot is entirely fictional and is not intended to represent actual historical events. The actions, thoughts, and dialogue of the historical characters featured in this story are fictional as well and not meant to reflect their actual personalities and behavior, although the authors have attempted to maintain a reasonable degree of accuracy.

In other words, none of what you're about to read really happened . . . but it could have.

Chapter 1

Exuberant shouts filled the air as a blaze-faced black stallion with four white stockings bucked and sunfished like mad in a desperate attempt to unseat the rider perched perilously on his back.

People crowded around the corral to watch the spectacle inside the fence. Most were men, but the group included several women as well.

The sweating rider had lost his hat, revealing that he was a young, fair-haired cowboy. He clung desperately to the horse's back as the animal pitched back and forth, leaped up and down, and switched ends with blinding speed.

It was just a matter of time, John Slaughter thought, before his brother-in-law Stonewall wound up on his butt in the dust.

The man standing beside Slaughter nudged him with an elbow, grinned, and said, "Your young man is quite good. But Santiago's *El Halcón* will emerge triumphant in the end. You will see."

Slaughter—Texas John, some called him, since he

hailed from the Lone Star State—figured his guest was right, but he was stubborn enough to say, "Oh, I don't know. I wouldn't count Stonewall out—"

Before Slaughter could continue, Stonewall lost his grip and sailed off the horse's back. He let out a yell as he flew through the air, a shout that was cut short as he crashed down on his back.

Another young man had started to scramble up the corral fence as soon as Stonewall left the saddle. When he reached the top, he vaulted over and landed lithely inside the enclosure. He was in his middle twenties, a little older than Stonewall, with olive skin and sleek hair as dark as a raven's wing. He ran toward the still-bucking horse and called, "*El Halcón!*"

The horse responded instantly to the name, which was Spanish for "The Hawk." He stood still except for a slight quivering in his muscles that was visible under the shiny black hide. His nostrils flared in anger.

Santiago Rubriz walked up to the horse and caught the reins. He swung easily into the saddle and began walking the horse around the inside of the corral. The transformation was astounding. *El Halcón* now appeared gentle enough for a child to ride.

"A one-*hombre* horse, eh?" Don Eduardo Rubriz, Santiago's father, said to Slaughter.

"Not much doubt about that," Slaughter agreed.

On his other side, his wife Viola looked anxiously between the fence boards and asked, "Is Stonewall all right?"

Stonewall Jackson Howell, who was Viola Slaughter's younger brother, still lay on his back, unmoving. Slaughter felt a moment of apprehension. Stonewall had landed pretty hard. He might have broken something. Maybe even his head.

But then Stonewall groaned, rolled onto his side and then on over to his belly, and pushed himself to hands and knees. He paused there for a few seconds and shook his head as if trying to clear it of cobwebs.

Then he staggered to his feet, looked around, spotted the grinning Santiago on *El Halcón*'s back, and said, "Son of a gun!"

That brought a laugh from the spectators, most of whom were either American cowboys or Mexican *vaqueros* who worked here on the Slaughter Ranch in southeastern Arizona's San Bernardino Valley. The crew was divided about half and half in nationality and nearly all of them were fluent in both languages. That wasn't surprising, because the Mexican border was a mere two hundred yards south of this corral.

Santiago rode over to Stonewall and said, "You did very well, *amigo*. You stayed on him longer than I expected."

"That ain't a horse, it's a devil," Stonewall muttered. "Why don't you call him *El Diablo*?"

Santiago patted *El Halcón* and said, "Because when he runs at full speed, he seems to soar over the earth like a hawk riding the currents of the wind."

That statement made Stonewall's blue eyes narrow speculatively.

"Fast, is he? Well, I bet we got a horse or two around here that can match him—or beat him."

Santiago arched a black eyebrow.

"Are you proposing a race, my friend . . . and a wager?"

Stonewall had waltzed right into that trap, thought Slaughter. He considered warning his brother-in-law, then decided against it. Stonewall was a grown man, a top hand here on the ranch, and one of Sheriff John Slaughter's deputies when they were back in Tombstone. Let him make his own mistakes.

Stonewall picked up the hat he had lost when the horse started to buck, slapped it against his leg to knock some of the dust off it, and said, "You're dang right I'm talkin' about a race. As for a wager, we'll have to figure out the stakes."

"Very well," Santiago said. "We'll discuss it at the *fiesta* tonight, eh?"

"Sure," Stonewall agreed.

Viola turned away from the corral and said, "While my brother figures out some other way to make a fool of himself, why don't we all go back to the house? The sun's getting rather warm, and we can sit on the patio in the shade."

That sounded like a good idea to Slaughter. He linked arms with Viola and used his other hand to usher Don Eduardo and the don's American wife Belinda along the path that led beside a grove of cottonwood trees back to the sprawling ranch house.

The four of them made striking pairs. Both men were handsome, dignified, and considerably older than their beautiful young wives. There were contrasts, however. Slaughter was compactly built, below average height but muscular and possessed of a vitality that belied his years and the salt-and-pepper beard on his chin. Don Eduardo was taller, leaner, with a hawk-like face that was clean-shaven except for a thin mustache.

The two women were both lovely, but Belinda Rubriz was blond and blue-eyed while Viola Slaughter had dark hair and flashing dark eyes.

Their coloring wasn't the only difference. Belinda was from Boston, the daughter of a banker who had done business with the wealthy Don Eduardo, and had the pampered air of a young woman who had never done a day's work in her life.

Viola, on the other hand, was a cowgirl born and bred. She had been riding almost before she could walk, and she could handle a rifle better than a lot of men. Cool-nerved in the extreme, not much in life ever threw her for a loop—a quality that had come in very handy during times of trouble in the past.

John Slaughter loved her to the very depths of his soul and always would.

Like Viola, Belinda was a second wife. Don Eduardo's first wife, Santiago's mother, had been dead for many years. Slaughter had learned that during his correspondence with the Mexican rancher. Their letters had been concerned for the most part with the business arrangement they were making, but a few personal details had slipped in on both sides.

As Slaughter looked through the trees now, he saw grazing in the distance the concrete proof of their arrangement in the small herd of cattle Don Eduardo had brought up here from his *hacienda* ninety miles below the border.

Those cattle were some of the finest specimens Slaughter had ever seen, and he was paying a suitably pretty penny for them. He was eager to introduce the stock into his own herd and improve the bloodline.

Don Eduardo and his entourage, including his wife and son, had arrived with the cattle earlier today. Tonight, he and Slaughter would conclude their deal when Slaughter handed over the payment.

Then it would be time to celebrate. Slaughter had lived on the border long enough to adopt many of the Mexican customs, among them the idea that the chance for a party should never be wasted.

A white picket fence ran around the large compound that included the main ranch house, two bunkhouses, one with a kitchen attached where the meals for the crew were prepared, a chicken coop, and an ice house. An elevated water tank such as the ones found at water stops along the railroad stood to one side. Nearby, sparkling blue in the afternoon sunlight, was a water reservoir contained within a retaining wall built of rocks.

Here in southern Arizona, where summers were often hotter than the hinges of hell and moisture was a precious commodity, having plenty of water on hand was important. Luckily, the San Bernardino Valley got more rain than some areas and there were also artesian wells located on the ranch that helped keep the reservoir and the water tank filled.

In fact, the Slaughter Ranch was an oasis of sorts, and John Slaughter was justly proud of what he had built here. When his term as sheriff of Cochise County was up, he intended to hand the badge over to someone else and spend the rest of his days on this spread.

Viola led her husband and their guests to a flagstone patio at the side of the house. Tall cottonwoods cast cooling shade over the area. A servant came out a side door, and

Viola told her to bring a pitcher of lemonade and some glasses.

The two couples sat, and Belinda Rubriz said, "You have a lovely home, Mrs. Slaughter."

"Thank you," Viola said, gracious as always, adding with a smile, "You should call me Viola, though. We don't believe in a lot of formality around here."

"So, Señor Slaughter," Don Eduardo said, "is your brother-in-law correct? Do you have horses here on your ranch faster than *El Halcón*?"

"Well, I don't know," Slaughter said, letting a little of a Texas drawl creep into his voice. "I reckon Stonewall's right about how we can find out."

"And would *you* be interested in a small wager?"

Slaughter felt Viola's eyes on him. She knew that gambling was one of his weaknesses. Sometimes she tried to rein in that particular tendency.

Now, though, when he glanced at her, he saw her head move a fraction of an inch in an encouraging nod. She didn't believe in being reckless, but the honor of the Slaughter Ranch was at stake.

"Oh, I imagine we can work out something suitable," he said.

He and Don Eduardo both smiled in anticipation.

The servant came back with the cool, tart lemonade, which never tasted better than on a hot afternoon like this. When Slaughter's glass was full, he lifted it and said, "To good friends and good times."

"A most excellent toast," Don Eduardo said. "To good friends and good times."

The afternoon couldn't get much more pleasant, Slaughter mused as he swallowed some of the lemonade.

And that made a shiver go through him that had nothing to do with the temperature.

He was old enough to know that if a man ever let himself believe things couldn't get any better, that was when all hell was liable to break loose.

Chapter 2

In the foothills of the Chiricahua Mountains northwest of the Slaughter Ranch, a man lowered the spyglass through which he had been peering. His dark eyes gleamed in anticipation under the blue bandanna tied around his forehead to hold back the crudely cropped, shoulder-length black hair.

He was dressed in a blousy blue shirt, breechcloth, and high-topped boot moccasins. A strip of cloth dyed bright red was tied around his lean waist as a sash. He carried a knife tucked into that sash. A Winchester leaned against the rock by which he stood.

The man lifted his arm, pointed toward the southeast, and said in his native Apache, "There lies the ranch of the one called Slaughter. We will go there tonight and spill much blood."

The fifteen warriors to whom he spoke erupted in yips and shouts of excitement. Several of them lifted their rifles above their heads and pumped the weapons up and down.

A few yards away, a white man stood watching with

his hat tipped forward so that the brim shaded his face. Normally a white man who found himself in the company of sixteen bronco Apaches would be getting ready to fight or die. Probably both.

He'd be praying, too, either way, but this *hombre*'s lips didn't move except to curve into a sardonic smile.

"You're really gettin' 'em worked up, Bodaway," he said in English to the leader of the war party. The Apache had lived on a reservation and had even worked for a time as a scout for the cavalry, so he had no trouble speaking or understanding the white man's tongue.

"You know I am called *El Infierno*," the war chief said with a glare. "The Fires of Hell."

"Sure, sure," the white man said. "I'd forgotten how you *hombres* sometimes take Mex names."

Ned Becker hadn't forgotten at all. Calling *El Infierno* by the name he'd been given when he was born was Becker's way of reminding the Apache that they had known each other since they were boys.

Indians had long memories, sure enough, but sometimes if their blood got hot enough, they conveniently "forgot" that they had promised not to kill a fella. Especially a bloodthirsty bunch like these renegade Mescaleros.

Becker went on, "I know the ranch is too far away for you to see it from here, even with that telescope, but my scouts report that Don Eduardo is there with his herd of crossbreeds. They'll be celebratin' tonight, you can take my word for that."

"This man Slaughter is said to be a good fighter. He will have guards."

"Sure he will," Becker agreed. "But they'll be thinkin' about how they're missin' the barbecue and the wine and the dancin', and they won't be as alert as they ought to be. Your men should be able to slip past them."

Bodaway gave the white man a cold look.

"My warriors are like spirits in the night," he said. "No one will see them until they are ready to be seen."

Becker nodded and said, "Fine. You hold up your end of the deal and I'll hold up mine."

They understood each other. Indians liked to bargain. Becker knew that. That and his old friendship with the war chief had made him bold enough to ride into Bodaway's camp hidden in these rugged, isolated mountains when most men wouldn't have dared do such a thing.

Ned Becker wasn't most men, though, as those who had been unlucky enough to cross him had found out.

He was almost as dark as the Apaches, but black beard stubble covered his lantern jaw. His eyes under the pulled-down hat brim blazed with hatred. He kept those fires banked most of the time because he knew it was dangerous for a man to let his emotions get out of control.

But every now and then the flames inside him leaped up and threatened to consume him from the inside out if he didn't cut loose. When he did, somebody usually died.

Becker figured if anybody ought to be known as The Fires of Hell, it was him. He wasn't going to argue about it with Bodaway, though. The war chief was too useful to risk making him mad.

"Remember, hit 'em hard and fast," Becker went on. "That'll draw Slaughter's crew and Don Eduardo's men away from the herd. My men and I will take care of everything else."

Bodaway's lip curled slightly in disdain. To an Apache's way of thinking, stealing more cattle than you could eat was a waste of time and effort. For that matter, they would rather steal horses, since a warrior could ride a horse—and they preferred the taste of horse meat to beef.

"You will deliver the rifles?" he said to Becker.

"In two weeks or less," the outlaw promised. "Just as we agreed. Fifty brand-new Winchesters and a thousand rounds of ammunition for each."

Bodaway nodded in solemn satisfaction. Offering him money wouldn't have accomplished a damned thing, Becker knew. The Apaches didn't have any use for it.

But the lure of rifles had been more than the war chief could resist. Only a few of Bodaway's men were armed with Winchesters. Most of the others carried single-shot Springfields taken from dead cavalrymen. A couple even had muzzle-loading flintlocks that had been handed down for generations after being stolen from fur trappers farther north.

Most of the Apaches were on reservations now, but isolated bands of renegades still hid out in the mountains. It was Bodaway's dream to mold those groups into a band large enough to do some real damage to the cavalry and to the white settlements in the territory. With modern rifles to use as a lure, he might well succeed in bringing together all the bronco Apaches.

In the night, he probably thought about doing all the bloody things Cochise and Geronimo had never been able to accomplish. Becker knew what that was like.

He had a dream of his own.

His old friend Bodaway didn't know anything about that, and there was no reason to tell him. As long as Bodaway and his men did what Becker needed them to do, that was the only thing that mattered. If they did . . .

If they did, then Becker's long-sought vengeance would be right there in front of him where he could reach out and grasp it at last.

Evening settled down on the San Bernardino Valley, bringing some cooling breezes. Viola Slaughter loved this time of day. It gave her great peace and happiness to step out into the dusk and gaze up at the spectacular wash of red and gold and blue and purple in the sky as the sunset faded. Often she stood there drinking in the beauty of nature and listening to the faint sounds of the ranch's activities winding down for the day.

Today wasn't like that, however. The sunset was as gorgeous as ever, but the air was filled with the sound of preparations for the evening's festivities.

Servant girls chattered as they brought plates and silverware from the house and set them on the tables under the cottonwoods. Cowboys and *vaqueros* called to each other and laughed from the great spit where a beef was roasting over a crackling fire. Fiddlers and guitar players tuned their instruments for the dancing later. Children from the families of the ranch hands ran around playing and shouting. Among them were some Indian youngsters. The peaceful Indian families in the area knew they were always welcome when the Slaughters had a party. Everyone was welcome, in fact. That was just the way it was on the Slaughter Ranch.

Viola's husband came up behind her, slipped his arms around her waist, and nuzzled her thick dark hair.

"I say, you've done a fine job with this *fiesta*, as usual," John Slaughter told her.

Viola leaned back in the comfortable embrace of his arms and laughed.

"I haven't done much of anything, John, and you know it. The people who work for us deserve all the credit."

"Without your planning and supervision, there wouldn't even be a party," Slaughter said. "And *you* know *that*."

She turned to face him and asked, "What do you think of Don Eduardo?"

"A fine fellow. Very straightforward." Slaughter shrugged. "A bit arrogant, perhaps, but that's common with these grandees. It's the Spaniard in 'em, I suppose. Europeans have a weakness for the aristocracy."

"What about his wife?"

"Doña Belinda? She's all right, I suppose. We don't really have anything in common with her, what with her being from back east and all."

"Maybe that's why I'm not sure I like her," Viola said quietly.

"What?" Slaughter looked and sounded surprised. "I thought you liked everyone."

"Not everybody," Viola said, a little tartly now. "She's pleasant enough, I suppose, but I'm not sure I trust her."

"Well, luckily you don't have to," Slaughter pointed out. "Her husband seems trustworthy enough, and he's the one I'm doing business with." Slaughter stepped back, slipped his watch out of his vest pocket, and opened it to check the time. "In fact, I ought to get back inside. I'm supposed to meet Don Eduardo in my study and deliver the payment for those cows to him. Then we can get the *fandango* started."

"All right, go ahead," Viola said as she patted her husband's arm. "I'll see you when you're finished."

Slaughter nodded, put his watch away, and turned to stride back into the house with his usual vigor. He was not a man to do things in a lackadaisical manner, whether it was pursuing lawbreakers as sheriff, working with the hands here on the ranch, or making love to his beautiful young wife.

Viola checked with the servants to make sure the preparations were going as they were supposed to, then walked out to talk to the *vaqueros* and see that the meat would be ready. Assured that it would be, Viola started back toward the house.

Her route took her near the elevated water tank. She was surprised to see movement in the shadows underneath it. The area where the *fiesta* would be held was brightly lit by colorful lanterns hanging in the trees, but their glow didn't really reach this far. Twilight had deepened until the gloom was nearly impenetrable in places.

Viola had keen eyes, though, and she knew it was unlikely that any of the servants or the ranch hands would be around the water tank right now. She gave in to curiosity and walked in that direction, moving with her usual quiet grace.

As she came closer she heard the soft murmur of voices, but she didn't recognize them and couldn't make out any of the words. She started to call out and ask who was there, but she stopped before she said anything.

Her natural caution had asserted itself. If whoever was lurking under the water tank had some sort of mischief in mind, it might not be wise to let them know she was there.

Instead she stuck to the shadows herself and slipped closer, and then stopped as she began to be able to understand what the two people were saying.

They spoke in Spanish, the man with a fluency that indicated it was his native tongue. The woman's words were more halting as she tried to think of how to express what she wanted to say.

It was perfectly clear to Viola that they were lovers, and passionate ones at that. After a moment they both fell silent, and she assumed that was because they were kissing.

She had recognized the voices and understood the words as well. One of them belonged to Santiago Rubriz.

The woman was his stepmother, Doña Belinda.

Viola knew there had to be a reason she didn't like or trust the blonde from Boston, she thought as she stood there in the darkness, her face warm with embarrassment from the secret she had unwittingly uncovered.

Chapter 3

Before Don Eduardo came in, Slaughter had already worked the combination lock on the massive safe bolted to the floor in his study. All he had to do now was twist the handle and swing the heavy door open. He reached inside and pulled out a pair of leather saddlebags, grunting a little at their weight.

The saddlebags clinked meaningfully as Slaughter deposited them on the desk.

"Payment in gold, as we agreed, Don Eduardo," he said to his visitor. "Double eagles. Feel free to count them if you'd like."

Rubriz waved a hand dismissively. "I trust you, Señor Slaughter," he said. "I pride myself on being an excellent judge of character, and I have no doubt whatsoever that you are an honest man."

"I appreciate that," Slaughter said with a faint smile. "Unfortunately, not everyone I've dealt with in the past has felt that way."

"Then they were mistaken." Don Eduardo's shoulders rose and fell in an eloquent shrug. "Such things happen."

"Be that as it may, if you'd like to count the money, it won't offend me."

"And I say again, it will not be necessary. Besides—" Don Eduardo's eyes twinkled with good humor, but a glitter of steel lurked there as well, Slaughter noted. "If you were to try to cheat me, as the old saying goes, I know where you live, señor."

That brought a laugh from Slaughter, a laugh in which his visitor joined. Don Eduardo picked up the saddlebags, hefted them approvingly, and went on, "We may consider our arrangement concluded. Now that it is, if I might request a favor of you . . ."

"Of course," Slaughter said.

"If you would not mind keeping this locked up in your safe until we depart tomorrow, I would be in your debt."

"Certainly, if you'd prefer it that way," Slaughter said. He reached out and took the saddlebags from the don.

"It's not that I don't trust my people, or yours," Rubriz said as Slaughter locked the double eagles in the safe again. "But I wish to enjoy the evening's festivities without the slightest hint of worry in my mind."

"Can't blame you for that. It should be quite a shindig."

"I hope my wife enjoys it. Belinda has had a bit of trouble adjusting to our Western ways since coming to live at my *hacienda*. She finds us somewhat . . . uncivilized."

"Sorry to hear that," Slaughter muttered.

Don Eduardo waved an elegantly manicured hand. "I'm sure it is only a matter of time until she becomes accustomed to life on the ranch," he said. "But for now, I'm glad she has the friendship of such a fine lady as Señora Slaughter. That will make it easier for her to adjust."

Slaughter just nodded. He couldn't very well say

anything about what Viola had told him earlier. Anyway, he was certain that despite how his wife might feel about Doña Belinda, Viola would treat her with the utmost courtesy and kindness. To do otherwise would be to go against everything she believed about being a good hostess.

Slaughter came out from behind the desk and suggested, "Why don't we go and see how the preparations are coming along? I reckon it ought to be time pretty soon to get this *fandango* started."

"An excellent idea," Rubriz agreed. Together, the two men left the study.

Viola didn't want to move for fear of making a noise and giving away her presence. It was bad enough that she had stumbled upon this illicit rendezvous. She didn't want Doña Belinda and Santiago to know that she was aware of their affair.

After a few more moments that seemed longer to Viola than they really were as she waited in the shadows, Belinda and Santiago moved apart. Belinda murmured an endearment in Spanish and then added in a mixture of Spanish and English, "Later, *mi amor*. When your father is asleep, I will come to you."

"*Sí*," Santiago breathed. "I will count the seconds until then."

In the darkness, Viola rolled her eyes. All too often, young men in love sounded as if they were reading lines from a second-rate melodrama.

Santiago faded away quietly, disappearing into the warm, early evening gloom as he headed toward the house.

Viola expected Belinda to follow him—after a suitable interval, of course—but instead the woman stayed where she was in the shadows under the water tank. Viola began to get restless.

She jumped a little as Belinda said in a quiet but clear voice, "You can come out now. I know you're there."

Viola didn't budge. She hoped the other woman would decide that she had been mistaken.

Instead, Belinda said, "There's no need to pretend, Mrs. Slaughter."

That took Viola even more by surprise. She stepped forward and said, "How—"

"How did I know it was you?"

Viola was close enough now that even in the poor light, she could see the faint gleam of Belinda's teeth as the blonde smiled.

"I smelled your perfume," Belinda went on. "I remembered the scent from earlier."

"I wasn't wearing it then," Viola said.

"Maybe not, but enough of it lingered about you that I noticed. I'm observant about things like that."

"I'm observant, too," Viola said. Her tone was a little sharp now. "Sometimes I notice things that I wish I hadn't."

"How much . . . did you see?" Belinda asked with only the faintest of catches in her voice.

"Enough. You and your stepson—"

"Please," the other woman broke in. "You don't have to tell me. I was here, after all."

The note of wry humor in Belinda's voice irritated Viola even more. She was not a stiff-necked prude. In fact, according to her mother, she had always been a bit too earthy for her own good.

But she also had a code she lived by and a firm sense of what was right and what was not. There was no excuse for a woman to be carrying on with her own stepson.

"What you do is your own business, Doña Belinda," Viola said coldly. "But I hope you understand that I won't tolerate any improper behavior under my own roof."

Belinda sighed. "You don't understand," she said.

"That's what people always say when they know they're doing something wrong."

"Have you never gotten carried away by your emotions and done something you shouldn't have?"

"I married a man considerably older than myself when I was still a teenager," Viola pointed out. "My family didn't think that was a good idea."

"But you did it anyway, didn't you?"

"I was in love. I still am."

"Then you can sympathize." A worried note entered Belinda's voice. "Surely you won't say anything—"

"To your husband? You don't think Don Eduardo deserves to know the truth?"

"I don't think he deserves to be hurt for no good reason!"

The vehemence of Belinda's response surprised Viola. She said, "You sound almost like you love him."

"I do love him. I just—" Belinda broke off with an exasperated sigh. "Arguing isn't going to do any good. All I can do is ask you not to tell my husband and to throw myself on your mercy, Mrs. Slaughter."

A moment of awkward silence passed. Finally, Viola

said, "A lot of work went into this party, and I don't want it ruined. Since you and your husband are leaving tomorrow, I don't see any need to say anything to him about this matter."

"Thank you," Belinda said. The words sounded heartfelt and sincere.

"But surely you can . . . conduct yourself with propriety . . . for one night," Viola added.

"Don't worry. We won't do anything to bring shame on your house."

Viola felt a flash of anger. It almost sounded as if Belinda were mocking her. But she had already promised not to tell Don Eduardo what she had seen and heard, and she wasn't going to go back on her word.

"I'll see you again in a few minutes," she said. "We'll act as if nothing happened."

"All right. Thank you again."

Viola didn't say anything. She turned and walked away. She would be glad when this night was over, she thought.

And she would be even happier when their guests from below the border were gone.

Stonewall spotted Santiago Rubriz on his way back to the house and hailed him.

In the light from the lanterns in the trees, Santiago looked a little flushed and breathless. Stonewall wasn't sure what he might have been doing to cause that, but it didn't really matter. Stonewall had something else on his mind.

"Have you been thinkin' any more about that race?" he asked.

A grin stretched across Santiago's face.

"I have been thinking about nothing else, *amigo*," he said. "Have you settled on a horse that you think will put *El Halcón* to the test?"

"Yeah. We got a roan we call Pacer that's mighty fast. I'd like to match him against *El Halcón*."

"And will you be in the saddle, my friend?"

"You're dang right I will," Stonewall declared. "Fact of the matter is, I rode Pacer in the race at the last Fourth of July picnic in Tombstone."

"And did you win?"

"Well . . . no," Stonewall admitted. "But we came in second, and there were ten horses in that race. The horse that won nipped us by a nose, right at the finish line."

"Then I'm glad you and Pacer will have a chance to redeem yourselves." Santiago shook his head. "It's too bad you're destined to lose again."

"We'll just see about that." Stonewall frowned and went on, "But when? Your pa's headed back to his *rancho* in the morning, right?"

"That's true. My stepmother, however, is not what you would call an early riser. We probably won't leave until midmorning. Perhaps we can hold our race at dawn?"

"That's a good idea," Stonewall enthused. "Fellas fight duels at dawn, don't they? We'll have it out, only with horses, not pistols."

Santiago clapped a hand on his shoulder and laughed. "Yes, that's much more civilized," he agreed. "And no one dies."

"I better not drink too much tonight," Stonewall said.

"I'll need a clear head in the mornin' if we're gonna be racin'. How long are we talkin' about? A mile?"

"That's fine with me."

Santiago's easy agreement made Stonewall wonder if he should have chosen a different length for the race. But it was too late now. The deal was done . . . except for the stakes.

"What are we bettin'?" he asked.

"I thought that was understood," Santiago said. "The stakes are our mounts, *amigo*. Whoever wins walks away with the other man's horse."

Chapter 4

Slaughter and Don Eduardo had just emerged from the house when the don's wife reached the other side of the patio. She hurried to meet them and laid a hand on her husband's arm.

"Oh, Eduardo, everything is so beautiful," Belinda said. "Señor and Señora Slaughter have gone to great lengths to celebrate our visit."

"As well we should, ma'am," Slaughter said. "It's not every day we have a lady such as yourself on the ranch, all the way from Boston."

She shook her head and laughed lightly. "I'm not from Boston anymore," she said. "I'm from Mexico now."

"This is what I have longed to hear," Rubriz said. "You accept my home as your home."

"Well, of course it is," Belinda told him. "We're married, aren't we?"

"We most certainly are."

With that, Don Eduardo leaned down and kissed her with a passionate intensity that was clearly visible.

When her husband stepped back, Belinda went on,

"At any rate, Señor Slaughter, you have a wonderful lady here on the ranch in your wife, no matter where she's from. I never met a more gracious and caring person."

"Well, that's certainly true," Slaughter agreed. "Meeting Viola was a great stroke of luck for me. Convincing her to become my wife was an even greater one." Slaughter looked around. "Have you seen her recently?"

"Not in the last few minutes. I'm sure she's around somewhere, making sure that everything is done properly for the party."

"No doubt about that. I believe I'll go and find her. I'm sure things will be getting under way soon. If you two would like to freshen up, I can have one of the servants take you back to your quarters."

"That would be excellent, Señor Slaughter," Don Eduardo said.

"Please, call me John."

"Texas John, is it not?" Rubriz asked with a smile.

"That's true. Arizona is my home now, but I'm still a proud son of the Lone Star State. Always will be."

Slaughter beckoned to one of the servants and told the girl to escort Don Eduardo and his wife to their quarters. She lowered her gaze and murmured, "*Sí*, Don Juan."

When they were gone, Slaughter looked around, pleased at the preparations he saw. He was even more pleased when he spotted his wife coming toward him a moment later. Viola looked slightly flushed but as lovely as ever. She had probably been scurrying around making sure everything was done right, thought Slaughter.

"There you are, my dear," Slaughter said. He took both her hands in his. "I trust all the preparations are to your satisfaction?"

"What? Oh, yes, the party. It's fine."

She was definitely distracted by something. Slaughter frowned slightly and asked, "What's wrong?"

Viola gave a little laugh and said, "I never could hide much from you, could I, John? It's nothing for you to worry about, I promise."

"You're sure?" Slaughter pressed her.

"Absolutely certain. In fact, I'm going to put it out of my mind myself." She squeezed his hands and smiled at him. "We're not going to worry about anything this evening except having a good time."

There was enough food for an army, as the old saying went, and by the time people began filling their plates, it seemed as if an army had descended on the Slaughter Ranch. Word of the celebration had gone out to all of John and Viola Slaughter's friends on neighboring ranches and in the town of Douglas, eighteen miles to the west. Everyone was invited, and most of them had shown up for the festivities.

Slaughter and Viola sat at the main table with Don Eduardo, Doña Belinda, and Santiago. Their plates were piled high with barbecue, beans, potatoes, greens, and cornbread. Attentive servants saw to it that wineglasses never ran dry.

Eventually Slaughter had to push himself away from the table. He patted his belly and said, "I believe I could live for a month on what I've eaten tonight."

"It was an exceedingly fine meal," Don Eduardo agreed. "My compliments to Señora Slaughter."

"Oh, I didn't have much to do with it," Viola said. "The cooks deserve all the credit."

Belinda said, "You'll have to visit us at our ranch. We'd love to return the favor, wouldn't we, Eduardo?"

"*Sí*, of course," Rubriz said. "The two of you will be most welcome at any time."

"We'll take you up on that," Slaughter promised.

He noticed that Viola didn't chime in and agree with him. Not only that, he also thought he saw a hint of coolness in her eyes. That told him it was unlikely they would be accepting Belinda's invitation anytime soon, and her attitude puzzled him slightly. Normally Viola was a very sociable person and loved visiting friends.

Then he recalled what she had said earlier and figured that she didn't consider Belinda Rubriz to be a friend. Slaughter was still puzzled over the reason for that, but he didn't suppose it was any of his business.

Not long after the meal was over, the musicians who had stationed themselves on the other side of the road, near the cottonwoods that bordered a large stretch of open ground, fired up their fiddles. The Mexican guitarists joined in, and within moments the jaunty strains of a lively tune filled the air. It was a siren song that drew the guests away from the tables and their empty plates. They streamed across the road and began dancing.

Belinda put her hand on her husband's arm and said, "Come and dance with me, Eduardo."

"You know my leg is a bit too stiff for that, my dear," Rubriz told her. "Santiago, lend a hand here. Dance with your stepmother."

"Of course," Santiago said as he got to his feet. Slaughter thought he showed a noticeable lack of enthusiasm for the task. Stiffly, Santiago held his hand out and Belinda took it as she rose from the table. He led her across the road to the area where the dancing was going on.

Slaughter heard a faint sniff from where Viola sat beside him. He looked over at her and asked quietly, "Are you all right?"

"I'm fine," she said. "Shall we dance, John?"

"We shouldn't leave Don Eduardo alone—"

"Please," Rubriz interrupted. "Do not let me hold you back, *por favor*. By all means, Juan, dance with your lovely wife. The two of you should enjoy this beautiful evening."

"Well . . . all right, then," Slaughter said. He stood and extended his hand to Viola. "If you would do me the honor, Mrs. Slaughter?"

"I'd be happy to, Mr. Slaughter," she said as she smiled at him and took his hand.

Viola knew it was all an act, the way Belinda and Santiago were carrying on toward each other. Their coolness, their demeanor of not actually liking each other all that much, all of it was intended to fool Don Eduardo. To keep the image of his wife and his son locked in a passionate embrace from ever even entering his mind.

And it seemed to be working, otherwise he never would have been so casual about telling the two of them to dance together.

"You're thinking about something again," Slaughter said as he held her close to him and they turned in time to the music. "And it's not me or the tune the fellows are playing."

"I'm sorry, John. It's true I'm a bit distracted tonight."

"It's Belinda, isn't it? You said earlier that you didn't like her."

For a moment Viola considered telling him what she had discovered. After all, she had promised Belinda only that she wouldn't say anything about the affair to Don Eduardo. She hadn't mentioned anything about whether or not she would tell her own husband.

But that would violate the spirit of the promise, if not the letter, she decided. John wasn't very good at hiding his feelings, either. If he knew the truth, he might not be able to act the same toward their guests.

Viola didn't want a scene, didn't want anything to ruin the evening for everyone else.

So she said, "I'll tell you all about it later, John, I promise. But not until the time is right."

When their visitors were gone, she added silently to herself.

Slaughter sighed and nodded.

"Very well," he told her. "If there's one thing I've learned over the years we've been together, it's that I'd be wasting my time and energy arguing with you." He pulled her even closer and nuzzled her ear. "It's much more pleasant agreeing with you."

"Later you'll see how much more pleasant it can be," she whispered.

"I'll hold you to that, my dear," Slaughter said.

Stonewall slipped away from the party and went along the tree-lined path to the barn and corrals. It was difficult for him to leave when there was dancing going on, especially when there were so many pretty señoritas eager to go for a spin around the "dance floor" with him.

But he couldn't stop thinking about the race with Santiago Rubriz in the morning. He wanted to go check on Pacer and see how the roan was doing.

Stonewall wouldn't have admitted it to anybody, but he had his doubts about being able to beat *El Halcón*. Santiago's horse was something special. Stonewall knew that, but his own stubborn pride had prodded him into issuing the challenge. Once he'd done that, it was too late to take it back.

But Pacer was a heck of a horse, too. They had a chance, Stonewall told himself. That was all he had ever asked out of life.

As he walked through the darkness, Stonewall reflected on how he'd be making evening rounds right about now if he'd been back in Tombstone, where he served as one of his brother-in-law's deputies. Slaughter had left Tombstone in the capable hands of his chief deputy Burt Alvord while he made this trip to the ranch to meet Don Eduardo and accept delivery of the cattle he'd bought.

Stonewall had told Slaughter he would stay in town if that's what the sheriff wanted, but it had been a half-hearted offer. He knew there would be a big party to celebrate Don Eduardo's visit, and Stonewall hated to miss out on a party.

Slaughter knew that, too, and had told his brother-in-law to come along. Stonewall hadn't wasted any time in agreeing.

A lantern burned in the barn, its warm yellow glow

spilling out through the open double doors. A couple of ranch hands sat on three-legged stools in the broad center aisle between the stalls, using a crate for a table as they played cards. They looked up and nodded greetings to Stonewall.

"Surprised to see you here, youngster," one of them said. He was a wizened wrangler named Pete who had been around the Slaughter Ranch for years. "Figured you'd be at the *fandango*, dancin' with all the pretty girls and tryin' to convince 'em to slip off into the trees with you."

"Maybe they all told him no," the other cowboy suggested with a grin.

Stonewall said, "As a matter of fact, there are at least a dozen gals up yonder I could be sparkin' right now if I wanted to. But I got a race in the morning to uphold the honor of the ranch, and that's more important. I came down to check on Pacer."

"He's fine," Pete said. "You insin-yoo-atin' that I don't know how to take care of a hoss? I been handlin' horses more'n twice as long as you been alive, boy."

"I know that. I just wanted to take a look at him for myself."

Pete waved a gnarled hand at the stalls and said, "Go ahead and he'p yourself. Ain't nobody gonna stop you."

Stonewall walked over to the stall where Pacer stood. Even in the dim light from the lantern, the horse's hide seemed to glow with a reddish fire. He tossed his head and whickered a greeting to Stonewall, who reached over the gate to scratch between Pacer's ears.

"You're gonna run your heart out in the mornin', aren't you, big fella?" Stonewall murmured.

Pacer didn't answer, of course.

Stonewall stood there a few moments longer, talking quietly to the horse in encouraging tones that he knew were aimed as much at himself as they were at Pacer. The roan appeared to be in fine shape. He had left the party for nothing, Stonewall thought.

"Who the hell—" Pete suddenly said.

Stonewall heard the note of alarm in the wrangler's voice and turned his head to look just as Pete came up off the stool and took a step toward the barn's entrance.

Then there was a quick fluttering sound followed by a thud, and Pete swayed back a step and half-turned as he clutched at the shaft of an arrow buried in his chest. He made a plaintive gurgling noise as bright crimson blood trickled from a corner of his mouth.

The other cowhand yelled and jumped to his feet just in time to catch an arrow in the throat. The arrowhead went all the way through his neck and emerged out the back of it, accompanied by a flood of gore. He collapsed on the hard-packed dirt like a puppet with its strings cut.

Pete fell to his knees but stayed upright for a second while he continued fumbling at the arrow in his chest. Then he fell over onto his side and didn't move again.

Stonewall stood in front of Pacer's stall, momentarily frozen in shock and horror. He had been talking to both of those men only minutes earlier, and now they were dead, struck down by a threat that came out of the darkness.

Three men stepped from the shadows into the lantern

light, filling the barn's entrance. Stonewall stared at them, at the bow one of them held and the rifles in the hands of the others, recognizing the fierce faces of Apache warriors who had come to the Slaughter Ranch to kill.

And unless he did something mighty quick, he was next.

Chapter 5

Hector Alvarez tried not to resent the fact that he was stuck out here guarding this herd of cattle instead of being at the main house half a mile away enjoying the *fiesta* Señor and Señora Slaughter had thrown for their guests.

Somebody had to watch the cattle and keep them from straying. The animals were in a strange place, after all, having been driven up here from the Rubriz ranch south of the border. They might take it into their heads to try to go back there. Cows were funny creatures. You never could tell for sure what they might decide to do.

So three of Señor Slaughter's hands and three of the *vaqueros* Don Eduardo had brought with him had been chosen to ride night herd. As one of the youngest of Slaughter's men, and one who had been working on the ranch for less time than most of the others, it made sense that Hector had been picked as a night herder.

But that didn't mean he had to like it.

Hector could see the lights in the distance, shining brightly and merrily on those lucky enough to be enjoying the good food, the music, and the dancing. From time to time when the night breezes were right, he could hear the sprightly strains of the fiddles. He even thought he heard laughter now and then, but that might have been his imagination.

The slow, gentle thud of hooves came toward him. The nighthawks crossed paths occasionally as they endlessly circled the herd, and Hector knew that was probably what he heard.

Even so, he reined in and waited, and as he did he placed his right hand on the butt of the old Colt Navy .36 he carried in a crude holster at his waist.

A voice softly hailed him in Spanish, asking who he was. Hector gave his name, then added, "I ride for Don Juan Slaughter."

The rider came closer and said, "And I ride for Don Eduardo Rubriz, so you can take your hand off that gun, young one."

"How did you—" Hector began.

"How did I know you were ready to draw on me?" The man laughed. "Because I heard your voice and knew you weren't very old and figured you were probably nervous. And my eyes are good—like those of the cat. In fact, they call me *El Gato*."

"They do?" Hector asked, impressed by the name.

"No, you young fool!" The man laughed again and went on, "My name is Hermosa. No one has ever called me *El Gato*. So don't start, all right?"

A match flared to life. Hermosa had turned in the saddle, leaned over, and cupped his hand around the match to shield the flame before he snapped it alight with his thumbnail. It was a sensible precaution to take around cattle.

Hermosa held the match to a thin brown cigarette he had rolled. Then he snuffed out the flame between thumb and index finger.

That one moment of light was enough to reveal a lean, leathery face with a wide mouth framed by drooping mustaches. Hermosa was old, or at least he seemed that way to Hector, who had yet to see twenty summers.

Hermosa didn't take the quirly out of his mouth but rather asked around it, "Have you run into any trouble out here tonight?"

"None," Hector answered. "Everything is peaceful."

"Good. That's what we want."

Hector gave in to impulse and asked the older man, "Don't you wish you were back at the house so you could go to the party?"

"Bah. A bunch of noise and commotion."

"And food and wine and dancing and pretty girls—"

"All things that are important to a young man. I prefer a good horse, comfortable boots, and a warm place to sleep."

"A man who feels like that is barely alive," Hector said without thinking. As soon as the words were out of his mouth, he realized that he might have insulted Hermosa—and the hard planes of the *vaquero*'s face had a cruel slant to them, Hector recalled.

Hermosa didn't seem to have taken offense, though. He puffed on his smoke and said, "Barely alive is still better than dead."

"I suppose." Hector thought it might be a good idea

to change the subject. "What is it like to work for Don Eduardo?"

"Good. He is a hard man, but he treats his people fairly. Life on his ranch is the only thing I have ever known. And my father worked for his father, back in the days when Don Vincente founded the *rancho* with his partner. Before we started our own. Many years ago, boy. Long before you were born."

"You've spent your whole life in the same place?" Hector could barely wrap his mind around that idea.

"It's not so bad," Hermosa said as he snuffed out the butt of the quirly and snapped it away. He added dryly, "You get used to it."

"I'd like to go places," Hector said. "Faraway places. I'd like to see big cities and gaze out over the sea. But tonight I would settle for going to that *fiesta*."

Hermosa growled, "You're young. There will be other *fiestas*." With that he lifted his reins and nudged his horse into motion. "We had better get back to our jobs," he said.

Hector heaved a sigh, stared longingly at the lights glittering at the ranch house, and said, "I suppose—"

He stopped short as he heard several sharp reports. The sounds were muted somewhat by distance, but they were unmistakable.

Gunshots.

Hermosa lifted himself in his stirrups, muttered an exclamation, and said, "Don Eduardo." He dug the rowels of his fancy spurs into his mount's flanks and sent the horse leaping forward as he called over his shoulder, "Stay here with the herd, boy!"

"But—" Hector began as worry for John Slaughter and the lovely Señora Slaughter filled him.

"Stay here!" Hermosa ordered again, and then he was gone, galloping away into the darkness.

Hector hesitated. He didn't have to follow the commands given to him by Don Eduardo's man, but on the other hand, Señor Slaughter had ordered him to watch the herd.

Torn between concern for his employer and his desire to do as Slaughter had told him, Hector agonized for a moment before deciding that he would stay here with the cattle. He was convinced it was the right thing to do.

Besides, Hector had no doubt that whatever the trouble was, John Slaughter could handle it.

Stonewall wasn't armed. He hadn't figured it would be necessary to bring a gun to a *fandango*.

But he knew there was a shotgun inside the tack room. Pete kept it there to chase off the wolves that occasionally came down from the mountains.

Those Apaches were more dangerous than any wolves, Stonewall knew.

He made a desperate leap for the tack room door, which stood open about a foot. As he moved, one of the raiders fired. The man's rifle was an old single-shot weapon. Stonewall heard the bullet hum past his ear like a bee, rather than the high-pitched whine of rounds fired by more modern rifles.

An arrow flew past him as well and lodged in the jamb as his shoulder struck the door and knocked it open the rest of the way. He half-stumbled, half-fell into the tack room and spotted the shotgun hanging on pegs beside the door. As he reached for it, one of the Apaches bounded toward him with a strident yell.

Now that a gun had gone off, there was no longer any need for stealth. Stonewall had a sinking feeling that these three renegades weren't the only ones on the ranch tonight.

The Apache charging him couldn't see the shotgun hanging on the wall just inside the door. He had jerked a knife from the colorful sash around his waist and raised it high as his face contorted with hatred. Clearly, he planned to kill Stonewall in hand-to-hand combat.

Stonewall had no interest in going *mano a mano* with the warrior. He jerked the scattergun from the pegs, swiveled toward his attacker as he used his thumb to ear back both hammers, and touched off the right-hand barrel.

The load of buckshot traveled only a couple of feet, so it was still bunched up as it slammed into the Apache's chest, shredding his blousy shirt and blowing a fist-size hole clean through him. The charge's impact was great enough to lift the warrior off his feet and throw him backward.

The intruder crashed down on his back with his shirt on fire from the tongue of flame that had licked out from the shotgun's muzzle. He would never get any deader.

Another rifle blasted and a slug chewed splinters from the doorjamb near where the arrow had lodged. Stonewall swung the shotgun up and fired the second barrel at the two men in the barn's entrance. They dived back into the darkness. Stonewall couldn't tell if he had hit either of them.

He retreated into the tack room and kicked the door shut. A box of shotgun shells sat on a shelf. He reached into it and grabbed a handful. It took him only a couple of seconds to break open the gun, dump the spent shells, and slide fresh ones into the barrels. As he closed the shotgun, he heard more gunfire, confirming his hunch that the ranch was under a general attack.

He needed to be out there with his friends and relatives, defending their home.

But if he stepped out of the tack room, he might run right into a rifle bullet or an arrow.

What happened next took the decision out of his hands. He smelled smoke wafting under the door.

The sons of bitches had set the barn on fire.

Slaughter had brought Viola back to the table after the dance ended. Belinda and Santiago had returned as well. Belinda sat close to her husband, while Santiago slouched several chairs away, toying with a glass of wine.

After seeing that Viola was seated, Slaughter walked over to the young man and asked, "Did you and my brother-in-law settle the details of that race you were talking about this afternoon?"

Santiago's interest perked up. He smiled and said, "It is all arranged, Señor Slaughter. We will race at dawn, Stonewall's Pacer against my *El Halcón*."

Slaughter picked up one of the chairs, reversed it, and straddled it.

"That ought to be something to see. I can tell by looking at him that horse of yours is fast."

"*Sí*, very fast," Santiago nodded.

"But Pacer's got some speed, too. I'll enjoy watching them." Slaughter looked around. "Where is Stonewall?"

Santiago shook his head and said, "I have not seen him."

"I thought he'd be out there dancing," Viola said.

"Perhaps he is nervous about the race," Don Eduardo suggested. "Señor Slaughter . . . Juan . . . I was wondering . . . perhaps you would care to make a small wager on the outcome?"

"I might be persuaded to do that," Slaughter replied. "What sort of stakes were you thinking of?"

He was destined not to know Rubriz's answer, because at that moment a terrified scream ripped through the festivities and made the musicians abruptly fall silent. Slaughter bolted to his feet, looked around, and saw one of the young women who worked for them running toward the house, panic-stricken.

A shot rang out. Slaughter automatically identified the whipcrack report as that of a rifle.

The servant threw out her arms as her mouth opened in a wide "O" of shock. She stumbled and pitched forward on her face. Slaughter saw the bright red stain on the back of her white shirt and knew she had been shot.

Screams and shots and high-pitched whoops suddenly filled the air, along with more gunshots.

Instinctively, Viola leaped to her feet and cried, "John!"

Before she could say anything else, Slaughter tackled her and bore both of them to the ground. The tables and chairs would provide a little protection as long as she stayed low.

"Stay down!" he told her as he looked around. A few

feet away, Don Eduardo had pulled Belinda to the ground, too. He knelt beside her with a derringer in his hand. Slaughter hadn't known that the don was armed, but it didn't surprise him.

As a matter of fact, Slaughter had a gun himself, a short-barreled, single action .38 Smith & Wesson he carried in a holster under his left arm, hidden by his jacket. As he stood up he drew the revolver and looked around for somebody to shoot.

That didn't take long. Chaos filled the area that had been used for dancing, as the couples there scattered in the face of an attack by what appeared to be at least a dozen renegade Apache warriors. Some of the men were trying to fight back, but they were unarmed and a few had already fallen. Slaughter spotted one of the Apaches raising a knife high above his head. The renegade was about to plunge the blade into the chest of a man at his feet.

Even though the range was long for a handgun, Slaughter drew a bead and fired. He aimed at the Apache's chest, but the bullet went high. Just as well, though, since it entered the renegade's left cheek just below the eye and bored on into the brain, dropping the man like a stone before he could strike that killing blow with his knife.

"Santiago!" Don Eduardo bellowed.

Slaughter jerked around to see that the younger Rubriz was running toward the fight. Slaughter admired Santiago's courage, but the youngster's actions were rather foolhardy since he was unarmed.

Santiago had something in mind, though. He grabbed up an overturned chair, brought it crashing down on the ground so that it shattered, and charged on into battle, using a broken chair leg in each hand as clubs.

Slaughter saw that he couldn't risk any more shots—there was too great a chance of hitting one of the innocents—so he reached down and took hold of Viola's arm with his free hand. As he lifted her to her feet, he told her, "Take Belinda and get inside the house. You'll be safe there." He pressed the .38 into her hand. "Anybody tries to stop you, gun 'em down."

Viola acknowledged the order with a curt nod. Slaughter knew from the grim expression on his wife's face that she would do what he told her. Any Apache who got in her way would have a fight on his hands.

Viola ran to Belinda's side and told her, "Come with me."

The blonde didn't respond at first. Clearly she was too terrified to move. Her husband had to take hold of her, lift her to her feet, and shove her toward Viola.

"Go with Señora Slaughter," he told her. "I love you, Belinda. Never forget that."

"Eduardo—" She clutched at his coat.

"Go!"

Belinda obeyed, stumbling along beside Viola as the other woman held her arm to steady her. Rubriz turned toward Slaughter, opened his mouth to say something, and then jerked up the derringer and fired instead.

Slaughter heard the bullet go past him and thud into something behind him. He turned to see one of the Apaches collapsing with a hole in the center of his forehead where Don Eduardo's slug had struck him.

The warrior had been armed with a Henry rifle. Slaughter snatched it from the dead man's hands and brought it to his shoulder as he said "Much obliged" to Don Eduardo.

"You have fought these bronco Apaches before?" Rubriz asked.

The rifle in Slaughter's hands cracked. One of the Indians across the road spun off his feet as the bullet ripped through him.

"Many times," Slaughter said in response to the don's question. "But they haven't dared attack the ranch in quite a while."

"We should turn this table on its side and use it for cover," Don Eduardo suggested.

"Good idea," Slaughter said. He lowered the Henry and held it in one hand while he used the other to help Don Eduardo tip the table onto its side. Platters of leftover food, plates, silverware, wineglasses, all went flying.

The mess could be cleaned up later—if they survived.

Slaughter knelt behind the table and fired several more shots from the Henry. The sight of two Apaches collapsing rewarded his efforts.

Don Eduardo crouched beside him and said, "Where is Santiago? I don't see—"

"There," Slaughter said as he spotted the younger Rubriz. Santiago was using the broken chair legs to fight off an Apache who was attacking him with a knife. He blocked the thrusts and tried to strike back, but the warrior was too quick, too experienced in such combat. The Apache's foot shot out, hooked behind one of Santiago's knees, and jerked him off his feet.

"Santiago, no!" Don Eduardo cried as he saw his son fall. The don straightened up in alarm and then fell back.

At the same time, Slaughter fired and blew away a

chunk of the Apache's skull before the warrior could plunge his knife into the fallen Santiago.

"I got him," Slaughter said. "Santiago's all right."

Don Eduardo didn't respond. Slaughter turned to see the don lying there with a hand pressed to his side as blood welled between his fingers.

Chapter 6

Through the tack room door, Stonewall heard the terrified shrieks of the horses and knew the smoke had spooked them, too. He couldn't let them burn, and if he stayed in here the flames would consume him as well.

Even if the Apaches were waiting for him, he had to get out of here.

With the shotgun held ready, he kicked the door open and lunged through it into the barn's center aisle, which was clogged with black, billowing smoke. He ducked his head, but that didn't really do any good. The stuff still stung his eyes, nose, and throat, leaving him half-blind, coughing, and choking.

He fought his way through the smoke, figuring that if he couldn't see the Apaches, they couldn't see him, either. As he came to each stall, he threw the latch open and flung the gate back to let the horse inside stampede out. The panicky animals would have a chance to escape, anyway.

When the renegades saw the horses emerging from the barn, they would figure out that he was letting them loose and know he was still alive. So they would be expecting him to come out, too, any time now.

Stonewall had a surprise in mind for them, though.

He wasn't going to emerge from the barn by himself.

He saved Pacer's stall for last, and when he came to it he saw the roan lunging back and forth within the sturdy wooden walls.

"Pacer!" Stonewall said. "Pacer, settle down. Settle down, boy, it'll be all right."

The words were punctuated by hacking coughs, so he supposed they might not be as reassuring as they would have been otherwise. There was nothing he could do about that. Something in what he said must have gotten through to the horse, though, because Pacer stopped trying to batter his way out of the stall. He threw his head up and down and whinnied as if asking Stonewall to do something, anything, about the inferno spreading around them.

The walls were on fire, and when the flames reached the hay in the loft, that fuel would turn the barn into a gigantic torch. It couldn't be saved. Stonewall glanced in the direction where the two bodies lay but couldn't see them because of the thick smoke.

He would have liked to get Pete and the other cowboy out of here, but that wasn't going to be possible. He would be doing good to save himself. As he swung the stall gate open, he continued talking to Pacer in calm, steady tones. If the roan bolted, Stonewall wouldn't be able to stop him.

Pacer didn't run. Stonewall opened the gate wide and used it to help him throw a leg over Pacer's back. He leaned forward over the roan's neck, held the shotgun in one hand and Pacer's mane with the other, and banged his heels on the horse's flanks.

Pacer took off like a shot.

Instinct must have guided the horse through the smoke toward the barn entrance. Pacer burst out into the open. Stonewall's eyes were streaming tears from the smoke; he couldn't see a thing. He was doing good just to stay mounted, riding bareback like he was.

Fresh air flooded against his face. His vision began to clear a bit as he heard rifles cracking. Some of the Apaches were shooting at him, he realized, but Pacer was moving too fast for them to draw a bead on him.

Stonewall galloped along the road through the cottonwoods that led back to the house. One of the attackers leaped into his path and fired a Winchester. The shot missed, but it spooked Pacer and made the roan shy violently. Stonewall almost fell off. Somehow he managed to hang on.

The Apache worked the rifle's lever for a second shot. Stonewall had no choice but to thrust the shotgun at him and fire it one-handed. The short-range blast blew the Apache's head off his shoulders, but the recoil ripped the weapon out of Stonewall's hand.

The thunderous blast also made Pacer rear up and paw at the air. This time Stonewall wasn't able to stay on. He slipped off the roan's back and crashed to the ground.

Slaughter knew that Don Eduardo must have been hit by one of the bullets flying around. He dropped to a knee beside the wounded man and asked him, "How bad are you hit?"

"I . . . I don't know," Rubriz gasped. "But don't worry . . . about me . . . Juan. Protect my wife . . . my son . . ."

"I'll do my best," Slaughter promised. "In the meantime . . ."

He set the Henry aside, whipped off his coat, and wadded it up. As he pressed it hard against the wound in Don Eduardo's side, he went on, "Hold this on there to slow down the bleeding."

"I will . . . be all right . . . *mi amigo*," Rubriz said. "Now go. Deal with those . . . damned Apaches."

Slaughter nodded and picked up the rifle. He turned back to the fight.

Not as much shooting was going on now. The battle had turned into mostly hand-to-hand combat. The actual number of attackers had been relatively small, Slaughter realized. The Apaches were outnumbered, and their only advantages had been surprise and the fact that most of the partygoers weren't armed.

Eventually the odds had worked against them, however, and as some of the Apaches had fallen, the guests and Slaughter's cowboys had snatched up the weapons the dead warriors had dropped. That had helped turn the tide even more.

Slaughter stalked across the road, seeking out targets and bringing the Henry smoothly to his shoulder to fire every time he spotted one of the renegades still on his feet. There was plenty of light for shooting because the barn was on fire, flames shooting a hundred feet into the air as they consumed the structure.

The barn could be rebuilt, but Slaughter hoped the horses had gotten out all right. And some of his men might have been in there, too, he thought grimly. If they had been killed, he would make sure their deaths were avenged.

Not one of the renegades would leave the ranch alive.

He looked for Santiago Rubriz and felt a surge of relief when he spotted the young man. Slaughter was even more relieved when he recognized the smoke-grimed figure Santiago was helping along.

"Stonewall!" he called. "Over here."

Stonewall and Santiago hurried toward him. Stonewall said, "John! Thank the Lord you're all right. Where's Viola?"

"I sent her and Doña Belinda into the house."

"My—my stepmother!" Santiago said. "Was she hurt?"

Santiago had seemed rather cool toward Belinda earlier, but clearly he was concerned about her safety now. Slaughter told him, "She was fine the last time I saw her."

"Thank God!"

"But your father . . . I'm afraid he was hit, Santiago."

The young man's eyes widened. He said, "Is he . . . was he—"

"I don't know how bad it is," Slaughter said. He turned and pointed. "Over there, behind the table where we were sitting earlier."

Santiago took off in that direction at a run.

The shooting had stopped completely now, but the area between the ranch house and the barn wasn't silent. Angry shouts and the moans of the wounded filled the air. Bodies, white and Apache alike, littered the ground.

Stonewall looked around at the carnage and said, "John, the Indians around here have been peaceful lately. What the hell was this all about?"

"I don't know," Slaughter said, "but I intend to find out."

Hector Alvarez was in agony as he sat on his horse and listened to the gunshots and watched the flames leaping up. From this distance, the fire was just a garish orange blob and Hector couldn't tell what was burning, but he thought it might be the barn.

Whatever it was, that didn't really matter right now. What was important was that Señor and Señora Slaughter and all of Hector's friends and fellow cowboys were in danger, and he wasn't doing a single thing to help them.

But his orders had been to stay with the herd no matter what happened. He prided himself on being a faithful *vaquero* and doing what he was supposed to.

Hermosa and the other nighthawks had disregarded their orders, though. They had galloped back to the ranch to find out what was going on and help if they could. Hector had heard the swift hoofbeats of their horses in the darkness and knew he was alone out here with the herd.

He thought about one of the maids who worked in the main house, Yolanda Ramos. She was about a year younger than Hector and very beautiful. He had walked out with her several times when neither of them was working, and once he had even been bold enough to kiss her. Nothing he had ever tasted had been sweeter than Yolanda's lips.

Soon, when they had known each other longer, Hector planned to ask Yolanda to marry him. He had hopes that she would say yes, and if she did, then they would live in one of the small cabins where Señor Slaughter's married hands made their homes. Yolanda would continue to work for Señora Slaughter—at least until her belly was too big with their first baby for her to do so.

There would be other babies, many of them, and Hector would grow old surrounded by the love of children and grandchildren and great-grandchildren and most of all his beautiful Yolanda. It was a dream that he held close to his heart and cherished.

A dream that would be destroyed if anything happened to Yolanda.

As that horrible realization sunk into Hector's brain, he knew he couldn't wait any longer. Orders or no orders, he had to make sure she was safe from whatever terrible thing was happening there at the ranch.

He had just lifted his reins when he heard hoofbeats nearby. Were Hermosa and the other nighthawks coming back? The shooting was still going on, and the fire still blazed.

Hector hesitated as large shapes loomed up in front of him. Men on horseback, he told himself. He put his hand on the butt of the .36 and called softly, "Hermosa?"

Something thudded against his chest as if someone had just thrown a rock at him. Whatever it was, it didn't bounce off like a rock, though. He reached up to feel, and as his fingers touched the leather-wrapped handle of a knife, pain welled up inside him, a greater pain than he had ever known.

He realized the blade was buried deep in his chest.

A numb weakness followed the pain. Hector tried to draw his gun, but his muscles refused to work properly. The Colt came out of its holster but then slipped from Hector's fingers. He swayed in the saddle and grabbed for the saddle horn instead. That steadied him for a second, but then he lost that grip as well and toppled off the horse.

A hot, salty flood filled his mouth. He knew it was blood, knew he was dying. He fumbled at the knife sticking out of his chest but couldn't dislodge it.

Fingers pushed his aside, gripped the knife, pulled it out. A shape loomed over him, a deeper patch of darkness in the night, and a man's voice said in English, "You should've gone back to the house with the others, kid. Might've stood a chance that way."

Hector's head fell to the side. Blood welled out of his open mouth. His lips moved, and he whispered, "Yolanda . . ." just before he died.

Chapter 7

Viola and Belinda had almost reached the house when one of the servants came shrieking after them with an Apache in pursuit. As Viola looked over her shoulder and saw what was happening, she remembered the poor girl who had been gunned down when the attack first began. She was determined not to let another of her people be killed.

She pushed the sobbing, stumbling Belinda toward the door and snapped, "Get inside."

Then she turned back, raised the Smith & Wesson, pulled back the hammer, and fired.

The Apache's head jerked back. His legs kept running for a couple more steps, then folded up underneath him. As the dead man tumbled to the ground, Viola stepped forward and caught hold of the hysterical servant.

The girl screamed and fought, not knowing or caring who had hold of her. Viola said, "Stop it!" then recognizing the girl she added, "Stop it, Yolanda! Stop fighting me!"

Her urgent words must have gotten through to the

servant's terrified brain. She stopped struggling and gasped, "Señora Slaughter?"

Viola pushed her toward the front door that Belinda had left open behind her. "Get inside. Find Doña Belinda and take care of her." Giving Yolanda a job to do might help her keep calm.

"What . . . what are you going to do, señora?"

"I'll make sure none of those Apaches get in," Viola said in a flat, hard voice.

As soon as Yolanda had hurried into the house, Viola stationed herself in the doorway and watched the battle unfold. Her heart seemed to twist in her chest when she saw the flames through the trees and realized the barn was on fire. She was afraid for the men and horses who might have been caught in there, but it was just one more worry on top of her fear for the safety of her husband and her brother.

With the iron-willed, icy-nerved determination that had proven so valuable in times past, she kept those fears tamped down deep inside her. She couldn't afford to give in to them while the outcome of the attack was still in doubt.

Fortunately, that didn't last too much longer. The shooting died away. The lanterns still burned in the trees, casting the same light they had before terror and death replaced dancing and gaiety. Viola's eyes searched desperately for John and Stonewall.

When she spotted them and saw that they appeared to be all right, the relief that surged through her was so powerful it made her gasp. Her knees went weak for a second before she stiffened them.

"Señora . . . ?"

Yolanda's voice made Viola turn. The maid stood there, calmer than before but obviously still very agitated.

"What is it?" Viola asked.

"I found Doña Belinda like you said, señora, but she . . . she collapsed. I cannot get her to wake up, señora. I think she is dead!"

By the time Slaughter and Stonewall reached Don Eduardo, Santiago was already kneeling at his father's side. He had lifted Don Eduardo and leaned the wounded man against him.

Rubriz's eyes were open. He gazed up at his son and asked in a weak voice, "Santiago . . . you are unharmed?"

"I'm fine, Papa," Santiago assured him. "Don't try to talk. Just rest."

Thin lines of blood had trickled from the corners of Don Eduardo's mouth. Slaughter hunkered on the other side of him and said, "Let me take a look, Santiago."

Rubriz still had Slaughter's coat pressed against the wound. Slaughter lifted it away. There was no strength left in Don Eduardo's fingers. Slaughter pulled the don's shirt out of his trousers and lifted it along with the short charro jacket Rubriz wore. When the bloody garments were out of the way, an ugly red-rimmed hole in his side oozed crimson.

Slaughter reached around and felt for an exit wound. When he didn't find one, he said, "The bullet's still in there. No way of telling how much damage it's done. We need to get him inside, stop that bleeding, and let him rest."

"The bullet must come out," Santiago said.

"Try to dig it out now and you'll finish him off," Slaughter said. "He needs to get stronger first. Tomorrow, maybe."

"He could have blood poisoning by then," the younger man argued.

Slaughter knew Santiago was right. This was a fine line they had to walk. Too much delay in getting the bullet out would prove fatal, but subjecting Don Eduardo to a lot of cutting and probing in the shape he was in now would kill him, too.

"We'll do everything we can for him, Santiago, I give you my word. I'll send a man to Douglas tonight for the doctor. They should be back by morning."

"Will my father still be alive by then?" Santiago asked bitterly.

"S-Santiago . . ." Don Eduardo rasped. "*Mi amigo* Juan . . . is right. What I need now . . . is to know that my wife . . . is unharmed."

"I sent her into the house with Viola," Slaughter told him. "We'll take you in there so you can see her. You need to be resting in a bed anyway."

Of course, moving the wounded man might be dangerous, too, Slaughter thought, but they couldn't leave him out here in the open all night.

Before he and Stonewall and Santiago could pick up the don, rapid hoofbeats pounded nearby. Slaughter thought the likelihood of another attack tonight was very slim, but he picked up the Henry rifle he had set aside and straightened to his feet anyway.

Several men rode up in a hurry. Slaughter recognized the rider in the lead as one of Don Eduardo's men, an older, saturnine *hombre* who had the look of a *bandido* about him even though Slaughter had no reason to think he was anything more than an honest *vaquero*.

The leader of the newcomers swung down from his saddle and said, "Don Eduardo—"

"I am all right, Hermosa," the don said. His voice sounded a little stronger now, but Slaughter had a feeling he just didn't want to seem any weaker than he had to in front of his men. "What about . . . the cattle?"

"They were fine when we left," Hermosa replied. "We had to make sure you were safe."

A shock went through Slaughter as he realized these were the men Rubriz had picked to watch over the herd while the party was going on. Not only that, but he spotted two of his own hands among them and recognized them as men who were supposed to be acting as nighthawks.

"Wait a minute," Slaughter said sharply. "Who's out there keeping an eye on the herd?"

"One of your young cowboys, señor," Hermosa said. "I told him to stay behind while we rode in."

"Son of a—" Slaughter bit back the rest of the curse. He turned to his men who had come in with the *vaqueros* and said, "Get down from those horses. Help carry Don Eduardo into the house. Mrs. Slaughter will know what to do. Stonewall, you up to coming with me?"

"Sure, John," Stonewall said. His voice was raspy from the smoke he'd inhaled in the barn. "What's wrong?"

"That's what I intend to find out."

The two confused cowboys dismounted and turned their horses over to Slaughter and Stonewall. Both saddles had scabbarded Winchesters strapped to them, so Slaughter left the Henry rifle behind. He set a fast pace toward the bed ground half a mile away, where the herd he'd bought from Don Eduardo was settling in.

As they rode, Stonewall said above the hoofbeats, "I think I've got it figured out now. That raid by the Apaches was just a distraction."

"That's what I'm afraid of," Slaughter said. "Raise hell, draw in all the men, then hit the herd."

"Apaches usually don't go in for rustling on a scale like that," Stonewall pointed out.

"No, but somebody could have gotten them to do it. Paid them off with rifles, maybe, or something else they'd want."

As Slaughter put this theory into words, he knew it made sense. He might be wrong—he hoped he was wrong—but he wasn't going to be surprised if he and Stonewall found that the cattle were gone.

They rode hard at first, then Slaughter slowed and told his brother-in-law, "Better get that rifle out. There's no telling what we're going to run into."

With Winchesters in hand, they advanced at a more cautious pace. Slaughter felt his hopes disappearing as he scanned the countryside in the light from the moon and stars and failed to find the dark, irregular mass that should have greeted him.

"They're gone," Stonewall said, his voice hollow. "All those cattle you just bought from Don Eduardo—gone!"

"Yes," Slaughter agreed grimly. "That appears to be the case."

He spotted something else, though. A single, much smaller shape huddled darkly on the ground. He pointed it out to Stonewall.

The young cowboy cursed. All the members of the crew were his friends. It was impossible not to like Stonewall, and he felt the same way about almost everybody he met.

"Take a closer look," Slaughter told him. "I'll watch for any trouble, but I don't think we're going to find any." His voice held a note of bitterness, too, as he added, "Whoever was out here a little while ago, they're all gone now."

Stonewall dismounted and walked over to the shape on the ground. He knelt and rolled the body onto its back. With a catch in his voice, he called, "It's . . . Hector Alvarez."

Slaughter sighed. Young Alvarez hadn't been working on the ranch for very long, but in the time he'd been here, he had demonstrated that he was a devoted, capable hand.

He was courting one of the maids who worked in the house, too, Slaughter recalled Viola telling him.

Now any future together they might have had was over, ripped away by ruthless men.

Somebody would pay for hurting his people, thought Slaughter.

"Can you tell what happened to him?" he asked.

"Let me strike a match," Stonewall said.

He snapped a lucifer to life and held it so that its feeble, flickering glow washed over the unfortunate Hector Alvarez. Even from horseback, Slaughter could see the large bloodstain on the young man's shirt.

"Doesn't look like he was shot," Stonewall said. "More likely he was stabbed. He must've let whoever it was get pretty close to him, to get stuck like that."

"Not necessarily," Slaughter said. "The killer could have been good at throwing a knife."

"Yeah, I guess." The match had burned down almost to Stonewall's fingers. He shook out the flame and dropped it.

"Strike another one," Slaughter told him. "Let's have a look at the hoofprints around here."

As Stonewall did so, he said, "Apaches aren't really horse Indians, like the ones back on the plains."

"No, they're not," Slaughter agreed. An Apache was just about as likely to eat a horse as he was to ride it. These renegades preferred to travel on foot. Some of their hideouts in the mountains were impassable even by horse.

"Only hoofprints I see are shod ones," Stonewall reported. "White men's horses. Looks like your idea of rustlers working with the Apaches was the right one, John."

"It's not a coincidence that this happened tonight," Slaughter said. "Not when Don Eduardo just delivered this herd today. Somebody knew these cattle would be here and came after them specifically."

"You reckon one of the don's men is workin' with the rustlers?"

Slaughter frowned in thought for a moment, then said, "Maybe, maybe not. They could have been keeping an eye on his ranch, waiting for the right moment to make a move against him. Some old enemy of Don Eduardo's, maybe."

"Or an enemy of yours," Stonewall suggested.

Slaughter shook his head. "Not likely. I have plenty of enemies, but I don't see how any of them would have known the don was bringing that herd up here. Not in time to set that up with the Apaches, anyway." Slaughter scraped a thumbnail along his jawline. "No, this is somebody who wants to get back at Don Eduardo for something. Unfortunately, since earlier this evening when that money changed hands, those are my cows that they stole."

"And that means . . . ?"

"That means I'm going to get them back," Slaughter said.

Chapter 8

Viola was practically holding her breath as she hurried after Yolanda. She would have sworn that Belinda Rubriz hadn't been wounded. What could have happened to her?

Maybe Belinda had been hit by a stray bullet on their way into the house and hadn't even realized it herself. Viola had heard of people being shot without knowing it.

The maid led Viola into the parlor, where Belinda was slumped on the floor in an untidy heap. Viola dropped to her knees beside the blonde and placed a hand on Belinda's chest, searching for a heartbeat.

To her great relief, after a few seconds she found it.

Belinda was alive, just unconscious.

"She's not dead," Viola told Yolanda, who crossed herself and offered up a quick prayer of thanksgiving. Viola went on, "Help me check her for injuries."

They looked the visitor over and found no sign of blood on her clothes. Viola checked her head, searching through the thick blond hair, thinking that maybe Belinda had been creased by a bullet. That turned out not to be the case, either.

Viola lifted one of Belinda's eyelids and saw that the blonde's eyes had rolled back in their sockets.

"It looks to me like she just fainted from fear and strain," Viola said.

"Do people really do that, señora?"

"High-toned ladies from Boston do, I guess," Viola said. "Help me lift her onto the sofa."

She took Belinda's shoulders while Yolanda grasped her ankles. Together they lifted her and placed her on one of the sofas in the parlor. Viola loosened Belinda's clothing.

"We'll give her some air and wait for her to wake up," she said. "That's about all we can do right now."

Heavy footsteps sounded from the house's main entrance. Yolanda whirled in that direction, put a hand to her mouth, and gasped, "Señora!"

Viola had slipped the .38 Smith & Wesson her husband had given her into a pocket of her dress. She reached in and grasped the gun now. She lifted it and had her thumb on the hammer as the shapes of several men appeared in the entrance to the parlor.

She relaxed slightly as she recognized Santiago Rubriz and Don Eduardo. Santiago was on one side of the don, holding him up, while one of Don Eduardo's *vaqueros* supported him on the other side.

The don's clothes had a lot of blood on them. His head sagged forward limply. He appeared to be unconscious.

Viola put the revolver away again as she hurried to meet the men.

"Señora Slaughter—" Santiago began.

"Put him over there," Viola interrupted as she pointed to the room's second sofa. "Was he shot?"

"*Sí*. Your husband said the bullet was still in him."

"I'll have a look at him," Viola said with an efficient nod. "I've patched up gunshot wounds before. There's a good doctor in Douglas, too, and a rider can be there in a few hours."

"*Sí, señora*, Señor Slaughter said he would send a man for the doctor."

As Santiago and the *vaquero*, an older, hawk-faced man, carefully placed Don Eduardo on the sofa, Viola asked, "Where is my husband?"

"He and your brother rode off in a hurry, señora," Santiago said. He stepped back from the sofa and added, "They did not say where they were going, but they seemed quite upset about something, especially Señor Slaughter."

John had plenty of reason to be upset, thought Viola. His home had been attacked, his friends and family endangered.

Texas John Slaughter wasn't going to take that outrage lying down.

Santiago seemed to notice his stepmother for the first time. His eyes widened at the sight of Belinda lying on the sofa, and he exclaimed, "*Dios mio!* Belinda! She is—"

He had started toward her, but Viola caught hold of his arm and stopped him.

"Your stepmother is fine," she said. "She just fainted."

Unless Belinda had told him earlier in the evening, Santiago didn't know that Viola was aware of their affair. Don Eduardo's men wouldn't know about it, either, and Viola was sure Belinda would want it to stay that way. Several of the don's *vaqueros* had crowded into the parlor, and they might become suspicious if they saw Santiago carrying on too much about his stepmother.

With a visible effort—visible to Viola, anyway—Santiago controlled his rampant emotions and asked, "You are sure she's all right?"

"I told you, she fainted. As soon as she wakes up, she'll be fine. Now, I need to tend to your father."

Santiago swallowed and nodded. He said, "Anything you need, we will help."

"I want to clean the area around the wound first. Yolanda, get some clean rags and a basin of hot water. I'll need some whiskey or something like that, too."

The piratical-looking *vaquero* asked, "Will tequila do?"

"I don't see why not," Viola said.

The man reached into a pocket inside the brown leather vest he wore and brought out a silver flask.

"Then we have that," he declared with a grim smile.

Viola took the flask from him and said, "I'm sure there are wounded people outside who need help, too. Go out there and see about making them comfortable. Those who are hurt the worst need to be brought in here."

The sharp tone of command in her voice might have rankled some men, especially one who didn't work for her and technically didn't have to do what she told him.

But the *vaquero* just smiled faintly again, touched the brim of his gray felt sombrero with a tobacco-stained finger, and murmured, "*Sí, señora,*" before he left the room.

There was no doubt who was in charge here at the moment.

Viola spent the next quarter-hour working on Don Eduardo, first using rags soaked in hot water to clean the blood from the area around the wound. She was gentle and tried not to hurt the don any more than she had to.

His eyes were closed. He had passed out, and he didn't come to as Viola tended to his injury. When the bullet hole was clean and open, she uncapped the *vaquero*'s flask of tequila and poured some of the fiery liquor into the wound, filling it until it overflowed in reddened streaks.

The tequila's fierce bite was enough to make Don Eduardo groan, even though he didn't regain consciousness.

Viola didn't know her husband had returned until Slaughter touched her shoulder and asked, "How is he?"

She turned quickly toward him and instead of answering his question asked one of her own. "Are you all right, John?"

"Fine," Slaughter replied with a curt nod. Viola saw anger and pain in his eyes, though. Not physical pain, she thought, but grief at what had happened here tonight. The people who worked for the Slaughters were like family, and some of them had been lost.

Slaughter nodded toward the sofa and asked again, "What about the don?"

"He's lost a lot of blood," Viola said. "But he seems to be breathing all right, and the last time I checked his heartbeat it was a little ragged but still strong. I don't think the bullet did a tremendous amount of damage inside, or else he wouldn't be hanging on like he is. He ought to be all right if we can get the slug out of him."

"That's what I thought," Slaughter said. "Do you want to go after it, or should we wait for Dr. Fredericks to get here from Douglas?"

"I'd rather let the doctor do it, if we can wait that long. You're going to send a rider?"

"Already did it, as soon as Stonewall and I got back. Orrie's on his way into town now, on the fastest horse we could find."

"Pacer," Stonewall added. He had come into the parlor behind his brother-in-law.

Slaughter glanced over at Santiago, who hovered near the sofa where his stepmother lay.

"Is that all right with you?" he asked. "We'll wait for the doctor to operate on your father in the morning?"

Santiago took a deep breath and nodded.

"If you think that is best, señor."

Slaughter frowned as he looked at the unconscious blonde and asked, "What happened to her?"

"Fainted," Viola answered dryly. "She'll come around."

"Oh."

From the doorway, the old *vaquero* said, "Señora, there are more people who need your help. Shall I have them brought in, as you commanded?"

"Of course," Viola said. "Yolanda, fetch blankets. We'll make pallets on the floor. Stonewall, help me move some of this furniture back to make room."

As the maid hurried out, Slaughter touched Viola's arm and asked quietly, "That's Yolanda? The one young Alvarez was courting?"

"That's right," Viola said. She caught her breath. "John, you said 'was' courting?"

With a bleak expression on his bearded face, Slaughter nodded.

"He was riding nighthawk. The others left him with the herd when the trouble started. Then he was jumped by wide-loopers who went after the cattle." Slaughter paused for a second. "They killed him."

Viola pressed a hand to her mouth and breathed, "No. That poor boy . . ."

"I'll tell the girl when she comes back—"

"No," Viola said. "I'll tell her, John. But later." A determined look came over her face. "Right now, we have wounded to take care of. There'll be time enough later to talk about what happened—and what we're going to do about it."

When the final tally was made, six people had been killed by the Apaches in the attack at the ranch: Pete the wrangler and the other cowboy, Jesse Harper, in the barn; the first victim at the *fandango* itself, a servant girl named Elena; two more of the ranch's cowboys, Al Fraley and Ben Baxter; and one of Slaughter's neighbors, a rancher named Carl Stevens. Hector Alvarez was the seventh victim, killed by the men who had stolen the herd.

In addition to the fatalities, nine men and three women were wounded, some of them seriously. That included Don Eduardo Rubriz.

Fifteen Apaches lay dead, here and there around the ranch. Slaughter believed that the renegades must have fought to the last man.

Viola and some of the other women stayed busy all night, nursing the wounded. Yolanda had cried when Viola broke the news of Hector Alvarez's death to her, but after a while she dried her eyes and went on helping, grim-faced.

Doña Belinda woke up after a while, but she was no help. She was still half-hysterical, especially after she saw her husband lying there so pale with makeshift bandages wrapped around his midsection. She fell to her knees beside him and would have grabbed him, but Viola held her back.

"You don't want to jostle him around any more than he already has been," Viola said. "We don't know exactly where that bullet is, but we know the don is hanging on the way things are. We don't want to cause it to shift and maybe hurt him worse."

"But . . . but he looks so bad," Belinda wailed. "Like he's already dead."

"But he's not, and we want to keep him that way." Viola looked around, spotted Santiago sitting across the room in a straight-back chair, his head hanging down and his hands clasped between his knees. He must have felt her eyes on him because he lifted his head and looked at her. Discreetly, she motioned with her head toward Belinda.

Santiago was good enough to have an affair with his stepmother, Viola thought. The least he could do was take care of her now and keep her out of everyone else's way.

Santiago sighed, stood up, and came over to the sofa where his father lay. He put his hand on Belinda's shoulder and said, "They are doing everything they can for him. We must let him rest."

It took a couple of minutes, but Santiago was able to persuade her to stand up and stop trying to climb onto the sofa with his father. He put an arm around her shoulders and started to turn her away.

Don Eduardo stopped them by whispering, "S-Santiago . . ."

Viola leaned over him, a bit surprised that the don had regained consciousness. She had halfway expected him to be out until the bullet could be removed.

"Don Eduardo, you must rest—" she began.

"My son . . . Santiago . . ."

"I'm here, Father," Santiago said.

Belinda tried to pull loose from his grip. She sobbed, "Eduardo."

Rubriz ignored her. His eyes didn't open, but he said, "Santiago . . . I think I heard talk . . . the cattle we brought . . ."

"Stolen," Santiago said grimly. "Señor Slaughter believes the Apaches were working with rustlers, that their attack was a distraction."

"*El Señor Dios* protect us . . . if those savages begin working with . . . *bandidos*. You must help . . . must help . . ."

"Must help what, Father?"

Rubriz lifted a trembling hand. Santiago let go of Belinda and stepped closer to clasp his father's hand in both of his.

"You must go after them," Don Eduardo rasped. "You must bring those cattle back . . . Our family's honor demands it."

Slaughter had been standing back, listening to the conversation. He stepped forward now and said, "I already paid you for those cows, Don Eduardo. Losing them is my problem. And I assure you, I intend to get them back."

"Take Santiago . . . with you," Don Eduardo pleaded. "Those thieves . . . they stole from me, too. They put my son and my wife . . . in danger. They must be . . . punished."

"Eduardo, that's crazy," Belinda said. "If you send Santiago after them, then you're putting him in danger, too."

"It's different," Santiago said. "I understand what he means." He squeezed his father's hand. "And I'll do it. I'll uphold our family's honor."

A trace of a smile crossed Don Eduardo's lips. Barely audible, he said, "That is good . . . I knew I could count on you . . . my son . . ."

The last word came out of him with a sigh. Belinda lifted both hands to her mouth and stared in horror as she said, "Eduardo!"

"He's still breathing," Viola told her. "He's just asleep again. Talking even that much wore him out. You should probably get some rest, too."

"I . . . I want to help. If there's anything I can do—"

"There's not," Viola said.

One of the last things she wanted right now was to have Belinda underfoot, weeping and wailing.

Santiago turned to Slaughter and said, "You heard what my father said, señor. When are you going after those rustlers?"

"At first light," Slaughter said.

"Then I will be going with you. I can bring most of our *vaqueros* with me, too. A few should be left behind, though, to protect my father since we don't know how long he will be here."

"I agree," Slaughter said. "And I appreciate the offer, Santiago."

"It's not an offer. It is my duty."

"All right. We'll ride together." Slaughter looked over at Stonewall. "Too bad you fellas won't get to have your race in the morning."

"I reckon this is more important," Stonewall said.

"*Sí,*" Santiago agreed. "And there will still be a race. Justice—against the men responsible for this tragedy."

Chapter 9

Ned Becker waited in the mouth of the canyon. A quirly drooped from his lips. From time to time his fingers brushed the leather-wrapped handle of the knife sheathed at his waist.

The knife he had used to kill that young *vaquero* with one deadly accurate throw.

A couple of hundred yards behind him, the cattle moved restlessly, making noises familiar to any man who had spent much time as a cowhand. They were tired and they were angry because they had been driven so hard to get here before dawn.

Now they could rest for a while, though, before some of Becker's men moved them on deeper into the mountains. It was still more than an hour until sunrise, and Becker didn't figure John Slaughter would start after him until first light.

It would probably take that long just to clean up the mess from that little visit by Bodaway and his Apaches, Becker thought as a wry smile curved his lips.

A footstep behind him made Becker look back over his

shoulder. In the shadowy canyon, he couldn't see the man who approached him, but he recognized the voice as that of his *segundo*, Herb Woodbury.

"You sure you should be out here alone waitin' for those redskins, boss?" Woodbury asked. "They could decide to double-cross you. Maybe cut your throat just for the spite of it. You can't never tell what them bloodthirsty savages'll do."

"Bodaway would never betray me," Becker said. "We've been friends for too long."

Woodbury came closer now, close enough that Becker could see him in the starlight. He was a tall, gaunt man with a sandy mustache that straggled across his upper lip.

"It ain't none o' my business, but I can't help but wonder how in blazes you wound up pards with a damn Apache."

"You're right," Becker snapped. "It's none of your business."

Woodbury started to fade back, muttering, "Sorry, boss—"

"But that's all right," Becker went on, his tone softening a bit. "Bodaway and I both grew up around army posts and reservations. His father, you see, was a scout who worked for the army and helped them hunt down his fellow Apaches."

Woodbury grunted. "Lord. That must not've set too well with the redskins who wanted to keep puttin' up a fight."

"No, it didn't," Becker agreed. "To many of the Apaches on the reservation, Bodaway's father was hated and reviled. It was inevitable those feelings reflected over on him, too. He grew up being despised."

"Reckon that's what makes him hate white folks so much now," Woodbury said.

"More than likely. He feels like he's got a lot to make up for. He'll never come in peacefully. He's had his fill of reservations."

"What were you doin' there?" Woodbury asked. "Your pa must've been one of the soldiers, I reckon."

"No," Becker said.

"Sutler, then? Civilian scout?"

Becker considered telling Woodbury to go back with the others and leave him alone. The man's questions were stirring up old memories that were better left alone.

Becker knew from experience that as long as he kept his past buried deep inside him, he could control it instead of the other way around. He could use the bitter hatred as fuel to drive him on.

On the other hand, no man could keep everything bottled up inside him forever. It might feel good to let some of it out for a change.

"My father was dead by then," Becker told his *segundo*. "It was my mother who worked around the forts and the camps. She cooked, did laundry, sold herself to the troopers."

He said the words casually, but there was nothing casual about the way something inside him twisted as he spoke.

"So you see," he went on, "it was natural for Bodaway and me to become friends. My mother was a whore, and his father was being paid to betray his people. We were alike in so many ways."

For a long moment Woodbury didn't say anything.

Then the outlaw said in a clearly uncomfortable voice, "Boss, I never meant to pry—"

"Don't worry about it, Herb." Becker's voice hardened again. "But know one thing: I won't be gossiped about. What I just told you, that stays between the two of us, understand?"

Becker heard the other man swallow. Woodbury said, "Sure, boss. I won't say anything to anybody."

Becker knew that he meant it, too. Woodbury was too afraid of him not to honor the request. Woodbury had seen him kill—savagely, suddenly, without warning.

No, Woodbury wouldn't say anything, Becker thought with a smile.

Then he stiffened as he heard an owl hoot somewhere outside the canyon.

Only it wasn't an owl, Becker knew. He recognized the sound from childhood. He turned, slipped a match from his vest pocket, and struck it with his thumbnail. He moved the flame back and forth in front of him three times, then snuffed it out and dropped the match at his feet.

Less than a minute later, a lithe figure trotted out of the darkness.

Alone.

Becker tensed even more. He had expected Bodaway to lose some men in the attack, but it appeared that the Apache war chief had arrived at this rendezvous by himself.

"Bodaway," Becker said quietly. "*El Infierno*."

Bodaway came to a stop in front of him and grunted.

"What happened?" Becker asked. "Your warriors—"

"All dead," Bodaway said, his voice flat and devoid of

emotion. "We took the white men by surprise, but they fought well. Especially a few. The little one with the beard slew many of my men."

"Slaughter," Becker said with a note of hatred. Until now he hadn't had anything personally against John Slaughter. His grudge was against someone else. But the rancher and lawman had made himself an enemy tonight.

Becker knew that was a little irrational. Of course Slaughter would fight back when his ranch was attacked. But Becker hated him for it anyway, the same way he hated anyone who dared to oppose his plans.

Setting that aside for the moment, Becker asked, "What about Don Eduardo? Your men knew he was not to be harmed."

"You ask too much, Becker," the Apache snapped. "No man's safety is guaranteed in the middle of a fight."

Becker suddenly felt as if he were standing at the edge of a high cliff, with everything falling away into nothingness at his feet. If Rubriz had been killed, that would ruin everything. He couldn't die without knowing the reason. He just couldn't.

"What happened?" Becker forced himself to ask. "Was he killed?"

"I do not know, and that is the truth, Becker. You told me what he looks like, and I saw such a man fall." Bodaway shrugged. "That is all I know."

Becker struggled to maintain his composure. This didn't really change anything, he told himself. He would still go through with his plan. Even if Rubriz was dead, that wouldn't finish things.

There was still more killing to do.

"All right. I'm sorry about your men, Bodaway. I'll honor our bargain, though. I'll get the rifles for you—"

"With no warriors, I have no need of rifles now," the war chief cut in. "Later, when I have raised another band. Then you will give us rifles."

"Of course," Becker agreed.

"But now . . ."

"Whatever you want, Bodaway, if it's within my power."

"I want to kill that little man, the one you called Slaughter. I want to strip his skin off inch by inch and burn him over a fire for a long time before I allow him to die."

Becker smiled and nodded and said, "I think that can be arranged."

The eastern sky was gray with the approach of dawn when Slaughter held a council of war in his study.

Stonewall was there, and so was the ranch's foreman, Jess Fisher. Slaughter had invited Santiago Rubriz, too, and Santiago had brought along the older, rakish *vaquero*, who he introduced as Augustín Hermosa.

"Jess, I'm leaving you in charge here on the ranch," Slaughter told the foreman. "I want you to pick out ten good fighting men to come with me after those cows."

Fisher, who had also served as one of Slaughter's deputies in Tombstone from time to time, frowned and said bluntly, "I'd rather go with you after those damned rustlers myself, boss."

"I know that. But I'm not going to ride off and leave the ranch unprotected. I'm not expecting any more trouble . . . but I wasn't expecting the trouble last night, either."

With obvious reluctance, Fisher nodded and said, "All right. When are you riding out?"

"No later than an hour from now," Slaughter said. "Sooner if we can get everything together."

"I had the remuda brought in, like you ordered earlier. You'll want to take extra horses."

"One per man," Slaughter agreed with a nod. "This shouldn't turn into a long chase. We can move faster than those cattle can. But I spoke to the cook about supplies, too. We'll take a couple of pack horses and carry enough provisions for several days."

Santiago spoke up, saying, "I can provide eight men, not counting myself. Our force will number almost two dozen. We should be more than a match for the thieves."

"We'll have to catch them first," Slaughter said. He looked at Hermosa. "You're Don Eduardo's foreman, aren't you?"

"Me?" Hermosa's shoulders rose and fell in a languid shrug. "I'm just a simple *vaquero*, señor."

Slaughter knew better than that. All he had to do was look at Hermosa to recognize that the *hombre* was a top-notch fighting man. He was glad they were going to be on the same side.

He turned his attention to Stonewall and said, "I suppose you're going to insist on coming along, too."

"Those Apaches tried to burn me up in the barn," Stonewall said. His voice was still a little hoarse from the smoke he'd inhaled. "And they were workin' for the varmints we're goin' after. So, yeah, you can dang well bet that I'm comin' along."

"Apaches don't really work for anybody," Slaughter pointed out. "But there's no doubt they had an arrangement with the men who stole that herd. It's unusual, no doubt about it, but the conclusion is inescapable. Those two things didn't happen the same night by coincidence."

It was agreed that the party going after the rustlers would assemble on the road in front of the ranch house. As soon as everyone was ready, they would start in pursuit.

Slaughter knew the trail ought to be easy to follow. The herd was a relatively small one, only about five hundred head, but that many cattle couldn't be moved without leaving plenty of signs.

"I want to see how my father is before we leave," Santiago said. "But we will be ready to ride, Señor Slaughter, have no doubt of that."

"I don't have any doubts," Slaughter told him. "The rest of us will be saying our good-byes, too."

The meeting broke up. Slaughter went to the parlor, where Don Eduardo was still resting on the sofa. He looked around but didn't see Viola. One of the servants tending to the wounded men noticed what he was doing and told him, "Señora Slaughter is in the kitchen, señor."

"*Gracias,*" Slaughter said. He went on out to the kitchen and found Viola supervising the packing of provisions for the men who were going after the rustlers.

She smiled at him and asked, "Will you be leaving soon?"

"Soon," Slaughter confirmed.

"I don't suppose it would do any good to tell you to be careful."

"I'm always careful," he protested. "I'm a cautious man."

"You can be," Viola admitted. "Maybe even most of the time you are. But then you get some crazy, reckless hunch, and nothing will do except that you follow through on it."

He grinned and said, "You mean like when I decided I was going to ask this wild young cowgirl to marry me?"

Viola laughed and then moved closer so she could rest her forehead against his shoulder.

"Honestly, John," she said quietly, "don't get yourself killed over some cows. You can always buy more cattle."

"That's true . . . but I can't buy the lives of the people who were killed last night. Murdered while they should have been enjoying themselves at that *fandango* you threw."

"And that's the real reason you're going after the rustlers, isn't it?"

Slaughter inclined his head in acknowledgment of her point.

"Just come back to me safely," she said. "That's all I've ever asked."

"And I always have. I always will."

Promises like that were easy to make, he thought.

Sometimes not so easy to keep. But he would do his best.

"You'll look after Stonewall?"

"Of course. But that brother of yours can look after himself, you know. I wouldn't say it to his face for fear of giving him a swelled head, but he's a fine young man."

"Yes, he is." Viola put her hands on Slaughter's arms and leaned in to kiss him. She didn't have to come up on her toes very far to do that, since he wasn't much taller than she was. "All right, let me get back to work. The sooner you chase down those rustlers, the sooner you can bring our cattle back and things can settle down here."

Slaughter nodded and went back out to the parlor. He found Santiago there, sitting on a chair he had drawn up next to the sofa where Don Eduardo lay.

"He seems to be resting fairly comfortably," Santiago said as he looked up at Slaughter. "Will the doctor be here soon?"

"Should be. I expect him and the rider I sent to Douglas by dawn, or at least not long after that. But that's only if Orrie was able to locate Dr. Fredericks right away. The doc could have been out somewhere on a call. In that case, Orrie would have to wait for him to get back to town."

"I have prayed for my father. That's all I can do." Santiago's face hardened. "Except for going after the men responsible for what happened to him."

"Where's your stepmother?" Slaughter asked.

"She's gone to her room to rest. She didn't want to leave my father's side, but I convinced her."

"I reckon there's really not much she could do. Viola will let her know if they need her help."

"Your wife is a fine woman, Señor Slaughter."

Slaughter chuckled and said, "You're not telling me anything I don't already know, son."

He could count on Viola to take care of things here at the ranch. Otherwise, he never would have been able to chase off after those rustlers like he was about to.

He wasn't acting in his capacity as a lawman in this case, but justice was going to be done anyway.

The sooner the better.

Chapter 10

Viola stepped out the front door of the ranch house and used her hand to shade her eyes from the glare of the sun rising to her left. Almost two dozen men were gathered on the other side of the picket fence that enclosed the house. They had mounted up and were ready to ride. Her husband, wearing a black Stetson, blue work shirt, and denim trousers, would take the lead.

The range clothes were considerably different from the suit that the nattily dressed John Slaughter usually wore, even here on the ranch, but they were much more appropriate for chasing down rustlers.

Santiago Rubriz, in tight trousers, charro jacket, and steeple-crowned sombrero, was much more dapper. His face was pale and drawn, though, which prevented him from looking dashing.

He was mounted on *El Halcón*. The blaze-faced black stepped around nervously. With her ranch woman's experienced eye, Viola wasn't sure the horse was the best animal for the job of chasing down rustlers. *El Halcón* was fast, no doubt about that, but he might not have the staying power this task would require.

But that was none of her business, Viola told herself. Her concern at the moment was keeping the ranch safe while John was gone, as well as taking care of the people who had been wounded in the Apache attack.

Dr. Neal Fredericks still hadn't arrived from Douglas. It was pretty obvious by now that something had happened to delay him.

If the doctor didn't show up soon, Viola knew she would have to try to remove the bullet from Don Eduardo. Every hour the chunk of lead stayed inside him lessened his chances for survival.

She had already said her good-byes to her husband. They had caught a moment alone in the house and shared an embrace and passionate kiss. The difference in their ages that had caused some people to look askance at their marriage had never meant a thing to them. They loved each other wholeheartedly, always had, always would.

From the back of his horse, John lifted a hand to her in farewell. She returned the wave, trying to ignore the pang of worry that went through her. She already missed him, and he wasn't even gone yet. She couldn't even begin to comprehend what it would be like if something happened to him and he never returned.

"Let's move out," Slaughter called. Santiago repeated the order in Spanish for the Rubriz *vaqueros*, even though Slaughter's command of the language was as fluent as a native's. In the absence of Don Eduardo, though, his men looked to Santiago for leadership.

Viola hoped the young man could provide it. If he

didn't, that might wind up putting John Slaughter in danger.

Maybe this whole affair would help Santiago grow up a little.

That thought was in Viola's mind when someone tried to hurry past her. She looked over, saw Doña Belinda, and caught hold of the blonde's arm to prevent her from rushing out to the road.

"Let go of me," Belinda said. "He's leaving. I didn't get a chance to say good-bye to him."

"If you're talking about your stepson, you can still wave to him," Viola said. "If I could trust you to give him a motherly kiss, you could go out there. But since I can't . . ."

Belinda glared at her and demanded, "Who are you to judge me? I've heard about you. You married a grown man—a widower—when you weren't much more than a child."

Viola struggled with the impulse to slap this woman from back East. She said, "I was old enough to know what I wanted, and it's worked out. We have the happiest, strongest marriage I know. And I've always been faithful to him."

"You can get off your high horse," Belinda said coldly. "You don't know anything about me and my marriage."

"I know more than I wish I did."

"I love my husband," Belinda went on as if Viola hadn't said anything. "I wanted to help take care of him. You wouldn't let me."

Maybe she had a point about that, Viola thought. Maybe the dislike she felt for Belinda had prompted her to keep the woman at arm's length, even from her own wounded husband.

Right now, though, Viola didn't care. Her husband and brother were riding away, quite possibly to risk their lives. The group of riders had covered about a hundred yards, moving at a fast lope as they headed for the place where they would pick up the trail of the stolen herd. Dust rose in the air from their horses' hooves, blurring their dwindling figures.

"You might as well go on back in the house," she told Belinda. "They're gone . . . and all we can do is pray that they'll be safe while we wait for them to come back."

Slaughter led the way to the spot where the herd had been bedded down the day before. The group had to pass the place he and Stonewall had found the body of Hector Alvarez. Slaughter didn't pause, but he pointed it out to the others and said, "At least one of the fellas we're going after is good with a knife, so be ready for that."

"I don't intend to let any of 'em get close enough to me to use a knife," Stonewall said.

The *vaquero* called Hermosa plucked a Bowie knife from a sheath at his waist and said, "I can handle a blade fairly well myself, Señor Slaughter. Perhaps I will meet up with this *hombre* who killed young Alvarez."

That would probably be a good fight to see, thought Slaughter.

Finding the trail the cattle had left when they were driven away was no problem. The tracks led almost due north. If they continued in that direction, eventually they would reach the Chiricahua Mountains on the other side of Cave Creek. If they curved west, they would get to the mountains sooner, and if they went east they would find themselves in the wasteland of southern New Mexico Territory.

Whatever direction the rustlers took, Slaughter intended to stay on their trail. He set a brisk pace, but not fast enough to wear out the horses. They had extra mounts, but he wanted to keep all the horses in as good a shape as possible.

You never knew when you might need to make a hard run for some reason.

"I wish the doctor had gotten there before we left," Santiago said. "My mind would rest easier if I knew my father was going to be all right."

"He's in good hands," Slaughter told the young man. "My wife has tended to many wounded men before. If the doctor doesn't show up soon, she'll do what needs to be done."

"I suppose you're right. And my father is a very strong man, very tough. He has been shot before, you know."

"No, I didn't know that," Slaughter said. "I'm not surprised, though. He mentioned in one of his letters that he started his ranch almost thirty years ago. Northern Mexico's still pretty rugged today, but it was really wild back in those days. Not much around except Apaches, Yaquis, and *bandidos*."

"That is true," Santiago said, "but it was none of those who shot him. It was his own partner. An American named Thaddeus Becker."

* * *

As the sun rose, Ned Becker told the eight men who would be taking the cattle deeper into the mountains, through twisting canyons to the high, isolated pasture where they would be kept, to get ready to move out.

Eight men would have their hands full driving the herd, but it could be done. That left eighteen gunhands to accompany Becker on the next part of this job.

Or maybe he had nineteen men, he thought as he approached the spot where Bodaway hunkered on his heels next to the ashes of a campfire, soaking up what little warmth still came from it in this chilly dawn.

"What are you going to do now, Bodaway?" Becker asked his old friend.

The glance the Apache lifted to him was almost as cold as the desert air around them.

"I will start looking for more warriors to fight the white men," Bodaway said, as if the answer to Becker's question should have been completely obvious.

"That can wait a while. Why don't you come with me? I know we were supposed to split up after this rendezvous, but there's no reason to do that now."

"You mean since all my men are dead."

"I'm sorry about that, I truly am," Becker said in response to the flat comment. He knew what Bodaway had to be thinking, and he wanted to head that off if he could. "In a way it's my fault they're dead. I understand why you'd feel that way. You were there at Slaughter's ranch because of me. I knew you'd probably lose a few men, but . . ." Becker sighed and shook his head. "Damned if

I ever thought you'd lose all of them. I really didn't, Bodaway."

The Apache regarded him through dark, slitted eyes for a long moment before saying, "All the way here, I thought I would kill you as soon as I saw you. As you said, I blamed you for their deaths. I wanted to avenge them by killing you. But that would not bring them back . . . and you did not take their lives. Slaughter and his people did. The Mexican don and his people did."

"That's right," Becker said, trying not to sound too eager to exploit what Bodaway had just said. "And you can take your vengeance on them if you come with me."

Bodaway straightened to his feet. He asked, "Will they not come after the cattle?"

"Slaughter will. I've heard enough about him to know that. I figured Rubriz would come with him, but you said he was wounded."

"Or killed."

"Or killed," Becker agreed with a shrug. "But I'm not going to accept that until I know for sure. I'd planned to make him come to me begging on his knees, but if he's still at the ranch that'll work out even better."

Bodaway frowned slightly and said, "I never really understood what you mean to do."

That was because he had never really explained it to anybody else, not even Woodbury or any of his other men, Becker thought. The details of the plan had remained fluid in his mind, capable of being changed to take circumstances into account, and as things were turning out, that was good.

Bodaway was perhaps the only person cunning enough to follow his reasoning, though, so he said, "Your raid on the ranch was a distraction to allow us to steal Don Eduardo's herd."

Bodaway nodded.

"But the rustling was a distraction, too, to lure nearly everybody away from the ranch. I figured Don Eduardo would come along with Slaughter and try to get the herd back. That way I could take some of my men and circle around and go back to the ranch. There wouldn't be enough of Slaughter's crew there to stop us from taking over."

"But you thought the Mexican would not be there."

"Yeah, but his wife would be. With her as a hostage, Rubriz will do anything I tell him to, even give himself up to me so I can torture him."

Bodaway nodded gravely and said, "This is much hate in you, to go to so much trouble instead of just killing the man."

"Just killing him's not enough. I want Don Eduardo Rubriz to suffer as much as possible, in as many ways as possible, before he dies."

"Why?" Bodaway asked.

"Because the son of a bitch murdered my father."

Chapter 11

Viola stood next to the sofa where Don Eduardo lay and looked down at his slack, pale face. If not for the fact that she could see his chest rising and falling, she might have thought that death had already claimed him.

An hour had passed since John and the others left in pursuit of the rustlers. The doctor still hadn't arrived from Douglas. Viola glanced at the big grandfather clock in one corner of the parlor to check the time.

She would give it another half-hour, she decided, and then she would have to try to extract the bullet from Don Eduardo's body herself.

A soft step sounded behind her. Viola turned and saw Belinda standing there.

"How is he?" the blonde asked.

"The same as before. He's sleeping."

"Unconscious, you mean," Belinda said in an accusing tone.

"I'm not sure I'd call it that. His body is doing everything it can to preserve the strength it has left."

"How long are you going to wait for the doctor?"

"I was just thinking about that," Viola admitted. "Another thirty minutes or so. That much time shouldn't make any—"

Before she could finish, a small Mexican boy, the son of one of the married *vaqueros*, ran into the room and said excitedly, "Señora, señora, someone comes."

"Who is it, Paco?" Viola asked.

"A man in a buggy, señora. That's all I know."

It was enough, Viola thought. She knew that Dr. Neal Fredericks drove a buggy when he called on his patients. She put a hand on the boy's head for a second, said, "*Gracias*, Paco," and hurried to the door.

Belinda was right behind her.

Viola looked west along the road leading to Douglas and saw the buggy drawn by a tall, sturdy horse. A thin plume of dust rose into the sky behind it.

Another man rode alongside the vehicle. That would be Orrie, the cowboy John Slaughter had sent to town to fetch the physician. As they came closer, Viola recognized the horse Orrie was riding as Pacer, and seeing the roan confirmed her hunch.

"Is that him?" Belinda asked anxiously. She shaded her eyes with her hand, even though the sun was behind them. "Is that the doctor?"

"It is," Viola said.

"Thank God."

Viola looked at the other woman and said, "You sound like you mean that."

"You'll never understand how things are between my

husband and me," Belinda snapped. "Don't even waste your time trying."

"Fine," Viola said. Maybe she was being too judgmental, although she didn't think so. But either way, it didn't really matter right now. Saving Don Eduardo's life was the important thing.

Dr. Fredericks brought the buggy to a halt in front of the picket fence. Viola already had the gate open, ready for him. He climbed out of the buggy, a tall, heavyset man with a squarish head and close-cropped gray beard. He wore a gray suit and a flat-crowned black hat and carried a black medical bag.

"Good morning, Mrs. Slaughter," Fredericks greeted Viola as he came into the yard. "I hear you had quite a commotion out here last night."

"You could call it that," Viola said.

"I knew about your party and thought I might attend, but I was called away. It was Mildred Bankston's time. Triplets, can you believe that? It was quite an ordeal for everyone involved. Anyway, I didn't get back until long after midnight. That's why your man had to wait for me."

Belinda said, "Can't you stop talking and go inside?"

Fredericks looked at her and raised his bushy eyebrows in surprise. Viola said, "This is Doña Belinda Rubriz, doctor. Her husband is in the worst shape of those who were injured in the attack."

"Then by all means let's go have a look at him," Fredericks said. He gave Belinda a curt nod and added, "I'm sorry to be making your acquaintance under such trying circumstances, ma'am."

Belinda didn't say anything else. She followed Viola and the doctor into the house.

Viola took Fredericks straight to Don Eduardo. He pulled a chair over next to the sofa and set his bag on it, then untied the bandages and pulled them back to reveal the bullet hole in the wounded man's side.

Belinda gasped a little at the sight of it, but Viola thought the hole actually looked pretty good, considering. The flesh around it wasn't too red, and she didn't see any streaks running away from the wound, which would have been a sign that it was festering and spreading.

Dr. Fredericks seemed to agree with her. He said, "It appears you did a fine job here, Mrs. Slaughter. I believe your man said the bullet is still in the victim's body?"

"That's right. We didn't find any other wounds, so it has to be."

Fredericks nodded.

"The next thing to do is get it out. I'll give the don just a bit of laudanum to make sure he remains unconscious through the procedure."

"See?" Belinda whispered to Viola. "I told you he was unconscious, not just asleep."

Fredericks heard her anyway and chuckled.

"What you call it doesn't matter, Señora Rubriz. What's important is that your husband doesn't wake up and start moving around while I'm going after that bullet."

"Should we try to move him?" Viola asked. "We can put him on the dining room table so you can operate there."

Fredericks shook his head and said, "No, I'd prefer that he stay right where he is until we get that bullet out of him." He took off his hat and coat and started rolling up his shirt sleeves. "I'll be needing some hot water and clean rags."

Viola turned and nodded to one of the servants standing nearby. The woman hurried off to fetch what the doctor wanted.

"Now, before I start this procedure let me take a quick look at the other wounded, so I'll have an idea of what else I'll need to do this morning," Frederick said.

Ten minutes later, after checking his other patients, Fredericks perched on a chair next to the sofa where he could reach Don Eduardo and got ready to extract the bullet. He had a long, slender probe and a pair of forceps in his hands. Before he got to work he looked over his shoulder and said to Belinda, "You might want to step out of the room, madam."

"I'm not going anywhere," she declared. "I'm going to stay right here until my husband is out of danger."

"All right, but I warn you, there's liable to be more bleeding."

"I don't care. I'll be all right."

"Suit yourself."

Fredericks inserted the probe into the wound and began using it to search for the bullet. As he had warned Belinda, blood welled out of the bullet hole around the probe.

Viola heard a faint moan and glanced over at the blonde. She saw how pale Belinda was, how wide her eyes were, and how hard she was breathing as she watched the operation. Viola moved a little closer to her.

It was a good thing she did, because Belinda moaned

again and her knees buckled. Viola was there to catch her under the arms and keep her from falling.

Without looking up from what he was doing, Fredericks said, "Fainted, eh? That didn't take long."

"About as long as I figured it would," Viola said. "Doña Belinda seems to have a tendency toward passing out."

She motioned with her head, and a couple of servants hurried to take hold of Belinda and carry her over to an armchair. They lowered her into it gently.

A few minutes later, Fredericks held up a misshapen lump of lead that he gripped with the forceps.

"There it is," he said to Viola as he showed the bullet to her. "I believe, considering its location, that it didn't damage any major organs or fracture any ribs. The don was lucky. He lost enough blood to make him pass out, but as long as the wound is kept clean, with plenty of rest he ought to be fine."

"I'm glad to hear that, doctor."

Fredericks used one of the rags to wipe blood off his hands as he stood up.

"Now I'll get started on the other cases." He smiled and added, "When you and your husband throw a party, Mrs. Slaughter, it's always quite an event. I'll be sure to attend the next one—just in case my services are needed again!"

"Where the hell are they going with those cows?" Stonewall asked as the trail of the stolen herd continued to lead north toward the Chiricahuas. "Do they plan to drive 'em all the way up to Galeyville or around the mountains to Fort Bowie?"

Slaughter rode at the head of the group of pursuers with Stonewall on his right and Santiago Rubriz on his left. Santiago hadn't explained his earlier comment about his father being shot by an American partner, and Slaughter hadn't pressed him for details. He didn't figure it was any of his business. If Santiago wanted to talk about it, he could.

Instead Santiago asked now, "Could they sell the herd to the army at this fort? Soldiers always need beef."

"It would be a shame to use those cattle for beef," Slaughter said. "I bought them to improve the bloodline of my herd, so I want them around for a while."

"They still have my father's brand on them, not yours, Señor Slaughter," Santiago pointed out.

And since Mexican brands most closely resembled a skillet full of writhing snakes, those markings wouldn't mean anything to an army quartermaster, Slaughter mused. All the rustlers had to do was convince the quartermaster at Fort Bowie that the stock was legally theirs, and they might collect for it.

For that matter, Slaughter knew that the army sometimes turned a blind eye to the possibility that animals with Mexican brands might be what they called over in Texas "wet cattle," meaning they had been driven across the Rio Grande—usually in the dead of night.

As Santiago had said, soldiers needed beef, and the men charged with providing it often weren't too particular about where it came from.

Those thoughts ran through Slaughter's mind, and then he said, "That may be what they try to do, but it seems like a lot of trouble for what they'd make out of the deal. This is a small herd. The payoff won't be big enough once it's split up among them to make it worthwhile—especially since they had to run the risk of involving those Apaches, too." He frowned. "I have a hunch that there's something else going on here, but I'll be damned if I can figure out what it is."

"We'll just catch up to the varmints and ask 'em," Stonewall said.

Slaughter chuckled and said, "Yes, that might be the best plan."

They kept moving, stopping now and then to switch horses and let the animals rest a bit. The sun had risen high enough now to generate a considerable amount of heat.

It was during one of those pauses, while Slaughter had his hat off and was using his sleeve to wipe sweat off his forehead, that he noticed something. Several miles away to the east, a thin haze of dust rose in the air as if a large group of riders was on the move over there, heading south.

It couldn't be the rustlers doubling back, he told himself. The dust was moving too fast for that. They couldn't push those cattle at such a pace and hope to control them.

A cavalry patrol, he thought. That was a more likely answer. Possibly word of the Apache attack had reached Fort Bowie, and the commander there had sent a troop to check it out and chase any renegades who were left.

If that was the case, they were too late for that, Slaughter thought. By now all those Apaches would be buried in shallow graves.

He put the matter out of his mind for now and told the men to mount up. They were moving out again.

Whoever those riders in the distance were, they had nothing to do with the deadly errand on which John Slaughter found himself occupied today.

Chapter 12

Ned Becker knew that Bodaway was still curious about the origins of his vendetta against Don Eduardo Rubriz, but the Apache didn't ask any questions. Bodaway wouldn't; that wasn't the sort of man he was. He would wait for Becker to offer details, and if that never happened, Bodaway would just put the whole matter out of his mind.

As with his conversation about his mother with Herb Woodbury the night before, though, the idea of letting out some of the demons that gnawed on his brain and guts appealed to Becker. During a halt to rest the horses around midmorning, Becker went over to his old friend and said, "I'll tell you about it if you want."

"It is nothing to me whether you do or not," Bodaway answered without looking at him. He had been given a horse to ride, and he was checking the animal's saddle.

"My father was Rubriz's partner," Becker said. "He'd done some fighting in Mexico. He went down there on a filibuster and stayed to work for one faction or another. Those Mexes are hell on wheels when it comes to overthrowing their government. Doesn't matter who's in charge, there's always a revolution brewing."

Bodaway grunted. He was starting to look interested in spite of himself.

"He and Rubriz became friends somehow," Becker went on. "When the side Rubriz supported came to power, he wound up with a big land grant in northern Sonora. He asked my father to help him start a ranch there. Before they left Mexico City, though, they each got married. Their wives were high-born ladies with mostly Castilian blood."

Becker started trying to roll a cigarette as he talked, but when he mentioned his mother his fingers began to shake. She had gone from the pampered surroundings of a wealthy family in Mexico City to selling herself in an Arizona Territory cavalry camp. Was it any wonder he hated the man responsible for that downfall?

He crumpled the half-rolled quirly and threw it aside.

"They worked together side by side to establish that ranch," Becker continued. "They fought Indians and bandits and drought and sickness. And they made something out of the place. I was born there."

"You are fortunate the warriors of my people never visited your ranch," Bodaway said. "You probably would not have survived infancy."

Becker responded with a grim chuckle.

"I reckon maybe you and me were meant to be partners, Bodaway. That's why the Apaches never tried to kill my folks."

Bodaway just grunted.

Becker said, "Things went along all right for a while. No telling how long they would have stayed that way if

Rubriz hadn't started sniffing around my mother. It wasn't bad enough he wanted to cheat on his wife. He had to go after his own partner's wife."

"This is none of my affair," Bodaway said.

The story had started to spill out of Becker, though, and he didn't want to stop it. He said, "When my pa found out what was going on, he wanted to take me and my mother and leave the ranch. But he couldn't bring himself to just walk away from everything he'd done. He had put as much time and hard work into the place as Rubriz had. He told Rubriz he had to buy out his half. If he didn't, then my father was going to send word to my mother's family back in Mexico City about what was going on, and to the family of Rubriz's wife, too."

Several more of Becker's men had drifted up and started listening to the tale. Becker was in the habit of keeping everything bottled up, so their presence almost made him stop.

But then he decided that they had a right to know. They wouldn't just be getting a payoff for this job. They were helping him right a wrong. For once in their mostly misbegotten lives, they were doing a good thing.

Sure, some innocent folks had wound up dead already because of Becker's plan, and more would surely die before it was over, but that couldn't be helped.

Vengeance trumped everything else.

"Rubriz was afraid of both families back in Mexico City. In those days they had more money and power than he did. So when my father threatened him, he should have backed off. I guess he just wanted my mother too much, though. He pretended to mend fences with my pa, then lured him out on the range one day and—"

Becker had to stop and swallow hard before he could go on.

"Rubriz shot my father in the back," he grated after a moment. "Pa managed to turn around and get off a shot of his own. He wounded Rubriz and got away from him. But he was hurt bad and barely made it back to the ranch before he died. He lived long enough to tell my mother what had happened, though. She was afraid Rubriz would try to hurt me, too, so that I couldn't grow up and settle the score. She took me and ran, to save my life. She figured Rubriz would expect her to head for Mexico City and her family, so she went the other way to fool him. We wound up in Arizona Territory. She planned to circle around and get back home, but we didn't have any money or food and Ma . . . Well, Ma had to do things so we could survive. After that, she was too ashamed to go home, so we got by any way we could." Becker shrugged and concluded, "You know the rest, Bodaway. Wasn't long after that you and I met."

One of the other men spoke up, asking, "Is that story true, Ned?"

"Would I have told it if it wasn't?" Becker snapped.

Bodaway said, "You have good reason for wanting this man Rubriz to suffer. But it will not bring back your father, or change any of the bad things your mother endured."

"I figured you'd understand about a blood debt if anybody would," Becker said.

"I understand," the Apache said. "And I stand ready to help you get what you want. But what you want may not be what you think it is."

"It'll do. As long as Don Eduardo Rubriz dies screaming

in agony, knowing that everything he holds dear is dead, it'll do."

Several of the other patients at the ranch had serious injuries, though not as life-threatening as Don Eduardo's had been, so by the time Dr. Neal Fredericks had finished tending to everyone, the hour was approaching midday.

"I hope you'll stay and have lunch with us before you start back to Douglas," Viola told him.

Fredericks nodded as he rolled down his shirt sleeves and fastened them. He was standing beside the pump behind the house where he had just spent several minutes scrubbing blood off his hands.

"I'd be glad to, Mrs. Slaughter," he said. "I appreciate the invitation. It's been rather a long morning." Fredericks canted his head to one side and added, "Longer for you, though, I expect. Just how long has it been since you had any sleep?"

"Oh, I don't really know. Thirty hours or more, I suspect."

"At least, I'd say. I'm going to prescribe a nice long nap for you after we've eaten."

"Someone needs to keep an eye on Don Eduardo and the other wounded," Viola protested.

"And someone can. Someone else. The don's wife, for example. Surely she's capable of taking care of him."

Viola couldn't stop herself from letting out a lady-like snort.

"I wouldn't be so sure of that," she said.

"It would take a blind man not to see that the two of

you don't care for each other," Fredericks commented as they started toward the back door. "Why the hostility?"

"Some people just don't get along, I guess," Viola said. She was still reluctant to expose Belinda's secret, even though she had only sworn not to tell Don Eduardo.

Anytime a secret was shared, it was well on its way to not being a secret anymore, she thought.

"I suppose it shouldn't come as a surprise," the doctor mused. "The two of you come from very different backgrounds, after all. Other than being married to older men, I wouldn't think you'd have much in common." He added, "And I'm not saying anything bad about you being married to an older man, by the way. I know you and John well enough to know how well-matched you are."

"Thank you, doctor. Not everyone has always felt that way."

As they went inside, Yolanda came to meet them. The maid's features still looked a bit drawn with grief over the death of Hector Alvarez, but she had been busy all day and Viola knew that must have helped her cope with the loss.

"Señora, Don Eduardo is awake," Yolanda reported. "He is asking for Doña Belinda."

"Where is she?" Viola wanted to know.

"In her room, maybe?" Yolanda shook her head. "*Quien sabe?*"

"I'll go see. But first I want to look in on Don Eduardo."

They went into the parlor, which was still serving as a makeshift hospital. Don Eduardo was not only awake, he was also trying to sit up on the sofa. One of the other maids leaned over him and told him in Spanish that he should rest.

"The young lady is right, sir," Fredericks said as he strode up. "You risk further injury by carrying on like this."

"Who are you?" Don Eduardo demanded as he glared up at the physician.

"Dr. Neal Fredericks. I'm the one who removed that bullet from you."

"Then I owe you my gratitude, doctor, but not my obedience. Where is my wife? Where is my son?"

Don Eduardo was a little wild-eyed, Viola thought. He was flushed, too, and breathing hard.

"Doña Belinda is around here somewhere," Viola told him. "I'll find her and let her know you're awake, but you really should lay back and rest."

"What about Santiago?"

Viola was a little surprised that he didn't remember telling Santiago to go with John. He must have been a little out of his head at the time.

"He went with my husband after those men who stole the herd of cattle you brought up here," she explained.

"The cattle . . . ?" The confused expression faded from Don Eduardo's face. He sank back against the pillows and went on, "Ah, I remember now. The Apaches were just to keep everyone busy while the real evildoing went on."

Viola would have said that killing innocent people was more evil than rustling cattle, but she knew what the don meant.

Rubriz went on, "You say Santiago went after the thieves as well?"

"You insisted that he should."

Don Eduardo closed his eyes and murmured, "Good.

The honor of our family demands it. May *El Señor Dios* watch over the boy."

Now that the don was calmer again, Fredericks reached down and rested a hand briefly on his forehead.

"He seems to have developed a bit of a fever," the doctor told Viola as he straightened. "Well, that was always a possibility and one of the things we needed to watch out for."

"What should we do now?" she asked.

"All we can do is keep him as cool and comfortable as possible and let his body fight it. He needs to stay calm, too, so why don't you go find his wife?"

Viola nodded. As she left the parlor, she heard Fredericks telling one of the servants to fetch a basin of cool water and some clean cloths, so she could bathe Don Eduardo's face.

The first place Viola checked was the room that had been intended for the don and doña's use if things had gone as planned. She knocked on the door twice and was about to give up when she heard a faint response from within.

"What is it?"

Viola opened the door. She saw that the curtains had been pulled tightly closed, but enough of the midday light came in through cracks around them that she had no trouble spotting Belinda on the big four-poster bed. Belinda was fully dressed and lying on top of the comforter.

"Your husband is awake and asking for you," Viola said. "Also, he's running a little fever."

Belinda sat up sharply and said, "What? I knew I shouldn't have trusted that backwater quack—"

"Dr. Fredericks is a very competent doctor," Viola

said. "I have no doubt that he could practice in Boston if he wanted to and do just fine. Instead of worrying about that, why don't you come and see if you can help?"

Belinda swung her legs off the bed and stood up. As she straightened her clothes she glared at Viola and said, "You've no right to talk to me that way. I'm a guest here, remember?"

"Trust me, I remember." Viola didn't add that it was her own stubborn hospitality that kept her from slapping some sense into the blonde. "The doctor said Don Eduardo needs to remain calm. You don't need to go in there acting angry and upset."

"All right. I understand." Belinda's chin jutted defiantly. "I'm getting tired of you judging me, though."

"Then how about in the future I just steer clear of you as much as possible?"

"I think that's a very good idea."

The two women left the room. As a tense silence hung between them, Viola led the way back to the parlor.

Belinda went straight to the sofa where her husband lay. One of the servants sat in a chair beside Don Eduardo and wiped his face with a cool, damp cloth. Smiling, Belinda said, "Why don't you let me do that, dear?"

The maid turned the job over to her, and as Belinda stroked the cloth over Don Eduardo's face, he looked at her and said, "My darling, are you all right?"

"Of course I'm all right, Eduardo," she told him, "and you will be, too, very soon now. Just lie there and rest and let us take good care of you."

Rubriz sighed. His eyes slowly closed as the taut lines of his face relaxed.

Standing back a ways, Fredericks said quietly to Viola, "See, she's doing him some good already."

Viola had her arms crossed over her chest as she struggled to keep an expression of dislike off her face. She said, "I suppose so."

"Let's leave the two of them alone."

Viola nodded and turned away. She needed to go see about getting a midday meal ready, she remembered.

Before she could do that, Jess Fisher appeared in the doorway, holding his hat in one hand. Viola knew instantly from the ranch foreman's worried expression that something was wrong.

She went over to him and asked, "What is it, Jess?"

"There's a good-size bunch of riders coming in," Fisher said.

Viola's spirits rose for a second when she heard that. She said, "John and the others are back already?"

"No, ma'am," Fisher said, his face turning even more grim. "Best I can tell, these fellas are strangers—and they don't look like the friendly sort."

Viola's breath seemed to catch in her throat. More trouble was exactly what they didn't need right now.

But trouble never waited until it was convenient. She said, "Get as many of the men together as you can. If these visitors are looking for a fight, that's exactly what we'll give them."

Chapter 13

Slaughter and the other men ate in the saddle, making a skimpy midday meal out of tortillas and bacon brought from the ranch. They were in the foothills of the Chiricahua Mountains now. The trail of the stolen herd had led to a canyon that wound through the hills and gradually climbed higher.

There was something odd about the sign they had found at the mouth of the canyon. The droppings indicated that the cattle had stopped there for a while, probably to let them rest after the hard nighttime run that had brought them to this point.

Slaughter could understand that, but what didn't make sense was that the tracks indicated the herd had been driven back and forth a few times, right there in the same area. He had pointed that out to Stonewall and asked, "What do you make of that?"

The young man just frowned, shook his head, and said, "I don't know, John."

The *vaquero* called Hermosa leaned forward in his saddle and said, "They were trying to hide something,

Señor Slaughter." He waved at the vast muddle of hoofprints. "What man could make any sense out of that?"

Hermosa was right, Slaughter realized. The tracks made it impossible to be sure how many men were with the herd.

As soon as that thought leaped into his head, Slaughter's keen brain carried it further. He muttered, "Some of them could have turned back."

"Why would they do that?" Stonewall asked.

Slaughter didn't have an answer for that question, but he couldn't help thinking about the dust he had spotted a few hours earlier. It worried him now more than it had then.

But there was nothing he could do. The tracks of the herd led deeper into the mountains. There was no denying that. Everything else was sheer speculation. He couldn't know for sure that the rustlers had split up, or if they had, where the second bunch was headed.

As Viola had pointed out, though, he was well-known for following his hunches. That applied equally in all areas of his life—lawman, rancher, gambler.

He gave in to one of those hunches now, saying, "Stonewall, I want you to go back to the ranch."

"What?" The young man looked shocked. "But I'm chasin' after those rustlers with you, John."

"We have a good-size force. We can afford to lose one man." Slaughter looked at Hermosa. "Or two."

"What do you have in mind, Señor Slaughter?" the *vaquero* drawled.

"I want the two of you to get back to the ranch as quick as you can and make sure there's no trouble there."

"What trouble would there be?" Stonewall asked. "We wiped out those Apaches."

"There's something deeper going on here," Slaughter pointed out. "We know that, we just don't know what it is. But I'd feel better about things if I knew there were a couple of good men headed back to the ranch."

Stonewall didn't like the idea of going back at all, not when the rustlers and the stolen herd were still ahead of them. Hermosa, though, just murmured, "With all due respect, Señor Slaughter, I ride for Don Eduardo, not you."

"And I represent my father," Santiago said. "I don't know if Señor Slaughter is right, Hermosa, but if he wants you and Stonewall to return to the ranch, I think that is what you should do."

Hermosa's shoulders rose and fell in an eloquent shrug.

"Of course, señor."

Still grumbling, Stonewall had gone with Hermosa. Slaughter hated to lose a couple of good fighting men, but his gut told him Viola might need help.

The rest of the group had pressed on, and now as the heat grew even more oppressive in the early afternoon, Slaughter could tell from the tracks that the cattle had slowed. The hoofprints were fresher. He and his men had cut considerably into the rustlers' lead.

"You know this country much better than I do, Señor Slaughter," Santiago said as he rode alongside. "Where do you think they are taking the herd?"

"Well, they're not headed for Galeyville or Fort Bowie," Slaughter said. "If they were bound for either of those places, they wouldn't have come into the mountains like this. Although I suppose they could still reach the fort if they know of some pass through the Chiricahuas. But it would have been faster if they had gone around." Slaughter scratched his bearded jaw. "It's almost like they're just trying to lead us up here. That's another reason I'm worried that some of them might have doubled back to the ranch."

"How many men are there now?"

"No more than a dozen, I reckon. But the house is sturdy. We've had to fort up in it before. My wife comes from pioneer stock, too. If there's trouble, she won't panic. Anybody comes riding in on the prod, she'll give 'em a hot reception."

"I wish I knew that my father was safe. And . . . my stepmother."

Slaughter heard the hesitation in the young man's voice and said, "It's none of my business, but you don't like Doña Belinda very much, do you?"

"My father loves her. I would not want her to come to any harm."

"I reckon maybe she got a little more than she bargained for when she moved out here. This part of the country isn't nearly as civilized as Boston."

Santiago shook his head and said, "I don't know anything about that. I have never been to Boston. My father has, but not me."

"Well, maybe you'll visit Doña Belinda's family someday."

"Perhaps," Santiago said, but he still sounded doubtful.

A few more minutes went by as they followed the herd's tracks through a broad, steep-sided canyon. As Slaughter looked ahead, he saw that the canyon took a turn around a fairly sharp bend several hundred yards in front of them.

A place like that would be a pretty good spot for an ambush, he thought. Considering the trickiness the rustlers had already demonstrated, he wouldn't put such a thing past them at all. Because of that, he reined in and motioned for the others to do likewise.

"I think we'd better do a little scouting," he said. "I'll go have a look around that bend."

"I'll come with you," Santiago volunteered without hesitation.

"Better not," Slaughter said. "If anything were to happen to me, somebody will need to take charge."

Santiago looked surprised by that statement. He said, "You would entrust such a task to me?"

"You're Don Eduardo's son. His men will follow you. So will mine, if I tell them they're supposed to." Slaughter crossed his hands on his saddle horn and turned a level gaze on the young man. "Are you up to the job, Santiago?"

"I—I will do my best to be, Señor Slaughter."

Slaughter shook his head and said, "Trying's not good enough. You either do it or you don't."

Santiago's backbone stiffened. He gave Slaughter a curt, solemn nod and said, "I will not let you down, señor."

"That's more like it." Slaughter lifted his reins and got ready to heel his horse into motion again.

Before he could do that, he heard a rumbling sound, like an approaching thunderstorm. The sky was clear, however, except for a few puffy white clouds against the crisp, startling blue.

The other men heard it, too, and a worried mutter went through their ranks. Slaughter was about to tell them to settle down when a cow bolted around that bend in the canyon up ahead. Another animal followed it, then another and another . . .

As the rumbling grew louder and a cloud of dust welled into the air, a solid line of spooked beef rounded that bend and thundered toward Slaughter and his companions. The herd they'd been chasing all day was now coming to them . . .

In the form of a stampede!

Viola hurried to get John's spyglass and then went back outside. Jess Fisher had told her that the strangers were coming from the northeast, so she climbed the ladder attached to the framework holding up the elevated water tank until she could see over the house.

This certainly wasn't a very ladylike thing to do, Viola thought as she wrapped an arm around the ladder to steady herself. She had never worried all that much about comporting herself properly, though. At heart she was still a wild cowgirl.

She spotted the group of riders in the distance, then lifted the spyglass to her eye and squinted through the lens. It took a second to locate them through the glass, but then the face of the leader sprang into sharp relief.

It was a beard-stubbled, hard-planed face. More details were hard to make out because the man had the brim of his hat tugged down fairly low. That threw a shadow over his features. Even so, it struck Viola as a cruel face.

She caught her breath as she swung the spyglass to one

side and saw the man riding to the leader's right and just behind him. His face was cruel, too, and it was easy to see because he wore no hat, only a bandanna tied around his head to keep his thick mane of black hair back. The man was an Apache. He didn't seem to be a prisoner. He looked more like an ally of the men approaching the ranch.

Viola used the spyglass to take a look at the other men. They all had the stamp of the owlhoot on them. Tough, brutal, ruthless men who would stop at nothing to get what they wanted. There were at least a dozen of them.

That meant the members of the crew John had left here at the ranch were outnumbered, but not by that much, Viola thought. And they had the advantage of being able to fight a defensive action, behind the thick walls of the house.

She closed the spyglass and climbed down as quickly as she could. As she went back to the house, she met Dr. Neal Fredericks at the front door. The doctor had his coat draped over one arm and carried his medical bag in his other hand.

"Doctor, you should get in your buggy and leave right now," she told him. She estimated that the riders wouldn't be here for another four or five minutes. That would give Fredericks time to get clear before any trouble started.

He frowned and said, "What's wrong, Mrs. Slaughter? You seem upset about something."

"There are riders coming in," she said. "I think they may be some of the rustlers who stole that herd of cattle last night."

"They've come back for more?"

"I don't know," Viola said. "I hope I'm wrong about

them. But in case I'm not, you should leave while you still can, doctor, before there's any trouble."

"You mean shooting," Fredericks said heavily.

"It could come to that."

"Then I'm not going anywhere," he declared. "My services may be required here."

"It may not be safe—"

"I didn't swear an oath to help people only when it was safe or convenient. You may have more wounded, so this is where I need to be." Fredericks grunted. "If it comes down to that, I know how to use a gun, too, not just how to patch up bullet wounds. It would go against my code to inflict them, unless it was absolutely necessary to prevent further harm."

Viola saw that it wasn't going to do any good to argue with him, and she didn't have time for that, anyway.

"All right, doctor, but go back inside and stay away from the windows. And thank you. I have to admit, I do feel a little better knowing you're here."

Fredericks disappeared inside the house as Jess Fisher emerged from the bunkhouse with eight more members of the crew. Each man carried a rifle, and most of them had holstered revolvers strapped around their waists as well.

"These are all the fellas I could round up, Miz Slaughter," Fisher reported as they trotted up to the fence. "You want us all inside, or should we spread out?"

"Who's the best marksman among you?" Viola asked.

One of the men stepped forward and said in a Texas drawl, "That'd be me, ma'am. Joe Sparkman."

None of the other men disagreed with Sparkman's assessment of his skills.

"All right, Joe," Viola said. "I want you to climb up on

top of that water tank. You have plenty of cartridges for that Winchester with you?"

"Yes, ma'am, a whole box of .44-40s."

"All right. I won't lie to you, it's a very dangerous position. You'll be more exposed than anyone else. But you'll have a better field of fire than any of the rest of us, too."

"Yes, ma'am." A grin creased Sparkman's leathery face. "I wouldn't rather be nowhere else."

He hurried off toward the water tank while Viola led the rest of the men into the house.

"There are too many windows and not enough of us," she said as she took a Winchester down from a rack of rifles in the front room. "We can't cover all of them. So you'll have to spread out and do the best you can. We'll try to cover all the approaches to the house. Luckily their numbers aren't overwhelming. They can't really hit us from more than one direction at once."

Yolanda stepped into the arched doorway between the front room and the parlor. She said, "Señora, do you need more people to fight? Some of the servants know how to shoot."

"That's a good idea," Viola said. She didn't really expect any of the maids to hit anything, but they had plenty of rifles and ammunition. The women could make a lot of racket, anyway, and maybe the attackers would believe the ranch house's defenses were stronger than they really were.

She was getting ahead of herself, Viola thought. She didn't know for sure those men intended to attack the place, no matter what they looked like. Even the fact that they had an Apache warrior with them didn't have to mean they were hostile. Some Apaches worked as scouts for the army, didn't they? Maybe this was one of them.

She was like a little girl whistling on her way past a graveyard, hoping the tune would ward off evil spirits, she told herself. Reason and logic meant little in a situation such as this. Viola trusted her instincts a lot more, and they insisted that those men were trouble.

She told Yolanda, "Bring any of the women who want to fight in here and let them get rifles. Then help the men cover the windows. The rest of you should help the wounded get as far out of the line of fire as possible."

The rifle Viola held didn't have a round in the chamber. She worked the Winchester's lever to rectify that and then strode toward the front door.

From the window where he had taken up position, Jess Fisher said in an alarmed tone, "Ma'am, what're you doin'?"

"This is my house," Viola said as she held the rifle at a slant in front of her, across her chest. "I'm going to go greet our guests."

Chapter 14

"We gonna ride in shootin', boss?" Herb Woodbury asked as they approached the ranch.

"No need for that," Becker said. "I'm sure they've spotted us by now. They know we're coming. We'll keep this as civilized as we possibly can."

From beside him, Bodaway said, "The woman knows."

Becker glanced over at the Apache and asked, "What do you mean?"

"The woman climbed the ladder on the water tank and looked at us through a telescope. I saw her."

Becker laughed.

"You've got better eyes than I do, *amigo*. I missed that. But I was right, they know we're here, and if the gal you saw had a spyglass, she probably got a pretty good look at us. So she has a pretty good idea that we're not friendly."

Woodbury muttered, "With this bunch o' cutthroats, I reckon not."

"Still, I'm going to try talking to her first. You never know what people will agree to until you ask them."

Bodaway just grunted, but the sound was packed with skepticism.

They came in past a row of cottonwood trees and a building made of adobe bricks that had two sides and a covered dogtrot in the middle, in the style of Texas cabins. It appeared to be empty at the moment.

Becker reined in and signaled a halt. He said, "The rest of you stay here. I'm going on up alone."

"I don't know how smart that is, Ned," Woodbury said. "They could be holed up in there with a bunch of rifles."

"I'm sure they are. That's exactly why I want the rest of you to stay here instead of riding right up into their gunsights."

"Yeah, but what about you?"

"The Slaughters are law-abiding people. Hell, he's the sheriff of Cochise County! Mrs. Slaughter's not going to gun down a man who just wants to parley."

Woodbury grimaced and said, "I hope you're right. If you ain't, you'll be just askin' to get ventilated by ridin' up there like that."

"I'll take the chance," Becker said. He hitched his horse into motion again.

Despite his confident tone, he felt his nerves crawling as he rode toward the ranch house. He didn't think anybody in there would start shooting without talking to him first and finding out what he wanted, but like everything else in life, there were no guarantees of that.

He had just reined to a stop in front of the gate in the picket fence when the front door opened and a woman stepped out of the house carrying a rifle.

Becker's first impulse was to reach for his gun, but he stopped himself from doing that since the woman wasn't pointing the Winchester at him. She held it ready in front of her.

She was damned good-looking, too, with a trim figure and dark hair that at the moment was pulled back in a loose knot behind her head. Her chin lifted in a show of stubborn defiance. Becker could tell that she was cautious but not scared of him, not really.

That was a mistake on her part. She needed to be scared of him—scared enough that she would cooperate and let him have what he had come here to take.

The woman lifted her voice and said, "Normally when someone rides up to my gate, I tell them to get down from their horse and come inside. I think it would be better if you stay right where you are, though."

"You're Mrs. Slaughter?" Becker asked.

"I am. Who are you?"

Becker didn't answer the question. Instead he said, "I'm looking for Don Eduardo Rubriz, and his wife and son if they're here."

"I didn't ask who you were looking for," the woman snapped. "I asked who you are."

He didn't see how it would do any harm to tell her. He was going to have to reveal his identity anyway, in order to get the full measure of revenge on Rubriz. The don had to know it was Thaddeus Becker's son who was responsible for the hell on earth that was about to descend on him.

"My name is Becker, Ned Becker," he said. "If you tell Don Eduardo that I'm here, he'll know the name."

For the first time, he saw a trace of indecisiveness on the woman's face. She was prepared for war, but she wanted to hope that maybe he had come in peace.

That wasn't the case, of course, but Becker was willing to let her think that for the time being.

"Stay where you are," Mrs. Slaughter said again. She turned her head slightly to speak over her shoulder without taking her eyes off of Becker. "Yolanda, go tell Don Eduardo that a man named Ned Becker is here."

A thin smile curved Becker's lips. The woman's words confirmed that Rubriz was here and still alive. Becker was sure the doña would be, too. She wouldn't have gone with Slaughter and the others after the stolen cattle. Santiago might be a different story, but Becker would deal with that when the time came.

"What do you want with Don Eduardo?" Mrs. Slaughter asked.

"I reckon that's between the don and me," Becker drawled. "You can rest assured, though, Mrs. Slaughter, that I don't mean any harm to you or your people."

"You don't mean any harm," she repeated. "But will you inflict it anyway if we get in your way?"

Becker's jaw tightened. He admired this woman for her beauty and bravery, but she was starting to annoy him.

Again he didn't answer the question she had asked him, choosing instead to ask one of his own.

"I heard the don was injured. How bad is he hurt?"

He knew that was a mistake as soon as the words were out of his mouth. The woman's eyes sparked with anger. She said, "You wouldn't know that unless you were here last night, or someone who was here told you about it. That Apache who's riding with you and your men, maybe?"

Anger of his own welled up inside him. He was wasting time here. He leaned forward in the saddle and said,

"I don't have anything against you, ma'am, but I'll have what I came here to get, one way or another. If innocent folks get hurt, that's on your head, not mine. Now bring Don Eduardo and his wife out here. You do that and we'll go on our way and leave you in peace."

That was a lie, of course. Becker didn't intend to leave any witnesses behind. When he was done here, when he rode away from this place, he planned to leave it burning. The flames would wipe out any trace that he had ever been here.

Mrs. Slaughter suddenly leveled the Winchester at him. She wasn't a large woman, but she held the heavy rifle rock-steady as she pointed it at him.

Becker stiffened and sat up straighter in the saddle, but he kept his hand away from his gun. He had no doubt that she would drill him if he gave her the slightest excuse to pull the trigger.

"Take it easy, ma'am—" he began.

"You've made a bad mistake, Mr. Becker," she said. "You think you hold the winning hand here, but you overplayed it. I don't know what your plan is and I don't care. All I know is that if you don't throw your gun away, climb down from that horse, and come in here, I'm going to kill you."

The herd of stampeding cattle filled the canyon almost from one side to the other.

Almost.

Some boulders littered the ground along the base of the canyon wall to the left, though. They were chunks and slabs of sandstone that had fallen from the wall in times past. Slaughter knew instantly that they represented the best chance for him and his men to escape the deadly onslaught of hooves and horns thundering toward them.

"Come on!" he shouted to the others as he yanked his horse around and kicked the animal into a gallop toward the rocks.

They might have been able to turn and outrun the stampede by heading back the way they had come. But they had been following this canyon for a couple of miles and Slaughter knew there was a good chance the runaway herd would overtake them before they could find a way out. If that happened, they were all doomed.

As usual when faced with danger, he had made the decision instantly, with no hesitation. A lot of men had died on the frontier from dithering around, and John Slaughter wasn't going to be one of them. If fate had finally caught up to him, it wouldn't be from lack of action on his part.

He glanced over his shoulder and saw that Santiago and the other men were close behind him. They understood what they had to do. They rode hard, leaning forward in their saddles and slashing their mounts with the reins.

Slaughter slowed as he neared the rocks. He pulled his horse aside and waved the others on. Like any good leader, his first concern was for the men who followed him. They raced past and crowded into the cluster of boulders.

The leading edge of the stampede was less than twenty yards away. The billowing dust cloud from it was already starting to reach Slaughter and the other men.

Slaughter swung down from the saddle and hauled his

horse behind a sandstone slab. All the men were clear now. The stampede reached the rocks and flowed around them like a brown tide. The noise was deafening, a rumble that assaulted the ears. It sounded like the world was ending.

The dust choked the men, clogged their throats and noses, stung their eyes, made it difficult to see anything. Their horses were all spooked, and they had their hands full keeping the animals under control.

Faintly over the racket, Slaughter heard men yelling and shooting. That would be the rustlers, he thought, driving the cattle through the canyon and using them as living weapons.

Those varmints were in for a surprise, Slaughter told himself grimly. They were about to discover that their would-be victims hadn't been trampled into raw meat after all.

The terrible rumbling diminished slightly. That told Slaughter most of the stampede had passed them already. The rustlers would be along very shortly. He called to Santiago, who crouched behind a nearby rock, "Get ready! We'll hit 'em when they go past us!"

Santiago nodded and turned to give the order to the next man. Slaughter hoped the command would spread to all the others in his group.

He reached up and pulled his Winchester from its saddle sheath. The dust was thinner now. He began to be able to see out into the canyon.

Several riders loped out of the sandy clouds, still yipping and shooting. Slaughter brought the rifle to his shoulder and drew a bead on one of the rustlers. It would have been easy to blow the man out of the saddle, and he was tempted to do just that.

But he was a lawman, he reminded himself, even if he wasn't wearing his badge at the moment, and there was a right way and a wrong way to do things. He raised his voice and shouted, "You men are covered! Throw down your guns and elevate!"

Instead of obeying the order, the startled rustlers twisted in their saddles and started blazing away at the men hidden in the rocks. That was the wrong thing to do. Slaughter fired, and so did Santiago and the other men. A storm of lead tore through the rustlers and knocked them off their horses.

"Hold your fire!" Slaughter called. If any of the thieves were still alive, he wanted a prisoner he could question. He left his horse with reins dangling and strode out from behind the slab of rock where he had taken shelter from the stampede.

The rustlers' horses had bolted, following the runaway cows. That left three shapes sprawled on the ground.

Only three, Slaughter thought. An unknown number of the rustlers were unaccounted for.

Maybe one of the wounded men could tell him where the others were.

He was about fifteen feet away from the men when one of them suddenly twisted halfway up from the ground and thrust a revolver at him. Smoke and flame gouted from the weapon's muzzle. Slaughter heard the bullet whip past his ear and reacted automatically. He fired his Winchester and saw the man's head jerk backward.

The rustler's gun slipped from his fingers and thudded to the ground as he rolled onto his back. By the time

Slaughter reached him, he was staring sightlessly at the lingering shreds of dust in the air. The bullet hole in the center of his forehead was like a third eye, but it was as blinded by death as the other two.

Pools of blood spread slowly around all three men, the sandy soil of the canyon floor soaking up the life-giving fluid almost as fast as it welled from the rustlers' bodies. Slaughter saw that the second man was dead, too, then was a little surprised when he heard a faint groan come from the third man.

Wary of another trick, Slaughter dropped to a knee beside the man, grasped his shoulder, and rolled him onto his back. The three crimson splotches of blood on the man's shirt—two on the chest, one on his belly down near his waist—were ample testimony that he no longer represented a threat. He was still alive, but barely, and that condition wouldn't last more than another minute or two at most.

The dying man was young, about Stonewall's age. Dark beard stubble covered his cheeks and jaws. His eyes were set in hollows that seemed to be made even deeper by the agony that gripped him now. Slaughter could tell by looking at him that he'd had a hard life.

That was no excuse for taking up rustling as a trade, though. Slaughter said, "You're dying, son. What's your name?"

The man's eyelids fluttered open. His mouth moved. It took a lot of obvious effort for him to force out, "St-Stoney . . . Carter."

"Listen to me, Stoney," Slaughter said. "We'll see to it that you're laid to rest properly, but you have to tell me what this is all about. Why did you steal those cattle?

Were the Apaches working with you? Where's the rest of your bunch?"

Slaughter put more emphasis on the last question. That was the most important one. He didn't think these three men had been handling that herd by themselves. There had to be more of them somewhere close by.

He hadn't forgotten that dust cloud he had seen, either, or the worry that some of the rustlers might have doubled back to the ranch for some reason.

Carter didn't reply. His eyes were still open but unfocused. Slaughter said, "Stoney! This is important. What's this all about? Did some of your men turn around and go back to my ranch?"

The youngster was slipping away in front of Slaughter's eyes. He didn't think Stoney Carter was ever going to say anything again.

But then the dying rustler whispered a word. Slaughter was leaning close over him, or else he wouldn't have heard it.

He heard and understood, though, and that one word was enough to make Slaughter stiffen and catch his breath. It was a name . . .

"Becker!"

Chapter 15

Stonewall and Hermosa had taken a couple of extra horses with them so they could switch back and forth and keep up a fast pace. Even though Stonewall hadn't wanted to turn back, now that he had he was beginning to get worried. He knew how smart his brother-in-law was, and he trusted John Slaughter's instincts, too.

If Slaughter thought something might be wrong back at the ranch, there was a good chance that it was.

Hermosa wasn't a very talkative companion. He rolled one quirly after another and smoked them as he rode. Stonewall was nervous, though, and when he got that way he talked even more than usual.

"You think whoever's behind this has got some grudge against Don Eduardo?" he asked the *vaquero* as their horses splashed across the shallow water of Cave Creek.

"Why not someone with a grudge against Señor Slaughter?" Hermosa asked. "He is the sheriff, is he not? I never saw a lawman who did not have an abundance of enemies."

"Oh, I reckon John's got enemies, all right," Stonewall

admitted. "Plenty of 'em, I'd say. And not just from him bein' sheriff, either. He had his share of trouble with folks while he was bringin' cattle over here from Texas and settin' up his ranch. Why, there was one *hombre* who accused him of rustlin'! Can you imagine that?"

"Was he guilty?" Hermosa asked dryly.

"What? You mean, was he a rustler? John Slaughter?" The disbelief was obvious in Stonewall's voice.

"Today's honest, upright man may not have always been that way," Hermosa said with a shrug. "And every story is different depending on who tells it."

"I reckon that's true," Stonewall said, only slightly mollified. "But you probably wouldn't like it if I started talkin' about Don Eduardo bein' some sort of outlaw."

Hermosa glanced sharply over at him and said, "Make no mistake about it, *amigo*, Don Eduardo has done things of which he is not proud. Things that many men would look down upon. But he has always stayed true to himself and the things he wished to achieve."

"You'd know, wouldn't you? You've been ridin' for him a long time."

"Many years. I was with him when he founded his ranch. He and his partner."

"Partner?" Stonewall repeated with a frown. "I didn't know anything about him havin' a partner."

"It was long ago. And it ended badly. But there were two of them, Don Eduardo and a *gringo* friend of his. And their wives." Hermosa shook his head. "If the women had not been there, things might have turned out very differently."

Hermosa fell silent. Stonewall allowed that to go on

for a minute or so, then burst out, "Come on! You've got to tell me the rest of the story."

"It is none of your affair, *amigo*. Of the people who were most intimately involved, they are all dead and buried now . . . except for Don Eduardo. Let him keep his pain to himself."

Stonewall frowned and said grudgingly, "Well . . . all right. I guess you're right, it's not any of my business."

Hermosa nodded. He took the stub of a cigarette from his lips and snapped it away, then started building a new one. As he rolled the smoke, he said, "It was long ago, but Don Eduardo still says prayers for the dead . . . all of them." He struck a match, held it to the tip of the quirly, and added from the corner of his mouth, "Even the man who tried to kill him."

From where Viola stood on the porch, just outside the front door, she heard the gasp from the parlor and the startled exclamation, "Becker!"

Clearly the hard-faced stranger was right: the name meant something to Don Eduardo.

There would be time enough later to find out what this was all about, Viola thought. For now, the moment had come to play her trump card.

Before Ned Becker could do anything else, she pointed the Winchester at him and ordered him to throw down his gun and surrender.

It didn't seem that likely that he'd do it, but you never could tell. Sometimes a man's personality changed when he found himself looking down the barrel of a gun.

Not this one, though, Viola saw despairingly. Becker

regarded her coolly from under the pulled-down brim of his hat. He didn't make a move to disarm himself or get down from the horse.

Instead he gave her a smug, infuriating smile and said, "We both know you're not going to pull that trigger, Mrs. Slaughter."

He wouldn't be aware of it, but that was just about the worst thing he could have done. The arrogant mockery made her temper blaze up inside her. Her finger started to tighten on the trigger as she shifted her aim slightly to put a bullet through his right shoulder.

Before she could fire, something struck the rifle with stunning force and ripped it out of her hands. She cried out, as much from shock as from pain, and threw herself backward as she saw Becker clawing at the holstered revolver on his hip. Viola fell through the door and kicked it shut.

Jess Fisher was there to drop the bar into the brackets on either side of the door, sealing it from outside. As soon as he had done that, he turned to her and said, "Mrs. Slaughter, are you all right? Blast it, your husband'll kill me if you're hurt!"

Viola sat up and shook her throbbing hands.

"I'm fine, Jess," she said. "What happened?"

"Hard to tell from in here, but it looked like somebody shot that rifle out of your hands."

Viola thought that was what had happened, too. She held up her hands and looked for blood, but she didn't find any. The bullet had hit the Winchester but missed her.

"That was a hell of a shot!" she exclaimed in a mixture of anger and admiration.

She heard a swift rataplan of hoofbeats from outside.

One of the ranch hands called from a window, "That fella's lightin' out, Miz Slaughter. You want me to let him go or try to knock him down?"

"Let him go," Viola said. There hadn't been any more shots. "Maybe they'll decide the house is too well-defended and leave."

She knew how unlikely that was. She had gotten a good enough look at Ned Becker to recognize the hatred burning in his gaze. Whatever grudge against Don Eduardo had brought him here, he wasn't going to just ride away and forget it.

Viola wanted to know more about that grudge, although she didn't see how the knowledge would change anything in this situation. She climbed to her feet and went to the parlor. Her fingers still stung a little, but they didn't hurt too badly.

Don Eduardo was sitting up on the sofa now with bandages wrapped tightly around his midsection. Belinda stood close enough that she could rest a hand on his shoulder.

Dr. Fredericks was nearby, too, with a worried look on his face. He spoke first, saying, "I heard one of the men ask you if you were all right, Mrs. Slaughter. What happened?"

"Someone shot the rifle out of my hands," Viola explained.

Fredericks let out a low whistle of surprise. He said, "I didn't think you ever ran across trick shooting like that except in Wild West Shows and dime novels."

"Those men have at least one excellent marksman among them," Viola agreed.

"But you're not hurt?"

She held her hands up and turned them so the doctor could see both front and back of each hand.

"You're lucky," Fredericks said. "You could have lost a finger."

"And it would have been my fault," Don Eduardo said.

"You didn't pull the trigger," Viola pointed out.

"No, but those men are here because of me. The one who spoke to you . . . he said his name is Ned Becker?"

"That's right. I take it the name is familiar to you?"

Don Eduardo sighed and nodded.

"It is one I have not heard in many years," he said. "A name that makes me ashamed to hear it now."

Belinda protested, "That's not fair. You don't have anything to be ashamed of, Eduardo."

Rubriz shook his head and said, "There are things about me you do not know, my dear. Things that happened long before the two of us met."

"If they happened before we met, then I don't care about them," Belinda said with a stubborn toss of her blond hair.

"You should," Don Eduardo said, "because they may mean the death of us all."

Becker slowed his horse and swung down from the saddle while the animal was still moving. His angry gaze swept over the men gathered behind the brick building that shielded them from the view of those in the ranch house.

"Who fired that shot?" he demanded.

"Talk to your Apache *amigo*," Herb Woodbury said with a nod toward Bodaway, who stood there with a

Winchester cradled in his arms. The war chief's face was as expressionless as ever.

Becker confronted his old friend and said, "I didn't give the order to start shooting."

"You would have rather I let the woman shoot you?" Bodaway asked coolly.

"She wasn't going to shoot me," Becker insisted. "She wouldn't have pulled the trigger."

"You're wrong. If I had not fired, you would be dead now, or at least wounded. I know when someone is about to kill."

"She's a woman, for God's sake!"

Bodaway actually smiled. His lips curved only a tiny fraction of an inch, but it was a smile.

"Have you not lived enough years to have learned how dangerous a woman can be?" he asked.

Becker blew out an exasperated breath and moved a hand in a curt, dismissive gesture.

"All right, what's important is that we know now Rubriz is in there," he said. "Mrs. Slaughter spoke to someone inside and had them tell the don my name. So he's here, and he's alive. I can still take my revenge on him. All we have to do is convince Mrs. Slaughter to turn him over to us."

Woodbury said, "I don't know if she'll do that, boss. She strikes me as a pretty stubborn woman."

"She'll do it if she wants to save her life and the lives of those other people in there," Becker insisted. "For now, spread out. Keep to cover, but search the place. I want to know if there are any other ranch hands around here, or if they're all forted up inside the house. That's what I'm betting on, but I'd like to be sure before I decide what we're going to do next."

Woodbury nodded and started pointing at the other men in turn, singling them out and telling them where to go.

"And keep your damn heads down," he added. "You waltz right into a bushwhackin', it won't be nobody's fault but your own."

Within minutes, only Becker and Bodaway were left at the adobe brick building. Becker went into the covered dogtrot and peered through the windows into the rooms on each side.

"I'll be damned," he said to the Apache. He pointed through the glass. "Look in there. Desks and chalkboards, by God. This is a schoolhouse. Slaughter must have somebody teaching all the little Mex brats that belong to his *vaqueros*."

"It is said that sometimes the Apaches come here, too," Bodaway mused. "Not all of my people are enemies to John Slaughter. Some are his friends."

"I don't care about that. He can be friends with all the Apaches he wants to, as long as he stays out of my way."

"I have heard as well that Slaughter is a good tracker," Bodaway said. "Once he starts on someone's trail, he never turns back until he catches his quarry."

"You're talking about those fellas I sent on ahead with the herd? I hope Slaughter stays after them. That's the whole idea, to keep him away from here until I've done what I came to do."

"They will be outnumbered. They will not have much chance to escape."

"You think I care about those cows?" Becker scoffed.

"I came to settle a debt, that's all. Why do you think I've been holding up banks and trains for the past five years? I saved my share of the loot from those jobs so I could afford to pay Woodbury and those other fellas. So I could afford those rifles I promised to you—the rifles you're still going to get, by the way. I did all that because money doesn't mean a damn thing to me, Bodaway." Becker stared across the open space between the school and the ranch house. "All I want is right in there. The head of Don Eduardo Rubriz, the man who murdered my father."

Chapter 16

Slaughter had promised the dying Stoney Carter that he would be laid to rest properly after he crossed the divide. He kept his word, even though the delay chafed at him.

Slaughter had brought along a couple of folding prospector's shovels, thinking there might be a need for them, and several of the men had taken turns scraping out shallow graves for the young outlaw and the other two rustlers. Those graves had dirt mounded over them now.

Hat in hand, Slaughter spoke a brief prayer over the dead men. He, Santiago, and the cowboys who had dug the graves were the only ones here. Slaughter had sent the rest of the bunch to round up the herd.

With the burying done, Slaughter clapped his hat back on his head and turned to Santiago. He fixed the young man with a hard, level gaze and said, "The two of us have to talk."

Santiago frowned and asked, "What about, señor?"

Slaughter didn't answer directly. He figured some

privacy would be best for this conversation, so he jerked his head for Santiago to follow him and said, "Come on."

They strode away, far enough to be out of easy earshot of the other men. Santiago still looked puzzled.

"What is this about, Señor Slaughter?" he asked again. "I thought we would either pursue the other rustlers or take the herd and head back to the ranch."

"We'll do one of those things, all right," Slaughter said, "but first I want to know the reason behind all this trouble."

Santiago appeared even more confused. He shook his head and said, "How would I know?"

"I didn't tell you the last thing that boy said before he died. It was a name. Becker."

Santiago stiffened. His face took on a grim cast.

"Earlier you said something about a man named Thaddeus Becker," Slaughter went on. "You mentioned that he was your father's partner, and that sometime in the past he shot Don Eduardo. But you didn't finish that story, and I think it's high time you did."

"Some things are private," Santiago said. "They should be kept within the family."

"I can respect that . . . but not when it brings trouble to my home and endangers people I love. When that happens I've got a right to know what's going on."

"It was all many years in the past," Santiago said with a stubborn shake of his head. "It cannot possibly have anything to do with what is happening now."

"Then how did Carter know the name Becker?"

"There could be many men with that name—"

"You don't believe that any more than I do," Slaughter said sharply. "Look, son, I don't want to pry in your family's personal business, but we've got to figure out what's going on here so we'll know what to do next."

For a moment, Santiago stared at him in stubborn defiance. But then the young man sighed.

"All right," he said. "I suppose you have a right to know. But I cannot tell you everything, Señor Slaughter, simply because I do not know it myself."

"Fair enough," Slaughter said with a nod. "Just tell me what you do know."

"Many years ago, my father befriended an American named Thaddeus Becker. Becker was in Mexico because he had come there with a man named William Walker, an adventurer who tried to take over the country."

Slaughter nodded. He had heard of Walker, the notorious filibuster and would-be dictator.

"Becker and Walker had a falling out, but Becker remained in Mexico, selling his services as a military man to the highest bidder. Eventually he fell in with a rebel faction that included my father. When that faction came to power, my father and Becker took advantage of their newfound wealth and power to establish a ranch in northern Sonora."

"The same ranch your father has now," Slaughter said.

Santiago nodded.

"They brought their wives with them. High-born ladies from influential families in Mexico City. It was a hard, dangerous time. Bandits roamed the land, and Yaquis from the mountains raided the ranch on numerous occasions. But they were strong and met all the challenges until . . . until Thaddeus Becker's wife decided that she wanted my father."

"I can see where that would cause some trouble," Slaughter said.

Santiago nodded and went on, "My father turned aside her advances, of course, but in her anger at being refused, she told her husband that my father had attacked her. Becker was furious. He wanted to dissolve their partnership. My father and mother both did everything they could to save the friendship. Becker pretended to put all the hurt feelings aside, but really he was planning his revenge. One day, while they were out on the range, Becker shot my father with no warning. I don't know what he planned. Maybe he intended to say that a bandit ambushed my father. No one would have been able to prove otherwise. He must have believed that my father was dead, because he turned away, no doubt to return to the ranch. But my father regained consciousness and shot him."

"In the back?" Slaughter asked with a frown.

"You must understand," Santiago said, "my father believed he was dying. That was the only way he could strike back at the man who had slain him. After he fired, he passed out again. His *vaqueros* found him lying there later that day. They had gone to look for him after Becker returned to the ranch, mortally wounded. I don't know what he said to his wife before he died. A pack of lies, though, surely."

"But you don't know that's exactly how things happened," Slaughter pointed out. "The way you told the story, the two men were out there alone."

Santiago nodded and said, "That is true. But I believe my father."

Of course he'd take Don Eduardo's word for it, thought Slaughter. Just about any son would.

"My father was badly wounded," Santiago continued. "For many weeks, my mother nursed him back to health."

"What happened to Becker's wife?"

"No one knows. She disappeared from the ranch after her husband's death and took her son with her."

"You didn't mention a son," Slaughter said.

Santiago nodded again.

"His name was Ned. He was several years older than me. I remember him only vaguely."

"Ned Becker," Slaughter mused. "You don't know if he's still alive?"

"I have no idea," Santiago said. Slaughter was convinced the young man was telling the truth.

"If he was alive, that might explain some of this. Lord knows what his mother might have told him over the years. She could have blamed his father's death and anything else that happened on Don Eduardo. She could have filled his head with hate, to the point that by now he's wanting some revenge."

"You really think Ned Becker could come back from nowhere and do all this, Señor Slaughter?"

"Stoney Carter said Becker's name."

"Not Ned."

"Can you think of another Becker it might be?"

Santiago shook his head and admitted, "No, what you say makes sense, señor."

"And Ned Becker wasn't nowhere all this time," Slaughter said. "He was somewhere . . . somewhere nursing the resentment he feels toward Don Eduardo."

Now that Slaughter had put the theory into words, he was convinced that he was on the right trail. If the long-lost Ned Becker was behind the attack on the ranch and the rustling of the herd, then his ultimate goal had to be . . .

Revenge on Don Eduardo.

And Don Eduardo was back at the ranch.

Turning to his men, Slaughter ordered in a curt, grim voice, "Saddle up. We're heading south."

"What about the rest of those rustlers, boss?" one of the cowboys asked. "They've got to still be up ahead in these mountains somewhere."

"I know," Slaughter said, "and I don't like letting them get away. But if I'm right, the man who put them up to it isn't with them anymore. The story's too long and complicated to go into it now." Slaughter reached for his horse's reins. "I want to be back at the ranch by nightfall—"

The sinister whine of a bullet slapping past his ear and the sharp crack of a rifle sounded at the same time, and a split-second later more shots blasted, their echoes filling the canyon.

"Help me up," Don Eduardo said as he struggled to stand. "Help me up, I say!"

"Eduardo, stop," Belinda said. Her hands fluttered uselessly in front of her. "Please, you can't get up. You have to rest—"

"Your wife is right, sir," Dr. Fredericks said as he stepped forward to rest a firm hand on Rubriz's shoulder. "You've lost a great deal of blood, and if you open that wound again, you'll lose more. I don't think you can afford to do that."

Don Eduardo sank back on the sofa cushions and glared around at them.

"I am to blame for what is happening here," he insisted. "I should be the one to put an end to it. I will go to this man Becker—"

"Don't be a blasted fool," Viola said.

Don Eduardo gave her a shocked, angry look. Clearly, he wasn't accustomed to anyone speaking to him like that, especially a woman.

Viola Slaughter wasn't like most of the women he had known, however. She returned his gaze without flinching and went on, "Even if you surrendered to him, do you really think he's going to let the rest of us live? With all due respect, Don Eduardo, I looked into the man's eyes, not you. He's a killer, pure and simple. Whatever he's got planned, when he's done with you he'll come after the rest of us and try to finish us off."

A frown creased the don's forehead. He asked, "Do you truly believe that, Señora Slaughter?"

"I have no doubt of it," Viola said.

Don Eduardo sighed.

"Then I have no choice but to accept your judgment. I have not seen Ned Becker since he was a boy, many years ago. But I can imagine he would grow into a man who hates me enough to do these things."

"But why?" Belinda asked. "That makes no sense, Eduardo. What could you possibly have done to make this man hate you so much?"

A stubborn expression came over Don Eduardo's face as he said, "I will not talk about it. Not here, not now."

"You don't think your wife deserves to know the truth?"

He looked up at her and said, "Perhaps if we survive this ordeal, my dear, then I will tell you what you want to know. But for now there are some things I will keep to myself, including Ned Becker's reasons for wanting to see me dead."

Viola said, "Whether you explain or not, Don Eduardo, we're left in the same position—defending this house."

"Give me a gun and help me to a chair beside a window. I can shoot."

"It may come to that," Viola said, "but not yet."

From the front room, Jess Fisher called, "Rider comin', Miz Slaughter!"

Viola hurried out of the parlor and joined Jess at the window. She crouched low, not wanting to give that sharpshooter a target, and watched as a man galloped along the lane that ran between the fence and open ground where the party had taken place the previous evening.

"Want me to see if I can knock him off that horse?" Fisher asked as he squinted over the barrel of his Winchester.

"No, hold your fire," Viola ordered. She raised her voice so the defenders in the other rooms could hear her. "Hold your fire until we see what he wants."

The rider didn't slow down as he raced past the fence. As he neared the gate he drew back his arm and threw something that sailed toward the house.

"It's a bomb!" Jess Fisher yelled in alarm. He snapped

his rifle to his shoulder as the thrown object clattered on the porch.

"No!" Viola caught hold of the barrel and kept him from shooting until the rider had galloped on past and gone out of sight, probably to circle around and rejoin his companions. "It looked like a rock or something with a note tied around it."

"Are you sure about that, ma'am? I'd hate to have the place blow up."

"You and me both, Jess." Viola backed away from the window, not standing up until she was clear of it. "We need to find out what it was."

"Could be a trick to get us to open the door," the foreman suggested.

"Maybe . . . but I don't think so. Give me your rifle."

Reluctantly, Fisher did so.

"Now take the bar off the door and open it," Viola went on. "Stand back when you do, though, so they won't have a good shot at you."

"What about you?"

Viola hefted the rifle and said, "I'll be ready if they try to charge the house."

Fisher still looked like he thought this was a bad idea, but he went to the door, took hold of the thick beam that served as a bar, and lifted it from its brackets. He grasped the knob, twisted it, and swung the door wide, standing behind the panel as it opened into the house.

Viola's heart hammered in her chest. In spite of what she'd told Fisher, she couldn't be certain this wasn't a trick of some sort. She had the Winchester pointed toward the door as it opened.

A chunk of rock a little bigger than a man's fist lay on the porch. A folded piece of paper had been wrapped around it and tied into place with a piece of string.

"I was right," Viola said. "It's a message."

She stepped toward the opening. Fisher said, "Careful, ma'am. I'll go and get it."

"No," Viola said. "No one is going out there."

She got down on her knees and inched forward. By thrusting the rifle out with one hand, she was able to hook the front sight against the rock and drag it toward the door without exposing herself. When it was close enough, she set the rifle aside, darted a hand out, grabbed the rock, and threw herself backward. Fisher shoved the door closed and dropped the bar across it again.

Viola climbed to her feet, untied the string, and removed the note from the rock. She handed the chunk of stone to Fisher, smiled, and said, "Here you go, Jess. Better hang on to it. You might need to throw it at one of the varmints."

"If one of 'em gets close enough, I'll dang sure do it, ma'am," the foreman promised as he weighed the rock in his hand. "This thing's heavy enough to bust somebody's skull open if you hit him just right with it."

Viola carried the note into the parlor without unfolding it. Everyone in there was waiting tensely. Belinda put what they were all feeling into words by asking, "Well? What was it?"

Viola held up the piece of paper and said, "They sent us a message." She unfolded the note and read the words printed there in a bold, easy to read hand. Her face grew more solemn as she said, “Becker is giving us until nightfall to turn you over to him, Don Eduardo.”

The don sat forward again and said, “See, it is like I told you. I should surrender—”

“That’s not all,” Viola said. “It’s not just you he wants. Becker says that we have to give him Doña Belinda, too—or he’ll kill everybody on the place and burn it to the ground.”

Chapter 17

Slaughter knew that he and his men were too exposed, standing out in the open this way next to the graves. He grabbed his horse's reins and said, "Head for the rocks!"

Those boulders had protected them from the stampede. They were the only real cover in the canyon. As Slaughter ran toward them, pulling his horse along with him, he searched for the source of the shots.

Bullets kicked up dirt around the men's feet as they hurried toward shelter. One of Slaughter's cowboys suddenly cried out in pain and stumbled.

Slaughter started to turn back to help him, but the man waved him on and said, "Keep goin', boss, they just nicked my leg!"

The cowboy took only one more step before he rocked back, making a strangling sound as crimson flooded from his throat. A bullet had ripped it open. He let go of his horse and flopped to the ground, writhing and jerking as he bled to death in a matter of a few heartbeats.

Rage filled Slaughter, but he kept moving. He couldn't do the man any good now except for avenging his death, and getting himself killed wouldn't accomplish that. In fact, it would just assure that the man had died for nothing.

Bullets ricocheted off the rocks as Slaughter, Santiago, and the remaining ranch hand, a man named Dixon, darted among them. Slaughter handed his reins to Dixon and motioned for Santiago to do likewise.

"Hang on to the horses, Chuck," Slaughter told the man as he pulled his Winchester from its sheath. "Stay back as close to the canyon wall as you can. Santiago, let's see if we can figure out where those bushwhackers are."

Slaughter's eyes swept the canyon as he crouched behind one of the boulders. The gunfire had stopped a moment earlier, but he figured the ambushers were just waiting for a good shot again.

The shots had come from farther up the canyon, the direction in which Slaughter and his companions had been pursuing the rustlers before the thieves stampeded the herd back at them. Slaughter was convinced the bushwhackers were the other men who had been driving the stolen cattle north. He had no way of knowing how many of them there were.

He could speculate about their motives, however, over and above wanting to avenge their comrades who'd been killed in the aftermath of the stampede. Slaughter had a hunch that Ned Becker had ordered the men to do everything in their power to delay the pursuers and keep them away from the ranch. That fit in with Slaughter's theory about what Becker was doing.

Becker didn't want to be disturbed while he went after his twisted revenge on Don Eduardo Rubriz.

"Did you see where the shots came from, Señor Slaughter?" Santiago asked.

"No, but when they start shooting again, I'm hoping I can spot their smoke."

"Be ready to watch, then," Santiago said, and with no more warning than that, he stood up and opened fire, spraying bullets wildly up the canyon.

Slaughter yelled, "Get down, you fool!" but Santiago was too far away for him to do anything else. He would have tackled the young man if he had been closer, but he couldn't reach Santiago without going out into the open.

A bullet spanged off the boulder in front of Santiago, but the ricochet missed him somehow. Slaughter spotted a puff of smoke from the rimrock on the other side of the canyon about fifty yards north from their position and sent three shots toward it as fast as he could work the Winchester's lever.

At least one of them found the target, although in a case like this, Slaughter was under no illusions that he was a better marksman than the bushwhackers. It was luck or fate that guided his shots.

A man rose sharply to his feet and lurched into view, dropping his rifle as he did so. He pitched forward off the edge of the rim and turned over in midair as he plummeted to the canyon floor.

The thud as he struck the ground made an ugly sound.

Slaughter glanced over and saw that Santiago had dropped back down behind the boulder.

"That was a damn fool stunt you just pulled!" Slaughter told the young man.

"It worked, though," Santiato said. "And now we have one less enemy."

Slaughter couldn't deny that. And a moment later Santiago's tactic paid an unexpected dividend. Slaughter heard hoofbeats and realized at least two horses were heading north at a fast rate of speed.

From farther back in the rocks, Dixon called, "Sounds like they're lightin' a shuck outta here, boss."

Slaughter agreed, but he said, "Let's keep our heads down for a few minutes anyway, just in case it's a trick."

There were no more shots, and after five minutes, Slaughter risked standing up and moving out into the open. He didn't draw any fire as he walked over to the dead cowboy, a man named Callan.

Slaughter knelt beside the man just to make sure he was dead, although he didn't really have any doubt. No one could lose that much blood and survive. Callan's eyes were open, staring sightlessly at nothing.

Slaughter straightened and let out a grim sigh.

"We've got another grave to dig. We'd better get at it."

"You think the others are gone?" Santiago asked as he and Dixon emerged from the rocks.

"Seems like it."

Dixon said, "If you want to go take a look around, Mr. Slaughter, I'll take care of buryin' Callan."

Slaughter nodded. "All right, Chuck. That's a good idea. Come on, Santiago."

Slaughter and Santiago mounted and rode up the canyon, rifles held ready for use. They went around the bend where the rustlers had held the herd until the pursuit caught up to them, and another hundred yards farther on, Slaughter and Santiago came to a narrow, twisting trail that led up to the rim on that side.

Slaughter nodded toward the trail and said, "Let's go take a look."

Cautiously, they rode to the top. When they reached

the rim, they had no trouble locating the spot where the bushwhackers had waited. They found empty rifle cartridges littering the ground, as well as the stubs of several quirlies.

"Three horses," Slaughter said as he pointed out the tracks. "They took the extra one with them when they lit out, and it looks like they were in a hurry to put this part of the country behind them."

"The odds were no longer in their favor," Santiago said.

"Yes, that's the way it seems to me, too. From the looks of everything we've found, it appears that Becker sent six men on with the herd and took the rest of the bunch with him. I'd say the two who were left didn't care for the idea of being sacrificed on the altar of Ned Becker's revenge."

"What do we do now?"

"We'll catch up to the herd, leave a few men to drive it on back to the ranch, and the rest of us will go on ahead and get back as soon as we can." Slaughter glanced at the sky. "I started to say earlier that I wanted to get there by nightfall, but I doubt if we can do that. But we've wasted enough time. If our guesses are right, they could use our help back there, and the sooner the better."

Joe Sparkman lifted his arm and used the sleeve to wipe sweat off his forehead. He had been up here on top of the water tank for a couple of hours, with no shade from the sun, and the heat from the sun was intense.

It would be nice if he could lift the hatch in the top of the tank, lower himself into the cool water, and float around for a while. That would cool him off. But he couldn't keep an eye on what was happening from inside the tank.

As far as he could tell, the varmints who had laid siege to the ranch didn't know he was up here, and Sparkman wanted to keep it that way for as long as possible. Not for his own protection, although he sure as hell had no wish to die here today, but rather because he thought he could do the most good for Mrs. Slaughter and the others in the house if he took the outlaws by surprise when he finally announced his presence by drilling some of the bastards.

Joe had come close to shooting the fella who had ridden up to the front gate. It would have been easy to do while the gent was palavering with Mrs. Slaughter.

But that would have been cold-blooded murder. Sparkman was no saint, but he drew the line at such things.

So he'd waited, and for a second it looked like he'd made a bad mistake when he thought that Mrs. Slaughter had been shot. Texas John would go on a rampage if anything ever happened to that little gal.

Thankfully, he'd caught a glimpse of her a short time later when she opened the door to retrieve that note one of the outlaws had tossed up on the porch, so he knew she was all right. That was a big load off his mind.

Now he'd settled down to waiting again.

Hot, tedious waiting.

He was no strategist, just a cowboy from Zephyr, Texas, who'd discovered at an early age that he had a natural shooting eye. He had supplied countless squirrels and jackrabbits for his ma's stew pot when he was a kid.

But he was beginning to get a hunch that the outlaws were going to wait until dark to make their move. They could get around easier then without being seen. They might be planning to sneak up on the house.

Sparkman figured he'd better do something to spoil that plan while he still could.

The varmints were holed up behind the schoolhouse. Sparkman could look over the ranch house roof and see the Texas-style adobe brick building a couple of hundred yards away. Cottonwood trees grew behind and to one side of it, and the outlaws were using those for cover, too.

But from time to time he spotted some of them moving around. As Sparkman thought more about it, he decided that the *hombre* who had ridden up to the gate to talk to Mrs. Slaughter must be the leader.

Cut off a snake's head and the rest of it died, he thought. Any good ol' Texas boy knew that. Sparkman's eyes narrowed as he looked over the barrel of his rifle and waited to catch a glimpse of the boss owlhoot. His vision was exceptionally keen. Even at this distance he thought he could spot the man again.

And when he did, that would be the time to take his first shot. Kill that fella and the others might give it up as a bad job. Maybe not likely, but there was at least a chance of that happening.

Sparkman waited with the patience of a born hunter. He recalled the time he had waited almost an entire night, not moving a muscle, for a coyote that had been getting into his ma's chicken house and carrying off a hen every night. Finally the slinking critter had showed up, and Sparkman drilled him with a single shot from the hayloft in the barn. He'd hung that varmint's tail from the fence around the vegetable garden, proud of what he'd done.

If he could save the lives of everybody here on the ranch, it would be even better.

Caught up in those thoughts, he might not have heard anything behind him—even if there had been anything to hear.

But as it was, the form that pulled itself swiftly onto the top of the water tank moved in utter silence. The only thing that warned Sparkman he had company was a flickering shadow in the corner of his eye.

His heart leaping in alarm, he rolled onto his back as fast as he could. That saved his life, at least for the moment. The knife that the Apache had been about to drive into his back struck the tank's top instead and the point imbedded itself in the wood.

Sparkman tried to swing the Winchester's muzzle up and around so he could get a shot off, but the Indian knocked the barrel aside with a swipe of his other arm as he struggled to wrench the knife free.

Sparkman struck upward with the rifle's stock instead. He aimed the blow at the Apache's face, but the man twisted and the butt caught him on the shoulder.

That was enough to knock the Apache to the side. Sparkman kicked him in the belly. The cowboy knew he was fighting for his life, and that desperation gave him strength and speed he didn't know he had.

Unfortunately he was battling a man for whom fighting and killing were as natural as breathing. The Apache writhed out of the way when Sparkman tried again to hit him with the rifle. His left hand shot out, gripped Sparkman by the throat, and drove the back of the cowboy's head against the tank.

The blow stunned Sparkman, caused his vision to go

blurry for a second, and made the world spin crazily around him. By the time he recovered his wits, the Apache had wrenched the knife loose and held the blade at Sparkman's throat.

Sparkman expected to die right then and there. The keen edge sliced into his skin and he felt the warm trickle of blood down his neck.

But the Apache held off and didn't put enough pressure on the blade to slice into Sparkman's throat.

Instead he leaned close over the cowboy, his face only inches away from Sparkman's, and asked, "How many are in the house?"

It was hard to talk with a knife at his throat that way, but Sparkman managed to gasp, "You can . . . go to hell!"

The Indian pressed a little harder on the knife and went on, "Santiago Rubriz. Is he here at the ranch?"

Sparkman didn't see how it would hurt anything to answer that one. He said, "No. He went with . . . Texas John . . . after those damn . . . rustlers." Sparkman breathed raggedly through his clenched teeth for a second, then added, "You fellas better . . . light a shuck . . . before Slaughter gets back. You'll be mighty sorry . . . if he catches you."

The Apache smiled. If anything, it made him look uglier and more evil.

"What about Don Eduardo?"

"I don't know . . . a damn thing. And I wouldn't tell you . . . if I did."

"Then there is no reason to keep you alive."

Sparkman's heart jumped again. He wanted to cuss the Apache again, but there was no time for that. He felt the knife bite deep into his throat, burning hot and icy cold at the same time, and his body bucked up from the pain. He saw his own blood spout up like a fountain as his panic-stricken heart pumped it out through the gaping wound.

He knew he would never see Texas again. In fact, the last thing he saw was his killer standing up, knife in hand, blood dripping crimson from the blade . . .

The only thing that gave Joe Sparkman any comfort as he crossed the divide was the knowledge that his death would be avenged.

John Slaughter would see to that.

Chapter 18

Becker saw Bodaway walking through the cottonwood grove and frowned. He realized he hadn't seen his old friend for a while.

"Where have you been?" Becker asked.

"Getting rid of a problem," Bodaway replied.

"What problem?"

"The rifleman hidden on top of the water tank."

Bodaway pointed to the tank, the top of which was visible in the distance, rising higher than the roof of the ranch house.

"Wait a minute," Becker said with a frown. "One of Slaughter's men was up there?"

Bodaway grunted and said, "I would not have had to kill him if he wasn't."

"How did you know?"

"I saw the barrel of his rifle when he pointed it at you."

"At me?" Becker asked, surprised.

"While you were at the fence talking to the woman."

Becker felt a little shiver go through him. He wasn't

surprised that he'd been covered while he was parleying with Mrs. Slaughter, but the idea that a sharpshooter had targeted him from the top of the water tank was unexpected. Putting a man up there was actually a pretty smart move.

But evidently it hadn't paid off, because Bodaway had disposed of the *hombre*.

"So you killed him?"

Bodaway shrugged.

"What did you do with him?"

"Left him up there. What else would I do with him?"

There were still a couple hours of sunlight left. The body would start to stink by nightfall, lying out in the sun that way.

Maybe the people in the house would smell it, Becker thought. The idea made him smile a little. Nothing like the stench of death to make somebody's spirits fall. Maybe some of the defenders would start to think about giving up.

Not that it would really matter in the long run if they did. They were all going to die anyway.

Herb Woodbury came up to Becker and Bodaway and said, "The boys are startin' to wonder what we're gonna do, boss. Are we waitin' until the sun goes down to make our move?"

"That's right," Becker said. "Once it's dark I want a couple of men to get up close enough to the house to throw torches through some of the windows. If we set the place on fire inside, they won't have any choice but to come out."

"And we shoot 'em down when they do," Woodbury guessed.

"Have you forgotten why we're here?" Becker asked with a frown. "I want Don Eduardo and his wife alive."

Bodaway said, "The boy is not here."

Becker looked quickly at him and asked, "You mean Santiago?"

"I asked the man on the water tank about him. He said the boy went with Slaughter after the cattle."

Becker rubbed his jaw and said, "Well, that's pretty much what I figured. That makes it even more important for us to capture the don and doña and Mrs. Slaughter. The others will be coming back sooner or later, and we'll need hostages to make them surrender, too."

"Gonna make a clean sweep of it, eh?" Woodbury said.

"Whatever it takes to make sure Rubriz dies knowing that I've taken everything from him. That means his wife and son have to die first."

Bodaway said, "And the white men claim that Apaches are cruel."

For a second that comment annoyed Becker. Then he looked closer at Bodaway and realized that despite the solemn expression on his old friend's face, the Apache had just made a joke. Becker threw back his head and laughed.

Then he grew more serious, too, and said, "Nothing is too cruel for the man who murdered my father."

* * *

"Let me go out there," Don Eduardo said as he struggled to stand up. "That is the only chance any of you have to survive this madman's scheme."

"Eduardo, don't be insane," Belinda said. She put a hand on her husband's shoulder. "You know it wouldn't do any good. You heard what Mrs. Slaughter said."

Viola held out the note to Don Eduardo and said, "You can read it for yourself. He wants both of you. And don't think for a second that if he got you, he would spare the rest of us. Becker's a natural-born killer."

"No!" the don responded with unexpected vehemence. "She made him that way, that woman. That evil woman!"

He was breathing hard. Dr. Fredericks came up on his other side and said, "You'd better take it easy, Don Eduardo. You've been through a rough time of it, and you're in no shape to work yourself into such a state."

With an angry frown, Rubriz leaned back on the sofa. Belinda perched on the edge beside him and took his hand. He lifted her hand in both of his and gently pressed his lips to the back of it.

"I am so sorry that you are in danger, my dear," he said. "This is my fault. I should never have trusted either of them."

"Either of them?" she repeated with a puzzled frown.

"Thaddeus Becker . . . and his wife." Don Eduardo sighed. "Although, to be fair, Thaddeus was a good man at one time. We fought side by side for freedom against the oppressors of my country. True, at first Thaddeus joined with us because he believed our side would emerge triumphant in the end, and he might become rich if he was one of us. But by the time that came about, he believed in our cause, I know it."

Viola thought the don might be wrong about that. A man who fought for money, or even for the hope of profit, seldom changed his stripes.

But she hadn't been there, she reminded herself. She had no way of knowing what had really been in Thaddeus Becker's heart and mind.

"It was Lusita," Don Eduardo went on. "She was the one who changed him. He saw her in Mexico City, at a ball to celebrate our victory, and lost all reason. It was the same ball where I met my own beloved Pilar." He looked over at Belinda. "I am sorry, I should not mention her—"

"Of course you can mention her," Belinda said. "I know you loved her. Of course you did. From everything you've told me, she was a wonderful woman. And she was Santiago's mother, so of course you still have feelings for her."

"They do not diminish my love for you."

Belinda leaned over and kissed him on the cheek. She murmured, "I know that."

Viola frowned slightly. She had spent the past eighteen hours intensely disliking Doña Belinda Rubriz, and now the woman had to go and act like a decent human being. Her affection for her husband seemed genuine.

But if it was, how could she be unfaithful to him with her own stepson?

"Lusita was quite taken with the dashing *gringo* adventurer, I suppose," Don Eduardo went on. "But I should not bore you with this story."

"No, go on," Belinda urged him. "Anything that helps me get to know you better is all right with me, Eduardo."

And talking kept the don sitting there relatively quietly and resting, thought Viola. She glanced at Fredericks, and the doctor gave her a slight nod. He approved of Don Eduardo telling them about his past, too.

"You understand, these are things that have weighed on my heart and soul for many years. We were happy at first, there at the ranch: Thaddeus and Lusita, Pilar and me. But Lusita always had, how do you say it, a wandering eye. She claimed to love Thaddeus, but she thrived on the attention of men. It seemed to be like air and water to her, a necessity of life."

"I've known women like that," Belinda said.

She had probably been a woman like that in the past, Viola thought, then chided herself for being so judgmental.

"Thaddeus loved her so much, he could not see what she was really like," Don Eduardo said. "Or if he did, he persuaded himself to ignore it. But he gave no sign that he knew, even when she . . . even when she decided that she wanted to seduce me, his own partner and comrade-in-arms."

"You resisted her, of course."

"Of course," Rubriz said. "Then when she became with child and presented Thaddeus with a fine son, I hoped that motherhood would force Lusita to put everything else behind her. That she would devote herself to her husband and the little boy. And for a time it seemed that would be so."

Viola said, "That little boy was Ned Becker, the man who's out there laying siege to this house now?"

With a solemn nod, Don Eduardo said, "Yes, it must be so. That is the name I remember him by. I have not seen him in many, many years. In truth, I thought that he was probably dead. I knew from friends in Mexico City that Lusita never returned to her family after she took the boy and left the ranch, after Thaddeus Becker's death."

Viola's head was spinning a little from trying to keep up with everything in Don Eduardo's story. It was a good example of how messy and complicated life could get for some people. She was glad that she had met the love of her life at a relatively early age and spent so many years happily married to John Slaughter.

"I wanted to believe that Lusita was just impulsive and misguided," the don continued. "But that hope was colored by memories of earlier, happier days. When she lied to her husband and made him believe that I had attacked her, she forced Thaddeus to take action that ultimately resulted in his death. I have no doubt that wherever they went after that, she filled her son's head with lies about the things I had done. She must have blamed me for what happened to Thaddeus, when I was only defending myself. And now Ned has come to reap the evil his mother sowed."

"Maybe you could talk to him," Belinda suggested. "Maybe if you explained the truth about everything, he'd see that he's wrong to hate you."

Don Eduardo looked at Viola and said, "You talked with him, señora. Did he seem to you like the sort of man who would listen to reason?"

"Not at all," Viola answered without hesitation. "He's been nursing his hate for too long. I don't think he could put it aside now. It's all he has left."

Don Eduardo spread his hands and said to his wife, "You see? There is nothing to be done. We must wait."

"Wait and hope that John gets back here in time,"

Viola said. "That . . . and be ready to fight for our lives if we don't get any help."

The sun was nearly down when Stonewall and Hermosa came in sight of the ranch. John thought there might be some sort of trouble here, so Stonewall was more nervous than he would have liked to admit. He had been watching for smoke in the sky that would indicate burning buildings and listening for the sound of gunfire, although it was beyond him why any of the rustlers would have doubled back to attack the ranch.

Instead, the place looked quiet and peaceful in the fading light. From a distance, Stonewall could make out the trees, the roof of the house, the water tank standing to one side a little higher than anything else.

He and Hermosa reined in, and Stonewall heaved a sigh of relief.

"Looks like John was wrong for once," he said. "That sure doesn't happen very often. I reckon we can ride on in—"

Hermosa reached over and gripped his arm.

"Wait," the *vaquero* said.

"What is it?" Stonewall asked with a frown. "Everything looks fine to me."

"Look there." Hermosa pointed. "Above the water tank."

Stonewall squinted, and as he did, he made out several dark shapes wheeling through the air. They were little more than dots at this distance, but he had seen such things often enough in the past to recognize them.

"Those are buzzards," he said.

As he watched, one of the carrion birds dipped down

toward the water tank and disappeared. It must have landed on top of the tank, Stonewall realized. The other buzzards continued to circle.

"Something is dead up there," Hermosa said, his voice flat.

"Maybe a . . . a rat?" Stonewall suggested as a ball of sick fear began to form in his belly.

Hermosa shook his head and said, "Not a rat. One of the *zopilotes* would have picked it up and carried it off by now. What's up there is too big for them to lift."

"Well, an animal of some other sort, then," Stonewall said, but even he could hear how hollow his voice had become.

"An animal, yes," Hermosa repeated with a grave nod. "A man."

"We can't be sure about that. Anyway, what in blazes would a man be doing on top of the water tank?"

"A man might be up there to work on it. But a dead man?"

Hermosa's shoulders rose and fell in an expressive shrug.

Stonewall took off his hat and scrubbed a hand over his face. It seemed like a week since he'd had any sleep, and he'd been in the saddle for so long that every muscle in his body ached. But for a second there he had felt a lot better when he thought everything was fine on the ranch after all.

Hermosa had kicked that right out from under him. Everything the *vaquero* said was correct. There had to be a dead man on top of the water tank.

That might well mean the trouble here was already over. Viola might already be—

Stonewall swallowed hard and clapped his hat back on his head. He wasn't going to believe that anything had happened to his big sister until he had undeniable proof of it. Viola had always been extremely capable of taking care of herself, so Stonewall was going to assume she was fine.

Thanks to Hermosa's keen eyes, though, he knew they couldn't afford to go riding in openly, as if nothing were wrong.

Hermosa seemed to be thinking the same thing. He asked, "Which approach has the most cover?"

Stonewall scratched his jaw in thought for a moment, then said, "It'll take longer, but we need to circle all the way around to the south, across the border. There are more trees and buildings if we come in that way. If we can make it to the barn and the corrals, we'll have a good view of the front of the house from there, and maybe we can tell what's going on."

Hermosa nodded in agreement with the plan, then glanced at the sky and said, "It will be dark in an hour or so. Trouble often comes with the twilight."

"If it does," Stonewall said, "we'll be ready for it."

Chapter 19

Night fell quickly in Arizona Territory once the sun dipped below the horizon. Normally that wasn't a problem, but Viola hated to see it happen tonight.

The darkness meant they couldn't see the enemy coming.

And come they would, she thought as she knelt at one of the front windows and watched the dusky shadows gathering.

It was getting even darker inside the house. When the maids started to light the lamps, as they normally did at this time of day, Viola had told them to stop and added that they should blow out the ones they'd already lit. She didn't want any of the defenders silhouetted against the glow so they would be even better targets.

A footstep beside her made Viola look around. Dr. Fredericks stood there, crouching a little so he could look out the window.

"Better move back, doctor," she said. "There's no telling when they might start throwing lead through these windows."

Fredericks retreated quickly. He said, "I'm afraid you have more experience at this sort of thing than I do, Mrs. Slaughter. I deal with the aftermath of trouble. I rarely find myself squarely in the middle of it like this."

"I know, and I wish you weren't here now. Not that I don't appreciate any help you can give us—"

"I know what you mean," Fredericks said. "I could have driven away and not been trapped here." His voice took on a determined tone as he continued, "But I have patients here, so I'm glad I stayed. I have every confidence that we're all going to be all right."

"So do I," Viola said.

That was stretching the truth, she thought, but she knew better than to give up hope. She had come through some dangerous situations before, and John hadn't always been at her side during those times, either.

"I don't know much about this sort of thing," Fredericks went on. "What do you think they'll do?"

Viola had been pondering that quite a bit herself. She said, "Unless their numbers are overwhelming, I don't believe they'll launch a full-scale attack on the house. If they had that many men, they would have already done it. So it's more likely they'll try to drive us out into the open. The best way to do that is with fire."

"Fire," Fredericks repeated. Viola heard the worry in his voice. "You mean they'll try to set the house on fire."

"That's right."

"Flaming arrows on the roof, perhaps, to borrow a trick from the savages?"

Viola shook her head and said, "The roof is slate. It won't burn easily. They might try to shoot flaming arrows through the windows or get close enough to throw torches through them. It'll be up to us to keep them from succeeding."

"The other people who are wounded could probably get out of the house if they had to, but Don Eduardo shouldn't be moved too much," the doctor said. "It could be very dangerous for him." Fredericks paused. "But not more dangerous than staying in here while the place burns down around him, of course."

"Maybe it won't come to that. We'll do our best to see that it doesn't."

"You know," Fredericks mused, "if this man Becker wants Don Eduardo and Mrs. Rubriz alive, he can't just massacre everyone wholesale. He'll have to take prisoners."

"Only until he has the ones he wants," Viola pointed out.

"And then everyone else . . ."

"Will be a problem to be disposed of," she said.

A large rock cairn jutted up from the flat ground covered with scrub grass. Stonewall and Hermosa crouched behind it, each man peering past the cairn toward the barn and corrals about two hundred yards away.

The cairn marked the border between the United States and Mexico, and right now it provided some cover for Stonewall and Hermosa, too. Stonewall hoped that in the fading light their shapes would blend in with that of the marker in case anyone happened to look in this direction.

"I see no one moving around," Hermosa said quietly. "Perhaps the ranch is deserted."

"Maybe. That might not be a good thing, though."

Stonewall hadn't seen any signs of life as they approached, either. They had left their horses a quarter of a mile behind them and proceeded on foot for about half that distance before dropping to hands and knees and crawling the rest of the way to the border marker.

Stonewall listened intently. He didn't hear anything. A cloak of silence seemed to have been dropped over the ranch. That was unusual in itself. There were evening chores to do, and a lot of times there was horseplay going on around the bunkhouse. The quiet was ominous.

"We need to get closer," Stonewall said. They had brought their rifles with them, so he picked up his and went on, "You stay here and cover me. When I get to those trees"—he pointed to the cottonwoods that grew near the barn—"I'll stop there and you can come on across."

"The ground between here and there is wide open," Hermosa pointed out. "Anyone who looks in this direction will see you."

"Yeah, I know, but we're not doin' any good out here. I reckon we'll just hope that anybody around the place who ain't friendly will have their eyes on the house instead of back here."

The *vaquero* didn't argue with that. He simply picked up his Winchester and gave Stonewall a grim nod.

Stonewall tugged his hat down tighter on his head, then burst out from behind the border marker and ran toward the trees. He zigzagged a little, just in case anybody was trying to draw a bead on him.

Running in boots wasn't easy. Like most *hombres* who had practically grown up in the saddle, Stonewall figured that any job a man couldn't do from horseback usually wasn't worth doing.

This evening, though, he had no choice. He summoned up all the speed he could as he ran with the rifle held at a slant across his chest.

His heart hammered wildly in his chest, and not just from the exertion. His muscles were braced for the shock of a bullet at any second.

That shock never came. He reached the cottonwoods and slid to a stop among them, pressing his back to one of the tree trunks.

After standing there a moment with his chest heaving as he tried to catch his breath, he took off his hat and waved at Hermosa. From here, Stonewall couldn't see the *vaquero* behind the border marker even though he knew Hermosa was there.

Hermosa emerged from the cairn's shelter and loped toward the trees. Now that Stonewall had crossed the stretch of open ground without drawing any fire, Hermosa obviously didn't feel quite as much urgency. Despite that, his long legs covered the ground quickly, and he joined Stonewall in the trees.

Stonewall gestured toward the barn and said in a half-whisper, "We can get in there now and take a look at the house. I'll go first."

"Be careful," Hermosa advised. "If there are bad men around, some are likely to be in there."

"Yeah, I know. But there's only one way to find out."

Bending low, Stonewall ran through the gloom, past the corral, and up to the back of the barn. There was a door here. He had it open and slipped through in a matter of heartbeats.

The hinges squealed a little more than he liked, though.

He stopped just inside the barn. The shadows were thicker in here. The double doors at the front were almost completely closed, but not quite. When he looked along the center aisle he saw a thin line of grayish light, indicating the gap between the doors.

Stonewall listened again but didn't hear anything out of the ordinary. Several milk cows were kept in stalls in here, and he heard them moving around a little. They seemed restless, and one of them mooed plaintively. A couple of others joined in.

Those simple sounds told him something. The cows hadn't been milked this evening, and they weren't happy about it.

That was the last bit of evidence he needed to tell him something was very wrong here. A chore like milking the cows never would have been neglected otherwise.

He sniffed the air. Manure, straw, animal flesh . . . those were the only things he smelled. Tobacco smoke would have told him that someone was in here.

Of course, just because nobody was smoking a quirly in the barn didn't mean he was the only human occupant, he reminded himself. Maybe somebody was just being careful not to give away their presence.

Stonewall started toward the double doors.

His booted feet made no sound on the hard-packed dirt of the center aisle. The walk through the barn wasn't long, but his nerves were stretched so tight it seemed to take him an hour.

Finally he was at the doors. He leaned forward and

peered through the gap. From here he could look across the two roads and the large open area where the party had been held the previous night and see the house behind the picket fence.

In this poor light, he couldn't tell if any smoke rose from either of the two chimneys. The house sat there dark and quiet, flanked by a couple of outbuildings and the water tank, some tall cottonwoods looming behind it, several shorter trees and shrubs in front of it.

Stonewall regarded this place as his home, but it sure didn't feel very welcoming at the moment.

He was about to return to the back door and hiss at Hermosa, indicating that the *vaquero* should join him, but before he could turn away from the door he heard a faint noise close behind him. It was only a tiny scrape of boot leather against dirt, but that was enough.

Stonewall dived down and to the side as something swished over his head. He heard a grunt and then somebody stumbled into him.

Whoever this man was, he might be a friend, attacking Stonewall because he didn't know who he was. Stonewall didn't want to hurt him until he found out what was going on here.

Then the man let out a harsh, vile curse and Stonewall didn't recognize his gravelly voice. Stonewall lowered his head and lunged forward. His shoulder rammed into the man's legs. Stonewall hooked an arm around his knees and heaved. The man let out a yell as he went over backward and crashed to the ground.

Stonewall scrambled onto his knees and swung the Winchester one-handed, hoping the barrel would strike his attacker in the head and knock him out. The blow missed, however, and Stonewall had to put his other hand down to catch himself as he lost his balance.

That left his chin hanging out in the open for the kick that the man swept around at him. The blow knocked Stonewall across the aisle. He lost his hat and the rifle as he rolled over a couple of times and came up hard against the gate across the front of one of the stalls.

He started to pull himself up but froze as he heard the unmistakable sound of a revolver being cocked.

"Who the hell are you, mister?" the gravelly voice demanded. "Speak up or I'll start shootin'."

Stonewall didn't say anything. He figured the stranger didn't really care who he was. He just wanted Stonewall to say something so he could shoot at the sound of his voice.

Now that the man had committed himself and given away his own position, though, he couldn't afford to wait very long. Sure enough, only a couple of seconds went by before the man's nerve broke and he squeezed the trigger. Stonewall saw Colt flame bloom in the darkness as the sound of the shot assaulted his ears. The bullet thudded into a board somewhere as Stonewall threw himself onto his belly and palmed out his own Colt.

The gun roared and bucked in his hand as he triggered twice, bracketing the spot where he had seen the muzzle flash. He figured the man had ducked one way or the other after firing.

His ears were ringing from the shots, but he heard a choked scream. The man fired again, but the shots were wild, spasmodic, as if his finger was jerking the trigger with no conscious thought. He emptied the gun, and then Stonewall heard something hit the ground with a soggy thud.

He pushed himself up but had to grab the stall gate with his free hand to keep from falling again. That kick to the jaw had shaken him up more than he realized at first. As he stood there he heard rapid footsteps slap against the dirt and lifted his gun to shoot again if he needed to.

"Stonewall!"

That was Hermosa's voice. Stonewall sagged a little as he recognized it.

"Here," he called. "But be careful, I don't know how many of them are in here."

No more shots sounded. A moment later the *vaquero* gripped Stonewall's arm and asked, "You are all right, *amigo*?"

"Feel like a mule kicked me, but other than that I'm fine," Stonewall told him. "I think there must've only been one fella in here, and I'm pretty sure I got him."

"One more thing you can be sure of," Hermosa said grimly. "If there are more of them, they know now that we're here."

The shots made Becker stiffen and turn his head. He had been looking toward the house, but now he gazed toward the southwest.

"Did those shots come from the barn?" he snapped.

"Sounded like it," Herb Woodbury replied.

"Who's over there?"

"Walt Bryce, I think. Maybe he thought he saw somethin' and got spooked."

"No," Becker said, "I counted seven shots." He turned to the Apache. "Bodaway—"

"I will find out what happened," Bodaway said before Becker could finish. The Apache faded away into the shadows.

Once Bodaway was gone, Becker said to his *segundo*, "We're not going to wait any longer. The men have the torches ready?"

"Yeah, but those folks in the house are gonna be on edge now," Woodbury said. "It'll be harder to sneak up on 'em."

"Do it anyway," Becker ordered. "It's time to put an end to this."

Woodbury hesitated, then said, "Boss, you've already waited a long time for your revenge. Maybe it wouldn't hurt anything to wait until the redskin gets back and we find out what's goin' on."

"No," Becker said, his voice as hard and cold as ice. "Have the men set the place on fire now. It's judgment day for Don Eduardo Rubriz."

Inside the house, Viola's heart seemed to jump into her throat when she heard the shots. She could tell they came from the barn.

"Jess," she said to the foreman, who knelt at one of the other windows, "did we leave anybody out there?"

"Just Joe Sparkman on top of the water tank, ma'am,"

Fisher replied. "Everybody on the place except for him and the men who went with your husband is in this house."

"It couldn't have been Joe, so who were they shooting at?"

"Beats me. Shadows, maybe."

Viola didn't think so. She couldn't be sure, but she thought she'd heard two different weapons going off. She had been around enough gunfights to know one when she heard it.

Did that mean help had arrived? Was John back?

She didn't know, but for the first time in a while she actually felt hopeful again—but also more frightened because for all she knew, her husband might be in danger or even hurt.

"Keep a close eye out," she told Fisher. "That might have been a signal, and even if it wasn't, it might prod them into starting something."

"Yes, ma'am."

Time stretched out maddeningly as several minutes ticked by. The echoes of the shots had died away, leaving the ranch cloaked once more in that sinister silence.

Then Fisher exclaimed, "There!" and straightened up. The rifle in his hands cracked as he thrust the barrel through the open window.

Viola kept her attention focused on the area outside the window she was covering. She saw a sudden flare as someone snapped a match to life.

"Watch out!" Fisher called. "They've got torches!"

Viola squeezed off a shot and felt the rifle buck against her shoulder. As she worked the Winchester's lever she saw a small explosion of flame in the darkness. It spun toward her and she had to throw herself backward to keep from being hit by the torch as it sailed through the window.

The blazing brand landed on the floor, bounced a couple of times, and came to a stop. Viola smelled kerosene from the torch as the rug began to burn.

Chapter 20

"We need to get back outside where we can move around," Hermosa told Stonewall. "We do not want to get trapped inside this barn."

That sounded like good advice to Stonewall. Without wasting time checking on the man he had shot, he and Hermosa turned and hurried out the barn's rear door as soon as Stonewall found the rifle he'd dropped.

They headed for the trees. More shots split the gathering night, these coming from the direction of the house.

Alarm made Stonewall's heart slug heavily in his chest. He knew Viola was probably in the house, trying to defend it from whoever the intruders were. He wanted to reach her, to make sure his sister was all right.

But if he charged blindly into the middle of the fracas it was more likely he would just get himself killed, and that wouldn't be any help to Viola at all.

Stonewall spotted a garish orange glare through the trees that made his already taut nerves constrict even more. He pointed it out to Hermosa and whispered urgently, "They're tryin' to set the house on fire!"

"It seems they are trying to make those inside flee."

"How can we stop 'em?"

"It may be too late for that."

The *vaquero*'s voice was grim, and Stonewall saw why. The flames were growing brighter. From here it looked like the house might already be on fire.

Rifle reports came from the northeast. Stonewall looked in that direction and spotted the flicker of muzzle flashes several hundred yards away. He pointed them out to Hermosa and said, "That's where the schoolhouse is. The kids of the married hands have classes there whenever John's got somebody around who can teach 'em."

"It appears to be where the invaders have taken cover," Hermosa said. "Is there a way to get behind it without crossing open ground where we would be seen?"

The question made an idea leap into Stonewall's head. He said, "There's a ditch that runs parallel with the road. If we stay pretty low, we can follow it most of the way and they shouldn't be able to spot us."

Hermosa nodded and said, "Let us go."

Stonewall dashed through the darkness. Full night had fallen now and the moon hadn't risen yet, so they had that on their side, anyway. But the silvery light of millions of stars was scattered down over the landscape. They could have used a few clouds to block that starlight, but the sky was dazzlingly clear, as it often was in this part of the country.

Stonewall reached the ditch, which was about five feet deep and six wide, and dropped into it. It had been dug to bring water to the trees near the barn when one of the infrequent rains fell. That hadn't occurred in a good while, though, so the sandy bottom was dry as a bone.

Stonewall crouched low and moved along at a fast trot with Hermosa following close behind him. The ditch ran for approximately five hundred yards, ending at the little lane beside the ranch cemetery.

The two men had covered about half that distance when a dark shape suddenly loomed up in front of Stonewall.

He barely had time to realize somebody was there before the man lunged forward and crashed into him, driving him back into Hermosa. The surprise attack knocked both of them into the bottom of the ditch.

Stonewall had the presence of mind to thrust his Winchester straight up and ram the barrel into the attacker's belly. Foul breath spewed into his face.

Hermosa writhed free of Stonewall's weight and surged up to tackle the man who had jumped them. As the two of them locked in hand-to-hand struggle, Hermosa gasped to Stonewall, "Go on! Help your sister!"

Stonewall didn't want to leave Hermosa, but he figured if anybody could take care of himself, it was the *vaquero*. Besides, Viola's safety had to come first. Stonewall scrambled to his feet, leaped past the two men, and ran along the ditch.

The shooting continued from the direction of the house as he reached the end of the ditch and climbed out to race past the cemetery. He was farther east now than the place where the schoolhouse sat, so the men using the adobe brick building for cover wouldn't be likely to see him as he circled in behind them.

He spared a thought for Hermosa and hoped the *vaquero* was all right. Then he turned his attention to the task before him. He was only one man and knew he would be outnumbered, but that might not matter if he could take his enemies by surprise and get the drop on them.

As he slipped into the trees behind the schoolhouse, he heard horses nearby, blowing and stamping. It made sense that whoever was attacking the ranch would leave their horses back here where they were more out of harm's way.

Stonewall catfooted among the cottonwoods and made his way carefully toward the animals. When he was close enough he could see them, a large, dark, restless mass. He thought one of the gunmen might be watching the horses, but apparently they were just tied back here.

Unsure whether to be disappointed or relieved—Stonewall had thought he might jump the horse guard and knock the man out of the fight, but that also would have meant the risk of getting caught himself—he moved closer and murmured to the horses so he wouldn't spook them even more. He took hold of a pair of taut reins, followed them to the sapling where they were fastened, and untied them. The horse pulled away.

One by one, Stonewall untied the other mounts. He didn't try to stampede the horses because that would have drawn attention to him. Instead he just let them drift away. Whoever the invaders were and whatever they wanted, they wouldn't be able to make a quick getaway now.

With that done, he moved closer to the schoolhouse. He had counted fourteen horses. The man he had shot in the barn and the *hombre* he and Hermosa had run into in the ditch accounted for two of their owners.

That left an even dozen men to carry out the assault on

the house. Some of them had crept close enough to throw torches at the house and try to set it on fire.

Thankfully, they didn't seem to have succeeded. The orange glow that had blazed up briefly had died back down. The defenders must have put out the fire.

That didn't mean this bunch of killers would give up, however. They would try something else, unless Stonewall managed somehow to stop them.

He didn't get the chance to try. He heard something behind him, started to turn in the hope that Hermosa had disposed of his opponent and caught up to him, but instead he caught a glimpse in the starlight of a cruel, savage face framed by black hair bound back by a bandanna.

Apache!

That was Stonewall's last thought before something exploded against his head and sent him tumbling down into an all-consuming blackness.

Viola reacted instantly when the rug blazed up from the kerosene-soaked torch. She grabbed one edge of the rug, lifted it, and threw it over the flames.

Then she lunged on top of it, snuffing out the fire with the rug and her own weight.

This wasn't the only place the attackers had succeeded in getting a torch inside the house, though. She heard shouting in some of the other rooms that told her the defenders there were battling other blazes.

With the stink of kerosene and burned rug in her nose, she grabbed the rifle she had dropped and leaped back to the window. She saw a man drawing back his arm to throw another of the burning brands and snapped a shot at him.

Instinct guided the bullet. The man cried out, spun around, and dropped the torch at his feet as he collapsed. The grass along the fence was fairly dry at this time of year. It caught fire and sent flames dancing along the man's body.

The fact that he didn't move told Viola she had killed him. That might bother her later, but at the moment it left her unmoved. The man had attacked her home. As far as she was concerned he deserved whatever happened to him.

"Mrs. Slaughter, are you all right?"

The urgent question came from Dr. Fredericks behind her. Without looking around she said, "I'm fine, doctor. What about everyone else?"

"No one is hurt except for a few minor burns."

"The other fires?"

"They're out—for now. We were lucky they didn't spread too much. Your house sustained some damage, though."

"Damage can be repaired," Viola said. "A house can be rebuilt, if it comes to that. As long as we don't lose any more people, that's all I really care about."

She watched over the windowsill as the grass along the road continued to burn. The fire was bright for a few minutes, but then it began to die down as the fuel was exhausted. The smell of smoke lingered in the air.

From the window where he was posted, Jess Fisher said, "I don't see anybody else moving around out there. Looks like they've all pulled back except for that fella you drilled, Mrs. Slaughter."

As the smoke drifted over the house, Viola caught a whiff of a sickly sweet smell that made her stomach turn over unpleasantly. She knew it came from the body of the man she had killed, which had been charred by the flames around it. She gagged a little at the thought.

"Mrs. Slaughter?" Fredericks asked.

"I'll be fine," she managed to say. "Don't worry, doctor."

"It's the smell, isn't it? It always got to me, too, during the war. I was a surgeon in the Union army, you know. It wasn't the things I saw in the field hospitals that bothered me the most, although Lord knows they were bad enough. It was always the smells."

Viola took a handful of .44-40 cartridges and concentrated on thumbing them through the Winchester's loading gate. Once she took her mind off what had happened, she found that her stomach calmed down quickly.

She had a job to do—defending this ranch—and she couldn't allow anything to interfere with that.

No matter how many men she had to kill.

Becker paced back and forth angrily behind the schoolhouse as Woodbury tried to explain how the defenders must have been able to put out all the fires before they spread too much.

"I can see that," Becker interrupted. "I can see that the damned house isn't on fire like it's supposed to be. Did that failure cost us any men?"

"Pony Chamberlain didn't make it back," Woodbury said as he shook his head ruefully. "One of the boys told me Pony got hit just as he was about to throw his torch.

He dropped it and it set fire to the grass around him instead. He must've been dead, 'cause he didn't move while it burned him."

"Serves him right for letting himself get shot," Becker muttered. Then he saw the surprised, upset look on his *segundo*'s face and knew he had gone too far. He added, "We'll make the bastards pay for killing him."

That seemed to mollify Woodbury. He nodded and said, "We damn sure will." He paused, then asked, "What are we gonna do now, boss?"

That was a frustrating question. Nothing they had tried so far had worked.

Before Becker could answer, Bodaway emerged from the trees carrying something draped over his shoulders. As the Apache came closer, Becker's eyes widened in surprise. Bodaway's burden was the body of a man, either unconscious or dead.

Bodaway came up to Becker and Woodbury and dumped the body in front of them. In the starlight, Becker could tell that the man was young, with fair hair and a dark smear of blood across his face from a cut on his forehead.

"Who's this?" Becker demanded. "I thought all of Slaughter's people were holed up in the house."

"I found this one and another man trying to get behind you," Bodaway explained. "This one had reached the trees and turned your horses loose before I caught up to him."

A curse exploded from Becker's mouth. He turned to Woodbury and ordered, "Go get those horses rounded up."

Woodbury hurried to obey as Becker turned back to his old friend.

"Is he dead?" he asked as he nodded at the young man lying on the ground.

"Not this one. I left the other in a ditch over there." Bodaway waved vaguely toward the barn.

"What about those shots earlier?"

"Your man in the barn is dead, as you thought."

"So we've lost two men," Becker said. "That's got to stop. Why didn't you go ahead and kill this son of a bitch?"

"I thought you might be able to make use of him. He is Señora Slaughter's brother."

That came as a surprise to Becker, too. He said, "How in the world do you know that?"

"Last night, before my men and I raided the party, I overheard some of the people talking while I was still hiding in the dark. I learned then that Viola Slaughter is his sister."

A smile tugged at Becker's thin lips as he looked down at the unconscious young man.

"Well, now," he said, "that was good thinking on your part, Bodaway, bringing him here alive instead of killing him. This little bastard might just come in handy."

Chapter 21

Stonewall wasn't out cold for long. He was a little surprised when he regained consciousness to find that he was still alive.

When the last thing you saw before you passed out was the cruel face of a bloodthirsty Apache warrior, you didn't really expect to wake up again.

It was obvious he wasn't dead, though. Not with the way his head hurt from being walloped like that. Unless that pounding racket was Satan's own imps playing a drum inside his skull instead of his own pulse.

No, he heard human voices somewhere nearby. He was definitely alive.

But that didn't mean he was all right. He could still be in a mighty bad spot. The next step was to open his eyes and find out exactly what was going on.

Easier said than done. Each eyelid seemed to weigh at least a thousand pounds, and he lacked the strength to lift them.

Finally he pried them up, and when he did he saw that he was lying on the ground with trees around him.

Figures moved vaguely nearby. Those were the men he'd heard talking a moment earlier, he thought.

They didn't seem to be paying much attention to him. Maybe he could get up and slip away into the night. It was worth trying.

Or it would have been if he could move, he realized. As he tested his muscles, he discovered that he was tied hand and foot. Someone had pulled his arms behind his back and lashed his wrists together. Likewise a length of rope was bound around his ankles.

They hadn't gagged him, though. He could yell all he wanted to—for all the good that would do. He didn't figure there was anybody close by who would want to help him.

Actually, it might be better if they didn't even know he had come to, he decided. That way he stood a better chance of eavesdropping on his captors and figuring out his best course of action.

Sooner or later he would get a chance to make a bold, unexpected move, he told himself, and when the proper moment came, he needed to be ready.

At first he thought his eyes were adjusting to the starlight, but over the next few minutes as everything became brighter and took on a more silvery hue, Stonewall realized the moon was coming up. He could make out his surroundings a little better. The dark mass about fifty yards away became the double-cabin schoolhouse where the kids on the ranch were taught their lessons.

He even saw the Apache who had captured him, talking to a tall, lean man who held himself like he was the boss around here.

That *hombre* would soon find out how wrong he was, Stonewall told himself. When John Slaughter got back, everything would be different. He was the only boss on this ranch.

Except for Viola, of course.

The two men stopped talking and turned to walk toward him. Stonewall slitted his eyes as he watched them approach. He didn't move a muscle or give any other sign that he was conscious.

Turned out that was wasted effort on his part, because the first thing the tall white man did when he walked up was to draw back his foot and kick Stonewall in the side. The brutal blow made Stonewall gasp and jerk.

"Wake up, if you're not already," the man said. He hunkered on his heels next to Stonewall. "You hear me, boy?"

"I . . . hear you," Stonewall grated through the pain in his side. Felt like the son of a buck might've cracked one of his ribs.

"I know you're Stonewall Howell, John Slaughter's brother-in-law, so don't even think about lying to me. Where's Slaughter?"

"I don't know."

The man stood up and kicked him again, this time in the left shoulder. Pain shot down that arm for an agonizing few seconds before it went numb.

"I told you not to lie to me. You went with Slaughter when he chased after those rustled cattle. Why are you back here so soon?"

"My horse . . . went lame."

"That's a lie, too. Slaughter would have taken extra

horses. And even if it were true, why would that other *hombre* come back with you?"

So they knew about Hermosa. Stonewall wondered if the Apache was the man they had run into in the ditch. If he was, the Indian's presence here didn't bode well for Hermosa.

"Did Slaughter send you back?" the man went on. "Did he know there was going to be trouble here at the ranch?"

"Mister . . . John Slaughter's my boss . . . not just my brother-in-law. I don't ask him . . . to explain himself . . . I just do . . . what he tells me."

"So he told you to come back. Well, I thought as much. I don't suppose it really matters what tipped him off. I've heard that Slaughter is a pretty smart man. Now here's the important question."

The man placed his foot on Stonewall's shoulder, the one he had kicked a few minutes earlier, and bore down on it. Stonewall groaned as he felt his bones grinding together under the pressure.

"How far behind you is Slaughter? When will he get here?"

Stonewall couldn't answer because the pain in his shoulder made him throw his head back as a grimace stretched his mouth. After a moment his captor let up, and as the weight went away, the pain eased.

"I don't . . . know," Stonewall panted in a whisper. "I really . . . don't."

The man hunkered beside him again and said, "You think what I've been doing to you is bad? This man beside me, he's called *El Infierno*. The Fires of Hell. The name suits him, too. If you don't tell me what I want to know, I'm going to turn you over to him and let him ask the questions for a while. You think you'll like that any better?"

Anger welled up inside Stonewall. This *hombre* thought he could just waltz in here, kill people and raise all sorts of havoc, and then demand answers. Stonewall said, "Why don't you . . . go to hell?"

The Apache moved a step closer.

The white man raised a hand to stop him and said, "No, that's all right. I know you'd enjoy working on him, Bodaway, but we don't have time to waste. There's too good a chance Slaughter is headed back and will get here before morning."

He straightened and prodded Stonewall in the side with a boot toe. It wasn't really a kick this time, but it hurt anyway.

"Get him on his feet," the man ordered. "We can make use of him whether he talks or not."

Stonewall didn't like the sound of that.

Viola didn't know what Becker would try next, but with the rising of the moon she doubted if the invaders would attempt to sneak up on the house again. The moon was three-quarters full and cast a lot of light over the area around the ranch house.

She had started wondering about Joe Sparkman up on the water tank. She hadn't heard any shots from there during the earlier skirmish, and she was afraid Becker's men might have spotted him and killed him.

If that turned out to be true, it was one more score against Ned Becker that would need settling. Viola hadn't even known Sparkman's name before today, but if he was dead, he had died fighting for the Slaughter Ranch and he would be avenged.

Dr. Fredericks came up to the window where Viola had posted herself and said, "Don Eduardo wants to talk to you."

"I'm a little busy," Viola said without taking her eyes off the stretch of ground in front of the window.

Fredericks chuckled and held out his hand. He said, "Give me the rifle. I'll spell you long enough for you to go talk to the don. I told you before, I know how to use a gun."

Viola had to admit to herself that it would feel good to get up and move around a little. She had been kneeling here for quite a while. She made up her mind and handed the Winchester to Fredericks, then grasped the side of the window to brace herself as she stood up. She made sure to stay out of a direct line of fire.

"I'm not as young as I used to be," she commented as stiff muscles protested the movement.

"My dear lady, you're a child compared to most of us."

"I don't know about that. I'd say that Doña Belinda is a little younger than me. Is she still with her husband?"

"She's asleep in one of the chairs." Fredericks paused. "That may be why the don asked to speak with you. I think he was waiting for her to doze off."

Viola wasn't sure what that meant, but there was one way to find out. She nodded to Fredericks and went into the parlor. She didn't need a lamp to find her way around. She knew every square inch of this house, and even if she didn't, enough moonlight came in through the windows to reveal the shapes of the furniture.

Don Eduardo was sitting up on the sofa with pillows propped behind him. Fredericks must have thought that was all right since he'd just been in here. Viola went over to the sofa, perched on the arm, and said, "The doctor told me you wanted to talk to me, Don Eduardo."

He nodded and slowly lifted an arm to point at a wing chair set against the wall. Viola could make out Belinda's huddled form as she slept, claimed again by exhaustion.

"I thought while my wife was asleep I should take the opportunity to speak with you again, Señora Slaughter."

"Something you don't want Doña Belinda to hear?" Viola smiled. "If you're planning on flirting with me, Don Eduardo, you should realize by now that I'm a happily married woman."

The don laughed quietly and said, "I do realize that, señora. I only wish my Belinda was as happily married."

Viola tried not to wince. She hoped that he wasn't about to confide in her. She didn't want to hear his suspicions that his wife was cheating on him. In these desperate circumstances, if he did that she wasn't sure she could keep what she knew to herself.

"Her husband is a very stubborn man, though," Rubriz went on.

"Are you saying that my husband isn't stubborn? Because if you are, you don't know John Slaughter very well."

"No, I was talking only about my determination to do what must be done. I have to turn myself over to Ned Becker. If you will help me, señora, we can accomplish that while Belinda sleeps, so she will not try to stop me."

Viola didn't try to hide her irritation as she said, "We've already talked about this. We're not going to give

Becker what he wants. Anyway, it wouldn't do any good, since he's said that we have to surrender Doña Belinda to him as well as you."

"I am the one he really wants," Don Eduardo insisted. "I am the one he blames for his father's death. It was many, many years after that tragic occurrence before I even met Belinda. She had nothing to do with it. Surely once he has me in his power, he will see that and be satisfied."

"Satisfied to kill you, you mean."

Carefully, probably because of the bullet hole in his side, Don Eduardo shrugged.

"If such is to be my fate, I will regret it, of course. But I have enjoyed my life for the most part and if it is destined to end now, I can accept that."

"If my husband was here, he would tell you that we make our own destinies, Don Eduardo. John has always lived by that code."

The don let out a weary sigh and said, "People have died, Señora Slaughter. How many, I don't know, but more than should have because of me. It is my wish that no one else should die because of Ned Becker's hatred for me."

"That argument might work if I really believed he would let the rest of us go. But that's never going to happen, and we both know it. He's a madman. If he gets his way, he'll kill us all, to cover his trail if for no other reason."

The moonlight was bright enough for Viola to see the tired but determined expression on the don's face. She wished he would stop wasting his energy arguing with her. She tried another tactic to get him to understand.

"Anyway, what would you do if your home was attacked and a lunatic wanted to kill one of your guests?" she asked. "Would you step back and let that happen?"

He glared at her for a few seconds, then abruptly laughed. "You are an intelligent woman, Señora Slaughter. You appeal to my sense of honor, knowing that it means more to me than almost anything else in the world. Only two things mean more: my wife and my son."

Who are cuckolding you, thought Viola. That became less urgent, though, in a life-or-death situation such as the one in which they found themselves.

She stood up and said, "I'm sorry, Don Eduardo, we're not going to allow you to surrender—"

"Mrs. Slaughter," Dr. Fredericks said from the parlor doorway with a note of urgency in his voice. "Mr. Fisher says you need to come back in here right now."

That set Viola's heart to tripping faster. Something was happening, and under the circumstances she doubted if it could be anything good.

As she hurried past Fredericks, she told him, "Keep an eye on Don Eduardo. Don't let him do anything foolish."

"You can depend on me," Fredericks assured her as he handed over the rifle.

Viola took the Winchester and went over to the window where Jess Fisher was crouched.

"What is it?" she asked the foreman.

He nodded toward the road in front of the house and said, "They showed up out there a minute ago. I passed the word for everybody to hold their fire."

She looked through the window and gasped as she saw three figures standing in the road. The moonlight was bright enough for her to recognize Ned Becker as one of them. One of the other men appeared to be an Apache warrior.

And the third man, standing between Becker and the Indian with his hands tied behind his back, Becker's gun to his head, and the Apache's knife to his throat, was her brother Stonewall.

Chapter 22

Stonewall bit back a groan of despair as he stood there in the road between Becker and Bodaway. He hated the fact that he was being used as a weapon against his own sister.

Surely Viola was smart enough not to give these bastards what they wanted, no matter how much they threatened him. Even if she cooperated, they would double-cross her and kill everybody. He was sure of it.

"Mrs. Slaughter!" Becker called. "You hear me in there?"

"I hear you."

That was Viola's voice, all right, and the faint tremble in it told Stonewall that she was mad. Not scared, as somebody else might think if they heard it, but deep down, nail-chewing, blood-spitting mad. Stonewall knew that because he had been on the receiving end of such anger from her before. Not often, but enough to never forget it.

"You better listen to me," Becker went on. "You can see I've got your brother. My thumb on the hammer of this gun is all that's keeping me from blowing his brains out, so don't get any ideas about trying some fancy trick shot. Anyway, even if you managed to kill me without this gun going off, my friend here would cut the little bastard's throat wide open before I even hit the ground."

"We're holding our fire," Viola said. "What do you want?"

Becker laughed.

"Why, you know that as well as I do. I want Don Eduardo and his wife, and I want you to surrender, as well. I plan to make a clean sweep of this when Rubriz's son gets back, and I don't want your husband interfering with that."

"You've gone to all this trouble and killed all those people for nothing, Becker," Viola responded. "Don Eduardo wasn't responsible for your father's death. Whatever your mother told you about what happened years ago was a lie."

Becker stiffened. Stonewall felt the muzzle of the man's gun press harder against his head. For a second he thought that Viola's words might have just gotten him killed.

Becker controlled himself enough not to shoot. He yelled, "You're a lying bitch! Rubriz is a murderer, and he has to pay for what he did. I'll see to it that he loses everything he holds dear before he dies! He'll be begging me to kill him and put him out of his misery!"

So that was what was going on, Stonewall thought. Some sort of loco vengeance quest. It made sense now, or at least as much sense as a scheme hatched by a lunatic could make.

Viola said, "If you let my brother go and ride away,

you can make it into Mexico before anyone can stop you. The authorities down there probably won't come after you. This senseless killing can stop here and now."

"It's not senseless," Becker insisted. "It's justice. Rubriz deserves to die for his crimes, and anybody who gets in the way of that, well, it's just too bad about what happens to them."

Talking wasn't easy with the Apache's knife against his throat, but Stonewall croaked, "Mister, you're wastin' your time. I've known my sister all my life, and she's the stubbornest woman on the face of the earth. She'll never give you what you want."

"Not even to save your life?" Becker asked as his lips twisted in a snarl.

"Not even for that," Stonewall said. He knew it was true, too. Viola would never back down in the face of evil.

"Well, that's her mistake. She'll see that I'm not bluffing." Becker's voice shook with the depth of his anger. "Bodaway—"

Stonewall figured Becker was about to order the Apache to cut his throat. He tensed, readying himself to make a desperate, last-ditch move that probably wouldn't accomplish a damned thing.

Before Becker could finish what he was about to say, Viola called, "Wait!"

An arrogant grin spread across Becker's face in the moonlight as he said, "So, you're ready to listen to reason, are you, Mrs. Slaughter?"

"You're the one who needs to listen," Viola said. "You've overplayed your hand again, Mr. Becker. If you kill my brother, we won't have any reason to hold our fire. You and your Apache friend will be riddled with lead before you can take two steps." She paused. "I'd say what we have here is a standoff . . . and the only way for you to break it is to release my brother, back away, and get off this ranch."

Becker's breath hissed angrily between his teeth. He said, "You're a fool. Do you think I'll give up my revenge that easily?"

"You can't get your revenge if you're dead," Viola pointed out.

She was right, of course. Becker had believed he could waltz in here and terrorize his way into getting what he wanted.

It hadn't occurred to him that he would run up against a woman with a backbone of tempered steel. No matter how this turned out, Stonewall was proud of his sister.

The tension in the air would have continued to stretch out until it snapped, and there was no telling what sort of explosion might have resulted from that.

But before that could happen, an unsteady figure stumbled out of the shadows next to the house, extended shaking hands toward the men in the road, and called, "Ned! Ned, please don't do this! Don't hurt these people when the one you really want is me!"

"Rubriz!" Becker exclaimed.

The gun barrel came away from Stonewall's head as Becker's instincts made him jerk the weapon toward the don.

In the same instant, the front door of the ranch house slammed open as Doña Belinda charged outside screaming, "Eduardo!"

The Apache's knife moved away from Stonewall's neck just slightly, and he knew this would be his only chance.

He lowered his head and rammed his shoulder into the man beside him.

Don Eduardo's sudden appearance outside took Viola by such surprise that for a moment all she could do was stare at him as he stumbled erratically toward the road.

Then Belinda rushed through the front room, threw the door open, and ran outside as well before anyone could stop her.

"Everyone hold your fire!" Viola shouted as she lunged to her feet and headed for the door, too.

Maybe she could grab Belinda and wrestle the blonde back inside before something happened to her.

As she emerged from the house, she caught a glimpse of Stonewall fighting with the Apache. She wasn't sure her brother was a match for the savage warrior, but she didn't have time right now to try to help him. She went after Belinda instead, who had just about reached Don Eduardo.

Unfortunately, so had Ned Becker. Becker could have gunned down Don Eduardo easily by now, but obviously just killing him wasn't enough to satisfy the crazed need for revenge that Becker felt.

Don Eduardo leaped between Becker and his wife and cried, "Belinda, get back!" She ignored him and grabbed his arm instead as he almost fell.

Becker was close enough to lash out with the gun in his hand. The barrel slammed against Don Eduardo's head and battered him to his knees as Belinda screamed. Viola lifted her rifle but couldn't get a shot at Becker because as Don Eduardo collapsed, Belinda threw herself at Becker and clawed at his face with her fingernails. She was directly in Viola's line of fire.

Viola had no idea what else was going on around the ranch house. All hell could have been breaking loose for all she knew. She ran closer, hoping to get a clear shot at Becker even though she knew that if she killed him, the rest of his men would probably open fire on her.

Becker swung his left arm in a backhanded blow that cracked across Belinda's face and sent her spinning off her feet. Then he lunged at Viola. She fired the Winchester, but Becker twisted aside at the last second and the bullet screamed harmlessly past him. He grabbed the rifle barrel and wrenched it aside.

The next instant a blow exploded against the side of Viola's head. The Winchester slid from her suddenly nerveless fingers. She felt herself hit the ground, then knew nothing after that.

Stonewall panted as he struggled against the Apache called Bodaway. His left hand was locked around Bodaway's right wrist, holding the knife away from his body. Stonewall's right hand had hold of Bodaway's throat. He dug in his thumb and fingers as hard as he could.

But Bodaway's left hand gripped Stonewall's throat, cutting off his air, and Stonewall knew it was a race to see who passed out first. The Apache was lithe and incredibly strong, a man whose business in life, basically, was killing.

Stonewall was young and strong, too, though. He just didn't know how long he could hold out. Already crimson rockets were exploding behind his eyes.

The sound of a shot nearby made Stonewall flinch. From the corner of his eye, he had seen Viola run out of the house a few seconds earlier, and he was afraid she might have been hit.

That distraction was enough to allow Bodaway to switch tactics. He let go of Stonewall's throat and hammered a fist into his temple instead. That blow was enough to stun Stonewall, already on the verge of passing out from being choked. His grip slipped off Bodaway's wrist, and he expected to feel eight inches of cold, deadly steel penetrating his throat or chest.

Instead Bodaway slammed the knife's handle against Stonewall's head. That finished the job of knocking him unconscious for the second time tonight.

If he had been awake, Stonewall wouldn't have given good odds on the chances of him waking up this time, either.

As soon as Mrs. Slaughter fell unconscious at Becker's feet, out of the line of fire, a rifle blasted from the house and a bullet whistled past his head. He crouched and looked around. Bodaway had just knocked Stonewall Howell to the ground.

"Leave the kid!" Becker called to his old friend. "Grab Mrs. Slaughter instead."

Becker then bent down, took hold of Belinda Rubriz's arm, and jerked her to her feet.

"You're coming with us, Don Eduardo," he ordered, then shouted, "Herb, give us some cover!"

Instantly, a barrage of rifle fire ripped out from the schoolhouse. Bullets slammed into the ranch house and forced the defenders to duck. Becker ran toward the school, forcing a stumbling Don Eduardo in front of him at gunpoint while he dragged the half-senseless Belinda.

Behind them trotted Bodaway with Viola Slaughter's unconscious form draped over his shoulders as Stonewall had been earlier. Even without the covering fire provided by Herb Woodbury and the other outlaws, the people in the house wouldn't have been able to shoot for fear of hitting Viola.

Things hadn't gone exactly according to plan, Becker thought, but they never did. The key to his genius lay in his ability to adapt his plan to the circumstances, whatever they might be.

A few moments later, he and Bodaway reached the schoolhouse with their prisoners. Stonewall Howell had been left behind, but that was all right. Becker had traded Stonewall for his sister, and that was a swap he would make any time.

John Slaughter would have been concerned about his brother-in-law's safety, of course, but he would be even more worried about his wife.

"Boss, are you all right?" Woodbury asked as the firing slacked off now that Becker and Bodaway were safe.

"I'm fine," Becker replied. "We've got what we need. We can get out of here now."

Woodbury frowned in confusion and said, "I thought we were gonna burn the place to the ground and kill any witnesses."

"That's not necessary. I've decided that we're going to finish this somewhere else."

Bodaway said, "Barranca Sangre."

Becker nodded.

"That's right. Slaughter's going to bring Santiago Rubriz there—alone—if he ever wants to see his wife alive again." He gave the whimpering Belinda a shove toward Woodbury and continued, "Hang on to her and see that she doesn't get away. You won't like what happens if she does, Herb."

Woodbury holstered his gun and took hold of Belinda with both hands. She shuddered and tried to pull away from him, but his grip was too strong.

Don Eduardo said, "You don't have to do this, Ned. Take me and let Belinda and Señora Slaughter stay here. They have nothing to do with your grudge against me."

"Forget it," Becker snapped. "You're all going. This isn't going to be over, Rubriz, until you've lost everything just like I did."

"You cannot mean that."

"The hell I don't." Becker looked at the Apache and went on, "Keep an eye on things while I write a note to leave for Slaughter. I want to be sure he knows exactly what to do to keep his wife from dying." Becker smiled. "At least . . . to keep her from dying too soon."

Chapter 23

Slaughter, Santiago, and the other men caught up to the hands driving the herd back to the ranch late in the afternoon.

Slaughter paused long enough to ask one of the cowboys, "Were you able to round up all the cattle after they scattered to hell and gone like that?"

The man tipped his hat back and nodded. "Yeah, I think so, boss. Pert-near all of 'em, anyway. What happened up yonder in the mountains? Did you catch up to those rustlers?"

"We did," Slaughter said grimly. "A couple of the scoundrels got away, but they were running so hard I doubt if we'll ever see them in this part of the country again."

"I reckon that means the others didn't get away."

"That's right. And we found out what this is all about, too." He didn't offer any further explanation, just asked, "How many men will it take to drive this herd back to the ranch?"

"Well . . . it'd be a lot of work, but four men could probably handle 'em, I reckon," the cowboy replied.

"All right. You'll be one of those four, Hal. Pick three more. The rest are coming with me back to the ranch as fast as we can get there."

"There really is trouble back there?" the cowboy asked with a worried look on his weatherbeaten face.

"I'll be surprised if there's not," Slaughter said.

A short time later, with a larger force behind him now, Slaughter was on the move again. When he looked at the sun hanging low in the sky, he knew it would be long after dark before they could reach the ranch. He hoped that whatever Ned Becker had planned, Viola and the men left behind at the ranch could handle it until reinforcements arrived.

As Santiago rode beside him, the young man said, "I'm sorry my family's history has brought danger to your family, Señor Slaughter. All this had nothing to do with you."

Slaughter grunted and said, "Wrong place at the wrong time, as the old saying goes, I suppose. Becker must have known that he couldn't make a move against your father on his own ranch. Don Eduardo was too well-defended there. He waited until the don was away from home and thought that would be easier."

"But that was foolish on his part, waiting until my father was visiting the famous Texas John Slaughter."

With a bleak, icy smile, Slaughter said, "The jury's still out on that. So far I haven't managed to do a hell of a lot to disrupt Becker's plans, whatever they may be."

"How could you know what to do when we didn't find out he was involved with this until a short time ago?"

Santiago had a point there, but it didn't make Slaughter feel any better.

Nothing was going to accomplish that until he got home and saw for himself that his wife was safe.

Slaughter pushed men and horses as hard as he could, but it was still hours after sundown by the time they approached the ranch. Stonewall and Hermosa should have gotten there quite a while earlier, though, so he hoped they had been able to give Viola a hand in case of trouble.

Stonewall was young but not green. He had considerable experience as one of Slaughter's deputies, as well as being a top hand on the ranch. And Hermosa was a fighting man through and through, in Slaughter's judgment.

Slaughter had been watching the sky to the south. He knew the sort of orange glow that appeared whenever something big was on fire . . . like a ranch house. He hadn't seen anything of the sort, so that gave him hope.

He called a halt when he judged that he and his companions were about half a mile from their destination. As he leaned forward in the saddle he listened intently.

Santiago must have been doing the same thing, because after a moment the young man said, "I don't hear any gunfire."

"Neither do I," Slaughter said.

"That is a good sign, surely."

Slaughter shook his head and said, "Not necessarily. It may just mean that the fighting is over."

And that everyone there is dead, he added to himself, but he couldn't put that dire thought into words.

Slaughter heeled his horse into motion again. He rode

at a more deliberate pace now. It was possible that some sort of ambush was waiting for them at the ranch, and he didn't want to charge blindly into it.

As they came closer he saw lights. Lots of lights, in fact, as if every lamp in the house was ablaze. That was cause for alarm in itself. Under normal circumstances, by this time of the evening everyone on the ranch would be settling down for a good night's sleep.

Slaughter's nerves wouldn't take it anymore. He kicked his horse into a gallop that didn't end until he hauled back on the reins and swung down from the saddle at the gate in the fence in front of the ranch house. Santiago and the rest of the men weren't far behind him.

The people in the house must have heard the hoofbeats. Slaughter hoped to see Viola step out of the front door and come onto the porch.

Instead it was the burly figure of the doctor from Douglas, Neal Fredericks, that appeared. Fredericks stood on the porch and wiped his hands on a rag.

In the light that spilled through the doorway and the windows, Slaughter saw the crimson splotches on the rag and knew they were bloodstains.

He threw the gate open and hurried into the yard.

"Doctor," he called. "What's happened here? Where's Viola?"

"I have bad news, John," Fredericks said as Slaughter bounded up the steps to the porch.

Slaughter's hand closed tightly around the doctor's arm. Fredericks winced a little but didn't pull away.

"By God, don't tell me she's dead," Slaughter said. "Don't you tell me that."

"I don't know. She was alive when she left here, that's all I can be sure of."

"When she . . . left here?" Slaughter repeated, confused now. "Where in blazes did she go?"

"A man named Becker took her, along with Don Eduardo and Doña Belinda."

"No!" That shocked cry came from Santiago, who leaped down from his horse and charged up to the porch. "That cannot be!"

"I'm sorry, son, but that's what happened," Fredericks said. "Who are you?"

Slaughter said, "This is Santiago Rubriz, Don Eduardo's son." He struggled to control his raging emotions and went on, "You'd better start at the beginning and tell us what happened, doctor."

For the next few minutes, Fredericks did exactly that. Slaughter had to bite back both curses and groans as he heard about how Viola had been captured by the raiders, along with Don Eduardo and Doña Belinda.

Santiago interrupted to ask, "My stepmother, was she hurt?"

"Knocked around a little, but that's all, as far as I know." Fredericks frowned a little. "Your father was in much worse shape."

"You got the bullet out of him, though," Slaughter said.

Fredericks nodded and said, "Yes, but he lost a lot of blood. He was very weak and couldn't afford to lose any more. If that wound of his opened up again . . ."

The doctor's voice trailed off and he shook his head. His meaning was all too clear.

Something else occurred to Slaughter. He said, "My brother-in-law Stonewall and one of Don Eduardo's *vaqueros* were on their way here ahead of the rest of us. Have you seen any sign of them?"

Fredericks pointed over his shoulder with a thumb that still had bloodstains on it.

"In the parlor with the rest of the wounded," he said.

Slaughter stepped past the doctor and went inside. As he came into the parlor he spotted Stonewall sitting on a straight-backed chair as one of the maids wrapped a bandage around his head. The young man exclaimed, "John!" and would have stood up if Slaughter hadn't motioned for him to keep his seat.

Stonewall didn't appear to be in too bad of a shape. The same couldn't be said of Hermosa, who lay on the same sofa where Don Eduardo had been recuperating the last time Slaughter saw him. Thick bandages swathed the *vaquero*'s midsection. His eyes were closed. He looked dead, except for the fact that his chest was rising and falling lightly.

Slaughter and Santiago went over to Stonewall. He gestured toward the bandage on his head as the maid stepped back.

"Don't worry about this," Stonewall said. "I got knocked out a couple of times, but that's all. My head's too hard for that to have done any real damage."

"Tell us what happened," Slaughter snapped.

Stonewall provided his version of events, then added, "I figured that blasted Apache had killed Hermosa, but he was still alive when Doc Fredericks and Jess Fisher found him out yonder not far from the schoolhouse. Hermosa must've crawled out of the ditch after he tangled with the Apache, and that Apache left him for dead."

Fredericks said, "Any normal man would have been

dead. He'd been stabbed at least five times. To be honest, I'm shocked he's still alive. His insides must be made of rawhide, just like his outsides."

Slaughter stepped over to the sofa and looked down at the wounded *vaquero*. He told Fredericks, "Do everything you can for him, doctor."

"I will, don't worry about that."

"Was anyone else killed?"

"We found a man on top of the water tank," Fredericks said. "His throat had been cut."

"That was Joe Sparkman," Jess Fisher said gloomily. The ranch foreman had come into the room while Slaughter was talking to Stonewall. "Miz Slaughter put him up there to do some sharpshooting, but I reckon that damned Apache found him before he ever got a chance to take a hand."

Slaughter shook his head and asked, "Who is this Apache all of you keep talking about?"

"His name's Bodaway or something like that," Stonewall said. "From the way he and Becker act, they're old friends. I hear tell that Becker's got a bad grudge against Don Eduardo, and that's what caused all this ruckus."

"Ned Becker is a madman," Santiago said. "That is the only way to describe him."

"He may be a madman," Fredericks said, "but he's got a plan." He held out a folded piece of paper. "We found this message over by the schoolhouse, held down with a piece of broken brick. They used a bandanna and a sharp stick to make a flag they planted right beside it, so we couldn't miss it."

Slaughter took the paper and unfolded it. A fairly long message was written on it in a compact, precise hand.

Ned Becker might be an outlaw, a murderer, and a lunatic, but apparently he was also an educated man, because it was his signature at the bottom of the missive.

Since the maid had finished bandaging Stonewall's head, the young man stood up and came over to join Slaughter, Santiago, and Fredericks beside the sofa where the unconscious Hermosa lay. The others watched Slaughter tensely as he read the message.

After a moment, Slaughter looked up from the paper.

"Becker is very clear about what he wants," Slaughter said. "I'm to bring Santiago with me, and the two of us—alone—are supposed to cross the border at dawn tomorrow and ride south until someone meets us. From there we'll be taken to the place where Becker is holding Viola, Don Eduardo, and Doña Belinda. If I turn Santiago over to him, he says he'll let Viola and me leave and return here unharmed."

"I don't believe that for a second, John," Stonewall said. "That fella's loco, and the Apache's worse. We killed all of his war party when they raided the ranch last night. He'll want vengeance for them."

"You're not telling me anything I don't already know," Slaughter said. "And I sure wouldn't trust Becker's word after everything he's done." He looked at Santiago. "You're the last one he wants. What do you say about this?"

"I would gladly turn myself over to him if I thought it would save the lives of my father and . . . and stepmother. But I think Becker intends to kill all of us."

Fredericks said, "Judging by some of the things I heard him say to Mrs. Slaughter, I think you're right, young man."

"But what else can we do?" Santiago went on. "We

don't know where Becker has taken the prisoners. If we're going to have any chance to rescue them, we have to play along with him."

Slaughter scratched his bearded chin and said, "Two of us against Becker, the Apache, and the rest of the gang? We won't have much of a chance."

Stonewall said, "I can bring some men and follow you, John. We'll be close by, close enough to help when the time comes."

Slaughter shook his head and held up the paper. "Becker's smart enough that he'll have somebody watching us. He'll know if there's a party following Santiago and me, and he's liable to kill Viola if we try to trick him."

"Well, dadgum it!" Stonewall burst out. "What else can we do? There's no other way to find out where they're holed up."

Slaughter didn't have an answer for that, but it was in the silence following Stonewall's angry words that a faint voice spoke up.

At first Slaughter couldn't tell where the voice came from. Then he looked down at the sofa and realized Hermosa was awake and trying to say something. He motioned for the others to remain quiet and dropped to one knee beside the sofa so he could lean closer to the *vaquero*.

"Are you trying to tell us something, Hermosa?" he asked.

The *vaquero*'s eyes were mere slits of pain as his lips moved. Slaughter heard him breathe two words of Spanish.

"Barranca . . . Sangre."

"Barranca Sangre," Slaughter repeated. He looked up at the others and translated loosely, "Blood Canyon."

"I don't know where that is," Stonewall said. "I never heard of it."

"Nor have I," Santiago put in.

Hermosa whispered, "T-Tequila . . ."

"Will it hurt him, doctor?" Slaughter asked.

"It'll be painful, but it won't do any more damage than has already been done," Fredericks said.

Slaughter turned his head and told one of the maids, "Bring a glass of tequila."

The young woman hurried to obey. When she brought back the tequila a minute later, Slaughter took it and carefully held the glass to Hermosa's mouth. He trickled a little of the fiery liquor between the *vaquero*'s lips.

Hermosa sighed in apparent satisfaction. The tequila seemed to have an almost instant bracing effect. His voice was stronger as he said, "I know . . . Barranca Sangre. I heard the man say to the Apache . . . that was where they were going."

"How did you manage that?" Slaughter asked.

"The Apache thought . . . he killed me. But I . . . fooled him . . . I did not die . . . and when I could . . . I crawled out of the ditch . . . and went after him."

"Impossible," Fredericks said. "No man as badly wounded as this one could have been worried about going after his enemies."

"With all due respect, doctor, that's exactly what I'd expect from a man like Hermosa."

The *vaquero* chuckled dryly. He said, "Hate is . . . powerful medicine, doctor."

"So you got close enough to hear them talking about where they were going," Slaughter said.

"*Sí* . . . but that is all. My strength . . . she deserted me."

"That's all right," Slaughter assured him. "You've done more good by staying alive rather than getting yourself killed. Where do we find this Barranca Sangre?"

"I can . . . take you there."

"Out of the question," Fredericks said. "And I'm not just being overly cautious. Put this man on a horse or even in a wagon and he'll be dead before you go a mile. I guarantee it."

An idea occurred to Slaughter.

"What about a map?" he suggested. "Do you think you could draw a map so we can find the place, Hermosa?"

"Bring me . . . paper and a pencil," Hermosa said. "I can . . . draw a map."

Slaughter nodded to the same maid who had brought the tequila, and once again she scurried off to fetch what Hermosa asked for.

"What good is this going to do?" Santiago wanted to know. "You already said that the men could not follow us, Señor Slaughter, because Becker would know about it."

"That's true," Slaughter said as he looked up at the men gathered around him. "But it might be a different story if Stonewall and the others were to get there first."

Chapter 24

Bodaway seemed to know where he was going, even in the dark. He led the group of riders as they penetrated deeper into the mountains across the border, in the upper reaches of the Sierra Madre Occidental.

Viola dozed off in the saddle from time to time. It seemed like forever since she'd actually stretched out on a bed and slept. It was unlikely that she'd get the chance to do so again any time soon, she thought—if in fact she ever did.

There was every chance in the world she was going to her death, and she knew it.

But she wasn't dead yet, so she still had hope. Becker was going to keep her alive as long as he had a use for her, and that meant until Santiago Rubriz was his prisoner as well.

John might catch up to them before that happened, Viola told herself. And if she got a chance to escape on her own without waiting for him, she would seize it.

Only if she could get the other two captives away, as well, though, and that seemed unlikely. Becker rode right beside Don Eduardo, leading the don's horse, and the man called Woodbury, who seemed to be Becker's second-in-command, had Belinda riding double with him, in front of his saddle.

The blonde wore a dull, defeated expression. She had been through too much. Her pampered existence hadn't prepared her for the danger and hardship she now faced. So she just shut her mind off to it, refused to think about what was going on. Viola could tell that by looking at her.

Don Eduardo, on the other hand, was still angry and defiant, but he was so weak it was a struggle for him to stay in the saddle. He wore a wool serape that one of Becker's men had given him, because when they left the ranch his only covering from the waist up were the bandages the doc had wrapped around him.

"I tell you again, Ned," the don said, "take me with you if you must, but I beg of you, allow my wife and Señora Slaughter to go back to the ranch."

"You begging me," Becker said mockingly. "I like that. The same way you begged my mother to be unfaithful to my father?"

"That never happened." Don Eduardo's voice was clear, although weak. "I never would have done such a thing to hurt my Pilar . . . or your father."

"You killed my father. You think that didn't hurt him?"

"I was defending myself. She had driven him mad . . ." Don Eduardo's words trailed off into a sigh. "No matter what I say, you will not believe it, will you, Ned?"

"Believe the word of a liar, an adulterer, and a murderer?" Becker let out a bark of cold laughter. "I don't think so."

"Then take your vengeance on me, but spare my wife and son."

Becker shook his head.

"They're part of this," he said. "We all are. We all have to play our roles."

"Mad . . ." Don Eduardo said under his breath.

Viola heard that, but if Becker did, he gave no sign of it. He kept riding, leading Don Eduardo's mount and following the Apache who rode about five yards in front of him.

The terrain was flat where they crossed the border, but within a few miles hills had begun to rear up from the arid, mesquite-dotted plains. Beyond the hills rose a range of low, rugged mountains. The riders were probably ten miles deep in those mountains by now, their path winding through canyons and climbing to passes. Viola looked to the east and saw a hint of rose in the sky.

The sun was on its way, rising as always, the universe going about its business no matter what the infinitely small creatures did who lived on this world.

Viola always felt insignificant when she was out in the middle of nowhere like this, and northern Mexico had plenty of nowhere.

How was John going to find her in this vast wilderness? She knew Becker planned to send a man back to meet John and Santiago and bring them to the gang's hideout, but John was too smart for that. He would know it was a trap and would come up with some other plan. Viola wouldn't allow herself to doubt, because doing so meant giving up hope, and she just wasn't the sort of person to do that.

So in the meantime she rode and wondered just how

exhausted somebody had to be before they collapsed in a stupor. If she didn't get some real sleep soon, she might find out.

Becker called a halt every now and then so the horses could rest. During one of those breaks, Woodbury dismounted, then turned back to help Belinda down from the saddle.

Her dispirited demeanor suddenly vanished. Her head, which had been drooping far forward, snapped up, and her foot lashed out. The heel of her slipper struck Woodbury in the chest and knocked him back a step. He still had hold of the reins, but Belinda jerked them out of his hand, leaned forward, and kicked the horse in the sides as hard as she could. She shouted encouragement to the animal as it leaped into a gallop.

The escape attempt took Viola as much by surprise as it did everyone else. She recovered quickly, though. All eyes were on Belinda, so Viola made a move of her own.

No one had been leading her horse, because she was surrounded by the hardcases who worked for Becker. Now she jerked the reins to the side and sent her horse lunging into the mount of the man next to her left side. As the animals collided Viola reached out and plucked the outlaw's revolver from his holster.

She twisted in the saddle and triggered a couple of shots, aiming over the heads of the men around her. She didn't want to kill any of them, just spook them so they would get out of her way.

She wasn't going to leave Don Eduardo behind. That meant she had to get him away from Becker. She drove through the gap in the ring of startled guards and dashed toward the vengeance-seeking madman.

"Hold your fire!" Becker shouted as he hauled his horse around to see what was going on behind him. He must have spotted the fleeing Belinda. "Get the don's wife!"

He didn't see Viola coming in time. She lifted the Colt and fired. This time she was shooting to kill.

She knew, however, that being on the back of a galloping horse didn't lend itself to much accuracy. Her bullet must have missed. Becker didn't seem to be hit. He lost his grip on the reins of Don Eduardo's horse, though, when the don jerked the animal to the side.

Becker roared a curse and launched himself from the saddle as Viola tried to gallop past him. He crashed into her, and she couldn't stay mounted, either. Both of them toppled to the ground, landing so hard Viola was half-stunned. She tried to wriggle away from Becker, but her muscles responded sluggishly and he was able to fasten a hand around her arm.

"You bitch!" he yelled as he punched her in the belly with his other fist. Viola curled up around the pain of the brutal blow. She had dropped the gun when she hit the ground, so there was nothing else she could do.

Becker came up on his knees and shouted at his men to go after Don Eduardo. Viola didn't think either the don or Belinda would be able to get away. Becker had too many men, Belinda wasn't an experienced rider, and Don Eduardo was too weak from his injury.

She was right. By the time she recovered enough from the punch to sit up, some of Becker's men had caught the escapees and were bringing them back, leading the horses. Belinda sobbed in futility. Don Eduardo just sat there, hunched over a little in his saddle.

Becker stalked over and glared at them as he said, "That was foolish."

"Why?" Don Eduardo asked. "Are you not going to kill us anyway? Perhaps this way we would have died quicker and easier than what you have in mind for us."

"You can count on that. My father didn't die easy with your bullet in his back, Rubriz."

"He shot first," Don Eduardo said, his voice thin and reedy but filled with determination to get the words out. "He thought he had killed me. To be honest, I believed I was dying, too. I struck back at him the only way I could."

"Lies, all lies," Becker snapped. "Before he died, he told my mother what really happened, and she told me."

"Your mother told you what she wanted you to hear, not the truth. She wanted to make you hate me and blame me for what happened, when it was really all her doing."

Still sitting a few yards away on the ground, Viola thought Becker was going to pull his gun and shoot the don right then and there. That was how furious the outlaw looked. But with a visible effort, Becker suppressed that impulse. He turned away and walked back over to Viola.

As he extended a hand to help her to her feet, he said, "I'm sorry, Mrs. Slaughter. I shouldn't have lost my temper with you. This is nothing personal where you're concerned."

Viola gripped wrists with him and let him pull her up. She let go of him, slapped some of the dirt off her long skirt, and said, "You made it personal when you attacked my home, Mr. Becker. You'd do well to remember that."

"Maybe I will. Right now, though, my only interest in you is being able to persuade your husband to cooperate and deliver Santiago Rubriz to me."

"John Slaughter will never cooperate with you," Viola said coldly.

"You'd better hope you're wrong," Becker said. "Because if you're not, there's a very good chance you're going to die sometime in the next twelve hours."

Their captors kept an even closer eye on them as they rode deeper into the mountains. After a while they turned east, went through a pass, and dropped down into a valley between the ranges that ran roughly north and south. To the east, on the far side of the valley, lay a canyon that cut through the mountains on that side.

The sun was almost up. As the group rode toward the canyon, the fiery orb peeked above the horizon. Viola caught her breath as she realized that the rising sun was framed by the notch formed by the canyon. The red sandstone cliffs and the garish crimson light made it look like the canyon was awash with blood.

"Barranca Sangre," Becker announced. "That's where we're going."

Viola felt a chill ripple through her at those words. The idea of going to a place called Blood Canyon would not be very inviting under the best of circumstances. As the prisoner of a madman, it was even worse.

Even though no one had asked Becker for an explanation, he seemed to like the sound of his own voice. He went on, "Bodaway's band lived here for a while, after they left the reservation in Arizona Territory. But the *Rurales* found the village and attacked it. They wiped out nearly everyone. Only Bodaway and a few warriors escaped. He spent the next year hunting down every man in that *Rurale* company and killing them all."

Viola could believe that. She had never seen any expression on the Apache's face other than cold, impassive hatred.

"One of the Mexicans lived for a little while after Bodaway was through with him," Becker continued. "He told the men who found him that looking into Bodaway's eyes was like looking into the flames of hell. That's how he got his name, *El Infierno*. It fits. His real name means Fire Maker."

"I'm not sure who you're talking to," Viola said. "None of us are interested in this."

Becker smiled at her.

"I just want you to know who you're dealing with. Bodaway always settles his scores. He lost fifteen good warriors when he raided your ranch."

"You were the one who told him to do it," Viola pointed out. "All to help you carry out this insane revenge scheme of yours."

"If you're trying to drive a wedge between us, Mrs. Slaughter, you're wasting your time. Bodaway and I are the only real friends either of us has left."

If the Apache heard that as he rode a few yards ahead of the others, he didn't show any sign. He continued leading the way into the canyon.

Viola could see all the way to the other end of Barranca Sangre. She estimated that it ran for a mile or more straight through the mountains. The group had covered about half that distance when a smaller canyon suddenly opened up to the left, running at right angles into the bigger one. The sandstone wall of the main canyon bulged out so that you couldn't see the smaller one until you reached its mouth.

The smaller canyon, fifty yards wide and maybe two hundred yards deep, ended at a blank wall of rock. A spring bubbled out of the sandstone at that point, creating a small pool and providing water for several cottonwoods and enough grass for the horses to graze. Half a dozen adobe *jacales* and a pole corral had been built near the pool.

"I've visited your home, Mrs. Slaughter," Becker said. "Now I have the pleasure of welcoming you to mine."

"This isn't a home," Viola said. "It's a hideout."

Becker shrugged and said, "Call it whatever you want. This is where we'll wait for your husband and young Rubriz."

They rode up to the huts and started to dismount. One of Becker's men riding beside Viola said, "You just stay right where you are until I tell you to get down, missy. Nobody else is tryin' any tricks today."

Viola didn't acknowledge the order, but she didn't swing down from the saddle until the outlaw told her to. Once her feet were on the ground, he took hold of her arm and marched her roughly toward one of the *jacales*.

Woodbury brought Belinda to the same hut. Both women were forced inside and the door closed after them. The door didn't have a bar or a lock on it, Viola noted, but she was sure at least one member of the gang would be standing guard outside all the time.

The *jacal* had no windows, but its roof was made of thatched limbs from the cottonwoods and there were enough cracks and gaps to let in some of the reddish light.

Belinda looked rather sickly in that illumination, and Viola supposed that she did, too.

The single room was sparsely furnished with a rough-hewn table, a couple of equally crude chairs, and two bunks, one on each side wall. The bunks had no mattresses, only folded blankets on top of woven rope. Viola thought they looked pretty uncomfortable.

Despite that, Belinda sat on one of them, swung her legs up so she could lie down, and rolled over with her face to the adobe wall.

For some reason that irritated Viola. She said, "We need to talk about what we're going to do."

"We're going to die, that's what we're going to do," Belinda said without looking around. "That man Becker and his pet Indian are probably going to torture me to death while they make Eduardo watch. Maybe you'll be lucky and he'll just put a bullet through your brain."

"Not if we get away first," Viola insisted. "You tried to escape earlier. You must not want to give up."

Belinda began to sob quietly. Her back shook a little from the crying as she said, "I didn't make it even a hundred yards before they caught me. That proved to me how hopeless everything is. We're doomed and you know it."

Viola bit back the angry response that wanted to spring to her lips. No matter how bleak the situation looked, she wasn't going to give up. She couldn't. She wasn't made that way.

And John wouldn't want her to. She could almost sense his presence beside her, hear him whispering in her ear as he told her to stay strong and fight back against her captors if she got the chance.

Belinda needed something to jolt her out of her despair.

Viola sensed that encouraging words wouldn't do a bit of good. But anger might, she decided, so she said, "How in the world did you wind up having a dirty little affair with your own stepson?"

Belinda jerked as if she'd been struck. She stiffened and rolled over on the bunk so she could look at Viola again. As she propped herself up on an elbow, she glared at Viola and snapped, "Don't talk about it like that. What's between Santiago and me isn't a dirty little affair. We love each other."

Viola folded her arms over her chest and said coldly, "Yet you married Don Eduardo."

"I love him, too."

"Of course you do," Viola said with obvious disbelief.

Belinda sat up and pushed herself to her feet. Her chin jutted out defiantly as she said, "It's none of your business, but it happens to be true. Don Eduardo is like a father to me. When he asked me to marry him, he made it clear that I wouldn't have to . . . fulfill any wifely duties . . . with him. He said he wanted a beautiful young woman to be the mistress of his *hacienda* and to brighten his days for the time he had left. That's all."

What Belinda was saying took Viola by surprise. She couldn't comprehend a marriage where husband and wife didn't share everything there was to be shared. Her union with John Slaughter had never been that way, that was for sure.

Belinda looked and sounded as if she were being completely sincere, though.

"So the two of you have never . . ."

"That's right." Belinda's face was flushed. "And it's not proper to talk about such things."

"But you and Santiago . . ."

"Santiago and I love each other. Someday we'll be married. But I haven't been unfaithful to my husband. You can believe that or not. I don't really care."

Viola didn't know what to believe anymore. She had jumped to a conclusion, and maybe she'd been wrong. A part of her was a little ashamed that she had been so quick to rush to judgment. Yet logically she knew that most people would have thought the same thing if they had seen Belinda and Santiago together under that water tank.

"I'm sorry," she said. "What about Don Eduardo? Does he know?"

"About Santiago and me, you mean?" Belinda shrugged. "We haven't told him. I think he suspects, though. He's never given me any indication that he's upset about it. Maybe he's just glad that once he's gone, Santiago will have someone."

Viola supposed a person could look at it like that. The whole thing still seemed rather incomprehensible to her, but not everyone lived their lives the same way. She reminded herself that plenty of people had believed she was loco to marry someone so much older than herself.

The conversation between her and Belinda might have continued, but at that moment both women gasped and jumped a little as an unexpected sound cut through the morning air.

Somewhere nearby in Barranca Sangre, someone had just unleashed a bloodcurdling scream.

Chapter 25

All the horses Slaughter and his men had taken in pursuit of the rustlers were worn out, so they had to get fresh mounts from the remuda. While that was going on the servants put together bags of provisions in case the men were gone for several days.

Slaughter hoped that wouldn't be the case. According to the map Hermosa had drawn, along with the things the *vaquero* had to say, the canyon known as Barranca Sangre was less than a twelve-hour ride across the border into Mexico.

That meant if luck was on their side, they might have Viola home safely by nightfall the next day.

If it took longer than that, there was a chance they wouldn't be coming back at all.

Slaughter sat down with Stonewall in the dining room to go over the plan. He spread out the map on the table and said, "You're sure you can find the place?"

"I think so, John," the young man said.

"You can't just think so. Your sister's life may well be riding on this."

"I'll find it," Stonewall declared.

"If you have any doubts about your health or your mental condition, Jess can lead the rescue party. You've been knocked out twice in the past few hours."

Stonewall grinned and said, "I told you, this skull of mine is too thick for that to be a problem. It's not even dented."

Slaughter didn't doubt that, but it was the brain underneath the skull he was worried about. Stonewall appeared to be fine, but getting hit in the head was a tricky thing. Slaughter had known men to seem fine after an injury like that, only to drop dead a few days later. Other men had been knocked out, even once, and although they lived they were never the same afterward.

"All right," Slaughter said, "but if you feel like you can't handle it, you turn things over to Jess. Viola's safety is more important than anything else, at least as far as I'm concerned. Although I want to rescue Don Eduardo and his wife, too, of course."

Stonewall nodded and leaned forward.

"Let me take another look at that map," he said. "I know I'll have it with me, but I want to be sure where I'm going."

They had to hope, as well, that Hermosa had known what he was doing when he drew the map. The *vaquero* was gravely wounded, more dead than alive, according to Dr. Fredericks, and there was no way of knowing if his directions were accurate—or if his so-called knowledge of Barranca Sangre was just a product of a fevered imagination.

"There is a little box canyon just off Barranca Sangre with a spring in it," Hermosa had told them, fortifying himself with sips of tequila. "For several years a band of Apache lived there, until the *Rurales* almost wiped them out. After that some prospectors came to look for gold and silver in the mountains and built *jacales* there by the spring to use as their camp. When no one saw them again for almost a year, relatives bribed the *Rurales* to look for the men. They were all still there in Barranca Sangre—or their bones were, anyway. The rumors I heard said that terrible things had been done to them, probably while they were still alive. Since then no one has dared to go there."

"How do you know about it?" Slaughter had asked.

"As a young man I was restless. I explored across northern Sonora whenever I had the chance. And I always listened to the stories told in hushed tones in *cantinas*."

"If it's true the place is, well, cursed," Stonewall had said, "how is it that Becker gets away with usin' it for his hideout?"

"There is no curse, not in the way you mean. There is only a survivor from that band of Apache, driven mad by hate and the need for revenge."

"The Apache who's workin' with Becker," Stonewall had exclaimed. "It's got to be him."

Hermosa had nodded, and even that much movement seemed to tire him greatly.

All of it made sense as far as Slaughter could tell. Anyway, he had no choice but to accept the *vaquero*'s story. Hermosa offered the only possible chance of turning the tables on the outlaws and rescuing the captives.

Slaughter's finger traced a path on the map as he and Stonewall bent over it.

"You'll need to take this way in," he said. "According

to Hermosa it splits off from the regular trail, the route that Becker is most likely to use because he'll want to get back to his stronghold as quickly as he can. This little trail is rougher, and you'll have to be careful getting up to some of the passes along the way. But you can approach the canyon from the north instead of the west, the way the main trail does. That'll put you above the spring and those huts around it. That's bound to be where Becker will be keeping the prisoners."

Stonewall nodded and said, "We'll be able to ambush 'em. Maybe wipe out the whole bunch in one volley."

"I wouldn't count on that," Slaughter cautioned. "But you should be able to even the odds enough that Santiago and I will have a chance to get to the prisoners. If we can do that, we'll keep them safe."

"How are you gonna put up a fight? Becker won't let you carry any guns in there, I'll bet."

"No, I'm sure he won't," Slaughter said. "But he and his men will have guns, and I'm counting on the chance that Santiago and I can get our hands on some of them."

Stonewall nodded solemnly and said, "It's gonna be mighty dangerous, especially for the two of you. You'll be ridin' right into a hornet's nest."

"That's why we'll be counting on you and Jess and the other men to do some stinging of your own," Slaughter replied with a grim smile.

A short time later, everyone was ready to leave. Stonewall and his group would ride out first, since the plan called for them to be in position above Barranca Sangre before Becker's emissary, whoever it was, brought Slaughter and Santiago to the hideout.

Once the men were mounted, Slaughter reached up, gripped his brother-in-law's hand, and said, "Good luck, son."

"You, too, John," Stonewall replied. He was riding the big roan Pacer, who'd had the day to rest after one of the hands rode him to Douglas to fetch Dr. Fredericks.

Santiago was there and shook hands with Stonewall as well. Then the riders, sixteen in all, left the ranch and headed south into Mexico.

"Will they be able to find the right trail in the dark?" Santiago asked as he and Slaughter watched the men ride away.

"It'll be close to sunup by the time they get to the place it branches off," Slaughter said. "We'll have to hope they can find it." He chuckled, but there wasn't much humor in the sound. "If they don't, you and I are going to be in a bad spot."

"I don't care. I'll dare anything to save my father and Belinda."

Slaughter thought it a little odd that the young man didn't refer to his father's wife as his stepmother or Doña Belinda, but at the moment that wasn't worth worrying about. They went back into the ranch house, where Slaughter conferred with Neal Fredericks.

"We're keeping you away from your practice in town, doctor," Slaughter said.

"I have patients here," Fredericks said. "There are a couple of midwives in Douglas who can take care of any birthing that needs to be done, and everything else will have to wait."

Santiago said, "I hope you can keep Hermosa alive, doctor. We owe him a great deal."

"I'm afraid that's almost out of my hands. Whatever has kept him alive this long is a higher power than any I can muster. But I'll do everything I can for him, I give you my word on that, young man."

As Slaughter was gathering up more ammunition, one of the maids approached him and said, "Señor Slaughter?"

"Yes, what is it?" he asked, then recognized her. "What can I do for you, Yolanda?"

"I know you go to rescue Señora Slaughter, and all my prayers for her safety go with you, señor. But is it a terrible thing if I pray that you deliver justice to the murderer of my Hector as well?"

Slaughter smiled, shook his head, and said gently, "No, Yolanda, it's not a terrible thing. Hector was a fine young man, and his death should be avenged."

"But can I pray for a man to die, even a very bad man like the one who killed Hector?"

"Just pray that Señora Slaughter and the rest of us return home safely," Slaughter told her as he patted her shoulder. "That's the best thing you can do."

If they did that, there was a very good chance that the murder of Hector Alvarez—and all the other crimes committed by Ned Becker and his friends—would be avenged.

Santiago led the big black horse called *El Halcón* out of the corral. The stallion was saddled and ready to ride.

Slaughter nodded in approval, but he qualified it by

saying, "I know that horse is fast and we're certainly liable to need that speed, but does he have the stamina?"

"He has the heart of a champion, Señor Slaughter. *El Halcón* will never falter."

"I hope you're right," Slaughter said. "Well, with any luck we won't need to make a run for it."

He had picked a big, rangy lineback dun for his mount. He had ridden the horse many times and knew that while the dun wasn't much for looks, it was strong and fast and would run all day if necessary.

Slaughter and Santiago swung up into their saddles and lifted hands in farewell to Dr. Fredericks, who stood on the porch watching them ride out, leading three saddled, riderless horses for the captives they hoped to rescue and bring back safely.

"Are you all right, Señor Slaughter?" Santiago asked as they left the ranch behind. "You have been going for a very long time without any rest."

"I'm a little tired," Slaughter admitted, "but that doesn't mean anything as long as my wife is in danger. I'll keep going for however long is necessary. I will say, though . . . when this is over a nice long nap will be most welcome."

"When our loved ones are threatened, our own comfort means nothing."

"We'll do everything we can to rescue your father, Santiago."

"And Belinda," the young man added.

There was that odd note in his voice again, Slaughter thought. He indulged his curiosity enough to comment, "No offense, but during the party the other night I got the impression you don't really care much for your stepmother."

"Certainly I care about her," Santiago said. "My father loves her. She is part of our family now."

"A lot of fellas don't like to see their mothers replaced."

Santiago laughed and said, "Believe me, Señor Slaughter, the very last thing Belinda has done is replace my mother."

Slaughter sensed that Santiago wanted to drop this line of conversation, so he didn't say anything else about Doña Belinda.

They had ridden past the border marker by now and continued south into Mexico. The moon and stars provided plenty of light for them to see where they were going, and Slaughter had no trouble letting those stars guide him in the right direction.

They talked only sporadically as they rode. Slaughter's mind was full of worry for Viola and, to a lesser extent, Don Eduardo and Doña Belinda. They had been guests in his house when they were kidnapped, and Slaughter considered the don a friend as well. Both of those things fueled the anger Slaughter felt at what Ned Becker had done.

Time had little meaning in a situation such as this. The eastern sky began to turn gray above the mountains that loomed in that direction. Slaughter knew that morning was only an hour or so away. He and Santiago had been riding most of the night.

"You're sure we are going the right way?" Santiago asked. "I thought perhaps Becker's man would have intercepted us by now."

"We're following the directions in Becker's note,"

Slaughter said. He patted his shirt pocket where he had put the folded paper. "There aren't many landmarks around here, but we've been going almost due south, the way he said." Slaughter eased back on the reins. "Let's stop and let the horses rest for a little while."

"I can keep riding," Santiago said.

"I know you can, but we don't want to wear out these animals." Slaughter patted the dun's shoulder. "They may wind up being more important than we are."

The two men dismounted. Slaughter had brought along several full canteens—nobody went anywhere in this arid country without carrying water—and used his hat to give the horses a drink. Then they let the animals graze a little on the sparse grass.

Santiago paced back and forth impatiently, ready to be on the move again. Slaughter just stood there breathing slowly, taking advantage of this opportunity to rest even though he couldn't sleep yet. After a while he poured a little water into the palm of his hand and used it to wash away the grit in his eyes.

The eastern sky had gone orange and gold. The sun would rise above the mountains soon. Santiago stopped his pacing, stared in that direction, and said, "Can we go now?"

"I reckon the horses have rested long enough," Slaughter said. He took hold of the horn and swung up into the saddle.

They had only gone another mile or so when Slaughter spotted a rider coming toward them from the mountains.

He pointed out the man to Santiago and said, "Looks like there's our escort."

"It's about time," the young man said. "I will try not to

shoot him, but it will be difficult, knowing what he was a part of."

"Maybe," Slaughter said, "but we need him, so keep a tight rein on your temper."

As the gap between them closed, Slaughter studied their guide. The man was a stocky hardcase wearing a broad-brimmed brown hat with a round crown. A serape was draped over his ax-handle shoulders. A spade beard the color of rust jutted from his slab of a jaw.

Slaughter and Santiago reined in when about twenty feet separated them from the outlaw. The man brought his mount to a halt as well and gave them what almost seemed like a friendly nod.

"Mornin'," he greeted them. "You're the fellas I've been waitin' for."

He didn't phrase it like a question, but Slaughter said, "That's right. I'm John Slaughter, and this is Santiago Rubriz."

"You're alone, the way you're supposed to be?"

"You already know that," Slaughter said. "You've been watching us with a spyglass from up in those hills, haven't you?"

That brought a grin to the man's bearded face. "I've heard tell that you're pretty smart, Slaughter. I reckon that's right. Yeah, the boss said not to take any chances with you. He figured you'd do like you were told because you want to see that pretty little wife of yours again, but there was always a chance you'd try to pull some sort of trick."

"No tricks," Slaughter lied. "I'm just interested in getting my wife back safely."

"How about you, boy?" the outlaw addressed Santiago.

"Your boss gave me no choice," he snapped. "You have my father and stepmother. I will do everything I can to keep them alive."

"Well, that's between you and Becker. I'm just the errand boy." The man scratched his beard. "They call me Red, by the way. Reckon you can see why."

"Owlhoots usually aren't very imaginative," Slaughter said dryly.

Red frowned and demanded, "Are you callin' me dumb?"

"You're not the one who came up with the name, are you?"

"Well, no, I ain't." Red shook his head. "Quit tryin' to mix me up. If you think I'll forget what I'm supposed to do, you're wrong. Now get down off those horses and shuck those guns. Where we're goin', you can't carry no weapons."

Slaughter glanced over at Santiago. He could tell that the youngster wanted to haul out his Colt and blast the red-bearded outlaw from the saddle.

But Santiago swallowed hard and then did what Red told him to do. Slaughter followed suit.

Within minutes, they were disarmed and Red had gathered up the rifles and pistols, stowing the handguns in a pack behind his saddle and lashing the Winchesters to one of the extra horses. Then he drew his own revolver and motioned for Slaughter and Santiago to ride in front of him.

"Straight toward them mountains," he said. "I'll tell you if you start goin' the wrong way. And rest easy, fellas. A couple of hours and we'll be where we're goin'. You'll get to see those folks you're so worried about."

"And they'll be all right?" Santiago asked. "We have your word on that?"

"Well . . . I reckon they'll still be alive," Red drawled. "That's about all I can promise you, though, especially where that old don's concerned."

Chapter 26

At the sound of the scream, Viola and Belinda both rushed to the door, which had a simple drawstring latch. Belinda reached it first, grabbed the string, and pulled. She jerked the door open.

Before they could take another step, two of the outlaws blocked their path. Each man held a rifle at a slant across his chest. The one closest to Belinda thrust the weapon at her in a hard shove that sent her staggering back against Viola. Belinda might have fallen if Viola hadn't caught and steadied her.

"You bitches ain't goin' nowhere," the other man snarled. "The boss said to keep you in there, and that's what we're gonna do."

"What's going on out there?" Belinda demanded in a hysterical voice. "What have you done to my husband?"

The two guards exchanged quick, ugly grins. The one who had shoved Belinda said, "The boss didn't say we couldn't let 'em take a look."

"No, I don't reckon he did," the other man agreed. He

backed off a little and pointed his rifle at the two women. "You can step into the doorway, but that's as far as you go."

The door opening was barely wide enough for both Viola and Belinda to stand there and look out at the outlaw camp. As they did, Belinda gasped and then sobbed. She lifted her hands to her face and sagged against Viola, who put an arm around the blonde's shoulders and steadied her.

About twenty yards away, under one of the cottonwood trees, Becker and Bodaway had pulled Don Eduardo's arms up and lashed his wrists to a low-hanging branch. They had removed the serape first so his bandages were visible again, and Viola saw a crimson stain spreading slowly on the don's side.

The rough treatment had opened the bullet wound. It didn't appear to be bleeding very fast, but Don Eduardo couldn't really afford to lose any more of the life-giving fluid than he already had.

The don's toes barely touched the ground as he hung there. The pain of having that much weight dangling from his arms had to be excruciating, Viola knew, especially in his weakened condition. His head drooped forward and he looked like he had lost consciousness.

"You monsters!" Belinda screamed at Becker and the Apache.

Becker stepped back and turned toward the *jacal*.

"Monster?" he repeated. "Hardly. A monster sets out to steal another man's wife. A monster shoots an innocent man in the back. I'm not a monster. I'm just a man who wants to see justice done."

"Your own warped version of justice," Viola said

coldly. "And you don't care how many truly innocent people you have to hurt to get it."

"Doesn't everyone have their own version of justice?" Becker shot back at her. "Who has the right to say that mine is any more warped than anyone else's?" He laughed. "And you should have figured out by now, Mrs. Slaughter, that there are no truly innocent people in this world. Not one."

Viola supposed she couldn't argue with his last statement. As for the rest of it, though, he was as loco as a hydrophobic skunk.

Becker evidently didn't want to argue. He gestured curtly at the women and went on, "Put them back inside. The don's all right for now. This is just getting started."

Viola was afraid he was right about that. The guards forced her and Belinda back into the *jacal* and the door slammed closed once again.

Belinda collapsed on the bunk where she had been earlier and sobbed. Viola sat down in one of the crude chairs and let her cry. She would have offered words of hope, but she figured they wouldn't do any good right now.

She wasn't going to give up, though.

Somewhere, help was out there, and it was only a matter of staying alive until it got here.

Was he lost? Stonewall frowned at the map in his hand and asked himself that question, but he didn't know the answer.

"What do you think?" Jess Fisher said. "Is this where we're supposed to be?"

"Yeah," Stonewall said as he folded the map and replaced it in his shirt pocket. "This is the trail."

He lifted his eyes and looked at the narrow path that zigzagged up the almost sheer side of a mountain.

"You sure?" Fisher asked. "This looks more like something a mountain goat would use."

"It's wide enough for a horse, and this is the way Hermosa drew it." Stonewall pointed to his left. "There's the sawtooth peak he put on the map, and over yonder is the flat-topped one. This trail leads up to a pass between 'em."

"All right. I trust you, Stonewall. This is the way we'll go."

Stonewall just wished he trusted himself. The possibility that he had gotten turned around somehow lurked in the back of his mind. Under other circumstances he might not have worried about it so much. He might have been content to wander around these hills and mountains until he found his way.

But his sister's life was on the line, along with the lives of Don Eduardo and Doña Belinda. He couldn't afford to make a mistake. He and the men with him had to beat John Slaughter and Santiago to Barranca Sangre so they could be ready when it was time to make their move. If they were late it could cost the others their lives.

Dithering around here wasn't going to do anybody any good, either, he told himself. He'd made his decision. It was time to stick to it.

"Let's go," he said as he lifted his reins and nudged his horse into motion. "I'll take the lead."

He walked Pacer onto the ledge. It was a natural formation, which meant its width varied and its surface was uneven in places. Pacer was a sure-footed mount, and he would need to be in order to make it up to the pass. Despite the urgency Stonewall felt, he knew he couldn't afford to rush the horse.

The sun was up already. Stonewall knew they ought to be farther along their route by now, but unfortunately there was nothing he could do about it other than keep pushing ahead and hope for the best.

The ground dropped away to Stonewall's right as he and Pacer continued to climb. He was widely regarded as fearless, but that wasn't exactly true. He didn't care much for heights. He was a flatlander at heart, and this land was anything but flat.

The ledge was a one-way trail, wide enough for only a single rider. Luckily it didn't seem to be heavily traveled, so he didn't think they were likely to meet anyone coming down.

As the path curved around a shoulder of rock, he took advantage of the opportunity to look behind him. Jess Fisher was second in line, about ten feet back, and then the other men strung out single file behind the *segundo*. Most of them looked tense and worried as the drop-off beside them increased, and Stonewall didn't blame them. If he never had to do anything like this again, it would be just fine with him.

After a few more minutes of following the torturous path, Stonewall felt relief flood through him when he spotted the pass up ahead. The ledge widened out into a broad, level trail that ran between two rocky upthrusts. Stonewall hoped that the descent on the far side of the pass wouldn't be as treacherous as the climb up here had been.

He turned his head to call to Jess Fisher and tell him that the end was in sight, and as he did a rifle cracked and a bullet whipped past his ear.

Stonewall heard a horse scream. He watched in horror as one of the animals farther back reared in pain. He knew the slug that had narrowly missed him had struck the animal. Whether or not the wound was fatal might not matter. The maddened horse's rear hooves skittered perilously close to the edge of the trail as the cowboy on its back struggled frantically to control his mount.

He wasn't going to be able to do it. The others all knew that. Jess Fisher yelled, "Jump, Corey!"

The man kicked his feet free of the stirrups and flung himself out of the saddle just as the horse slipped over the brink. As the animal twisted screaming through the air, Corey landed at the edge and clawed at the trail to keep himself from falling. He would have to save himself. On this narrow path, none of the others could reach him in time to help him.

Fisher reacted with the skill of a top hand. He plucked up the coiled lasso that hung on his saddle, shook out a loop in the blink of an eye, and cast it with the unerring accuracy of a man who had made thousands of throws with a rope. Corey saw it coming and thrust his right arm up through the loop just as he started to slide into empty space. He caught hold of it and hung on for dear life.

Fisher had already dallied the lasso around his saddle horn. The rope would take the weight of a thousand-pound steer, so it had no trouble supporting one cowboy.

All that happened in less time than it would have taken to tell about it. There were other dangers to deal with. Another shot rang out and the slug whined off a rock. This time Stonewall spotted the spurt of powder-smoke from the pass. At least one bushwhacker lurked up there.

That made sense if this was really the back door to Barranca Sangre as Hermosa claimed. Ned Becker could have been cunning enough to post a guard or two here.

Stonewall knew that he and his men couldn't let that stop them. He hauled his Winchester from its saddle boot and returned the fire, spraying the pass with lead as fast as he could work the repeater's lever.

He didn't really have any targets at which to aim—the ambushers were well hidden somewhere in the pass—but if he threw enough bullets in there and they started to ricochet around . . .

That tactic was rewarded by the sight of a man stumbling out from behind a rock with a rifle in his hands, obviously wounded. He tried to lift the weapon for another shot, but Stonewall was too fast for him. Stonewall drilled the bushwhacker, and the .44-40 slug lifted the man in the air and dumped him on his back in the limp sprawl of death.

As the echoes of the shots faded away, Stonewall heard swift hoofbeats.

There had been a second guard, and he was getting away.

Stonewall knew what the man would do. He would run back to Barranca Sangre as fast as he could and warn Becker that someone was approaching the canyon from the north. Those gunshots might have already done it, but the way the echoes bounced around off the slopes, there was a chance the sound wouldn't travel that far. They were still several miles away from the outlaw stronghold, Stonewall figured from his study of Hermosa's map.

As those thoughts flashed through Stonewall's mind, he was already acting. His boot heels jammed against Pacer's flanks and sent the big roan surging ahead. The trail was still narrow here, so Stonewall was taking a big risk by galloping his horse.

But letting Becker's man get away would be an even bigger risk. That would ruin the plan and likely result in Viola's death, along with Slaughter's.

Stonewall wasn't going to let that happen if he could prevent it.

He clutched the Winchester in his right hand and thrust it out to the side to help keep his balance as Pacer raced along the ledge. The trail began to widen, the drop-off became not as sheer, and suddenly Stonewall flashed into the pass. The rataplan of Pacer's hoofbeats rebounded from the rocky walls that rose on both sides.

Stonewall was glad he wasn't in danger of plummeting to his death anymore, at least for the moment, but that didn't mean he was out of trouble. As he emerged from the pass he spotted his quarry ahead of him, riding down a fairly steep trail that ran through a field of boulders.

The man twisted around in his saddle and fired a pistol back at Stonewall. The odds against hitting anything from the back of a running horse at this range, especially with a handgun, were almost too high to think about. But bad luck happened, and sometimes a bullet was guided by a capricious fate.

Stonewall hauled back on Pacer's reins and brought the roan to a stop. He lifted his rifle to his shoulder and aimed carefully, drawing a bead on the rider in the distance.

The outlaw was still in range of the Winchester. Stonewall let out his breath and stroked the trigger.

The rifle cracked and bucked against his shoulder, and as he peered over the sights he saw the rider suddenly swerve around a bend in the trail. A bright splash of silver appeared on a boulder where the bullet struck it. Stonewall's shot had missed.

And the varmint was out of sight now. Stonewall grated a curse and kicked Pacer into a run again.

The chase continued down the boulder-littered mountainside. Stonewall figured the rest of his bunch was following him by now, but that didn't really matter. This was a race between him and the man he was pursuing.

That thought made him remember the race he and Santiago Rubriz had planned to put on matching Pacer and *El Halcón*. That might never come about now, and Stonewall regretted missing the chance to compete against Santiago. There were a lot more important things to consider, of course, but it would have been nice to settle which of the horses was faster.

He caught a glimpse of the outlaw below him, where the trail had started to wind back and forth. An idea popped into Stonewall's head. A dangerous one, to be sure, but it might be his only chance to stop the man from warning Becker.

He veered off the trail and started cutting almost straight down the mountain.

Several times during that wild ride he thought Pacer was going to slip and go down, but the roan always caught his balance somehow as he lunged from rock to rock, over gullies, around outcroppings. The branches of a scrubby tree whipped at Stonewall's face, but he ducked his head and ignored them.

Taking this dangerous course allowed him to cut the outlaw's lead to almost nothing. He saw a big slab of rock thrusting out over the trail ahead of him. The man he was after hadn't come by here yet. Stonewall spotted him from the corner of his eye, galloping for all he was worth and swiveling his head around to check behind him.

The *hombre* didn't know the real danger was in front of him.

"Big jump ahead!" he called to Pacer. "But you can do it!"

Pacer's heart was gallant. Stonewall didn't ask him to slow down, so he didn't. He kept galloping full out and left the end of the rock slab in a soaring leap that carried both of them far out over the trail.

Stonewall had timed it perfectly. He left the saddle in a diving tackle that drove the outlaw off his horse.

The man hit the ground first with Stonewall on top of him. Even with the outlaw's body to cushion the impact, Stonewall felt like a mountain had risen up and swatted him. Dust swirled around them as Stonewall rolled over, but he couldn't cough. He didn't have any breath left in his body to do so.

He gasped a few times, swallowed some of the dust and choked on it a little, then pushed himself up and looked to the side. The outlaw lay on his back a few feet away, his head twisted and set at a funny angle on his neck. Dust started to settle on his widely staring eyeballs, but he didn't blink.

The man was dead, his neck broken in the fall.

Stonewall groaned and let himself slump back down.

His heart still pounded wildly and he had to fight to get his breath, but gradually he felt himself beginning to recover.

The sound of more hoofbeats made him look up. Pacer had landed safely and returned to him. The roan reached his head down and bumped Stonewall's shoulder with his nose.

"Yeah," Stonewall said in a weak voice. "I'm all right."

He heard more horses, and as he pulled himself upright by grasping Pacer's reins, he saw Jess Fisher and the other men riding toward him. Fisher called, "Stonewall, are you all right?"

"Yeah. Danged if I know how I didn't bust every bone in my body, but I don't think I'm hurt." He looked at the rest of the men and spotted the cowboy whose horse had fallen off the ledge riding double with another man. "Glad to see you made it, Corey."

"What do we do now?" Fisher asked.

"The same thing we set out to do," Stonewall replied with a note of grim determination in his voice. "We've got a rendezvous to keep at Barranca Sangre."

Chapter 27

After the outlaw called Red met Slaughter and Santiago, it still took them two more hours of riding to reach Barranca Sangre. That time seemed even longer than it really was to Slaughter as they followed a winding path through the mountains. These peaks might not tower like the Rockies, but they were still rugged enough to make for slow going.

Red was talkative, but it was just aimless chatter and didn't really help to pass the time. He wouldn't say anything about the captives except that they were fine when he left the camp. Slaughter had a hunch that Becker had ordered the man not to reveal too much.

Finally they descended into a valley and Red pointed out a canyon in the next range of mountains about two miles away.

"That's where we're goin'," he told them. "That's Barranca Sangre."

"How did it get the name Blood Canyon?" Slaughter asked. "It looks like a normal canyon to me."

"Right now it does, now that the sun's higher," Red

agreed. "But earlier in the mornin', right after the sun's come up and it's shinin' through there on those sandstone walls, the place looks like it's filled with blood. It's a lot redder than this beard o' mine."

"I'll take your word for it," Slaughter said. "After today I'd just as soon never see this place again."

That brought a laugh from Red. The outlaw didn't explain what he thought was funny, but Slaughter had a pretty good idea.

Red didn't think Slaughter and Santiago would ever be leaving Barranca Sangre.

The three of them rode on toward the mouth of the canyon. The high walls rose imposingly around them as they entered. Slaughter knew from talking to Hermosa that there was a much smaller canyon running into this one at right angles where the actual camp was likely to be.

That speculation appeared to be correct because Slaughter could see the entire length of the main canyon and it was empty except for rocks, tufts of hardy grass, and a few stunted bushes growing along the base of the walls.

Slaughter didn't spot the side canyon until they were practically on top of it. The natural formations of Barranca Sangre disguised it as cunningly as if someone had fashioned it that way. It was easy to see why the Apaches who had stumbled upon this place had decided to make their camp here. The isolation and the fact that it would be easy to defend made for a perfect hideout.

As soon as they rounded the shoulder of rock that partially concealed the entrance to the side canyon, Slaughter saw the *jacales* and the corral at the far end, around a pool where a spring bubbled out of the cliff face.

He also saw the motionless figure of Don Eduardo

Rubriz hanging like a dead man by his wrists from a branch of one of the cottonwood trees.

Santiago saw that, too, and couldn't control himself. He let out an inarticulate cry of rage and kicked *El Halcón* into a gallop. Red yelled, "Hey!" but he was too slow to stop Santiago.

The hoofbeats rang out loudly inside the confines of the canyon and gave Becker's men ample warning that someone was coming in a hurry. The men who were already outside grabbed their guns, and several others burst out of the *jacales* ready for trouble.

When a tall, dark-haired man ran out of one of the huts and shouted, "Hold your fire!" Slaughter figured that had to be Ned Becker. He hadn't laid eyes on the man until now.

Red half-turned in his saddle and leveled his revolver at Slaughter.

"Don't you go gettin' any ideas, mister," he warned.

"I'm just sitting here," Slaughter said coolly. "I want to save my wife, not get both of us killed."

Red grunted and motioned with the gun for Slaughter to keep going toward the end of the side canyon.

By now Santiago had reached his father. He yanked the horse to a stop and flung himself out of the saddle before *El Halcón* stopped moving. The outlaws closed in around him, though, and one of them slammed the butt of his rifle between Santiago's shoulder blades and drove him to the ground before he could reach Don Eduardo.

"That's enough," Becker said as he made his way through the ring of men and pushed them back. As they spread out, Slaughter caught sight of Santiago again.

The young man lay face down on the ground, writhing in pain from the blow that had knocked him off his feet.

"Get him up," Becker snapped. A couple of the men took hold of Santiago's arms and hauled him to his feet.

Becker stepped closer, and as his men held Santiago, he cracked a brutal backhanded blow across the young man's face.

Slaughter saw that from the corner of his eye, but most of his attention was focused on looking around the camp, hoping to catch sight of Viola. He didn't see her or Belinda, but he noticed two men standing outside one of the *jacales* with its door shut. They had to be guarding the hut, he thought, and that meant the two women were probably in there.

When Red motioned for him to rein in, Slaughter did so. He sat there and carefully kept his face impassive. For Viola's sake, he couldn't afford to give in to the raging emotions he felt. Instead he kept them buried as deeply as he could inside him. He watched as Becker confronted Santiago.

With a sneer on his face, Becker demanded, "Do you remember me, kid?" He laughed and went on before Santiago had a chance to answer, "No, of course you don't. You were just a baby the last time I saw you. Hell, I barely remember it myself."

Santiago stood there silently, his chest heaving. A trickle of blood ran from the corner of his mouth where Becker had struck him.

Becker leaned closer and thrust his face up next to Santiago's. Through clenched teeth, he said, "You're going to wish you never saw me again."

"I already . . . wish that," Santiago said.

Slaughter frowned as he looked at the two men staring at each other with such hatred. They were only a few years apart in age. Something struck him then about them, and his frown deepened. He couldn't quite figure out what it was.

Becker turned and jerked an arm toward the don.

"It looks like the old man's still passed out," he said. "Somebody wake him up. I reckon a bucket of water ought to do it."

While one of the outlaws went to fetch water from the pool, Becker sauntered over to Slaughter and Red. He grinned up at Slaughter and said, "So you're the famous Texas John."

"I'm John Slaughter. Where's my wife?"

"She's fine. You'll be seeing her soon. You've got a nice ranch, Slaughter, to go with that mighty pretty wife of yours."

"You don't need to hurt her," Slaughter said. "I've co-operated with you. I did exactly what you told me to do."

"That's right, you did. You brought me Santiago Rubriz." Becker glanced over at Slaughter's escort. "Did they come alone, Red?"

"As far as I could tell," Red said. "I checked their back trail for a long ways, and there was no sign of anybody followin' 'em."

Becker nodded and said, "That's good. I was hoping you'd be smart enough to do the right thing, Slaughter."

There was an unspoken threat in Slaughter's voice as he replied, "Like I said, I don't want anything to happen to Mrs. Slaughter."

"She's unharmed, I give you my word on that."

"Too bad the same thing can't be said for everyone else on my ranch."

Becker shrugged and said, "The course of justice often claims a few innocent victims along the way. It's regrettable, but it can't be helped."

The man who had gone to the pool came back carrying a bucket of water. Becker turned his attention back to Don Eduardo, but as he did he added to Slaughter, "You might as well get down from that horse. You're going to be here for a while."

"You could go ahead and give me my wife and let us get out of here," Slaughter suggested.

"Not yet. I want you to see these people get what's coming to them."

That confirmed Slaughter's suspicion that Becker intended to kill him and Viola no matter what they did. The man wasn't going to murder three innocent people in front of them and then let them go. That was what Slaughter expected, of course, so he wasn't surprised.

Becker swaggered back over to where Don Eduardo hung from the cottonwood branch. His men still held Santiago nearby. Becker nodded to the man with the bucket, who threw the water in Don Eduardo's face.

Rubriz gasped and sputtered and came awake from the shock. He flinched involuntarily, as if to get away from any more water thrown in his direction. The rude awakening had already been accomplished, though.

Even worse for the don, Slaughter thought, was the sight of his son in the hands of his enemies. Don Eduardo stared at the young man and whispered, "Santiago."

"That's right," Becker said in smug self-satisfaction. "Now I have all three of you. Your happy little family. I must admit, I'm surprised you and your wife didn't have more children, Rubriz. Were you too busy trying to force your way into the beds of other men's wives?"

Don Eduardo swallowed. Water still dripped from his face, but somehow he managed to summon up some dignity as he said, "My Pilar was unable to have more children. It was one of the great regrets of her life. She would have enjoyed having a large family."

"Well, some things are beyond our control, I guess. Like what's about to happen to you and your wife and son." Becker looked around at his men. "Bring the women."

At last Slaughter was glad to hear something Becker had to say. He wanted to see Viola with his own eyes and know that she was all right.

A couple of the outlaws went over to the men guarding the *jacal* with the closed door and spoke to them. Then three of them leveled their guns at the door while the fourth man opened it, said something, and stepped back quickly. If it was anybody except Viola in there, Slaughter would have thought they were being overly cautious.

Where his wife was concerned, though, it paid to be careful if you were her enemy. She could be tricky when she wanted to.

Not with the odds stacked this high against her, however. Viola came out of the *jacal* with Belinda, who seemed so shaken up by everything that had happened she could barely stay on her feet. Viola had her arm around the blonde's waist to support her as they emerged from the hut.

Then she saw Slaughter, and her eyes widened as their gazes met. He could tell she was excited to see him, but then she looked oddly disappointed.

Maybe that was because she'd expected him to come in here with all guns blazing and a salty crew of tough cowboys behind him. And to tell the truth, Slaughter had given that option some thought. He had decided that he stood a better chance of getting Viola out of here alive by taking a different tack.

As for him, he was so relieved to see she was all right that for a second he felt uncharacteristically weak in the knees. Viola was the most important person in his life. He wasn't sure how he would have ever gotten along without her. He hoped he never had to find out.

"Come over here, Mrs. Slaughter," Becker ordered. "Bring the doña with you."

"Come on, Belinda," Viola urged. She glared at Becker. "We have to cooperate . . . for now."

With the four outlaws close behind them, the women walked slowly toward the pool. Belinda kept her head down as if she didn't want to look at her husband until Don Eduardo said in a choked voice, "My love."

She finally lifted her eyes, and when she did, she must have seen her stepson because she exclaimed, "Santiago!"

"Yes," Don Eduardo said, sounding miserable. "I have doomed us all."

"You did nothing wrong, Father," Santiago said. "If anyone has doomed us, it is this madman with his twisted dreams of revenge."

"What we're doing here is justice, like I've said before," Becker insisted. He lifted a hand and pointed. "Strip the boy and stake him out right there, where the don and doña will have a good view. We're going to let Bodaway work on him for a while."

"No!" Belinda screamed. She tried to pull away from Viola, who tightened her grip.

"If you fight them, you're just playing into Becker's hands," she said. Belinda started sobbing and buried her face against Viola's shoulder.

Slaughter hadn't seen the Apache here in camp, but obviously Bodaway was still around if Becker was going to let him torture Santiago. Slaughter had seen what renegade Apaches could do to their captives. Santiago was in for a hellish ordeal, and it would be almost as bad for Don Eduardo and Belinda if they were forced to watch.

Slaughter glanced up at the rimrock and took his hat off. Red tensed and lifted his gun, which he was still holding.

"Take it easy," Slaughter said as he used his sleeve to wipe sweat from his face. "The sun's high enough that it's getting hot down here now."

"You'd better not have a gun or nothin' hidden in that hat," Red warned. The outlaw darted a nervous glance toward Becker. Clearly, he didn't want his boss to know that he hadn't thought to check Slaughter's hat for weapons.

Becker wasn't paying attention, though. He was watching in rapt attention as his men started ripping the clothes off a futilely struggling Santiago.

Slaughter put his hat back on. He had no way of knowing if Stonewall and the other men were up on the rim, but wiping his face with his sleeve was the signal they had agreed on. When Stonewall saw that, he knew it was up to him to open fire on the outlaws whenever he was ready.

It wasn't going to be easy, though, the way Becker's

men were grouped around the captives. Any shots aimed at them could endanger Slaughter and the others, too. Unfortunately, Slaughter knew he couldn't afford to wait any longer to give the signal.

Don Eduardo said, "Please, Ned, I beg of you, do not do this terrible thing. Go ahead and kill me. I'm an old man. I don't mind dying. Just let my wife and son and the Slaughters ride out of here unharmed."

"Nobody leaves until it's over," Becker snapped. "And the three of you will never leave. I'm going to destroy your family just like you destroyed mine, starting with your son."

Belinda was still crying as Viola held her. Slaughter waited for the crash of gunfire to drown out her sobs, but it didn't happen. No shots came from the rim.

Was Stonewall not up there? Had he and the rest of the men gotten lost and not even found the place? Slaughter was ready to make his move—he was going to dive at Viola and Belinda and tackle them to the ground, hopefully out of the line of fire—but he couldn't do anything until Stonewall opened the ball.

Becker's men had most of Santiago's clothes off now. Only a few tattered rags still clung to him. They started wrestling him toward the spot Becker had indicated, where one of the outlaws was using a mallet to drive picket stakes into the hard ground. Another man had some strips of rawhide they would use to lash Santiago's wrists and ankles to the stakes.

Clearly, Becker had done plenty of planning and preparing to put his crazed scheme into action.

Slaughter made an effort to keep what he was thinking and feeling from showing on his face. He didn't want to give anything away. But his nerves were stretching tighter and tighter as he waited for Stonewall.

Right from the start, he had known his plan was a gamble. There had been plenty of times in the past when he had wagered a great deal on the turn of a card or the roll of the dice.

He wasn't sure he had ever made a wager this big before.

One of the outlaws kicked Santiago's knees from behind so that the young man fell. His captors wrestled him onto his back. It took two men on each arm and leg to force him into position so that other men could begin tying him.

Belinda's sobs grew louder and more shrill. She was on the verge of hysterics, no matter how hard Viola tried to comfort her.

Bodaway emerged from behind one of the *jacales*. This was the first time Slaughter had seen him, too, although he might have caught a glimpse of the Apache during the fighting at the ranch two nights earlier. As Bodaway walked slowly toward Santiago, the men who had finished lashing the young man to the stakes stood up and backed away.

"Please, Ned, you cannot do this thing," Don Eduardo said to Becker. "You do not know what a terrible thing this is you are about to do."

Becker folded his arms over his chest and smirked as he said, "I know exactly what I'm doing, old man. I'm going to stand back and enjoy watching while Bodaway peels every inch of skin off your son's body. It'll take hours to kill him that way. He might not even die until nightfall."

"Noooo," Don Eduardo wailed. "You cannot!"

"Why not?" Becker demanded. "Give me one good reason."

Don Eduardo stared wild-eyed at him and howled, "Because he is your brother!"

Chapter 28

If Don Eduardo had suddenly sprouted wings and a tail, a more shocked silence could not have fallen over the canyon.

Slaughter wasn't surprised as completely as the others, however, because he realized now that was what he had noticed when Becker and Santiago were standing close together with their faces only inches apart. The resemblance between them had been plain to see.

Becker wasn't going to accept it, though. He shouted at Don Eduardo, "That's a damned lie!"

Don Eduardo shook his head wearily and said, "No, it is the truth. You are my son, Ned. Your mother, she was a very compelling woman. I . . . I fear I was not as strong as I should have been, the first time she approached me."

Becker just stood there, staring, shaking his head in angry disbelief.

After a moment Don Eduardo went on, "Thaddeus believed you to be his son, even after your mother insisted on naming you Edward. She . . . she said it was to honor your father's partner. I hoped that things would be different then. I thought that with you to care for, your mother would change." He sighed. "For a time it appeared that might be true, but in the end, she was still the same, determined to get what she wanted no matter what the cost. And this time it led to the bad trouble between your father and me that took his life."

"It's a pack of filthy lies," Becker insisted. His voice shook with rage. "She never would have done such a thing, no matter what she was forced into later by your treachery, Rubriz. I don't believe it, and it doesn't change anything."

Slaughter glanced around. He could tell from their faces, everyone else in the canyon accepted Don Eduardo's story, even if Becker refused to. They all had eyes. Now that the relationship between Becker and Santiago had been pointed out, the others could see the resemblance, too.

But Becker was right about it not changing anything. He was still in charge here. He jerked a hand toward his half brother's prone form and snapped, "Make him scream, Bodaway."

As expressionless as always, the Apache drew his knife from the sash around his waist and stepped toward Santiago.

The whipcrack of a rifle split the air.

Bodaway spun around and dropped the knife as the impact of slug striking flesh sounded like an ax splitting wood.

That shot had barely rung out when more followed it, filling the canyon with their racket.

Slaughter was on the move before Bodaway even hit

the ground. He lunged toward Viola and Belinda and spread his arms wide to encompass both of them. He grabbed them and pulled them down with him as he dived to the ground. Bullets buzzing like angry hornets filled the air.

"Stay down!" Slaughter told the women. "Viola, don't let her up!"

He would have preferred a more peaceful reunion with his wife, but there was no time to keep her in his arms. He scrambled onto his hands and knees and went after the knife that Bodaway had dropped when he was shot.

His hand had just closed around the knife's handle when strong fingers clamped on to his wrist. Slaughter jerked his head around and saw Bodaway lunging at him. There was blood on the Apache's torso from the bullet wound, but he was far from dead.

Bodaway tried to grab Slaughter by the throat with his other hand, but Slaughter blocked it with his forearm. The two men rolled over as they struggled. Slaughter drove a knee toward Bodaway's groin, but the Apache twisted away from the blow.

Slaughter was vaguely aware of shouted curses punctuating the continued gunfire. He knew a battle royal was going on around him. He wanted to know whether Becker was still alive or whether the shots from the canyon rim had cut him down.

But he couldn't afford to take his attention off Bodaway for even a split second, because he knew the Apache would kill him.

Somebody else would have to deal with Ned Becker.

* * *

Belinda screamed and shook as the shooting continued, but Viola was pretty sure the blonde hadn't been hit. John had gotten them out of the way very quickly when this particular hell broke loose.

She lifted her head and looked around. When the shooting started, Becker's men had scattered to hunt cover and now they were firing up at the rimrock with rifles and pistols. More lead slashed down from up there and a couple of the outlaws who hadn't concealed themselves well enough behind rocks and trees cried out and fell as slugs ripped through their bodies.

Viola had no way of knowing exactly who was up there, but she was certain John had planned things this way. Somehow, he had gotten men into position to attempt a rescue. She wouldn't be surprised if her brother Stonewall was among them. The young firebrand never wanted to miss out on any action.

Viola's breath caught in her throat as she spotted Ned Becker stumbling toward Don Eduardo with a gun in his hand. Becker shouted hoarsely, "I won't be cheated of my revenge! Whatever else happens, you're going to die, old man!"

John had told her to stay down, but Becker was about to shoot Don Eduardo and Viola knew she was the only one close enough to stop him. John was wrestling with the Apache, who was wounded but not dead.

"Stay here," she told Belinda, then surged to her feet, hoping she wasn't standing up in the path of a stray bullet.

Becker had his thumb looped over the hammer of his revolver and was raising it to shoot Don Eduardo when

Viola lowered her shoulder and rammed into him from behind.

She was a petite woman, but her life as a cowgirl had given her a considerable amount of wiry strength. The impact of her collision with Becker caused the outlaw to fly forward. He landed almost at Don Eduardo's feet. Somehow Becker managed to hang on to his gun. He twisted around, came up on his knees, and pointed the revolver at Viola, who lay a few yards away.

"You bitch!" Becker yelled.

Before he could pull the trigger, Don Eduardo lifted his legs and scissored them around Becker's neck, jerking him backward. That put even more weight on the don's wrists, but he hung on with grim determination.

"Señora Slaughter!" he gasped. "Take my wife and get out of here!"

That might be the best thing for them to do, Viola decided. She rolled over and leaped up.

But as she did, the still-struggling John and Bodaway rolled against her legs and knocked them right out from under her, dumping her on top of them.

Slaughter was shocked when Viola landed on him with a startled cry. He had told her and Belinda to stay down, but obviously that hadn't happened. And now she was in the middle of what amounted to a battle between two desperate wildcats.

That distraction allowed Bodaway to writhe out of Slaughter's grip. The Apache still had the knife. He slashed the blade at Viola's throat. Slaughter caught hold of the back of her dress and jerked her out of the way just in time. The razor-sharp edge missed her throat by no more than an inch or two.

Her hand shot out with fingers hooked like talons. They dug into Bodaway's eyes. For the first time the Apache showed a real reaction. He yelled in pain.

Slaughter's gaze fell on a chunk of sandstone about as big as two fists put together. He snatched it up and swung it over his head as he shouldered Viola out of the way.

Slaughter used the momentum of the roundhouse swing to drive the rock down as hard as he could into Bodaway's face. He heard the crunch of bone shattering. Bodaway spasmed, his back arching off the ground. His arms and legs twitched violently.

Then he sagged back limply. His eyes stared up sightlessly from his ruined face, which had been battered out of shape by the terrible blow.

Shots still rang out, but now there were fewer of them. Slaughter hoped that meant Stonewall and the men with him were winning the fight against Becker's outlaws.

He dropped the rock and grabbed the knife Bodaway had dropped in his death throes. Slaughter lunged over to Santiago and started sawing on the rawhide thongs binding the young man to the pickets. The knife's keen edge made it short work.

"John!" Viola cried.

Slaughter jerked around and saw Don Eduardo with his legs locked around Becker's neck, trying to choke him. Becker's face was dark red with trapped blood. But he still had his gun, and he managed to lift it above his head and fire a shot that ripped into Don Eduardo's belly.

Freed now, Santiago plucked the knife from Slaughter's

hand and drove himself at Becker with a roar of fury. Don Eduardo's legs fell away from Becker's neck, releasing him. Becker saw Santiago charging him and came up to meet him, gun spouting flame as he did so.

Santiago shuddered as the bullet struck him, but momentum carried him forward into Becker, who went over backward. The muscles in Santiago's arms and shoulders bunched as he drove the knife into his half brother's chest again and again, striking as deeply with the steel as he could.

Finally Santiago's injury caught up to him and he slumped atop Becker's body. The knife was buried in Becker's chest. The vengeance Becker had sought claimed him instead.

Slaughter scrambled up and lifted Viola to her feet. An eerie silence fell over Barranca Sangre as echoes of the shots rolled away and died.

"See to Belinda," Slaughter told Viola, then he hurried over to Santiago and Becker.

The outlaw was dead, no doubt about that. Slaughter grasped Santiago's shoulder and rolled the young man onto his back. There was a bloody bullet hole high on Santiago's left shoulder, but he didn't appear to be hurt too badly.

The same couldn't be said of his gutshot father.

Slaughter pulled the knife out of Becker's chest and went to Don Eduardo. The don's head lolled far forward as he hung from the cottonwood branch. Slaughter thought he was dead already, but Don Eduardo lifted his head and forced a smile onto his lips.

"My wife?" he whispered. "My son?"

Slaughter looked around. Viola and Belinda were helping Santiago to his feet.

"They're all right," Slaughter told the don. "They're going to be fine."

"Thanks to . . . *El Señor Dios* . . . and you, Don Juan. Thank you . . ."

The others reached them as Slaughter cut the ropes holding Don Eduardo up and lowered him gently to the ground. Santiago and Belinda dropped to their knees beside him, clutching him desperately.

"Do not . . . mourn me," he rasped. "I lived my life . . . good and bad . . . and the evil that came to me . . . was of my own doing."

"No," Santiago said. "It was not your fault—"

As if he hadn't heard, Don Eduardo went on, "The two of you . . . have given me much happiness . . . Now you must . . . comfort each other . . . be happy together . . . yes, I know . . . it is a good thing . . . those I love . . . should be together . . . as I am now . . . with your mother . . ."

His eyes closed, and he sighed a long, last breath.

Ned Becker's crazed hatred had claimed its final victim.

As Santiago and Belinda cried over Don Eduardo's body, Slaughter drew Viola into his arms and held her tightly against him. Her arms went around his waist with equal fervor. In the midst of this tragedy, they were together again, and that was something to be celebrated.

The sound of hoofbeats made Slaughter look around. He saw Stonewall and several of the other men from the ranch riding into the side canyon.

"Viola! John!" Stonewall cried as he hurried his horse toward them. He reined in, swung down from the saddle, and clapped hands on their shoulders. "I was afraid we weren't going to get here in time. You're all right, both of you?"

Viola nodded and said, "Of course we are. We're together, aren't we?"

Stonewall threw his arms around both of them in an enthusiastic hug.

After a moment, Slaughter said, "This, uh, isn't very dignified, Deputy."

"No, sir, it's not," Stonewall agreed. "But we're a long way from Tombstone, aren't we, Sheriff?"

Slaughter couldn't argue with that.

All of Becker's men were dead, picked off one by one by the riflemen on the canyon rim. They were left for the scavengers, and if anyone other than the coyotes and the buzzards ever saw the scattered bones, the sinister reputation of Barranca Sangre would grow that much more.

The only one buried in that lonely canyon was Ned Becker. Santiago insisted on it.

"He was mad, and he killed our father, but he was still my brother," the young man said.

That was a more generous attitude than Slaughter would have taken, but it was Santiago's decision to make.

Santiago, Belinda, and the don's men who had accompanied the rescue party took Don Eduardo's body back to his ranch, where he was laid to rest beside his beloved Pilar.

Two weeks later, Hermosa returned to the ranch as well, but he was alive, still recuperating from the wounds he had suffered at Bodaway's hands but growing stronger with each passing day. Dr. Fredericks insisted that the *vaquero* was a medical miracle. Hermosa just shrugged and said that he was too tough for some Apache to kill him.

And eight months later, John Slaughter, Viola, and Stonewall traveled to the ranch as well to attend the wedding of Santiago and Belinda. There was a great *fiesta*, and after they had eaten, the crowd adjourned to the race course Santiago had laid out.

Stonewall led Pacer to the starting line to join Santiago and *El Halcón*. With a big smile, Santiago said, "So, we will settle this at last, eh, *amigo*?"

"Sure, if that's what you want," Stonewall said. "I figure if I'd just got married, though, I could come up with somethin' better to do than have some ol' horse race."

"Yes, of course, but this is important, too. A matter of honor for us both."

"Maybe, but my honor's gonna be just fine no matter how this comes out."

Viola held a parasol to shade her from the sun as she and Slaughter stood with the spectators waiting for the race to begin. Belinda was with them, looking stronger and happier than she had in all the time they had known her.

"I may have misjudged her . . . a little," Viola had admitted to Slaughter. "She wasn't really doing anything Don Eduardo didn't want her to do, and she tried to be as honorable as she could about it. I still think she has some growing up to do, though."

"They can grow up together," Slaughter had said. "Santiago's a good man. They'll be all right."

Pacer and *El Halcón* both seemed eager to get started on this race. Stonewall and Santiago swung up into their saddles, and then Santiago looked around and called, "Señor Slaughter, will you start us off?"

Slaughter nodded and said, "It'd be my pleasure."

He walked out and stood next to the starting line, drawing his pearl-handled Colt as he did so.

"Get ready," he said as he lifted the gun. "All set?"

Grim, determined nods from the two young men.

"Go," John Slaughter said as he pulled the trigger and fired into the air. The two magnificent horses burst forward, galloping full out.

The race was on.

Keep reading for a special early excerpt!

A REASON TO DIE

A PERLEY GATES WESTERN

From bestselling authors William W. and J. A. Johnstone—the explosive adventures of Perley Gates, who's carving out his own legacy in the violent American frontier . . .

Restless cowpoke Perley Gates wanted nothing more than to track down the grandfather who abandoned his family years ago. What he found was the crazy old sidewinder barely hanging on after a Sioux massacre. The old man's dying wish was to make things right for deserting his kin—by giving his strong-willed grandson Perley clues to the whereabouts of a buried fortune in gold.

Finding his grandfather's legacy will set up his family for life. But it won't be easy. The discovery of raw gold in the Black Hills has lured hordes of ruthless lowlifes into Deadwood and Custer City—kill-crazy prairie rats, gunfighters, outlaws, and Indians—armed with a thousand glittering reasons to put Perley six feet under. All Perley wants is what was left to him, what he's owed. But with so many brigands on his backside, finding his grandfather's treasure is going to land Perley Gates between the promise of heaven and the blood-soaked battlefields of hell . . .

Look for it wherever books are sold . . .

Live Free. Read Hard.
www.williamjohnstone.net

Chapter 1

"It's a good thing I decided to check," John Gates said to Sonny Rice, who was sitting in the wagon loaded with supplies. They had just come from Henderson's General Store and John had wanted to stop by the telegraph office on the chance Perley might have sent word.

Sonny was immediately attentive. "Did he send a telegram? Where is he?"

"He's in Deadwood, South Dakota," John answered. "He said he's on his way home."

"Did he say if he found your grandpa?"

"He said he found him, but Grandpa's dead. Said he'd explain it all when he gets back."

"Well, I'll be . . ." Sonny drew out. "Ol' Perley found him. I figured he would. He usually does what he sets out to do."

John couldn't disagree. His younger brother was always one to follow a trail to its end, even though oftentimes it led him to something he would have been better served to avoid. He laughed when he thought about what his older brother, Rubin, said about Perley. *If there ain't but one cow pie between here and the Red River, Perley will most likely step in it.*

It was a joke, of course, but it did seem that trouble had a way of finding Perley. It was true, even though he would go to any lengths to avoid it.

"We might as well go by the diner and see if Beulah's cooked anything fit to eat," John casually declared, knowing that was what Sonny was hoping to hear. "Might even stop by Patton's afterward and get a shot of whiskey. That all right with you?" He could tell by the grin on the young ranch hand's face that he knew he was being japed. As a rule, Sonny didn't drink very often, but he would imbibe on some occasions.

Thoughts running through his mind, John nudged the big gray gelding toward the small plain building at the end of the street that proclaimed itself to be the Paris Diner. He was glad he had checked the telegraph office. It was good news to hear Perley was on his way home to Texas. He had a long way to travel from the Black Hills, so it was hard to say when to expect him to show up at the Triple-G. His mother and Rubin would be really happy to hear about the telegram. Perley had been gone a long time on his quest to find their grandpa. His mother had been greatly concerned when Perley hadn't returned with his brothers after the cattle were delivered to the buyers in Ogallala.

John reined the gray to a halt at the hitching rail in front of the diner, then waited while Sonny pulled up in the wagon.

"Well, I was beginning to wonder if the Triple-G had

closed down," Lucy Tate sang out when she saw them walk in.

"Howdy, Lucy," John returned. "It has been a while since we've been in town. At least, it has been for me. I don't know if any of the other boys have been in." He gave her a big smile. "I thought you mighta got yourself married by now," he joked, knowing what a notorious flirt she was.

She waited for them to sit down before replying. "I've had some offers, but I'm waiting to see if that wife of yours is gonna kick you out."

"She's threatened to more than once," he said, "but she knows there's a line of women hopin' that'll happen."

She laughed. "I'm gonna ask Martha about that if you ever bring her in here to eat." Without asking if they wanted coffee, she filled two cups. "Beulah's got chicken and dumplin's or beef stew. Whaddle-it-be?"

"Give me the chicken and dumplin's," John said. "I get enough beef every day. How 'bout you, Sonny?"

"I'll take the chicken, too," he replied, his eyes never having left the saucy waitress.

Noticing it, John couldn't resist japing him some more. "How 'bout Sonny, here? He ain't married and he's got a steady job."

She chuckled delightedly and reached over to tweak Sonny's cheek. "You're awful sweet, but still a little young. I'll keep my eye on you, though." She went to the kitchen to get their food, leaving the blushing young ranch hand to recover.

"She's something, ain't she?" John asked after seeing Sonny's embarrassment. "Can't take a thing she says seriously." He thought at once of Perley, who had made that mistake and suffered his disappointment. Further thoughts on the subject were interrupted when Becky Morris came in from the kitchen.

"Afternoon, John," Becky greeted him. "Lucy said you were here." She greeted Sonny as well, but she didn't know his name. "It's been a while since any of the Triple-G men have stopped in. Perley used to come by every time he was in town, but I haven't seen him in a long time now. Is he all right?"

"Perley's been gone for a good while now," John answered. "I just got a telegram from him this mornin' from Dakota Territory. Said he's on his way home."

"Oh, well, maybe he'll come in to see us when he gets back," Becky said.

"I'm sure he will." John couldn't help wondering if Perley had taken proper notice of Becky Morris. Shy and gentle, unlike Lucy Tate, Becky looked more the woman a man should invest his life with. He might be wrong, but John suspected he detected a wistful tone in her voice when she'd asked about Perley.

Before they were finished, Beulah Walsh came out to visit. John assured her that her reputation as a cook was still deserved, as far as he was concerned. He paid for his and Sonny's meal, and got up to leave. "We've gotta stop by Patton's before we go back to the ranch. Sonny's gotta have a shot of that rotgut whiskey before he leaves town."

"I never said that," Sonny insisted. "You were the one that said we'd go to the saloon."

"Don't let him bother you, sweetie," Lucy said and gave him another tweak on his cheek. "I know how you heavy drinkers need a little shooter after you eat."

"What did you tell her that for?" Sonny asked as soon as they were outside. "Now she thinks I'm a drunk."

"I doubt it," John replied.

Moving back down the short street to Patton's Saloon, they tied the horses to the rail and went inside.

Benny Grimes, the bartender, called out a "Howdy" as soon as they walked in the door. "John Gates, I swear, I thought you mighta gave up drinkin' for good."

"How do, Benny?" John greeted him. "Might as well have. We ain't had much time to get into town lately. Ain't that right, Sonny?"

"That's a fact," Sonny agreed and picked up the shot glass Benny slid over to him. He raised it, turned toward John, and said, "Here's hopin' Perley has a safe trip home." He downed it with a quick toss, anxious to get it over with. He was not a drinker by habit and took a drink of whiskey now and then only to avoid having to explain why he didn't care for it.

"Well, I'll sure drink to that," John said and raised his glass.

"Me, too." Benny poured himself one. After they tossed the whiskey down, he asked, "Where is he?"

"Way up in Dakota Territory," John said, "and we just got word he's on his way home, so we need to let the folks hear the news." He had one more drink, then he and Sonny headed back to the Triple-G.

The man John Gates had wished a safe trip home earlier in the day was seated a few yards from a crystal-clear waterfall. It was a good bit off the trail he had been following, but he'd had a feeling the busy stream he had crossed might lead to a waterfall. As high up as he was on the mountain, it stood to reason the stream would soon come to a cliff. It pleased him to find out he had been right, and it had been worth his while to have seen it. It was a trait that Perley Gates had undoubtedly inherited from his grandfather—an obsession for seeing what might lie on the other side of the mountain. And it was the reason he found himself in the Black Hills of Dakota Territory on this late summer day—that and the fact that he was not married and his brothers were. It didn't matter if he rode all the way to hell and who knows where. There wasn't any wife waiting for him to come home, so he had been the obvious pick to go in search of his grandfather.

His grandfather, for whom he was named, was buried in the dark mountains not far from where Perley sat drinking the stout black coffee he favored. He felt a strong kinship with him, even though he had not really known the man, having never met him until a short time before he passed away. Even so, that was enough time for the old man to determine that he was proud to have his young grandson wear his name, Perley Gates. The old man had been one of the lucky ones who struck it rich in the Black Hills gold rush before an outlaw's bullet brought his life to an end. Determined to make restitution to his family for having abandoned them, he hung on long enough to extract a promise from his grandson to take his gold back to Texas.

The gold dust had been right where his grandfather had said it would be. Perley had recovered four canvas sacks from under a huge rock before he'd been satisfied there were no more. With no scales to weigh the sacks, he guessed it to be ten pounds per sack. At the present time, gold was selling in Deadwood at a little over three hundred and thirty dollars a pound. If his calculations were correct, he was saddled with a responsibility to deliver over thirteen thousand dollars in gold dust to Texas, more than eight hundred miles away. It was not a task he looked forward to. The gold rush had brought every robber and dry-gulcher west of Omaha to Deadwood Gulch, all with an eye toward preying on those who had worked to bring the gold out of the streams. Perley's problem was how to transport his treasure without attracting the watchful eye of the outlaws. It would be easier to convert the dust to paper money, but he was not confident he would get a fair exchange from the bank in Deadwood, because of the inflation there.

To add to his concerns, he had accumulated five extra horses during his time in the Black Hills and he didn't want the bother of driving them all the way to Texas with no one to help him. With forty pounds of dust to carry, he decided to keep one of the horses to use as a second packhorse. His packhorse could carry the load along with his supplies, but with the load divided onto two horses, he could move a lot faster in the event he had to. His favorite of the extra horses would be the paint gelding that his grandfather had ridden. The old man had loved that horse, maybe as much as Perley loved Buck, so he didn't feel right about selling it.

With Custer City and Hill City reduced almost to ghost towns, he decided to ride back to Deadwood to see if he could sell the other four. Deadwood wasn't a good market for selling horses. Cheyenne would be a better bet, or maybe Hat Creek Station, for that matter, but he figured he hadn't paid anything for them, so he might as well let them go cheap.

With that settled, he packed up and started back to Deadwood.

"Evenin'. Looks like you're needin' to stable some horses," Franklin Todd greeted Perley when he drew up before his place of business.

"Evenin'," Perley returned. "Matter of fact, I'm lookin' to sell four of 'em if I can get a reasonable price. I'm fixin' to head back to Texas, and I don't wanna lead a bunch of horses back with me."

Todd was at once alerted to the prospects of acquiring four horses at little cost, but he hesitated for a moment, stroking his chin as if undecided. "Which four?" he finally asked.

Perley indicated the four and Todd paused to think some more.

"I really ain't buyin' no horses right now, but I'll take a look at 'em." Todd took his time examining the four horses, then finally made an offer of ten dollars each.

Perley wasn't really surprised by the low offer and countered with a price of fifty dollars for all four.

Todd didn't hesitate to agree. "These horses ain't stolen, are they?" he asked as he weighed out the payment.

"Not till now," Perley answered.

With an eye toward disguising four sacks of gold dust, he left Todd's and walked his horses past a saloon to a general merchandise establishment.

"Can I help you with something?" the owner asked when Perley walked in.

"I'm just lookin' to see if there's anything I need," Perley answered and quickly scanned the counters and shelves while taking frequent glances out the door at his horses at the rail. In the process of trying to keep an eye on his horses, his attention was drawn to several large sacks stacked near the door. "What's in those sacks?" He pointed to them.

"Probably nothing you'd be looking for," the owner replied. "Something I didn't order. Came in with a load of merchandise from Pierre. It's about four hundred pounds of seed corn. I don't know where it was supposed to go, but it sure as hell wasn't Deadwood. There ain't a level piece of ground for farming anywhere in the Black

Hills. I tried to sell it to Franklin Todd at the stable for horse feed. Even he didn't want it."

Perley walked over to an open bag and looked inside. "I might could use some of it. Whaddaya askin' for it?"

Too surprised to respond right away, the owner hesitated before asking, "How much are you thinking about?"

Perley said he could use a hundred pounds of it.

The owner shrugged and replied, "I don't know. Two dollars?"

"I could use some smaller canvas bags, too, four of 'em. You got anything like that?"

With both merchant and customer satisfied they had made a good deal, Perley threw his hundred-pound sack of seed corn across the back of one of his packhorses and started back toward Custer City. Although already late in the afternoon, he preferred to camp in the hills outside of Deadwood, considering what he carried on his packhorses.

He rode for a good nine or ten miles before stopping. When he made camp that night, he placed a ten-pound sack of gold dust in each of the twenty-five-pound sacks he had just bought, and filled in around it with seed corn. When he finished, he was satisfied that his dust was disguised about as well as he could hope for, and the corn didn't add a lot of weight with the amount necessary to fill the sacks.

He downed the last gulp of coffee from his cup and got to his feet. "Well, I can't sit here and worry about it all night," he announced to Buck, the big bay gelding grazing noisily a few yards away. "You don't give a damn, do ya?"

"That horse ever answer you back?"

Startled, Perley stepped away from the fire, grabbing his rifle as he dived for cover behind a tree, searching frantically for where the voice had come from. It didn't sound very far away.

"Whoa! Hold on a minute, feller," the voice exclaimed. "Ain't no need for that there rifle."

"I'll decide that after you come outta your hidin' place," Perley responded and cranked a cartridge into the cylinder of the Winchester.

"Hold on," the voice came back again. "I didn't mean to surprise you like that. I shoulda sang out a little sooner. I was just passin' by on the trail up there on the ridge and I saw your fire, so I thought I'd stop and say howdy." A short pause followed, then he said, "It always pays to be careful to see what kinda camp you're lookin' at before you come a-ridin' in. I'm comin' out, so don't take a shot at me, all right?"

"All right," Perley answered. "Come on out." He watched cautiously as his visitor emerged from the darkness of the trees above the creek, alert for any sign of movement that might indicate there were others with him. When he felt sure the man was alone, he eased the hammer back down, but still held the rifle ready to fire. Leading a dun gelding with a mule following on a rope, his surprise guest approached the fire. "You're travelin' these back trails pretty late at night, ain'tcha?" Perley asked.

"Reckon so," the man replied, "but with all the outlaws ridin' these trails lookin' for somebody to rob, it pays for a man alone to travel some at night." He looked around at the loaded packs and the horses grazing close by. "Looks like you're gettin' ready to travel, too, from the looks of your camp. I smelled your fire from the ridge back there. Thought maybe I might get a cup of coffee, but I see you're 'bout ready to pack up."

"I was thinkin' about it," Perley said. "Where you headin'? Deadwood?"

"Nope, the other way. I've seen Deadwood. I'm ready to go back to Cheyenne."

Perley studied the young man carefully for a few moments. A young man, close to his own age, he figured. There was nothing unusual about him, unless you counted the baggy britches he wore, that looked to be a couple of inches short, and the shirt that looked a size too big. Perley decided he was no threat. "Well, I've got plenty of coffee, so I reckon I can fix you up with a cup. What about supper? You had anything to eat?"

"As a matter of fact, I ain't. I had that thought in mind when I caught sight of your camp. I'd be much obliged. My name's Billy Tuttle."

"Perley Gates." He waited for the man to ask the name again, which was the usual response. When he didn't, Perley said, "Take care of your animals and I'll make us a pot of coffee. It's kinda late to go any farther tonight, anyway, so I think I'll just stay here. You like venison? 'Cause that's what I'm cookin' for supper."

Billy said that would suit him just fine. He'd been living on sowbelly and little else for the past couple of days.

Perley soon decided there was nothing to fear from his

surprise guest. As he had said, he was focused on getting back to his home in Cheyenne.

Perley guessed the young man was also short on supplies. "You any kin to Tom Tuttle there in Cheyenne?"

"He's my pa," Billy replied. "You know him?"

"I've done some business with your pa," Perley answered. "Matter of fact, I sold him a couple of horses when I stopped at his stable one time. He's a good man."

It didn't take long before Billy told the story of his attempt to make his fortune in Deadwood Gulch, a story that left him headed for home with empty pockets. It was a story all too common in boomtowns like Deadwood and Custer City.

"So you partnered up with a couple of fellows and they ran off with all the gold the three of you found?" Perley summed up.

"That's a fact," Billy confirmed. "It wasn't but about four hundred dollars' worth. Wouldn'ta paid us much when we split it three ways, but it was still a helluva lot more than I came out here with."

"I swear," Perley commented. "That's tough luck, all right. Did you know these two fellows before you partnered up with 'em?"

"No, I just ran up on 'em one mornin' and they looked like they could use a hand, so I went to work with 'em, building a sluice box. Wasn't long before we started strikin' color, and it wasn't long after that when I woke up one mornin' and they was gone. Cleared out while I was asleep."

It was hard for Perley not to feel sympathy for the unfortunate young man. He couldn't help thinking that

Billy's experience sounded like the kind of fix that he carried a reputation for. He thought of his brother Rubin saying *If there wasn't but one cow pie on the whole damn ranch, Perley would step in it.* He had to admit that sometimes it seemed to be true.

Maybe he and Billy had that in common. "So whaddaya plan on doin' now? Go back and help your pa in the stable?"

"I reckon," Billy replied, then hesitated before going on. "Pa ain't gonna be too happy to see me come home. I think he was hopin' I'd stay on out here in the Black Hills."

That was surprising to Perley. "Why is that?" Tom Tuttle impressed him as a solid family man. He had to admit, however, that he had only a brief acquaintance with him.

"The woman Pa's married to ain't my mama," Billy said. "Pa married her when my mama died of consumption. She's my stepmother and she's got a son of her own about my age. She's talked Pa into turnin' his business over to her son when Pa gets too old to run it, and I reckon I'm just in the way."

Perley didn't know what to say. In the short time he had dealings with Tom Tuttle, he would not have thought him to be the type to abandon his own son. He had compassion for Billy, but all he could offer him was common courtesy. "Well, I'm sorry to hear you have troubles with your pa, but if it'll help, you're welcome to ride along with me till we get to Cheyenne. I'm guessin' you ain't fixed too good for supplies."

"You guessed right," Billy responded at once. "And I

surely appreciate it. I won't be no bother a'tall. I'm used to hard work and I'll do my share of the chores."

"Good," Perley said with as much enthusiasm as he could muster. Truth be told, a stranger as a traveling companion was close to the last thing he wanted, considering what he was carrying on his packhorses. He didn't intend to get careless, even though Billy seemed forthright and harmless. Close to Perley's age, Billy might come in handy if they were unfortunate enough to encounter outlaws on the road to Cheyenne.

After the horses and Billy's mule were taken care of, the two travelers ate supper, planning to get an early start in the morning.

"Here," Billy insisted, "I'll clean up the cups and fryin' pan. I've got to earn my keep," he added cheerfully. After everything was done they both spread their bedrolls close to the fire and turned in.

Perley was awake at first light after having slept fitfully, due to a natural tendency to sleep with one eye open, even though he felt he had nothing to fear from Billy. He revived the fire and started coffee before Billy woke up.

"Here I am lyin' in bed while you're already at it," Billy said as he rolled out of his blankets. "Whatcha want me to do?"

"Just pack up your possibles and throw a saddle on your horse," Perley said. "We'll have a cup of coffee before we get started, eat breakfast when we rest the horses."

It didn't take long for Billy to load the few items he

owned on the mule, so when he finished, he came to help Perley. "What's in the sacks?" He saw Perley tying two twenty-five-pound sacks on each of his packhorses.

"Kansas seed corn," Perley answered casually. "I found a store in Deadwood that had about four hundred pounds of it. Ain't nobody in Deadwood wantin' seed corn, so I bought a hundred pounds of it at a damn good price. Gonna take it back to Texas and start me a corn patch. If I'd had a couple more horses, I'd a-bought all he had." He made a point then of opening one of the sacks and taking out a handful to show Billy. "You can't get corn like this in Texas."

Billy nodded his head politely, but was obviously unimpressed, which was the reaction Perley hoped for. Packed up and ready to go, they started the first day of their journey together, following the road toward Custer City, heading south.

The second night's camp was made by a busy stream halfway between Hill City and Custer. By this time, Perley's supply of smoked venison was down to only enough for another meal or two. Then it would be back to sowbelly, unless they were lucky enough to find some game to shoot. Perley was not inclined to tarry, considering the gold he was transporting. As somewhat of a surprise to him, he found Billy just as eager to put the Black Hills behind them, considering what he had said about his father.

Curious, Perley asked him, "What are you aimin' to do when you get back to Cheyenne? You think your pa really won't be happy to see you back?" He couldn't believe that Tom Tuttle would kick his son out.

"Oh, I ain't worried about that. I don't wanna work in the damn stable, anyway. I've got a few ideas I'm thinkin' about."

"What kinda ideas?" Perley asked.

"Yeah, what kinda ideas?" The voice came from the darkness behind them. "Maybe stealin' gold from your partners, stuff like that, huh, Billy?"

"Don't even think about it," another voice warned when Perley started to react.

He had no choice but to remain seated by the fire.

A tall, gangly man stepped into the circle of firelight. He was grinning as he held a double-barreled shotgun on them. "Come on in, Jeb. I've got 'em both covered."

In another second, he was joined by a second man, this one a bull-like brute of a man. "Hello, Billy. I see you got you another partner already. It took me and Luke awhile before we tracked you down. Seems like you took off so quick, you must notta realized you took all the gold, instead of just your share."

"Whoa, now, Jeb," Billy exclaimed. "You know I wouldn'ta done nothin' like that. Luke musta buried it somewhere else and forgot where he put it." He looked at the lanky man with the shotgun. "What about it, Luke? Ain't that what musta happened? You were awful drunk that night."

His question caused Luke to laugh. "I gotta give you credit, Billy, you can make up the damnedest stories I've ever heard."

Jeb, who was obviously the boss, said, "We'll see soon

enough when we take a look at the packs on that mule." He stared hard at Perley then. "Who's this feller?"

"His name's Perley Gates," Billy said, causing both of the outlaws to laugh.

"Pearly Gates," Luke echoed. "Well, ain't that somethin'? Looks to me like he's carryin' a helluva lot more than you are. Maybe ol' Pearly struck it rich back there in the gulch and now he's packin' it all outta here."

Perley spoke then. "If I had, I reckon I'd still be back there in the gulch, lookin' for more." Angry that he had been taken so completely by surprise, it didn't help to learn that Billy had fooled him, too. Not only was he a thief, he had brought his troubles to roost with him.

"Damn. He talks," Luke mocked. "We'll take a look in them packs, too."

"You're makin' a mistake, Jeb," Billy said. "Pearly ain't got nothin' in them packs but supplies and some kinda fancy seed corn he's fixin' to plant. If you think I stole your gold dust, then go ahead and look through my packs."

"Oh, I will," Jeb replied, "you sneakin' rat. Luke, go through the packs on that damn mule. There's five pounds of dust in 'em somewhere. That oughta be easy to find." When Billy started to get up, Jeb aimed his pistol at him. "You just set right there and keep your hands where I can see 'em."

Caught in a helpless situation, there was nothing Perley could do but sit there while Luke rifled through Billy's packs. When he glanced at Billy, he saw no sign of concern in his face. Maybe he really hadn't stolen their gold, but it sure seemed like his former partners were convinced that he had.

"Ain't no need to make a mess of my stuff just 'cause you was wrong," Billy complained when Luke started throwing his possessions around in frustration.

"Shut your mouth!" Jeb yelled at Billy. "Look in his saddlebags," he said to Luke then.

"I told you I ain't got your gold," Billy argued. "Looks to me like maybe you oughta be askin' Luke where that dust is. All I wanted was to get the hell outta that creek after you shot that feller. I figured you and Luke could have my share."

Jeb shifted a suspicious eye in Luke's direction. "I don't reckon somethin' like that mighta happened, could it, Luke? I mean, we was all drinkin' kinda heavy that night. Last thing I remember before I passed out was you holdin' that sack of dust and talkin' about what you was gonna buy with your share. When I woke up the next mornin', you was already up and Billy was gone."

"Hold on a minute!" Luke blurted out. "You're lettin' that lyin' son of a bitch put crazy ideas in your head. Me and you been ridin' together long enough for you to know I wouldn't do nothin' like that."

"You looked through all his packs and there weren't no sack of gold dust," Jeb reminded him. "Whaddaya suppose happened to it?"

"How the hell do I know?" Luke shot back, then nodded toward Perley, who was still a spectator at this point. "Most likely it's in his stuff. Billy musta put it on one of his packhorses." He turned and started toward Perley's belongings, stacked beside his bedroll.

"This has gone as far as it's goin'," Perley said, getting to his feet. "You've got no call to go plunderin' through my things like you did with Billy's. Billy just hooked up with me last night and he wouldn't likely just hand over five pounds of gold dust for me to tote for him, would he? You can take a look at what I'm carryin', but I'll help you do it, so you don't go tearin' up my packs like you did with Billy's."

His statement caused them both to hesitate for a moment, surprised by his audacity. Then they both laughed at his obvious stupidity.

"Mister," Jeb informed him, "you ain't got no say in what we'll do. It was bad luck for you when you joined up with Billy Tuttle. I'm tired of jawin' with both of you." Without warning, he said, "Shoot 'em both, Luke."

"My pleasure," Luke said and raised his shotgun to fire. Before he could cock the hammers back, he was doubled over by a .44 slug from Perley's Colt.

Jeb's reaction was swift, but not fast enough to draw his pistol before Perley's second shot slammed into his chest. He was already dead when his weapon cleared the holster and fired one wayward shot in Billy's direction.

Billy howled, grabbed his leg, and started limping around in a circle. "Damn, damn, damn . . ." He muttered over and over as he clutched his baggy trouser leg with both hands.

Perley holstered his .44 and moved quickly to help him. "How bad is it? Let me give you a hand."

"It ain't bad," Billy insisted. "I can take care of it. You make sure them two are dead. I'll take care of my leg."

"They're both dead," Perley said. "Now sit down and I'll take a look at that wound." He paused then when a peculiar sight caught his eye. "What the—" was as far as he got before he saw a tiny stream of dust spraying on the toe of Billy's boot, not understanding at once what he was seeing. When he realized what it was, he looked up to meet Billy's gaze.

"Looks like I sprung a leak," Billy said, smiling sheepishly. "The son of a bitch shot a hole in my britches."

Perley said nothing but continued to stare in disbelief.

Billy tried to divert his attention. "Man, you're fast as greased lightning. You saved both our lives. I ain't never seen anybody that fast with a handgun." He was hesitant to move his foot for fear of causing the gold to mix in the dirt beneath it.

Perley's gaze was still captured by the little pile of gold dust forming on the toe of Billy's boot. "You caused me to kill two men you stole gold from," he said, not at all pleased by the fact.

A little more apprehensive now that he had seen Perley's skill with a gun, Billy countered. "Let's not forget that they was fixin' to shoot us. There weren't no doubt about that. I saw 'em shoot a man at a placer mine and take that little five-pound sack of dust. That's when I decided that weren't no partnership for me."

"So you cut out and took the gold with you," Perley reminded him. "Looks to me like they had good reason to come after you."

"Well, they didn't have no right to the gold," Billy said. "'Specially after they killed him for it." When it was obvious that Perley was far from casual when it came to the taking of a man's life, Billy tried to change his focus. "I reckon you've earned a share of the gold, and I don't mind givin' it to you. I figure I've got about sixteen hundred dollars' worth. That 'ud make your share about eight hundred."

When there was still no positive reaction from Perley, Billy tried to make light of the situation. "And that ain't countin' the dust runnin' outta my britches leg." He hesitated to make a move, still not sure what Perley had in mind. "All right if I see if I can fix it?"

"I reckon you might as well," Perley finally said, not really sure what he should do about the situation he found himself in. He was still feeling the heavy responsibility for having killed two men, even knowing he had been given no choice. The one called Luke had been preparing to empty both barrels of that shotgun. There had been no time to think.

"I don't want any share in your gold," Perley said. "Go ahead and take care of it."

Billy's expression was enough to indicate that he was more than happy to hear that. He immediately unbuckled his belt and dropped his britches to reveal two cotton bags, one hanging beside each leg from a length of clothesline tied around his waist. Perley could hardly believe what he saw. Jeb's wild shot had drilled a hole straight through Billy's trouser leg and the cotton bag hanging inside.

"What about their horses and guns?" Billy asked as he

transferred the remaining dust in the damaged bag into the other one.

"What about 'em?" Perley responded, still undecided what he should do with Billy.

"I mean, hell, you killed 'em, both of 'em. I reckon you'd be right in claimin' you own all their belongin's." He glanced up quickly. "I sure as hell ain't gonna give you no argument."

While Billy was busy trying to recover every grain of dust that had poured through the hole, Perley took an extra few minutes to think it over. He had to admit that he didn't know what to do about it—a thief stealing from another thief. The part that worried him was the killings he had been forced to commit, and he blamed Billy for causing that. One thing he knew for sure was that he'd had enough of Billy Tuttle.

He told Billy, "I ain't ever operated outside the law, and I don't reckon I'll start now. Those two fellows were outlaws and you were ridin' with 'em, so I reckon whatever they done, you were part of it. You're sure as hell an outlaw, too. I reckon this is where you and I part ways. You take your gold and the horses, and anything else on those two. If your daddy wasn't Tom Tuttle, I might be inclined to turn you over to the sheriff back in Deadwood, but your pa doesn't need to know you got on the wrong side of the law. If you'll go on back to Cheyenne and start livin' an honest life, he'll never hear from me about you bein' mixed up with these outlaws. We'll go our separate ways and forget about what happened here. Can I have your promise on that?"

"Yes sir, you sure do," Billy answered in his most contrite manner. "I 'preciate the chance to get myself right with the law. I've sure as hell learned my lesson. If it weren't for you, I'd most likely be dead right now, so you have my promise." He hesitated for a few moments, then said, "I don't see no use in us splittin' up, though. It looks to me like it'd be better for both of us to travel together for protection. Whaddaya say?"

"I don't think so, Billy," Perley answered. "At least for me, I'll be better alone. Good luck to you, though."

Chapter 2

As Perley had insisted, they parted company, Billy to continue along the Cheyenne–Deadwood Stage Road, while Perley followed a trail leading west. He knew that it was less than a full day's ride in that direction to be out of the mountains and back in Wyoming Territory, so he intended to turn back to the south once he cleared the mountains. That way, Billy should be well ahead of him on the stage road to Cheyenne. In the long run, it would delay him on his trip back to Texas, but only for half a day or so of the two and a half to three weeks he figured to take.

His thoughts kept returning to Billy and the situation he had been caught in. Before they parted company, Billy had sworn that he had learned his lesson, and he was going to follow the straight and narrow from that point on. Maybe he would. It was hard to say, but Perley preferred to let Billy deal with his conscience by himself. He was already involved in the mixed-up young man's life far more than he had expected when Billy first rode into his camp.

Since Perley was not really familiar with the country he was riding through, he was dependent upon no more than a sketchy knowledge of the heavily forested mountains. For that reason, when he came upon a busy stream that appeared to head in the right direction, he followed its course down from the mountains. Luck seemed to be with him, for it eventually led him down through the hills and into the flatter prairie west of the Black Hills. He decided it best to camp beside the stream that had led him out of the mountains, and set out on a more southeasterly course the next morning. It would be an uneventful ride of a day and a half before he struck the Cheyenne stage road just north of Hat Creek Station.

"Well, if this isn't a fine surprise," Martha Bowman said when she saw him walk in the door of the hotel dining room at Hat Creek Station. "I thought you'd be back home on that Texas ranch by now."

"I'm on my way," Perley responded. "Just thought I'd stop in for one of those good suppers you folks fix."

She followed him over to the end of the long table in the center of the room. "Are you staying in the hotel?"

"Not this time," Perley said. "I'm puttin' my horses up at the stable for the night and I expect I'd best sleep with them."

She stepped back, pretending to be offended. "Was the

hotel bed so bad last time you were here that you'd rather sleep in the stable?"

He laughed and replied, "No, ma'am. It's just that Buck, my horse, is feelin' kinda puny, so I'd best keep an eye on him." Martha was a friend, and he trusted her completely, but he didn't think it a good idea to tell her he was more concerned about the four bags of seed corn in his packs.

"There you go, ma'aming me again," she scolded. "I thought we settled that last time you were here."

"Sorry, I forgot . . . Martha," he quickly corrected himself. "I wasn't sure you'd be here. Thought maybe you'd be married and gone."

She chuckled at that. "I've been too busy to even think about that. Besides, I thought I told you I'm particular about the man I marry, and he hasn't showed up yet."

He had never stopped to analyze his relationship with Martha Bowman or given thought to the fact that he was so free and easy around her. As a rule, he was shy around all women, especially one of Martha's beauty and grace. But Martha was different. He was comfortable in her presence and free from getting tongue-tied, as he often did when talking to any woman outside a saloon.

He was brought back from his thoughts when she asked if he wanted coffee. "Yes, ma'am," he replied, then quickly corrected himself. "Yes, Martha."

She left to fetch the coffeepot, shaking her head in exasperation. "I'll get a plate for you," she called back over her shoulder.

He was working on a slice of apple pie when Martha

found the time to sit and visit with him for a while. "I'll have a cup of coffee while I've got a chance," she said. "Is that pie any good?"

With a mouthful of it, he answered with a satisfied nod.

"I haven't tried any, myself," she continued. "Gotta watch my figure."

"Me, too," Perley said. "What's goin' on here at the ranch?" He was interested, since the ranch foreman, Willis Adams, had at one time tried to hire him.

"Nothing new that I know of," she answered. "There's hardly anybody staying in the hotel. A man and his wife waiting to catch the stage to Deadwood, and some man on his way to Cheyenne."

That caught Perley's interest. "Who's the fellow goin' to Cheyenne? Has he been here long?"

She shrugged. "I don't know. Young fellow. Checked into the hotel this morning. He's not waiting to ride the stage 'cause he's got some horses with him."

That was not good news to Perley. It could be a coincidence, but there were better odds that it could be Billy. Martha said he'd checked in that morning.

Why would he want to stay over another night here? Unless he just wants to enjoy some of that money he stole. Or maybe he's got something else in mind. That's a possibility. Billy already demonstrated a potential to bury himself in deep trouble. And since he stumbled into my camp, he seems to want to share it with me. Perley glanced up to find Martha staring at him.

"Where did you drift off to? I think I lost you there for a minute," she said.

"I reckon my brain ain't caught up with me since I left Deadwood," he joked. "I have to stop and wait for it once in a while." He couldn't help thinking he'd stepped in another cow pie. He wasn't even sure the man Martha was talking about was, in fact, Billy Tuttle. He didn't ask her if she remembered the man's name because he didn't want to hear her say *Billy Tuttle*.

At any rate, if it was Billy, he had a room in the hotel while Perley would be sleeping in the stable. If he was careful, there shouldn't be any occasion for Billy to know he was even there unless he bumped into him in the dining room.

"Well, I reckon I'd best get outta here and let you get back to work," Perley announced.

"Yeah, I guess I'd better, if I don't wanna lose my job."

"That's a fact," he said, knowing she was joking. Her father owned the hotel, so he was not likely to fire her.

"You gonna be back for breakfast?"

"I ain't sure. Depends on how early I get started in the mornin'." Any other time, he wouldn't have missed the opportunity to see her again.

He paid for his supper, said good-bye, and hurried out the door, unaware that she stood watching him until he disappeared around the corner of the building. The only thing he was thinking at that point was that maybe he shouldn't have left his packs unguarded in the stable for so long. Then he reassured himself that he had been right to not show any undue concern over the packs he had left in a corner of the stall. Besides, Robert Davis was the man responsible for watching the stable, and he was as trustworthy as you could ask for.

As Perley had figured, his packs and possessions were undisturbed when he got to the stable and Robert Davis was still there to keep an eye on things. He said he had a few things he wanted to take care of before he retired to his room on the back of the barn.

"I'll not hold you up any longer," Perley said.

"Well, I reckon you can just make yourself at home," Davis said. "I put fresh hay down in the other corner and you know where the water is. I'll see you in the mornin'."

After Davis left for the night, Perley spent a little time making sure his horses were all right. Then he arranged the hay in the corner opposite his packs and spread his bedroll on top of it, making a soft, comfortable bed. He could hear the loud voices coming from the saloon fifty yards away, but they were not enough to delay his falling asleep almost immediately.

Praise for the first Coffeehouse Mystery

ON WHAT GROUNDS

#1 Paperback Bestseller
Independent Mystery Booksellers Association

"The first book in Coyle's new series is a definite winner! The mystery is first rate, and the characters that leap from the page are compelling, vivid, and endearing. The aroma of this story made this non–coffee drinker want to visit the nearest coffee bar." —*Romantic Times*

"[A] clever, witty, and light-hearted cozy. Cleo Coyle is a bright new light on the mystery horizon." —*The Best Reviews*

"*On What Grounds* introduces Clare and the Village Blend. The setting is wonderful and New York is portrayed with absolute accuracy. Clare is a character I would love to see more of. She is honest but never brutal and her intelligence is what shines through. I will be looking forward to the next book in the Coffeehouse Mystery series!"
—*Cozies, Capers & Crimes*

"A great beginning to a new series . . . Clare and Matteo make a great team . . . Plenty of coffee lore, trivia, and brewing tips scattered throughout the text (and recipes at the end) add an additional, enjoyable element. *On What Grounds* will convert even the most fervent tea drinker into a coffee lover in the time it takes to draw an espresso."
—*The Mystery Reader*

"A hilarious blend of amateur detecting with some romance thrown in the mix . . . I personally adored this book and can't wait to read the rest of the series!" —*Cozy Library*

"A fun, light mystery. Recommended." —*KLIATT*

"For those who enjoy not only a mystery but a chance to learn about a favorite beverage and a chance to try out new recipes at home—this book is for you." —*Gumshoe Review*

Coffeehouse Mysteries by Cleo Coyle

ON WHAT GROUNDS
THROUGH THE GRINDER
LATTE TROUBLE
MURDER MOST FROTHY
DECAFFEINATED CORPSE

Decaffeinated Corpse

Cleo Coyle

BERKLEY PRIME CRIME, NEW YORK

THE BERKLEY PUBLISHING GROUP
Published by the Penguin Group
Penguin Group (USA) Inc.
375 Hudson Street, New York, New York 10014, USA
Penguin Group (Canada), 90 Eglinton Avenue East, Suite 700, Toronto, Ontario M4P 2Y3, Canada
(a division of Pearson Penguin Canada Inc.)
Penguin Books Ltd., 80 Strand, London WC2R 0RL, England
Penguin Group Ireland, 25 St. Stephen's Green, Dublin 2, Ireland (a division of Penguin Books Ltd.)
Penguin Group (Australia), 250 Camberwell Road, Camberwell, Victoria 3124, Australia
(a division of Pearson Australia Group Pty. Ltd.)
Penguin Books India Pvt. Ltd., 11 Community Centre, Panchsheel Park, New Delhi—110 017, India
Penguin Group (NZ), 67 Apollo Drive, Rosedale, North Shore 0745, Auckland, New Zealand
(a division of Pearson New Zealand Ltd.)
Penguin Books (South Africa) (Pty.) Ltd., 24 Sturdee Avenue, Rosebank, Johannesburg 2196, South Africa

Penguin Books Ltd., Registered Offices: 80 Strand, London WC2R 0RL, England

DECAFFEINATED CORPSE

A Berkley Prime Crime Book / published by arrangement with the authors

PRINTING HISTORY
Berkley Prime Crime mass-market edition / July 2007

Cover art by Cathy Gendron.
Cover design by Rita Frangie.
Cover logo by Rita Frangie.
Interior text design by Kristin del Rosario.

For information, address: The Berkley Publishing Group,
a division of Penguin Group (USA) Inc.,
375 Hudson Street, New York, New York 10014.

ISBN: 978-0-425-21638-5

BERKLEY® PRIME CRIME
Berkley Prime Crime Books are published by The Berkley Publishing Group,
a division of Penguin Group (USA) Inc.,
375 Hudson Street, New York, New York 10014.
The name BERKLEY PRIME CRIME and the BERKLEY PRIME CRIME design are trademarks belonging to Penguin Group (USA) Inc.

PRINTED IN THE UNITED STATES OF AMERICA

10 9 8 7 6 5 4 3 2

This book is dedicated with affection and admiration
to a brilliant sister and a fellow java lover—
Grace Alfonsi, M.D.

Acknowledgments

Special thanks to the woman and man behind the curtain—Editor Katie Day and Literary Agent John Talbot

Visit Cleo Coyle's virtual Village Blend at www.CoffeehouseMystery.com

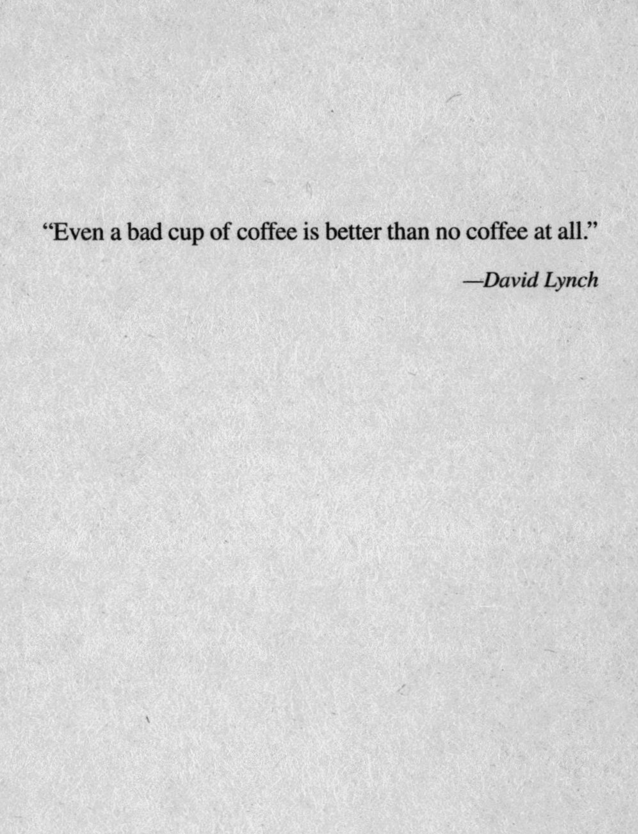

"Even a bad cup of coffee is better than no coffee at all."

—David Lynch

Prologue

In 1862 New York instituted its first gun control law, banning rifles to discourage hunting within the city limits. Over one hundred and fifty years later, at least one hunter failed to be discouraged.

Strolling along the wet, wide sidewalk of Sixth Avenue, this particular hunter found stalking prey a simplistic pursuit. Actually overtaking it, however, was a trickier matter. Unlike mouse or bird or lesser mammal, this prey wasn't small, and it wasn't weak. This prey was at least six feet in height and possessed muscles enough to fight back should it feel threatened.

Street after street, the two walked, pursuer and pursued, the little covert parade taking them from quiet Perry to bustling Bleecker then picturesque Grove, by pizzerias, novelty shops, bistros, bookstores, and boutiques.

The setting sun had swept in a passing storm, killing the reassuring warmth of the clear October day. Having failed to dress for the weather, the hunter shivered. The newly purchased windbreaker and Yankee cap were thin protection against the rapidly plunging temperature. But conditions weren't all bad. The location, at least, was an advantageous place to tail a pedestrian.

The narrow, winding lanes of this small historic district weren't nearly as congested as other parts of Manhattan—downtown's glass-and-steel Financial District, for instance, or the sardine-packed sidewalks of Midtown with its hordes of tourists stopping dead to take cell phone photos of twenty-story digital billboards and send them god knew where.

Here in this quaint little town within a town, genteel residents roved at their leisure, walking groomed dogs, carting home groceries, clustering on corners to chat with neighbors. All obstacles were easy enough to dart around in pursuit of the moving target, and the elegant brick row houses provided ample doorways to hide should the prey decide to double back.

But the prey never did. Not once did he glance over the shoulder of his fine suede jacket. With the compact umbrella now collapsed at his side, the dashing, accomplished, ebony-haired entrepreneur strode forward with confidence, even arrogance, like a bullet seeking a bull's-eye. He walked the way he lived his life, unmindful of the people around him, his primary concern penetrating the path ahead.

Before one last corner was turned, toward the Village Blend, the hunter pulled on the ski mask, then shoved down all remaining reservations, along with the bill of the brand new Yankee cap. Reaching into a jacket pocket, chilled fingers found cold courage—the hard handle of an unlicensed .38.

My little leveler, the hunter thought, less than a pound of metal, but with it the balance of power is about to tip in my favor . . .

One

FOR some of my customers, Greenwich Village is more a time than a place. They remember my neighborhood when Bob Dylan was young, when Allen Ginsberg howled poetry, Andy Warhol shot avant-garde films, and Sam Shepard waited tables while scribbling award-winning plays.

A few really old school hipsters like to go back even further (with or without the help of modern chemistry), to the days when rents for a one-bedroom flat were one hundred dollars a month, instead of the current two thousand, and Edward Albee was making a living delivering telegrams while he wrote *Zoo Story*. They see a young Marlon Brando, in black leather cruising the cobblestone streets on his motorcycle, and James Dean whiling away his hours at the Rienze coffeehouse that was once on MacDougal.

I certainly understand the appeal of mental time travel. Back then, the Village was the "Paris of New York," a passionate little bohemia, where hundreds of artists toiled in garret studios beside working-class immigrants. Poets scribbled all day and recited their masterpieces in cafes the same night, and young men and women, wearing black turtlenecks, argued intensely for hours about Nietzsche and Sartre over espressos and cigarettes.

These days, starving artists are living in the working class neighborhoods of Brooklyn and Queens. Any poets residing in the landmark, ivy-covered townhouses between Fourteenth and West Fourth are either drawing down trust fund annuities or temping for Wall Street law firms. And although young men and women still do argue for hours over espressos in my coffeehouse, cigarettes now carry a twenty-eight point violation by New York City's Department of Health and Mental Hygiene.

On the other hand, the caffeinated heart of Greenwich Village hasn't flatlined yet. Fueled by cabarets and bistros, Off-Broadway Theaters, and flamboyant gay pride, my neighborhood remains one of the most alive and eclectic parts of Manhattan. Where else can you see the 1852 house where Louisa May Alcott wrote *Little Women* sharing the same block as a body piercing and tattoo parlor?

Like the White Horse Tavern (founded 1880), Cherry Lane Theater (1924), Marshall Chess Club (1915), and Chumley's pub and restaurant (1927), the Village Blend stands as part of this neighborhood's dwindling continuity. For over one hundred years, the coffeehouse I manage has served the highest rated cup of java in the city. And when customers walk through our beveled glass door today—be they NYU college students, S&S advertising execs, Chase bank tellers, St. Vincent's paramedics, or Seventh Avenue street performers—they expect a warm, fresh, satisfying experience in a cup.

Most are also expecting stimulation, i.e. caffeine.

This, too, is a marked change from bygone days. When struggling painters and writers stumbled through the Blend's doors in the '50s and '60s, many were looking to pass out on the second floor couches. According to Madame, who'd been managing the place back then, she never minded.

The French-born, silver-haired Madame Dreyfus Allegro Dubois, herself a Village landmark, is now the Blend's owner. Her own acquaintance with despair (having lost mother, sister, and family fortune during her flight from Nazi-occupied Paris) is almost certainly what prompted her to enable alcohol-soaked playwrights and painters to treat the Blend as a second home. Back then, even after the aroma of her bold dark roasts would sober them up in the mornings, they'd go right back to the bottle the next night. So perhaps you can understand why, when I found the body slumped in our alleyway one night, I'd thought for a moment I'd gone back in time.

The man was too well dressed to be homeless, and I flashed on those stories Madame used to tell of so many artists and writers falling victim to the bottle or the needle. But this was no longer the Village of the '50s and '60s. A well-dressed gentleman passed out in an alley was practically unheard of. Residents in this area might still favor wardrobes the color of outer space, but few wanted to "drop out" anymore. They didn't want to get stoned, either. What they primarily wanted to get was "wired," which, in my circle of the universe, had as much to do with 24/7 connectivity as the act of sucking down premium priced Italian coffee drinks from dawn till midnight.

Like me, my customers universally loved the bean buzz, which is why, on the same night I'd found that slumped-over man in our alley, three of my best baristas were horrified when I called them together—not to observe the body, because I hadn't found it yet, but to taste a new kind of decaffeinated coffee.

Yes, I'd said it . . . the "D" word.

I, Clare Cosi, consecrator of caffeine, scorner of the neutered brew, had seen the decaffeinated light. Unfortunately, my baristas hadn't. Upon hearing the dreaded adjective, Esther, Tucker, and Gardner glared at me as if I'd just uttered an offensive political opinion . . .

"*Decaffeinated* coffee?"

"Say what?"

"Omigawd, sweetie, you've got to be kidding!"

We were all gathered behind the coffee bar's blueberry marble counter. Hands on hips, I stood firm, determined to reverse the barista revolt. "I know we've had trouble with quality in the past, but this is something new."

"Something new?" Esther echoed. "So it's *not* Swiss Watered-down?"

An NYU student, Esther Best (shortened from Bestovasky by her grandfather) hailed from the suburbs of Long Island. A zaftig girl with wild dark hair, she favored black rectangular glasses, performed slam poetry in the East Village, and maintained a Web profile under the upbeat pen name Morbid Dreams.

"No," I assured her. "These beans were not decaffeinated by the Swiss Water Process."

"Then it's the Royal Select method," Tucker presumed.

Tucker Burton was my best barista and a trusted assistant manager. For a few months earlier this year, however, the lanky Louisiana-born actor/playwright had landed a recurring role in a daytime drama, and I feared we'd lose him. Then the television writers had Tucker's character shoot his boyfriend and himself in a jealous rage—and I was back to enjoying the pleasure of his company.

"Isn't the Royal Select method the best way to decaffeinate beans these days?" he asked.

"No," I replied. "I mean, yes, that's probably the best method for the money—even though it's really just the

Swiss Water Process moved down to Mexico—but no, these beans weren't processed that way, either."

Esther sighed. "Meet the new decaf, same as the old decaf."

"C'mon, guys," I cajoled. "Keep your minds open."

"Boss, you know the quality of un-coffee just sucks compared to unadulterated beans, no matter what method you use to decaffeinate them. And decaf's not what this place is about anyway."

"Word," Gardner said. "Gotta agree with my Best girl."

In a rare show of sentiment, Esther responded to Gardner Evan's laid-back smile with the slightest blushing on her pallid cheeks. Gardner was from the D.C. area. The young African-American composer, arranger, and jazz musician worked for me part-time between gigs with his quartet, Four on the Floor.

"It's all about the caffeine hook up," he insisted, stroking his new goatee.

"Of course it is!" Tucker threw up his hands. "We're the crack house for the ADD generation."

My staff's reactions weren't entirely unexpected. Most baristas viewed asking for decaf on a par with asking a French chef to hold the butter. Even coffeehouse slang had labeled it a "why bother"?

Still, the last time I'd researched the subject for a trade journal article, I'd learned that fifteen to eighteen percent of coffeehouse customers wanted the lead out. The Village Blend was coming up short in that department. Over the years, we'd given a number of decaffeinated methods a shot on our menu, but maintaining the trademark Village Blend quality had been a challenge.

Decaffeination robs beans of their acidity (coffee speak, not for bitterness but the lovely brightness of flavor that keeps the drink from tasting flat). On top of that, the best decaffeination methods required fifty-five bag minimums. To manage that amount, the Blend had to rely on a third party roaster, since decaffeinated green beans had a significantly shorter shelf life than untouched beans. But that solution went against our century-old philosophy of micro-roasting daily.

The product quality sank so low, we just pulled it. At the moment, the only decaffeinated item we carried was "Coffee Milk" (coffee syrup mixed with moo juice, which we served hot or cold; skim or soy; regular or decaf). The drink was introduced to me by our new part-time barista, Dante Silva, regrettably absent tonight.

A compact guy with a shaved head and some interesting tattoos, Dante was a young painter with one modest gallery show to his credit. He was also born and raised in Rhode Island, where Coffee Milk was apparently the official state drink.

So even though I could certainly understand the skepticism on the part of Esther, Gardner, and Tucker when it came to the decaf coffee thing, I implored them to: "Keep your minds open, okay? There's a very good reason we're doing this."

Unfortunately, the reason we were doing this was *late*—that is, Matt was late, which wasn't like him. Not in the last few years anyway.

Matteo Allegro was an international coffee broker and the Village Blend's coffee buyer. One day in the future, after his mother, Madame, passed away (which I certainly prayed would not be anytime soon) Matt and I would become the legal co-owners of the Blend as well as the multimillion-dollar four-story Federal-style townhouse it occupied.

Neither Matt nor I had much in the way of savings, so both of us were committed to maintaining the business's viability. Our relationship, however, was not always on the best of terms.

A decade ago, when Matt was my husband, he was frequently late and often lied. The dashing, ebony-haired, extreme-sports globetrotter was also constantly wired, but not on caffeine. The train wreck of his life (and therefore mine) happened over a pile of cocaine.

Now whenever Matt was late for anything, I automatically tensed inside, a kneejerk of nostalgia, not for penniless artists painting in sun-washed garrets or actors in black leather cruising on motorcycles, but those lovely days in my own Village memories when I'd been trying to raise a young daughter while constantly asking myself where my husband was.

"Did you see the *Science Times* piece on caffeine?" asked Esther, bringing my attention back to the business at hand. "Apparently, it's the most widely used stimulant in the world—"

Tucker waved his hand. "I read that piece, too. Ninety percent of Americans ingest it daily, but they don't just get it in coffee. Soda, tea, chocolate—they all have caffeine, and—"

"My *point*, if you'd let me make it, is that caffeinated coffee stimulates frontal lobe activity in the brain, so working memory is improved. It also lights up the anterior cingulum, which controls your ability to focus attention, so I'm not dumping it anytime soon." Esther pushed up her black glasses. She tapped her wristwatch. "Boss, how long is this going to take? I'm giving a reading in ninety minutes, and I need to change."

"Aw, Best girl," Gardner winked. "Don't ever change."

Esther smirked. "Don't pull my chain, Bird man."

Gardner laughed.

Esther's impatience couldn't be blamed totally on her overstimulated anterior cingulum. Her shift had ended twenty minutes ago, and I'd asked her to hang around until Matt showed.

I reached beneath my blue Village Blend apron and felt for the cell phone in my jeans pocket. I pulled it out, flipped it open.

No messages.

My annoyance was changing to worry. Matt was over an hour late now. Had something happened to him? Why hadn't he called? I pushed the speed dial for his cell and reached his voicemail.

With a sigh, I went ahead with the tasting preparations. As I set up a second burr grinder beside our espresso machine, I made the quality-control point to my staff that when properly preparing decaf for service (as we were about to do again) one grinder should be used for caffeinated beans and a second for decaffeinated beans.

I ground the beans coarsely and measured the grinds into a large French press. The water was simmering on the burner, but I didn't want to pour until Matt arrived. Once again, I tried his cell number. I was just hitting speed dial when I heard the bell over the Blend's front door give a little jingle.

On this rainy Tuesday evening, only six of the Blend's nineteen marble-topped tables were occupied. In the last forty minutes, we'd had a mere two new patrons approach the coffee bar, so we were a little surprised by the arrival of a new customer, until we realized we hadn't gotten one. Coming through the door at long last, was my ex-husband.

Anxious to grill him, I closed my cell phone and set it down on the counter—an act I would soon regret.

Two

"WHERE were you? I couldn't reach you? What happened? Why didn't you call?"

A moment after barking these charming queries, I wanted to take them back. Matt and I functioned best when we communicated in a cordial, businesslike manner. The tone I'd just used had more attitude than a jilted fiancée on *Dr. Phil*.

Matt didn't appear bothered by it. He walked up to the coffee bar, flashing one of his confident, masculine smiles. "Sorry, honey."

Behind the counter, I tensed even more.

"Honey" was a term of endearment appropriate for a married couple. We were no longer married. I'd pointed this out several times. Matt never disagreed. He usually turned sheepish, saying it was a hard habit to break.

"Well, please try harder to break it," I'd told him just last week, "because you've clearly got a pretty steady 'honey' these days, and it's not me."

"I mean, you're right, Clare," Matt quickly amended. Beneath a new charcoal cashmere sweater and black camel hair jacket, his muscular shoulders shrugged. "I would have called, but I couldn't get a signal, and Joy wanted to come down for the tasting."

"Okay," I said. "But where . . . *wait*! Did you just say Joy's coming?"

"She's here. That's the reason I'm late."

My spirits instantly lifted. I hadn't seen my daughter in nearly three weeks, and I was used to her stopping by almost every day—if not to see her mom, then at least to get her vanilla latte fix.

"I was on the Upper East Side anyway," Matt explained, "and I checked in on her. She needed a ride downtown, so I hung around until her shift ended."

This was Joy's internship year in culinary school, which was why she was not taking classes in Soho. Instead, she was working all hours in the hot, new Upper Eastside restaurant Solange and over its even hotter gas burners. She'd be taking one more year of classes after the internship, guiding her through courses in restaurant management and marketing, and finally she'd graduate.

"Where is she then?" My head attempted to bob around my six-foot ex to see where the heck my daughter was hiding.

Matt jerked a thumb towards the front door. "She saw someone she knew on the next corner. She wanted to say hello."

Matt then began studying the customers in the coffeehouse. It didn't take long. There were only about a half-dozen men and women sitting at the Blend's cafe tables, reading books and magazines, going through work papers, or typing away on laptops.

"Where's my man, Ric?" he finally asked.

"Ric? Ric who?" asked Tucker Burton.

"Federico Gostwick." Matt checked his watch. "He was supposed to meet me here. Clare, have you seen him?"

"First of all, you didn't mention he was coming tonight. And secondly, I haven't seen him in over ten years."

I'd known Ric Gostwick fairly well back in my twenties when I was still married to Matt—in other words, ancient history. After we divorced, and I moved to New Jersey, Ric had quickly fallen out of my newly collapsed social circle.

"Maybe he dropped by already and I didn't recognize him," I said.

"Doubt it," Matt replied. "I'm sure you would have recognized him. He hasn't changed much at all, apart from his wardrobe. He's dressing a lot differently these days."

"No more ripped jeans and Sting T-shirts?"

Matt laughed. "Try tailored slacks, suede jackets, and Italian shoes."

"Yummy." Tucker laughed. "A *GQ* man."

"He didn't use to care about clothes." I met Matt's eyes. "Like somebody else I know."

Matt frowned and looked away.

"What's that about?" Tucker asked me.

"I can't imagine," I said.

Matt's gaze returned, this time to spear mine. "You know what it's about, Clare."

I did, actually. I just didn't like it.

Matt was a down-and-dirty Third World trailblazer. Meeting with coffee farmers on their high altitude plantations in Central and South America, East Africa, and Indonesia, he routinely traversed treacherous terrain and quasi-lawless territories, which meant he used to be more worried about packing proper hiking boots and a dependable weapon than displaying the latest designer duds on his athletic physique. Over the last year, however, that had changed.

At first, he'd begun dressing for success while trying to secure investors to expand our business. Then he became involved with Breanne Summour, disdainer-in-chief of *Trend* magazine. Our coffeehouse had a charming location, but Breanne's circles were among the stratosphere of international cafe society. Matt's travels with her were now taking him to different worlds, not just different countries.

She'd taken to dressing him differently, too. Using her relationship with top clothing designers, she'd been gifting Matt pieces of clothing worth thousands of dollars. One evening, I suggested in passing (admittedly, after a few *vinos* with dinner) that Breanne's infatuation with him had to be based at least partly on his willingness to be treated like a life-size Ken doll.

"I can't very well escort Bree to society events wearing old jeans and a sweat-stained safari hat," Matt had snapped in reply. *"I'll thank you to remember, Clare, that when I help her, she helps me. And when she helps me, she helps our business."*

As I continued glancing at the front door—not for any sign of Ric but of my one and only little girl—Matt checked his watch again. "I don't understand what could be keeping him. I thought by now he'd be here and you would have started the tasting for our best baristas. Is everyone here?"

"Dante Silva couldn't make it," I said. "He called and said he was running a fever so I told him to stay in bed."

"Dante who?" Matt asked.

"Oh, right. I hired him about three weeks ago, before you got back from Brazil. He's very good—trained at a coffeehouse near Brown."

"Sorry, guys," Esther broke in. "But if you don't start soon, I've got to bolt."

"Then let's start," Matt said, shrugging out of his exquisite camel hair blazer. While he pushed up the sleeves of his cashmere sweater, I poured the hot water (simmering but off the boil) over the beans in the French press, gave it a quick stir to start the brewing process, replaced the lid with the plunger in the raised position, and hit the timer (four to five minutes is optimal for the French press method).

As I set up cups on the counter, I enjoyed the aromatics of the brewing decaf. Seductive and sweet, they promised a rich, flavorful experience to come. The timer went off and I pushed the plunger down—the "press" part of this brewing method, in which a fine metal screen forces the denuded grounds to the bottom of the glass cylinder, separating them from the finished coffee.

A truly professional cuptasting or "cupping" was a much more primitive endeavor, involving slurping up wet grinds from spoons, spraying the entire palette, and spitting the mess back out again. Tonight, however, I simply wanted a few of my baristas' reactions to a finished cup.

I poured out the samples. The French Press produces a coffee thicker in texture than the drip method—although not as thick as espresso. For my part, the taste of this new coffee was bold and bright, with intense depth and complexity and a satisfying mouthfeel. In the world of decaffeinated, it was perfection, a triumph.

"This can't be decaf," Esther declared.

"Agreed," Gardner said. "Must be a mistake."

"Clare, did you get confused?" Tucker asked, glancing at the two grinders on the working counter below the marble coffee bar. "Maybe you burred the wrong beans?"

"No, Tucker. Those are the right beans," I assured him. "They really are decaffeinated."

"What process then?" Esther pressed.

"No process," Matt informed them.

My baristas' heads swiveled towards my ex. They gawked in silent confusion.

"These coffee beans were grown on a brand new hybrid plant," Matt explained, "a *decaffeinated* coffee plant."

"No way," Gardner murmured.

"Say again?" Esther asked.

"My friend Ric Gostwick made the breakthrough after years of horticultural experimentation," Matt continued. "His beans don't need decaffeination because they already are."

Esther blinked in shock. "You're kidding."

Matt laughed. "I just made the deal with Ric. We're announcing it together at the ICGE this week."

"What's the ICGE?" Esther asked.

"Omigawd, Esther!" Tucker cried. "There's something you don't *know*!"

"Put a designer sock in it, Tuck."

"Don't get snarky, goth girl."

"The ICGE is the International Coffee Growers Exhibition." Matt checked his watch again. "And if Ric were here, he would be explaining that he needs your help at the Beekman Hotel this Friday night for coffee service. He's going to hold a tasting for the international press."

"Hold the phone!" Tucker looked excited. "A press conference?"

"That's right." Matt smiled. "Ric will be unveiling his breakthrough. And he'll be announcing the news that the Village Blend and its international kiosks will be the exclusive rollout for his new decaffeinated beans. So be sure to wear your Blend aprons for the event."

Esther, Tucker, and Gardner stared with gaping mouths

at the news. I already knew, of course, but it was a thrill to see their stunned faces.

Matt grinned wider. His eyes met mine.

Like Jack and the Beanstalk, my ex had brought home a bag of beans. They weren't magic, but they might as well have been because they were the find of a lifetime, a fortune in a cup.

Oh, honey, you did it, I thought, but didn't dare say, especially the "honey" part. Then the bell over the front door jingled again.

"Hi, everyone!"

My daughter finally bounded in, her spirits as high as her chestnut ponytail. Everyone said hello as she stepped around the counter and reached down to give me a hug. I was barely five two, and Joy outdid me by a good four inches. Or, at least, she used to. At the moment, she looked about five nine.

"Have you grown in three weeks?"

She laughed. "It's the shoes."

I glanced down to see the three inch wedged heels. "You aren't working in those?"

"C'mon, Mom, don't be a nudge." She shot a brief, embarrassed glance at Esther, Gardner, and Tucker, presumably because I was talking to her like she was my child, which she was, so I really didn't see the problem.

"I changed after work. My sneakers are in here." She pointed to the backpack slung over her shoulder.

"How's it going at the restaurant?" I asked.

"Amazing! Tommy's been fantastic!"

"Tommy?"

"I mean, Chef Keitel. He's been so incredibly helpful to me."

"Incredibly helpful? Uh-huh. And I'll bet he's very tall, too, isn't he?"

"Yeah! Like six four! How did you know?"

I glanced at Joy's stacked wedges. "Just a guess."

Esther loudly cleared her throat. I looked her way and she tapped her wristwatch. "Sorry, I've got to bolt."

Esther and Gardner agreed to serve next week, and they both took off, Gardner heading north for a late night jam session, and Esther heading east to slam out her poetry.

As Tucker overwhelmed Matt with questions, and Joy began sampling Ric's decaffeinated beans, I cleaned up the cups and French press. I smiled, listening to their chatty enthusiasm. I felt it too, that energy and anticipation of being on the cusp of something new. I wanted to keep listening. Unfortunately, the under-counter garbage can was nearly overflowing.

I could have left it for Tucker, but I felt guilty. He was going to be alone for closing tonight as it was, since Dante had called in sick. The least I could do was help him out with some cleaning and restocking before I called it a night myself.

I lifted the green plastic lining out of the silver can and twist-tied it closed. Then I headed for the back door, which sat between our storage pantry and the service staircase.

Downstairs was the basement, where we kept our green beans and roaster. Upstairs was the Blend's second floor, a cozy area of overstuffed armchairs and sofas. The third and fourth floors were a private, duplex apartment where I lived, sharing off and on with Matt, whenever he was in town, which thankfully wasn't often.

As a police siren suddenly screamed to life right outside our tall front windows, I yanked open the heavy back door and stepped into the alley.

The Blend was pleasantly situated on a street corner. Our front faced brightly lit, well-traveled Hudson. Our long, side wall featured a line of French doors. Stretching the length of the first floor, the doors paralleled a quiet, residential side street with sidewalks wide enough to use for outside seating in good weather.

The back of the Blend was my least favorite part of the property. Like all alleys, ours was a gloomy strip of unadorned concrete that ran the length of the building. We kept our Dumpster back here, which was emptied twice a week by a private hauling company.

I moved toward it now through the chilly wet drizzle. Although New York enjoyed temperate Octobers, with days as high as seventy, tonight's weather had turned downright raw. The clouds were thick, and the early evening already looked darker than our Italian-roasted Sumatra. Eager to get back inside, I lifted the Dumpster's lid with one hand and heaved the green plastic bag inside the metal container.

For a split second, I glanced up, toward the end of the alley. That's when I saw it—a dim outline slumped against our building's brick wall.

My god . . .

I stood and gawked for a stunned five seconds. Then I let go of the Dumpster's lid, barely registering the earsplitting clang of the heavy metal.

There's a body, I realized. *There's a body in my alley.*

THREE

LONG after the fact, what I did next would seem less than brilliant. Okay, *yes,* in retrospect, I probably should have run back inside and yelled for help. I should have been too upset to be intrigued, but I wasn't.

Why exactly I felt no fear, I couldn't swear to. Maybe what I witnessed on 9/11 makes all other potential threats seem trivial. Maybe now that my daughter has left home, I'm done with being circumspect 24/7. Maybe it was simply a residual by-product of excessive caffeine consumption, but I'd reached a point in my life when potential threats no longer cowed me. Something spurred me forward . . . in this case, through the shadows behind the Blend.

For a moment, I couldn't make out much more than a silhouette at the end of the alley. The misty darkness was too thick, the streetlight's illumination stopping at the sidewalk. I considered this might be a homeless person, even though the homeless were much more prevalent in the funkier East Village than the more affluent West, and when they took to sleeping (or passing out) on the New York pavement, authorities picked them up and delivered them to city shelters.

Shelters weren't a picnic. The homeless avoided them for many reasons, including fear of theft—of what little property they had—and violence, or unwillingness to comply with the shelter's rules. But the imperfect system was better than some of the bleaker alternatives.

When I'd first managed the Blend, in my twenties, I'd come across a homeless man during a morning walk. I'd dropped Joy off at kindergarten and was in no hurry to return to our little apartment. Matt had stumbled in during the wee hours, zonked after an endless flight from somewhere—Hawaii, Mexico, Costa Rica . . . take your pick. Silly me wanted to surprise him by doing his unpacking, but I was the one who'd gotten the surprise. I'd found it buried at the bottom of his Pullman: a box of condoms.

For a few pathetic seconds, I'd tried to tell myself that my young husband had bought the box upon touchdown at JFK, anticipating his return to our bed. But it was far too easy to examine the box and see that there were not in fact twenty-four foiled packets inside, as the black box with the purple lettering proclaimed. There were fourteen.

During his three weeks away from me, Matt had used ten condoms—and I doubted very much he'd used them during the ninety-minute taxi ride from Queens to Manhattan.

It wasn't the last time Matt would stray. For years he would deny it. The condom box, he would later explain, was something he'd had on hand for weeks before the trip and packed in case I decided to fly out and join him for a weekend. I'd accepted such a lame excuse for the same reason all wives of cheating husbands do: I didn't want my marriage to end.

On that particular morning, the morning I found the

condoms, I was still too much in love with Matt. I also loved managing his mother's coffeehouse, baking for the customers, having little Joy play in the Blend after school, usually with my mother-in-law stopping in for a visit. Every busy morning and sunny afternoon felt achingly familiar, like the days of my childhood in Pennsylvania, when I practically lived with my grandmother in her Italian grocery.

That box of condoms was a live grenade thrown into the middle of my sweet, cozy life. I was shocked, hurt, furious. Matt was still snoring away in bed, and I wanted to throttle him in his sleep, throw the box at him, demand an explanation. But I didn't—

Little Joy was calling me. It was time to take her to school. So I took her. Then I took myself on a long walk along the river to think. The February morning was frigid, but I didn't care. I chose a path that would insure me some privacy to consider Matt, my marriage, and what I'd discovered. And then I discovered something else—a body.

I still remember how the corpse had been dressed, with so many layers of sweatshirts he couldn't close the buttons on his long, soiled overcoat. The coat was a finely tailored garment, the kind a CEO's new wife might have given away during the city's annual winter coat drive, gleefully making room in her husband's closets for more fashionable frocks.

A two-wheeled handcart stood beside the frozen man, overflowing with three bulging green garbage bags, presumably his only possessions. Newspapers covered his torso and legs, a collection of dailies others had read and tossed. One stiff hand gripped an empty bottle of vodka, the drunk's method for keeping warm, which killed you all the faster when you were out in the cold.

This was every struggling, transplanted New Yorker's

nightmare: to end up alone, destitute, living on the street. . . . I called 911 and waited for the ambulance to come, watched the paramedics zip him into a body bag and wheel him away on a stretcher.

There was no ID on the dead man, and I wondered who he'd been in life, how he'd fallen so far, whether anyone would cry over his death. Then I realized I was crying, since I'd been too late to care.

I wandered home, feeling weak and mortal, my anger chilled by dread. My grandmother had passed away by then, my father was serving time in a penitentiary for running an illegal sports book, and my mother had been gone from my life since I was seven.

If I left Matt, Joy would come with me. But would I be able to properly provide for her, give her what she might want or need? In the dead of winter, in my early twenties, I didn't think I could. And Matt was far from a harsh or aloof partner, quite the opposite. When he was actually around, he'd been an understanding companion, an adoring lover, and a doting dad. Like it or not, I was still very passionately in love with my husband.

Thus began my master's program in ignoring and pretending, tolerating and rationalizing: *Matt's not cheating. I buy his explanations . . . okay, Matt is cheating, but he says the sex means nothing, a physical experience with no more meaning than his mountain biking or rock climbing . . . Matt's drug use is no big deal. He has the cocaine under control . . .*

It would take me a decade to douse my burning infatuation for my larger-than-life husband, corral my runaway fears. At twenty-nine, I would finally build up the courage to quit the job I'd loved, managing the Blend for Madame, and move to New Jersey with Joy. A shaky collection of part-time employment followed, which led to a viable career as a freelance writer—first with a regular culinary column in a local paper, then trade magazine pieces, and even one article in the *New York Times*.

It would take me another ten years to forgive my child's father, decide and admit what I really wanted (this partnership in the Blend), and stop making my life about hiding and withdrawing, worrying and retreating, even when things looked dubious or dangerous . . . like now.

AS I continued to move through the shadows of my alley, I became more and more concerned about the slumped-over man. Was he just passed out? Knocked out? Or worse?

Within a few feet of him, I finally saw that he was too well dressed to be homeless. His gorgeous tan jacket was butter-soft suede; his fine brown slacks, the caramelized color of espresso crema. Neither appeared worn or ripped. He was propped in a sitting position against our back wall, his arms and legs limp.

I remembered Madame's stories—the poets and painters of ye olde hipster Village. But things had changed too much since the days of the beat generation. Today's West Villagers didn't get falling down drunk on a nightly basis. The residents of this era were all about civilized, progressive attitudes and sophisticated tastes. And it just wasn't sophisticated to get so blotto you peed in St. Luke's churchyard and vomited on your obscenely expensive Bruno Magli shoes.

The unconscious man appeared to be attractive, too, not just well dressed. His sturdy, clean-shaven chin rested on a solid chest. The stranger's head was bowed, his black hair cut just like Matt's, in a neat, masculine Caesar. In fact, if I hadn't seen Matt inside the Blend, I might have mistaken this man for my ex.

"Hello?" I called softly. "Are you all right?"

Brilliant, Clare, of course he's not all right.

Was he even breathing? I bent over the body, peered into his face and gasped. The man on the ground wasn't a stranger. It took me a few seconds, but the memory came back to me . . . the man in my alley was Federico Gostwick.

Matt was right, I realized. Ric looked as if he'd hardly aged one year, let alone ten. I could see he was breathing; and, thank goodness, he wasn't dead, but he obviously needed help.

My hand slipped under my apron. I felt around for the small, hard rectangle in my jeans pocket, but it wasn't there. My cell phone was missing. I couldn't call 911 because I'd left it behind the counter!

I was ready to dash back inside when I heard footsteps on the nearby sidewalk, crisp and quick, aggressive, purposeful. I turned my head toward the approaching passerby, and that's when I felt the shove—hard and deliberate.

I was half crouched over Ric, off balance already, and the violent push propelled me forward, into the old bricks. For a split second, I think I was out. I remember the slamming connection to the cold wall, then nothing for a moment. I blinked and realized I was down on the ground.

My hands moved under me, wet pebbles scratching my palms. My apron felt heavy, restrictive. I struggled to rise, but the ground seemed to tilt dramatically, like those old *Batman* TV shows when the villain was cackling with evil glee. I fell back again. The icy drizzle stung my face and hands, the nearby Dumpster smelled rank. I heard the distant scream of a police siren, glimpsed a navy blue baseball hat, the trademark NY logo embroidered above the bill.

For a split second the Yankee cap was there, resting near me on the concrete. Then it was gone, snatched away. I sat up quickly but saw no one close by—except Ric's body, still slumped against the wall.

The top of my forehead was throbbing as I scrambled to my feet. My breathing was fast and shallow. I was disturbed, angry, and yes, *finally*, I was scared. Still, I had to risk a look. Stepping carefully, I moved beyond the alley, hoping to catch the glimpse of a figure running away on the sidewalk or lurking in a nearby townhouse doorway.

I peered east down the dark, quiet street; then west, toward brightly lit Hudson. I searched for any sign—male or female, short or fat, tall or thin. But there was not one human being on the block. Not that I could see. The night's shadows had cloaked my attacker.

He . . . or she . . . had vanished.

Four

"Hand me your cell phone," I asked Matt five minutes later.

"Why?"

"Because I left mine behind the counter, and I'm calling 911!"

We were back inside the Blend. I'd already sounded the alarm. Matt had followed me outside, Tucker on his heels, and I'd led them to the end of the alleyway.

By then, Ric's eyelids had fluttered open, and he was making groggy, incomprehensible noises. Matt and Tucker helped him inside and lowered him into an easy chair by the fireplace so we could take a look at his condition.

Joy rushed across the wood plank floor when she saw us coming, bumping through our cafe tables, most of them still empty. Those few customers nursing cappuccinos and espressos lifted their heads from their laptops, newspapers, and trade paperbacks. But as we closed ranks around Ric and lowered our voices, they went back to minding their own business—a skill ninety-nine percent of New Yorkers have perfected.

(I'd once seen a four-hundred-pound man in a purple flowered muumuu belt out the entire first act of *Oklahoma* between Canal and 116th streets on the Number One train, and every rider in the subway pretended absolutely nothing out of the ordinary was happening. It wasn't that hard to believe. I'd been one of those riders pretending.)

As I tore off my wet, dirty apron, I quickly explained to Matt, Tucker, and Joy what had happened in the alley: that Ric was not passed out drunk; he'd been attacked, most likely by the same person who'd shoved me into the Blend's brick wall. That's when I asked Matt for his cell phone to call the authorities.

"Don't do that," Ric murmured to me.

"Don't do *what*?"

"Don't call 911."

I stared in confusion. Those three little numbers represented more than the date of an infamous terrorist attack. Once dialed, the common citizen could immediately summon his own little uniformed army, including a team of battle-hardened paramedics. It was a tax-funded service any medieval duke would have envied, and I was more than ready to take advantage of it. So why the heck wasn't Ric?

"Please," he said, "no police."

"But you need to report what happened," I said, "and get some medical attention—"

"I'm fine. Really, it's no big deal."

"Of course it's a big deal!"

Ric remained adamant, and I considered calling 911 anyway. After all I was assaulted, too, and right in my back alley. But then I stopped to consider . . . there might be reasons Ric was reluctant to deal with the NYPD.

"Is it your paperwork?" I asked. "Is your visa expired?"

Ric shook his head. "No. I'm legally here . . . I just don't believe we need to make a large matter of this . . . May I have something to drink?"

Everyone nodded, and Joy ran off to get Ric some water, but I refused to budge—physically or mentally.

Although I hadn't seen Federico Gostwick in years, I remembered a few things about the man. His striking good looks for one. With a British dad and Caribbean mom, he'd inherited an amazing combination of features: the patrician profile and six feet of height from his father; the olive complexion and thick ebony hair from his mother. Add fluid mastery of Spanish and Portuguese, English spoken with a slight British accent, and a romantic nature, and he had a recipe for (quite literally) charming the pants off any woman he met.

That gave me pause . . . had Ric known his attacker? Was it a jilted girlfriend perhaps or a jealous husband?

I lowered my voice. "I won't call the police," I told him. "But I want you to tell me every detail of what happened out there."

"Sure, love, but there's not much to tell . . ." He shrugged. "I was coming down the side street, on the way to your front door on Hudson, when someone approached me from behind. I remembered a sharp poke in my back, like the end of a gun shoving into my ribs. Then *bam* . . ."

Ric fell silent and rubbed the back of his head. There had to be more to this story, but he'd stopped talking. I glanced at Matt.

C'mon, help me out here.

I waited for my usually glib ex to ask some questions of his own, argue with his friend about his reluctance to call the police. In the face of my pointed stare, Matt said not a word.

With a frustrated exhale, I turned back to Ric. "What do

you mean *bam*?" I pressed. "Didn't your attacker speak? Ask for anything?"

Ric shook his head. "There was only this mechanical-like voice—"

"Mechanical?" Tucker repeated. He and I exchanged confused glances. "What do you mean?"

"You know, uh"—Ric's hand waved, some Spanish phrases followed, and then—"the kind you hear on answering machines?"

"Answering machines? You mean . . . a computerized voice like this?" Tucker asked, giving an impression that landed somewhere between Stephen Hawking and the automated teller who answers my bank's phone.

Ric nodded. "That's it, but it wasn't coming from a person the way you just did it. This voice sounded tinny, like it was being played on a recorder."

Tucker's nose wrinkled up on his angular face. He glanced at me. "That seems odd. A mugger with a prerecorded message?"

"Yeah, that's odd, all right," I said. "So, what did this mechanical voice say?"

Ric shrugged. "I have a gun in your back. Put your hands up."

"Did you?" I asked.

"Yes."

"Then what happened?" Joy asked. She'd returned by now and was handing Ric a cup of water.

As Ric sipped, he regarded Joy for a moment. "You look familiar . . ." His dark eyebrows came together. "I don't think we've met, have we?"

"That's our daughter," Matt replied.

"No! Not little Joy!"

Joy rolled her eyes. "Not little anymore, Uncle Ric."

"*Madre de dios!* You're a grown woman. It can't be that long—"

Matt folded his arms. "Over ten years, bucko."

"Look at her! She's just like her mama . . . beautiful."

"Shut up!" Joy blushed, waved her hand.

I couldn't decide if Ric's sweetness was genuine or a dodge. Joy was my daughter, so of course I thought she was beautiful . . . just not me.

"Ric," I loudly interrupted, "please finish telling us what happened back there. What did that prerecorded, mechanical voice tell you to do?"

The shrug came again, like a child reluctant to talk. "The voice said to step into the alleyway, that's all."

"And did you?"

"No," said Ric. "I stalled a second."

"Why?" Tucker asked. "Weren't you afraid of getting shot?"

"I thought perhaps I could sprint away, take my chances that there was either no gun or this person was a terrible shot. And that's when I heard the police siren, right around the corner on Hudson."

A few beat cops were regular Blend customers. Officers Langley and Demetrious stopped in almost every day for lattes and *doppio* espressos respectively, and I wondered if it had been their car. I remembered hearing that siren. It had been startling—instantaneous and close, as if the cruiser had just gotten the call from dispatch and hit the switch in front of the Blend.

"It must have spooked my mugger," Ric continued, "because the next thing I remember I was being hit hard on the head—and with something decidedly harder than my head."

Tucker tapped his chin. "Sounds like you were pistol-whipped."

Ric nodded. "I remember nothing after that, just waking up in the alley . . ."

"The mugger must have knocked you out, and then dragged you off the sidewalk." I turned to face Matt. "He was out cold," I whispered pointedly. "He could have a concussion."

Of course, I could have one, too, but I felt fine—no headache, drowsiness, or disorientation. Ric was another matter. He'd been unconscious a long time, and he'd been incoherent upon waking. It seemed to me he should be checked out ASAP.

Thank goodness Matt nodded in agreement. "Ric, I'm parked just down the block. Let me drive you over to St. Vincent's ER—"

"No, no, no ER! I'd be in there for hours for absolutely no reason. I'm fine. Really." Ric looked up at our concerned faces. "It's nice that you all care so much, but I'd really like to forget it happened." He handed Joy back the cup of water she'd brought him. "Thank you, love. But I'd like to warm up a bit. Perhaps I might trouble you for a hot coffee?"

Matt laughed. "You certainly came to the right place for that. Regular or decaf?"

"Decaf," Ric replied. "You have my beans, I take it? How did the baristas like the samples?"

Tucker spoke up. "Oh, we liked them. We like them *a latte*."

Ric smiled. "Good, good, excellent. And what is your name?"

"Tucker Burton." He gave a little bow, tossing his newly highlighted hair like a Shakespearean troubadour. "At your service."

"Ah!" Ric was obviously pleased by his enthusiasm. "I hope that will include coffee service then? Do you have any objection to helping us with our event at the Beekman Hotel at the end of the week?"

"Wouldn't miss it," Tucker assured him. "And my colleagues agreed to help you out, too. Two of them had to beat it before you got here, and the third one was supposed to be here, but he took the night off at the last minute . . ."

As Tucker continued to converse with Ric, Matt turned to me. "Clare, why don't you brew some fresh decaf for us?"

"Joy can do it." I glanced at my daughter. "Joy? Do you mind? The decaf beans are in the burr grinder marked with the green tape on the lid. Use the eight-cup French press. We'll all have some."

Joy nodded. "Sure, Mom."

The second her chestnut ponytail bounced away, I turned back to Ric. I was mystified by the man's calm. My first year living in New York, I'd been mugged on a subway platform by a skinny punk, who'd taken my purse with fifty dollars, credit cards, and lip gloss. The boy waved a knife, which never touched me, but the only thing I wanted to do after the incident (besides throw up and chug half a bottle of Pepto) was report the little creep's description to the police.

Crime is a violation. It's frightening and humiliating. It shakes your world. And after it makes you scared, it makes you angry—which it should because that's the way you begin to fight back.

Ric might have been eager to put this behind him, but I was far from satisfied; and, in my view, the bruise forming beneath my own brunette bangs gave me the right to make a few more inquiries.

"Ric!" I loudly interrupted for the second time.

Tucker and Ric halted their conversation. They stared at me as if I'd dropped a large tray at a quiet party.

"I'm sorry, but I have a few more questions."

Ric glanced pleadingly at Matt; and, brother, did I recognize that retro masculine "Can't you control your ex-wife?" expression.

Matt answered by showing his palms to the ceiling. By now, of course, he'd grown accustomed to the new me. After solving more than one homicide, I could no longer join my fellow New Yorkers in ignoring the singing four-hundred-pound muumuu-wearing man in the subway car.

"I don't believe you're thinking clearly, Ric," I said. "Since you were out cold, how do you know that you weren't ripped off?"

"Clare, Clare, Clare . . . you know you've changed since I last saw you. You're still just as beautiful, but I guess ten years is a long time. You used to be so easygoing . . ."

Easygoing? I thought. *Or a gullible pushover?*

Ric's gaze held mine. "How headstrong you've become."

The man's eyes were velvet brown, arrestingly intense with long, dark lashes. They were what women's magazines would call "bedroom eyes," but we weren't in a bedroom.

"The mugger could have rifled your clothes," I pointed out. "Have you checked them? Do you still have your wallet?"

"I have it, Clare," he assured me. "I touched my jacket as soon as I came around. My wallet's still here."

To demonstrate, Ric made a show of patting down the left breast pocket of his fine suede jacket. Then he opened it, reached inside, and pulled out his wallet.

"You see, love, no need to keep worrying that pretty head of yours."

"What about your other pockets?" I asked.

"Clare—" Matt began. I felt the light touch of his hand on my shoulder. I ignored it.

"It's all right, Matt," Ric said. "She's just being protective. She always was a little mother hen."

Which would make Matt what? I wondered. *Henpecked?*

"Look, Clare," Ric continued, "my passport isn't on me. It's back in my hotel room. I just have loose change and a handkerchief in my pants, and in this right pocket here the only thing you'll find is my—"

Ric was opening up his jacket again, this time on the right side, to show me that all was well, and I shouldn't worry my "pretty mother hen" head.

But all wasn't well.

"Omigawd!" Tucker pointed. "Your beautiful jacket."

The left side of Ric's jacket may have been fine and his wallet untouched, but the right was in tatters, its lining ripped, and whatever was inside the breast pocket was gone.

Matt stepped forward, his jovial expression gone, too. "What did you say was in that pocket?"

"My keycard," said Ric, locking eyes with Matt. "The key to my hotel room."

Five

"A keycard," Tucker said. "Good lord, that's a relief."

"A relief?" said Ric. "Why?"

"Those hotel keycards never have room numbers on them." Tucker waved a hand. "There's no way your mugger will know which room you were in."

My ex-husband remained silent; his expression had gone grim, and I knew he was finished with the laissez-faire attitude. I figured he was trying to decide whether to drive Ric directly over to the Sixth Precinct or summon the police to the scene by phone.

"Matt," I said quietly. "You should probably just drive him over—unless you don't want to lose your parking space, then you should just hail a cab."

Matt's brow wrinkled. "Why would I want to hail a cab?"

"Don't be dense. To take Ric to the Sixth Precinct so he can report the theft of his hotel key—"

"Excuse me," Matt shifted his gaze from me to Tucker

and back to me. "Clare, Tucker, I'd like a word with Ric *alone*."

"Oh," said Tucker. "Oh, sure! No problem. I'll just go help Joy with the decaf."

Tucker left. I didn't. "What's going on?"

With an audible sigh, Matt took out his cell and handed it to Ric.

"Thanks," Ric said, opening the phone.

As he began to dial, Matt took a firm hold of my elbow, and pulled me away. We stopped far from the warmth of the fireplace, against the exposed brick wall, beneath a collection of antique hand-cranked coffee grinders.

"Matt, tell me. What is going on? Who's Ric calling—"

"Clare, please," Matt whispered, his eyes glancing around to make sure no one was close enough to hear. "This was just a random robbery. Okay? Let it go."

"A random robbery?"

"Yes."

"By a mugger who uses a prerecorded message?"

"Yes."

"And doesn't take the muggee's wallet?"

"Yes."

"What's in Ric's hotel room, Matt?" I tilted my head sharply to see around my ex-husband. Ric was quietly talking into the cell phone. "Is he calling the police?"

"No. And I don't want you involved. I know you too well." Matt gestured to Joy, behind the coffee bar. "Just like your daughter."

"What's that supposed to mean?"

"You know what it means."

"No, I don't—"

"Do you know why Joy hasn't been by the Blend in weeks? She's dating someone new, and she doesn't want you to know."

"Why not?"

"Why do you think? She knows her mom's a bigger nose hound than Scooby Doo and she wants her privacy."

"Scooby Doo?" I shook my head. "Matt, I realize you missed most of Joy's upbringing, but in case you haven't noticed, she no longer watches Saturday morning cartoons—"

"Come on, Clare. We've been over this. I was young and stupid, okay? I was a lousy father and a terrible husband, and, believe me, I know what I've lost because of it . . ." Matt paused, his tone softening, his eyes holding mine. "You know, no matter what, I'd do anything for her . . . and you."

I looked away. "You're trying to change the subject. You're using Joy to make me back off of Ric—"

"I'm trying to make a point that Joy's an adult now. It's natural for her to want some privacy. So don't push too hard or you'll end up pushing her away."

Matt turned, ready to walk. I grabbed a handful of cashmere sweater. "Wait," I said. "I can help you. Why don't you think of it that way?"

Matt smoothed the wrinkles I'd made. "For one thing because Ric hasn't seen you in ten years. He's not going to trust you."

"He will if you tell him to."

The bell over the front door jingled. After years in the beverage service industry, Matt and I had the same Pavlovian response. We stopped our private conversation and glanced at the new customer. Once we saw who it was, however, our responses weren't even close to identical.

"It's Mike," I said, my mood immediately lightening.

Across the room, Detective Mike Quinn nodded in greeting. His usual glacial gaze warmed as it took me in. Then his attention shifted to Matt and the chill returned.

Matt tensed, a scowl cutting lines in his face that I hadn't seen before. "Since when did you start calling him *Mike*?"

"We're friends," I whispered. "You know that."

The lanky cop strode to the coffee bar, where he took a load off. Tucker began to make conversation with the detective, but he didn't bother filling his order. By now, all of my baristas knew the drill. When Mike Quinn came here for his usual, he had no interest in anyone making it but me.

"Do me a favor, Clare," Matt said. "Get your 'friend' his order and get him the hell out of here *tout de suite*."

Given my ex-husband's years of dealing with corrupt officials in banana republics, I understood why he distrusted the police. It occurred to me that Ric might feel the same. But Greenwich Village wasn't exactly a Third World hellhole, and in my experience the NYPD had always lived up to its "New York's finest" motto, especially Detective Quinn, who'd gone out on a limb for me more than once.

"But, Matt," I argued, "this is the perfect opportunity to ask Mike for help. If Ric is in some kind of trouble—"

"Don't tell him a thing."

Matt's words sounded resolved, but his brown eyes were filled with uncertainty. He was feeling guilty about something, I realized. He was feeling nervous, too, and that told me I had some bargaining power.

"Don't tell Mike a thing?" I put my hands on my hips and arched an eyebrow. "I can't promise you that."

Matt read me just as fast as I'd read him. "What do you want?"

"I want you and Ric to tell me everything you're holding back."

"Now? We can't. Quinn will—"

"Later. Tell me later."

Matt glanced back over his shoulder. Mike Quinn was

still chatting with Tucker. "Okay . . ." he agreed, "but not a word to Quinn tonight or the deal's off."

"And you have to take Ric to the ER," I added. "If he was pistol whipped, he could be hemorrhaging. He needs a CT scan or an MRI, but somebody's got to take a peek inside that thick skull of his."

Matt turned to look at his friend. "You're right. I'll take him . . . and what about you?"

"What about me?"

Matt surprised me by reaching out and brushing back my bangs. His thumb feathered across the darkening bruise.

"Does it hurt?" he whispered. "Don't you need to be checked out, too?"

Matt's touch was tender, warm, and sweet. I pushed it away.

"It's okay," I said.

The man's hands were dangerous. A year ago, they'd gotten me into bed, right upstairs, and I swore it would never happen again. Not ever.

"You're sure?"

"Yes!" I said, then lowered my voice. "I don't have a headache. No dizziness or sleepiness—if anything I'm more alert. Besides, I'm scheduled for my annual physical Thursday. I'll get checked out then."

Matt raised his chin in Quinn's general direction. "And you'll keep your boyfriend in the dark tonight?"

"He's not my boyfriend, Matt. He's a married man—"

"Didn't you mention that he and his wife just separated?"

"Yes, but they're not divorced yet. And he's still pretty raw."

Matt smirked, glanced at the detective again. This time Quinn glanced back at the same time. The men locked eyes for a moment.

"He'll put the moves on you inside of a week," Matt said, facing me again.

"Stop it, Matt. I told you, we're just friends."

"A week."

I pointed to Ric and glared, making it clear I meant business. "The ER. Or I spill."

"All right, we're going."

Then Matt headed one way, and I went the other.

Six

"The usual?" I asked from behind the coffee bar.

The detective nodded.

Mike Quinn was an average-looking Joe with sandy-brown hair, a slightly ruddy complexion, and a square, dependable chin. He had crow's feet and frown lines, favored beige suits, rust-colored ties, and gave sanctuary to a trench coat that had seen better years. He was also tall and lean with rock-solid shoulders and a working moral compass.

I couldn't imagine Mike as being anything but a cop. To me, he was like one of those concrete block warehouses people barely notice on a fair weather day but run screaming to for refuge in a Category Four.

And then there were his eyes. Nothing average there. Even when the rest of him appeared aloof or exhausted, Mike's eyes were alert and alive, taking in everything. Intensely blue, they were the shade of a Hampton's sky—which I had only recently discovered, having just spent my first summer there—and when they were on me, my blood pumped a little faster (even without caffeine).

Behind the counter, Joy had finished brewing that fresh French press pot of Ric's new decaffeinated beans.

"Make Ric's to go," I advised her. "He's heading out."

I was tempted to keep yakking. I wanted to ask her about that new boyfriend, the one she'd discussed with Matt and not me. It rankled that she was keeping secrets, but we'd been through some rough patches in the last year, and I could see where she might be sensitive about my meddling in her new "adult" life.

My ex-husband had been wrong about a lot of things, but I wasn't going to disregard his advice just because he could be a horse's ass in other quarters. He loved our daughter. And she loved him. And maybe, for once, Matt knew what was best.

Biting my tongue, I stopped the dozen grilling questions on the tip of it. Instead, I put an arm around her and thanked her for coming down to say hello.

"No problem, Mom," she said. "It's nice to see you." She hugged me then. It was unexpected but heartfelt, and it made me feel a thousand times better.

As she headed off toward Ric and her dad, I turned back to Quinn.

"We have something new tonight," I told him. "Beans from a prototype decaffeinated coffee plant. Would you like to try a cup?"

He arched a sandy eyebrow. "You think I come here for decaffeination?"

"Now you sound like my baristas."

"The usual," he said, his low gravelly voice like music. "That'll be fine."

It always gave me a kick to make Quinn's "usual." Before

he'd made detective, he'd been a hardened street cop, and even though he wasn't the sort of man to wear his machismo on his sleeve, I vowed never to tell him that in Italy his favorite nightly drink was considered a wussy breakfast beverage favored by children and old ladies.

The latte was also the most popular coffee drink at the Village Blend, as it was in most American gourmet coffee shops, so who was I to judge? Our double-tall version used two shots of espresso, steamed milk, crowned with a thin layer of foamed milk. (In a cappuccino, the foamed milk dominates.) And because we throw away any espresso shot older than fifteen seconds, we always prepare the milk first.

I cleared the steam wand and dipped it deep into the stainless steel pitcher. One trick for steaming milk (as I tell my new baristas) is to keep your hand on the bottom of the metal container. If it becomes too hot to handle, you're probably scalding the liquid. That's one reason I clip a thermometer to every pitcher (150 to 160 degrees Fahrenheit is the optimum range).

As I worked, I kept one eye on Matt, across the main room. He'd approached Ric, who was still sitting by the fireplace, speaking into the phone. When the man completed his call, Matt quietly spoke to him.

Without protest, Ric rose to his feet. The top of his head came dead even with Matt's. The two could have been brothers, I mused, with their perpetual tans, short-cropped raven hair, and womanizing ways. Then Ric swayed in place. The man was obviously still woozy from the blow to his head.

Matt offered an arm. "Take it easy," he said as he helped his friend negotiate the close-quartered sea of cafe tables.

As usual, our sparse gathering of patrons, barely looked up from their seats. Mike Quinn, on the other hand, tracked the two zigzagging males as if he were a fixed bird of prey.

"What happened to Matt's friend?" he asked, his gaze never wavering from the pair until the two men left the building.

I didn't want to lie, but I didn't intend to break my word either. "Oh, you can guess, can't you?"

Quinn turned back to me. "One too many decafs?"

I laughed—in an unnaturally high pitch. Since it was time to aerate the top of the milk anyway, I let the steam wand's gurgle drown out my disturbing impression of an overexcited munchkin from the land of Oz.

Now Quinn's gaze was fixed on me as I pulled two espresso shots and dumped both into a double-tall glass mug. Then I tilted the pitcher of steamed milk. Using a spoon, I held back the froth at the top, letting the velvety white warmth splash into the liquid ebony.

The Blend had a tasty variety of latte flavors—vanilla, mocha, caramel, hazelnut, cinnamon-spice, and so on—but Quinn was a purist. I finished the drink with a few spoonfuls of frothy light foam and slid it to him. He took a few long sips of his no-frills latte, wiped away the slight traces of foam on his upper lip with two fingers, and sighed like a junkie getting his fix.

I loved seeing the man's stone face crack, relaxed pleasure shining out like sun rays through a storm cloud. I noticed the shadow of a beard on his jaw line. The dark brown scruff made him look a little dangerous. Not for the first time, I wondered what it would be like to wake up next to him first thing in the morning. He caught me looking. I turned away.

For well over a year now, Mike Quinn had been a loyal friend. He was someone I'd trusted and confided in, someone who'd helped me get through difficult situations, a few of which had involved murder.

Mike had confided in me, too . . . often about his caseload and sometimes about the crumbling state of his thirteen-year marriage. He had two young children, a boy and a girl, and he'd wanted to stick it out for their sakes, but the last few years had been the worst. He'd tried marriage counseling, group therapy, and "couples' exploration" weekends. Finally, he decided to grit his teeth and just bear it until his kids were older, but his wife didn't feel the same. She was the one who made the final cut.

About a month ago, she announced that she wanted a divorce. She intended to marry the "new" man in her life—which translated to the latest guy in a string of affairs. And since New York State requires couples to live apart for one year before a divorce can be granted, she insisted their jointly-owned Brooklyn brownstone be put on the market immediately.

Mike's wife and kids were now preparing to move into the guest house on the new man's Long Island estate (the new man apparently pulled down in a month what a veteran detective made in a year), and Mike was living alone in Alphabet City. He'd taken a one bedroom rental, not that I'd seen it.

Did I want to? was the real question.

Yes! was my resounding answer.

I'd had a brief summer fling with Jim Rand, but we'd parted ways at the start of September. Now he was scuba diving thousands of miles away, although it might as well have been millions. Jim was the kind of peripatetic lover of adventure who couldn't stay in one place long enough to let a tomato plant take root, let alone a relationship, and I'd had his number from the moment I'd met him.

The attraction between me and Mike was something else, something more. Over the past year, we'd flirted regularly, laughed at each other's jokes, and shared many a long, quiet conversation. But as long as Mike was trying to make his marriage work, there was no way I was going to allow us to cross that platonic line.

Things were different now . . . and yet they still weren't right . . .

My ex-husband's little prediction about the man "making moves" on me was quaint, but I didn't believe it for a second. Mike Quinn had "gun shy" written all over him—and it had nothing to do with the .45 peeking out of his shoulder holster.

Although he was separated, he wasn't legally divorced, and he was obviously still stressed and disturbed about the end of his marriage. When would he be ready to move on? I didn't know. I couldn't even be sure he'd want me when he *was* ready . . .

Grabbing the portafilter handle, I gave it a sharp tug, unlocking the basket from the espresso machine. "So what's new tonight?" I asked, knocking the cake of used grounds into the under-counter garbage.

"You tell me."

I glanced up at him. *Damn those blue eyes.* "There's nothing to tell."

"Really?"

"Really."

"You're such a terrible liar, Cosi."

I looked away, noticed Joy's pot of decaf, and moved to pour myself a cup.

"You know . . ." Mike said lazily sipping his drink, "Tucker told me what happened."

I froze, midpour.

When Mike had come in earlier, he'd sat down at the coffee bar and made small talk with Tucker. Until now, I hadn't considered what they'd been talking about. Obviously, Matt hadn't either or he never would have made a deal with me.

I threw out the cup of decaf. For this, I'd need caffeine.

I dosed grounds into a portafilter, tamped, clamped, and pulled two shots. Then I poured the double into a cup and took it with me to face Mike across the marble bar.

"What . . . *exactly* did he tell you?"

"That someone mugged your ex-husband's friend in your back alley. Why didn't you call the police?"

"You're the police. And you're here."

"But you didn't call me."

"Matt's friend . . . he didn't want to report the incident."

"Why?"

"There are issues."

"What issues?"

I took another hit of caffeine. "I don't know yet, but Matt promises he'll tell me later."

Mike's gaze didn't waver. "Be careful, Clare."

"Of what?"

"A man who doesn't want to report a crime is usually a criminal himself."

I folded my arms. "Ric's the victim here, not the criminal."

Mike didn't try to argue; he simply continued drinking his coffee.

"We're going into business with this man, you see? He's the one who made that breakthrough with the decaffeinated plant I mentioned. . . ." I was trying to project confidence, but I could tell I was coming off defensive. "It's really an amazing thing, you know, for the trade? And Matt's known Ric for almost his entire life."

Mike glanced away. "Matt's not exactly pure as the driven snow."

"That's not fair. I mean, okay . . . I wouldn't call him an innocent lamb, but Matt's definitely no criminal. And I don't appreciate the snow crack." I closed my eyes and held up my hand. "Don't say it. I already know . . . *crack* is also a term for cocaine."

Mike drank more latte. "So what do you think happened?"

"I'm not supposed to discuss it with you."

"Solve a few homicides and you're flying solo, huh?"

"I made a deal with Matt. He agreed to take Ric to St. Vincent's ER now and tell me everything later—"

"—as long as you keep the details from me."

"What are you, a mind reader?"

"Some people are an open book."

"Meaning me? Now you sound like my ex-husband."

"Ouch."

"Listen," I leaned on the coffee bar, closing the distance between us. "Since you already know the basics, I don't see any harm in talking hypothetically."

"Hypothetical is my middle name."

"I thought it was Ryan."

"Aw, Clare . . . you remembered."

"Have you ever heard of a mugger using a prerecorded message?"

The detective put down his nearly empty latte glass. "You're not kidding, are you?"

I shook my head.

"I've had voices mechanically distorted in extortion cases, but never a street mugger. Not in my experience."

"That's what I thought."

Mike's lips twitched. "What else do you think?"

"If the mugger didn't want his or her voice recognized, then Ric might have recognized it, right? Which means—"

"Ric already knows this person."

"Or . . ." I murmured, "he's about to know this person."

"I don't follow."

"Ric's in town for the ICGE—it's an international trade show for the coffee industry. Later this week he's announcing his horticulture breakthrough, and it's going to shake up a lot of people."

"What does 'shake up' translate to? Will it ruin them?"

"No . . . at least not right away. Ric's deal is exclusive with the Village Blend, and we're a premium product. Something like this won't change the mass market for years. This discovery shouldn't be a total shock, either."

"Why not?"

"People have been working on creating a viable decaffeinated plant for a little while now—the interest was negligible at first but the percentage of decaf drinkers has skyrocketed in the last fifty years. It was something like three percent in the sixties, now it's close to twenty, and—"

"You don't have to tell me. It's a very old song, where there's a market, there's interest in exploiting it."

I nodded. "Yeah. Love it or hate it, so goes the capitalist formula for progress."

"So who's competing with your friend?"

"Some scientists in Hawaii are doing field tests on a genetically engineered decaffeinated plant. And back in 2004, there were rumors that Brazilian scientists from the Universidade Estadual de Campinas had identified a naturally decaffeinated Ethiopian coffee plant."

"What happened there? Why wasn't that a success?"

"Ethiopia supposedly raised issues over the ownership and that was the last anyone heard of it—the quality of those beans is still an unknown."

"Is Ric associated with that discovery?"

"No. Ric's living in Brazil now, but Matt tells me he did his own experimentation. He's been interested in botany since he hung out here at the Blend back in college."

"He went to college here?"

"He came as an exchange student from Costa Gravas

for a year or so. He lived in the Village and took classes at NYU and Cornell, I think."

"I thought you said he was from Brazil."

"He and his family are living in Brazil now, but he was born and raised on Costa Gravas."

"Where is that? Central America?"

"It's a small Caribbean nation, near Jamaica, Spanish and English speaking. It was a British colony, which explains Ric's surname. His father's side held land there for generations. But now the island is independent and self-governing. Ric's family left and went to Brazil. They reestablished their coffee farm there."

"Don't you know why his family left?"

"Not really. Matt and I were divorced when it happened, and I lost touch with Ric . . . until now."

"What kind of a guy is he, would you say?"

"What do you mean?"

"Is he the kind who makes a lot of enemies? Does he have a temper? A short fuse?"

"No. The man's as easygoing as they come. Five minutes after the mugging he was telling my daughter how beautifully she grew up."

"If he's not one to make personal enemies—"

"I didn't say that . . . I don't know him well enough, and . . ."

"What?"

"He's a pretty smooth operator with women. At least he used to be, back in the day."

Mike nodded. "Would he sleep with a married woman?"

"I don't know . . ."

"Crimes of passion are at the top of the charts in my caseload."

"I know . . . but it seems more likely that someone's after Ric's research."

"As well as his life?"

"I don't know that Ric's *life* is in danger. The mugger stole his hotel room keycard. But this person might have taken his wallet too—the mugging was interrupted."

"How?"

"I'm pretty sure a police siren spooked the mugger first, and then when this robber came back, I was there with Ric."

"Then you saw the mugger?"

"No. Before I had the chance, I was introduced to our back wall." I lifted my bangs, showing Mike my bruised forehead.

"God, Clare . . ."

I dropped my bangs, but he reached out to lift them again. With one hand, he held back my hair. With the other, he tested the bruise's discolored edges. The rough pads of his fingers were gentle, but the injury was sore.

I winced.

"Sorry . . ." he whispered. "Damn that ex-husband of yours. He should have called 911."

Mike appeared to continue examining the bruise, but the affectionate way he kept stroking my hair was starting to scramble my brains. He just wouldn't stop touching me, and for a moment I lost my voice along with my train of thought.

"It's okay," I finally managed. "Ric was the one who needed the ER. He was pistol-whipped pretty badly. When I first found him, he was unconscious."

Mike's hand released my chestnut bangs, but he didn't pull away. Slowly, gently, he began to curl locks of hair around my ear. As his blue eyes studied my green ones, he seemed to be thinking something over. Then one finger drew a line down my jaw, stopping beneath my chin.

If he had leaned just a little closer, he could have kissed

me. But he didn't lean closer. He leaned back, taking the heat of his touch with him.

"I've got news for you, Clare," he said quietly, "if the mugger hit him that hard, then it's not a simple robbery."

"What is it?"

"Attempted murder."

Seven

"Is the flatfoot gone?" Matt asked.

It was almost midnight. I'd just climbed the back stairs and entered my duplex to find my ex-husband pacing the living room like a recently caged tiger. His expensive duds were gone. He was back to the sort of clothes I was used to him wearing—an old, knobby fisherman's sweater and well worn blue jeans.

"Yes, *Mike's* gone," I said, tossing my keys onto the Chippendale end table. I was grubby and hungry, feeling the need for a jasmine bath and a PB and Nutella sandwich, if possible simultaneously. "Since our talk went on for a while, I sent Tucker home and closed myself. Unfortunately, two NYU Law study groups swung in around ten and nearly drank us dry. I had to kick the last of them out to lock up."

Matt seemed ready to retort with something snippy but stopped himself. After a few seconds of silence, he said, "You look tired . . ."

"I am."

"Are you hungry? I warmed up some of my stew for Ric. There's some left on the stove."

"Great . . ." I turned to head into the kitchen. Matt stepped by me, touching my arm. "Take a load off. I'll get it."

I wasn't going to argue. I'd set the bar low with the PB and Nutella simply because I was too tired to do anything more than slather my plain peanut butter sandwich with hazelnut-chocolate spread. I much preferred a hot, meaty snack—as long as I didn't have to cook it myself. And, it appeared, I didn't.

I dropped into a rosewood armchair, pulled off my low-heeled boots, and wiggled my sore toes inside my forest green socks. They seemed to disappear against the jewel-toned colors of the Persian area rug.

Madame had done an amazing job decorating this duplex. The richly patterned carpet provided a lovely counterpoint to the lighter motifs in the room's color scheme. The walls were pale peach, the marble fireplace and sheer draperies a creamy white. The chairs and sofa were upholstered in a finely striped pattern of mandarin silk. Anchored above my head, in the fleur-de-lys ceiling molding, was a pulley chandelier of polished bronze and six blushing globes of faceted crystal.

Whenever Matt was in town, which was rarely more than one week a month, he had the legal right to use this apartment, too. Neither of us owned it outright. Madame had merely granted us equal rights to use this antique-filled West Village duplex rent free.

I'd tried arguing with Matt, but he wasn't willing to give up his rights to the tasty piece of real estate with two working fireplaces and a newly renovated bath of Italian marble—and neither was I. Given the high cost of living in this neighborhood, and our own anemic savings accounts, we'd agreed on an uneasy truce.

Matt approached me with a warm bowl of his *carne con café*, a coffee-infused beef stew. He'd adapted the recipe from a traditional Mayan dish, which he'd enjoyed on one of his trips to El Salvador.

"Mmmmm . . ." I murmured, "smells like sustenance."

I dug in with gusto, appreciating the tang of the garlicky tomatoes and the brightness of the poblanos against the earthy combination of beef and coffee. Matt had placed a hunk of crusty French bread on top of the bowl. I dipped the bread in the thick, meaty gravy, and tore off a sloppy mouthful.

"How long have you been back?" I mumbled through my less-than-ladylike chomping.

"A little over an hour," Matt said. "I saw your cop boyfriend through the Blend's windows, so we came up through the alley entrance."

"He's not my boyfriend . . . and did you just say *we*?"

"Ric and I."

"Ric's here?"

"He's upstairs, in my bedroom."

"They didn't admit him at the hospital?"

"His scan checked out okay. No hemorrhaging. They wanted to admit him for observation, but he refused, and I wouldn't let him go back to his hotel."

"So we can keep an eye on him? Or because of the stolen keycard?" I asked.

"Both."

"Keeping an eye on him is easy. What about the keycard? Can the hotel change the locks?"

"They already have."

Matt moved to one of the windows, pushed back the sheers. Peering past the flower boxes, he surveyed the shadowy street. "Ric notified the Marriott before we left for the ER—"

"So that's why you lent him your cell phone?"

Matt nodded. "Tomorrow I'm going with him to his hotel. I'm checking him out of that midtown location and bringing him downtown, closer to us."

"Where exactly?"

"There are a few hotels I used to use regularly before I moved in here. I'll find out who has vacancies and check him in under my name."

"Who's after him, Matt?"

"I don't know."

Matt stalked to the fireplace, grabbed a poker, and adjusted the crackling log. The night was cold, the stairwell downright chilly. I was glad he'd warmed the living room with the modest blaze.

"Not a clue? Come on?"

"Ric's still pretending this is nothing serious, but he admitted to me in the ER waiting room that he felt as if someone's been following him."

"Has he seen anyone? Man, woman, old, young, large, small—"

"Just footsteps behind him, sometimes he'll catch a shadow. He's actually been in the city about three weeks, but it wasn't until this past week that he started receiving a number of strange calls at his hotel."

I sat up straighter. "What kind of calls? Someone with a mechanical voice again?"

"No. Whoever was calling just hung up when Ric answered."

"So someone's been watching him? Waiting for a chance to strike?"

"That's what I think. Even though he still claims tonight was a random mugging, he's agreed to stay here, as a precaution. He's had a pretty rough night. I think he's already asleep."

"In your bed?"

"Yes, of course."

I tensed. "And where were you planning to sleep?"

A year ago, Matt had thought that because we were sharing the same apartment, we would also, when the whim struck us, be sharing the same bed.

"I'll be sleeping here, Clare, on the couch."

"Oh . . . okay." My relief must have been more than a little obvious because Matt's brow knitted.

"What did you think I was going to say?"

"Nothing."

He studied me a moment. "I see . . . you thought I was going to suggest—"

"Forget it."

I set down the nearly empty bowl of stew, rubbed the back of my neck. The stress of the last five hours—from those bottomless-cup law students to Mike Quinn's downright torturous flirtation—had tightened my muscles into hard, angry knots. It was almost unbearable and I closed my eyes, dreaming of that jasmine bath I was too tired to draw.

Matt stepped closer. "You look tense."

"I am."

He moved behind me, settling his hands on my shoulders. "Are you sure you didn't want me to suggest some other sleeping arrangements?"

His voice had gone low and soft, his mood switching from edgy to seductive with the smoothness of a veteran Formula One driver shifting gears on a high-performance sports car. The effect wasn't aggressive or sleazy. With Matt, it never was. His seductions were always tender and sincere, which is why he always got to me.

He began a slow, expert kneading. I closed my eyes and my tight muscles seemed to sigh. They wanted more, even if I didn't—not from Matt anyway. It was Detective Quinn

I wanted. The flirting wasn't enough anymore. Now that Mike was separated, I wanted him to cross that invisible fence we'd both been dancing on for over a year.

As my mind recalled Mike's intense blue gaze, his caring touches, my body became more pliant beneath my ex-husband's hands. I released a soft moan and shifted, leaning forward to give him more access. Matt *was* familiar and convenient, his warmth a tempting offering on this cold October night.

His hands moved lower, down my spine. Gently, he pulled up my shirt, reached beneath it to caress my lower back. But as my ex continued to make my tendons sing, it slowly occurred to me that I was doing exactly what Matt had done during our ten year marriage.

The one-night stands hadn't meant anything, he'd claimed. They were just physical workouts, temporary warmth on lonely nights, substitutes—apparently—for me.

Wasn't I contemplating the same thing now, substituting one man for another? Did I really want to cavalierly sleep with an ex-husband who was very publicly involved with another woman?

Wake up, Clare!

I opened my eyes. "No . . ." I said. "I mean . . . *yes*, Matt, I'm sure you should sleep on the couch."

"But you thought of the other option, right?" Matt mellifluously pointed out, his hands continuing to rub. "It entered your mind."

The definition for mental health also entered my mind. It did not include walking down the same road and falling into the same hole, over and over again.

I still vividly remembered the last time I'd fallen into the Matt hole. Yes, I'd climbed out quickly enough the next morning, but this time was going to be different. This time, I could actually avoid the hole altogether.

"Matt, don't." I turned to meet his eyes, make it clear. "We're partners in business now, but that's all we are. I'm sure we shouldn't be sharing the same bed, okay?"

With a shrug, Matt removed his magic hands from my body. My still-aching muscles immediately cursed me as he turned back to the fireplace, which would definitely be providing him with more warmth than me tonight.

"Let's get back to Ric, okay?" I said.

"What do you want to know?"

Matt's tone was even. *Good.* I quietly exhaled, infinitely relieved there wouldn't be any residual hostility from my rejection. "I know you've known the man a long time, but . . ."

"But what?"

"Are you certain you can trust him?"

"What do you mean?"

"Well . . ." *How do I put this?* "Mike said a man who doesn't want to report a crime is usually a criminal himself."

"Mike said."

I grimaced. *One stupid back massage and my guard's completely down.*

"You broke our deal!"

"Calm down, Matt—"

"You told him about the mugging!"

Yep. He's definitely over the romantic thing now. "Matt, listen. Mike Quinn already knew."

"Like hell."

"Tucker told him."

"Tucker!"

"Don't you remember? When Quinn came in and sat down at the coffee bar? We never warned Tucker not to say anything. He mentioned the mugging. So . . . since Quinn already knew all about it, I figured—"

"You figured you'd discuss everything with him! What

can I expect tomorrow morning, a forensics unit at our back door?"

"Don't get crazy. Quinn's not saying a word. He couldn't anyway. There's no mugging if the victim refuses to go on the record that there was one. And I don't know why Ric is so reluctant to ask the police for help. Obviously, someone means him harm—"

"You don't know what you're talking about, Clare."

"Enlighten me then. You're obviously keeping me in the dark about something, what is it? Tell me, Matt."

"Why? So you can call up the flatfoot to discuss it?"

I might have come up with a decent retort at that moment, but the phone rang. Matt and I had become so used to getting calls on our cells that the land line's ringing on the end table startled us both into dead silence.

A beat later, we both reached for it, but I was closer.

"Hello?" I said.

"Hello?" *Female.*

"Yes?" I said.

"I'm looking for Matt."

The superior attitude (and not bothering to waste any time greeting me) would have told me who she was, even if I hadn't recognized her slightly nasal voice—no doubt the result of looking down her long, thin nose at nearly everything for decades.

I held out the receiver. "It's Breanne."

Matt could have stepped away with the wireless handset, but he didn't bother. He just stood in front of me, close enough for me to hear every word of hers as well as his.

"What's up?" Matt checked his wristwatch. "It's after midnight."

Laughter followed on the other end of the line. "Matteo, you're getting old."

"We're the same age, Bree, and it's Tuesday night."

"*Bishoujo* is launching a new fragrance. Those Japanese designers really know how to party. The event's still going strong at Nobu—"

"Sorry, I'm done in."

"Oh, darling, so am I! You know I'm just teasing. How did that little tasting of yours go with Federico?"

"It . . ." Matt hesitated. "Fine . . . it went fine."

"Good. He's such a charmer, just like you. . . . So you're obviously free now. That's why I had my driver swing by to pick you up."

"Pick me up?"

"We're parked right downstairs, next to the Blend."

"I'm not dressed—"

"Good." Throaty laughter followed. "That's the way I like you—"

Matt glanced at me, his face actually registering a flash of embarrassment. He turned away then, taking the wireless handset across the room. As he continued the conversation (which sounded to my ears more like an argument), I moved to the window, pulled back the sheers, and looked down into the street.

A black Town Car was parked beside the curb. A tall, blond woman was pacing back and forth, a cigarette in one hand, a cell phone in the other. The editor-in-chief of *Trend* magazine looked every inch the chic-meister. A stunning claret and black gown hugged her model-slender figure, a sleek sable wrap caressed one creamy shoulder, rubies dripped from her ears, and her upswept hair boasted an elaborate salon-designed tower that shouted labor-intensive do.

"Bree insists I come back with her," Matt told me upon hanging up.

"Well . . ." I shrugged, folded my arms. "You have to admit, a king-size penthouse bed with five-hundred-dollar sheets is a lot more comfortable than a narrow antique sofa."

"Yeah."

There wasn't much enthusiasm in my ex-husband's tone. It sounded more like obligation, and I wondered what was going on in his head. For almost a year Matt had been squiring the woman to launch parties, political fundraisers, and charitable events. Their photos had been splashed in *Gotham*, *Town and Country*, and the *Post*'s "Page Six." The publicity was a great boost to Matt's profile as he expanded our business. Yet, over the summer, he'd told me that he and Breanne were just "casual," and he had no intention of becoming enmeshed in her life.

As summer turned into fall, however, it seemed to me that Breanne was becoming increasingly manipulative and demanding. My ex-husband may have been using Bree for her connections, but she appeared to be exacting a price.

After hanging up, Matt went upstairs and returned with a small gym bag. He hadn't bothered to pack a change of clothes, just underwear and toiletries. Obviously, he had no intention of staying very long at Breanne Summour's penthouse.

"See you tomorrow, hon—" he began, then corrected himself as he pulled open the door. "Sorry. I meant Clare."

"Matt?" I called.

"Yeah?" He turned, one hand still on the doorknob.

"Does Breanne know about Ric and his breakthrough?"

"Of course, she knows. I introduced them last week."

"So you invited Bree to Friday's launch tasting at the Beekman Hotel, right?"

"Her magazine is going to cover it. *Trend* is very influential. One article can have a tremendous impact."

Pillow-talk publicity, I thought. "Did she, by any chance, know about Ric coming to the Blend tonight?"

"As a matter of fact, I was with her when I took the call from Ric earlier today. When he heard about my giving you his beans to taste test with our baristas, he said he wanted to drop by and see what they thought. Bree wanted me to go with her to some launch party tonight, but frankly I was happier coming to the Blend . . . until the mugging, that is."

I nodded and began to wonder about Breanne. Could she have set Ric up? Sent someone to rob him or worse? What would be her motive if she had?

I gave Matt a halfhearted smile as I considered voicing these suspicions. But I knew he'd blow his top before I finished talking. And he'd most likely be right. Notwithstanding my total dislike for the woman, Breanne Summour just didn't strike me as a criminal mastermind.

"See you tomorrow," I told my ex.

The front door closed, and I stepped to the window, watched the sidewalk below until a dark-haired male head appeared. Breanne wasted no time. She threw her burning cigarette into the gutter. Laughing loudly enough for me to hear three floors away, she snaked her long, slender arms around my ex-husband's neck and began passionately kissing him.

Matt's body remained tense as she ground against him, but he didn't push her away. His mouth moved over hers, and I knew what I was missing. Matt was an amazing kisser. A piece of me shifted with regret—but only a very little piece.

When he finally broke it off, he pointed to the Town Car. The two of them disappeared inside, and I watched the vehicle pull away. I continued watching until the misty gray shadows closed like a curtain on the car's red taillights.

Letting go of the sheers, I frowned, trying to guess Bree's endgame with my ex-husband. As long as he needed her influence, she could pull his strings.

But, an annoying little voice nagged in my head, *what would happen if Ric's breakthrough made Matt a fortune? Would he cut those strings completely? Was Breanne capable of quietly sabotaging Ric, just to make sure her prized boy toy didn't flee the sandbox?*

The hearth's fire was dying out, and the room had grown colder. I felt almost empty inside, hollowed out and exhausted. Rubbing my arms, I couldn't help thinking of Mike Quinn. . . . Was he sleeping now? Missing his wife? His kids? His old home in Brooklyn? Could he possibly be lying in bed, thinking of me?

I cupped my hand against my cheek and chin, where he'd touched me earlier, and wondered if it had crossed his mind to touch more of me anytime soon.

I could certainly push things . . . but he was a trusted friend, and I didn't want to lose that. I couldn't risk misreading him, or—as Matt had advised me about my own daughter—if I pushed too hard, I could end up pushing him away. Then again, maybe Matt was speaking from his own experience with Breanne.

A sudden yawn put an end to my tortuous conjectures. I picked up my bowl, put it to my mouth, and guzzled the last dregs of Matt's tangy ragout. Then I took the bowl to the kitchen, wiped my mouth on a paper towel, and headed up to bed.

At the top of the staircase, I remembered Ric. Quietly I opened the door to Matt's room. I stepped a little way into the darkness. The light from the hallway splashed onto the bed pillows, illuminating Federico Gostwick's ebony hair and handsome profile. I could see he was sleeping comfortably. His breathing sounded even, not labored, and I was glad. Then I closed the door and headed down the hall to my own bedroom.

"Attempted murder . . ."

Mike's words came back to me as I stripped off my clothes and pulled the extra-large Steelers T-shirt over my head. I thought again of how much Matt and Ric looked like brothers, and my mind began to worry that fact . . .

If the person after Ric means to harm him and makes a mistake, could Matt end up in the crosshairs?

The vision of Ric in the cold, wet alley came back to me then. I saw the man's slumped over body, but this time with Matt's face. The image sent a sick chill through me.

Matt was my business partner and my child's father. He and I were no longer husband and wife, but after all we'd been through together, I wasn't prepared for any harm to come to him. Unfortunately, I'd blown his trust this evening when I'd admitted talking to Quinn.

But I haven't blown it with Ric yet.

"Tomorrow morning," I whispered, settling under the covers.

Matt will be at Bree's, and I can talk to Ric without interference.

"One way or another," I mumbled as my head hit the pillow, "I'm going to get my questions answered. . . ."

Eight

"How about a fresh pot?"

Ric nodded.

When it came to mornings, I didn't consider myself conscious until I'd sucked down at least one mammoth cup of our Breakfast Blend. But Ric was off caffeine. At his request, I was about to brew up a pot of the Gostwick Estate Reserve Decaf in my apartment's kitchen. Ric said he'd been researching decaf so long, he'd grown to prefer it.

Since I was going to use a standard drip method this time out, I set the burr grinder between coarse (for French presses) and fine (for espresso machines). I could almost hear Detective Mike Quinn's voice over the grinder's noisy whirring—"*You know, Cosi, you might want to dial that same setting for your interrogation. Too coarse, you'll spook the subject. Too refined, you won't get what you need. Aim for the middle . . .*"

I'd already had hours to think about questioning Ric. I'd

been up since five thirty, taking in the day's bakery delivery downstairs and brewing urns of our Breakfast Blend.

BETWEEN six and seven, I'd served about twenty customers when the door jingled and in walked a welcome surprise—Dante Silva. The compact twenty-six-year-old strode right up to the coffee bar, looking a little uneasy. "Good morning, Ms. Cosi."

"You can call me Clare," I said, and not for the first time. "What are you doing here? You said you were running a fever last night."

"I was, but I stayed in bed, slept it off . . . I'm good to go now, and I thought I'd make up the time by pulling a double shift today. I wouldn't want to lose this job, you know? Rents are tough around here, even with the three of us in the two bedroom."

Dante lived on the Lower East Side near Teany (the recording artist Moby's restaurant) in a two bedroom apartment he shared with two female friends from college. He said each of the girls had their own bedroom and he spent most of his nights on the sofabed in the living room. "Most" of his nights had a sort of *Big Love* bigamist ring to it, but I never pried.

In the course of his barista chatting, I'd overheard him talk about a pipe dream of purchasing his own Soho loft—a pretty common wish for young painters who come to the big bad city expecting a sun-washed studio. The reality check, of course, was more than obvious with one glance at the *Times* real estate section. Those legendary spaces were priced for investment banker types, not aspiring artists working part-time at coffeehouses.

"Dante, calling in sick every now and then isn't going to

get you fired," I assured him. "But I'm glad you're here. Apron up."

"Excellent."

He clapped his hands and came around the counter. Stepping into the pantry area, he removed the backward Red Sox baseball cap from his shaved head and peeled off his long flannel shirt, revealing more than a few tattoos on his ropey arms. I actually liked his pieces of skin art. My favorites were the demitasse on the top of his left wrist and a Picasso-esque Statue of Liberty on his right forearm.

The day I'd met him, I'd asked what was up with the body art, and he admitted, with a great deal of pride, that he'd designed every tattoo he displayed. As a painter, he said he wasn't about to let anyone else stain the canvas of his own skin.

A new crowd of customers flowed into the store, and I put Dante on the espresso machine. "Take a few practice runs."

"Don't need to, Ms. Cosi," he said, tying on the Village Blend apron.

"Humor me, Dante. Take them."

To me, espresso-making was an art. Like a perfectionist painter, a superior barista was one who exhibited an expert hand and palate. From day to day, adjustments needed to be made. Even the weather was a factor. High humidity meant the espressos could run slower, and the beans would have to be ground somewhat coarser. Lower humidity meant the espressos could run faster, so a finer grind was required.

I didn't want one single inferior demitasse served under my watch, which was why I insisted Dante make some test shots. As I supervised, he ran through the process.

Initially, I'd been wary of Dante. When he'd approached me three weeks earlier, asking after employment, the guy's tattoos made me wonder just how fringe he was. I'd already lost two part-timers in two months, and I didn't want to spend time training someone who would start bugging out on shifts. But then he began talking, and I could see he was articulate, intelligent, and (this capped it) he'd already been trained. In his teen years, he'd worked at a coffeehouse in Providence, so he was an old hand at making Italian coffee drinks, not to mention handling thirsty urbanites with caffeine deficits.

During his first week, he was a little rusty at applying even pressure at the tamping stage. At least thirty pounds of pressure is needed when tamping down the freshly ground coffee beans into the portafilter—and if the cake of grounds is uneven when steaming water is forced through it, you're in for some nasty business. Water takes the path of least resistance, so the lower side of an uneven cake would end up over-extracted (too much water passing through), the higher side under-extracted (not enough water), and the result is a vile little schizoid cup I'd be embarrassed to serve to a paying customer.

Today there were no such problems. I sampled both of Dante's shots. The first was the tiniest bit over-extracted, but the second was perfect—from the viscosity to the roasty, caramelly flavor of the crema (that beautiful, nut brown liquid that separates from the ebony espresso like the head of a freshly tapped Guinness).

We worked in tandem after that. I greeted customers, manned the register, watched the levels on the Breakfast Blend urns. Dante pulled espressos and kept the stainless steel pitchers of milk steamed and frothed. Then we switched positions.

"I'm glad you came by, Dante."

"No problem."

"I still need two, even three more part-timers for coverage. I ended up closing last night, and I'm still dragging this morning."

"Why did you close? Wasn't Tucker scheduled for that?"

"Yes, but . . ." I stopped my running mouth. After letting my guard down with Matt, I wasn't about to start spewing last evening's details to my newest barista. "A friend of mine dropped by and our chatting ran late, so I just let Tucker go early."

"A friend? You mean that cop, don't you?"

"Detective Quinn. Yes."

Dante nodded. "Well, I guess you're right then. It's a good thing I came by . . ."

When Tucker arrived at seven fifty, the real morning crush began. We were soon swamped, with a line out the door until ten thirty. As the crowd finally thinned, I left the two of them alone with a vague excuse about needing to complete some paperwork. Then I headed upstairs with a basket of freshly baked muffins.

FEDERICO Gostwick hadn't been up long when I entered the duplex. He'd just showered, and I called upstairs, inviting him down for breakfast. His clothes were still at his hotel, so he threw on Matt's long terrycloth bathrobe and slippers. Then he shuffled into the kitchen, dropped down at the table, and sampled a warm cappuccino muffin—made for the Blend by a local bakery from one of my old "In the Kitchen with Clare" column recipes.

"Mmmm . . ." Ric murmured as he chewed and swallowed. "What nut am I tasting here? Wait. I can tell you . . ." He took another bite, closed his eyes. "Hazelnut?"

"That's right."

"Quite delightful, Clare . . . very rich texture."

"Sour cream. That's the secret."

As I brewed Ric's un-coffee, I continued with the general chit-chat, asking after his injury (it ached, but he would live), his night's sleep (very restful, thank you), and his trip here from Brazil (the JFK customs processing was detestable). Then I poured him a cup of his "why bother?" and started bothering—with the real questions.

"Did Matt happen to mention that I've had some pretty good luck investigating"—*how do I put it?* I thought—"suspicious things?"

Ric smiled, rather indulgently it seemed to me as I took a seat across from him at the small kitchen table.

"He told me I could trust you," Ric said.

"You can. I want to see you safe, you know?"

"Me, too, love, believe me."

"Then tell me why all the secrecy? Why won't you go to the police about last night? What is it you aren't telling me?"

Ric sipped his decaf, stared into the dark liquid. "This breakthrough of mine . . . it's very new."

"I know." *Hence the term "breakthrough."*

"There are a lot of people who may want my new coffee plant to grow for themselves."

"That goes without saying, but they can't get it, right?"

"Yes, the farm and nursery are in a remote location, but more important, my family and I have kept the research very private."

"Then last night, someone assaulted you. Think, Ric . . . do you have any enemies? Anyone who might want to see you hurt . . . or even killed?"

Ric laughed.

"What's funny?"

"You Americans watch too many crime shows. I've been counting them up on my hotel room's telly: true crime, fake crime, funny crime, scary crime . . . supernatural, mathematical, and neurotic. Twenty-four hours a day on U.S. TV, you can see someone getting killed twenty-four different ways."

"You're saying I'm a paranoid American?"

"I know you mean well, love. But nobody is trying to kill me. I know what the mugger wanted."

"What?"

"The cutting. I'm sure of it. So is Matt."

"Cutting?" I blinked. "What cutting?"

"It's the reason Matt and I don't want the police involved. We did something . . . how shall I put it? Not quite legal . . ."

Oh, lord. Mike was right. "What? What did you two do?"

"We smuggled a cutting of my hybrid *arabica* into the country."

"You *what*?"

"It was quite cleverly done, actually. A few weeks ago, I shipped it to Matt overnight, hidden inside a specially lined statue of Saint Joseph, which Matt broke open."

"He broke a religious statue?" I frowned. "That's bad luck."

Ric laughed. "Little Clare . . . you're as adorable as I remember."

"I thought you said I've changed, that I'm more 'headstrong' than you remember?" I made little air quotes around the word to remind him.

Ric shrugged. "You're that, too." He sipped his decaf. "And you still make heavenly coffee."

And you're still as smooth a charmer as ever.

The man was as attractive as ever, too. The rugged shadow of his beard framed a dazzling smile, dark chest hairs peeked out between the lapels of Matt's white terrycloth bathrobe, and the man's big, brown long-lashed eyes looked just as sleepy and bedroomy as I remembered.

But ten years was a long chunk of time. It had been enough to change things about me. I wondered what it had changed about Ric.

When I'd first met him, he'd been a laid back foreign exchange student. Although he'd been interested in his studies, he'd never appeared especially committed. I still remember him sauntering into the Blend for wake-up espressos at eleven o'clock, having missed an early lecture because of partying too late the evening before.

As far as I knew, the Gostwicks' highly profitable coffee farm had let Ric live the life of a *carioca,* a Brazilian term for a guy who preferred to spend his days hanging out at the beach, looking good, eating, drinking, and making love to whatever female admirers happened by. (I'd learned the word from Matt, who probably qualified as one since Rio's Ipanema Beach—i.e. "*Carioca* Central"—was pretty much his South of the Equator headquarters.)

I wondered what had changed Ric Gostwick. Obviously, something had pushed him into hunkering down and focusing on the coffee business so intensely he'd achieved a botanical breakthrough that others had been diligently striving and failing to accomplish for years. I also wanted to know why he was in such a hurry to get the cutting into the country.

"You really shouldn't have broken the law," I told him. "I don't understand why—"

"Getting a live plant into this country is full of government red tape, that's why," Ric countered. "Any plant parts intended for growing require a phytosanitary certification in advance from your United States Department of Agriculture."

"There's a reason for that."

"Yes, I know. Worries about the spread of pests and disease. But I can assure you the cutting is pristine."

"If you're caught, the fines are astronomical. I can't believe you took the risk!"

"It would have been a bigger risk to do it openly. They might have turned down the application, or worse, its inspection process could have gotten it stolen."

I might have argued that his worries were pure paranoia, but it would have been a tough sell. Historically, the only reasons coffee had become a global cash crop were because of theft and smuggling.

Ethiopians might have been the first to discover the plant growing wild in their country, but Arabs were the ones who first exported it. For years they held the monopoly on its cultivation. Foreigners were forbidden from visiting coffee farms, and the beans would be sent to other parts of the world only after their germinating potential was destroyed through heating or boiling.

Around 1600, a Muslim pilgrim from India smuggled the first germinating seeds from Mecca to southern India. Soon after, Dutch spies smuggled coffee plants to Holland from Mocha. (Mocha being the principal port of Yemen's capital Sana'a, hence the naming of Arabian *Mocha Sanani*, coffee beans world-renowned for their powerfully pungent flavor, with notes of wine, exotic spices, and cocoa.)

After the Dutch got hold of the plant, they began cultivating coffee in their colonies: Ceylon (now Sri Lanka), Sumatra, Bali, Timor, Dutch Guiana (now Suriname), and eventually Java.

But the larceny didn't end there. A coffee plant was shipped from Java to Holland for its Botanical Garden, and a number of visiting dignitaries were given cuttings as gifts. The mayor of Amsterdam made the mistake of giving Louis XIV of France the gift of a coffee cutting from this Java tree.

In Paris, King Louis put the coffee cutting under guard inside his famous Jardin des Plantes, Europe's first greenhouse, where it was cultivated into seedlings. A French naval captain, eager to sever France's dependence on the high-priced coffees of Dutch-controlled East India, stole a seedling and sailed it to Martinique, where its offspring allowed France to grow its own coffee.

And my former mother-in-law's favorite legend was the one in which a coffee cutting was smuggled to Brazil in a bouquet of flowers. The flowers were given to a dashing Brazilian diplomat by the smitten wife of French Guiana's governor. If the story is true, Brazil's billion-dollar coffee trade apparently sprang from an extramarital love affair and that single smuggled cutting bearing fertile cherries.

Given coffee's volatile past, I knew it wasn't a stretch for Ric to be concerned about the theft of his cutting, so I held my tongue.

"Matt and I agreed we couldn't take any chances," Ric said, "not until it's been properly patented."

"Patented." I blinked in confusion. "You can patent a plant? I didn't think you could do that."

Ric nodded. "It's possible, according to Ellie."

"Ellie?" It had been well over ten years, but I quickly recognized the name, especially when it was linked to Federico Gostwick. "Ellie Shaw?"

Ric sipped his decaf and nodded. "It's Lassiter now. She agreed to help me."

"Help you . . . how?"

"I never finished my BS in botany. Ellie did. She even went on to get a masters from Cornell with a focus on public garden management. In horticultural circles, she's known and respected, and she's familiar with the process of applying for a plant patent. One of her old professors is on the PVPO advisory board. So she agreed to help me secure it."

"PVPO?"

"Plant Variety Protection Office. It's part of your Department of Agriculture."

"But why not just apply in Brazil? Don't you have patent lawyers there?"

"Of course, but there are . . ." Ric shrugged—"complicating issues. Matt and I both agreed that the U.S. patent would solve our problems."

"Problems? I don't follow you. What problems?"

"Really, Clare, you shouldn't worry about this. Matt and I have made our deal. Next week we'll announce it, along with my breakthrough, and then we can all just sit back and get rich, eh? You don't have to—"

A tinkling melody interrupted Ric's equivocating. The tune sounded vaguely familiar. "What's that?"

"My cell . . ." Ric pulled it out of the robe pocket. "I downloaded a Sting ringtone." He grinned. "Can you guess the song?"

The melody wasn't on my mind, the so-called "problems" of Ric's patent issues were.

"It's 'Roxanne,' " he announced as he hit a button and put the phone to his ear. "Hello?"

Confused as to whether Ric was referring to the Sting tune "Roxanne" or the name of the person phoning, I sipped my own cup of decaf as he took the call.

"No, darling," Ric cooed into the phone after a minute of listening. "I had a breakfast meeting outside the hotel, a very early one."

He tossed me a little shrug, which I assumed was supposed to persuade me to overlook the fact that he'd just lied to the person on the other end of the line.

"Why don't you just contact me on my cell from now on. . . ." He listened some more and checked his wristwatch. "Of course . . . me, too . . . yes, darling . . . that sounds lovely, but you'd better make it later than that, all right? I've got an important meeting . . ."

Ric finished his call, and I asked who had called him.

"Oh, just a friend in the city."

"A female friend?"

"Yes."

The phone rang once more. It was Sting's "Roxanne," all right.

"Hello?"

Another vague call ensued with yet another "darling."

"Me, too," Ric purred. "And I'm looking forward to it, darling . . . but I'll have to get back to you on where . . . yes, soon . . . just be patient . . . me, too."

Ric hung up, and I raised an eyebrow with (as Matt used to tell me) nunlike judgment.

"Let me guess, another female friend in the city?"

"Why, Clare . . ." Ric's eyes widened in mock surprise, "you didn't tell me you were psychic."

"Funny. You're too funny, Federico."

"What can I tell you? It's a hazard having this much charisma."

"Not to mention humility."

Ric laughed. "I do love women."

"You and my ex-husband . . . hence the ex."

"Men who love women this much, they shouldn't marry."

"You're telling me." I was kidding, but Ric looked suddenly serious.

"This is something of an insight then?" he asked earnestly.

"Uhm . . . actually, I was joking. Don't you know why Matt married me?"

"Because he adored you, of course. Why else?"

"I was pregnant with Joy. I thought you knew?"

"No, Clare." Ric shook his head. "Matteo never said anything like that, not once, not ever."

Honest to God, I was stunned to hear it. For those last years of our marriage, I'd assumed Matt had told every friend and colleague that I was the ball-and-chain around his neck, that he'd been pressured down the aisle because of my expecting Joy.

Ric was one of Matt's oldest friends. If he hadn't told Ric the truth, then he hadn't told anybody.

"So Matt was less of a cad than I thought," I whispered. *Not much less, but enough to surprise me.*

"What do you mean?" Ric asked.

Might as well set the record straight. "Matteo's mother pressured him into proposing. I didn't know it at the time, but apparently she made him understand that she didn't want her only grandchild to be illegitimate."

Ric nodded, looked down into his cup again.

Had I said too much? I wondered. *Probably.* The easy-going Ric looked suddenly more uncomfortable than usual. Or was there more than simple discomfort? *It probably doesn't matter,* I decided. Not only was this stuff ancient history, it was off my interrogation subject.

"So anyway . . ." I said, forcefully injecting some lightness to my tone, "where exactly is this illegal alien cutting you smuggled in?"

"Upstairs." He tipped his chin toward the ceiling. "In Matteo's room."

"Great."

"Matt accepted the delivery, you see? Then I borrowed it for a short time to show to Ellie, but now it's back with Matt. We both believe it's quite necessary to show the cutting at Friday's little gathering at the Beekman Hotel."

I didn't argue. I knew there'd be international press

there, trade journal writers, all in town to cover the ICGE. They'd want photos, and having the cutting there would add credibility to their stories.

"Matt says it's important we get the word out," Ric continued. "And I agree. Once the photo and description of my cutting is in the press, theft will be much more obvious. A patent will give me the right to sue anyone who doesn't license from me the right to grow my hybrid *arabica*."

"But why did you wait until now to announce it? Why didn't you announce from Brazil?"

"There were some issues that needed to be . . . resolved. Like the patent I mentioned."

"And is it resolved?"

"Ellie is working all that out."

"Do you trust her?"

Ric laughed. "Of course!"

I wasn't finished asking questions, but Ric was clearly done giving answers.

"I must get dressed now. Matteo called earlier." He stood and made a show of tapping his wristwatch. "We'll be meeting in less than an hour. He is checking me into a new hotel, just to be on the safe side."

"But, Ric, who do you think is after the cutting?" I called as he headed out the kitchen door. "Who attacked you last night?"

"I'm sorry, love," he cooed with a shrug, "but I haven't got a clue."

"Would you mind if I talked to Ellie then?" I called after him. "Ric?"

There was no answer. I left the kitchen and went to the bottom of the short set of stairs, leading up to the bedrooms and bath. Ric had just crested the top. I could see the back of Matt's white terrycloth bathrobe.

"Ric!" I called again, rapidly climbing the stairs. "How do I get in touch with Ellie?"

"You worry too much, love!" was Ric's reply. "But thank you for the breakfast!" Then the door to Matt's bedroom was firmly shut to me.

Nine

I wanted to strangle Matt.

I also wanted to strangle Ric. That was a given. But I'd read Miss Manners years ago, and I was pretty sure subjecting guests in your home to death by choking was poor hospitality etiquette, no matter how infuriating they were.

Ex-husbands, however, were another matter.

Matt had made a deal with me. He'd promised to convince Ric to tell me everything in exchange for my keeping Quinn in the dark.

True, I'd broken my part of the bargain, but Matt clearly had, too. Instead of instructing Ric to open up, he'd obviously warned the man about his "nose-hound" ex-wife.

There was no doubt in my mind that I'd just been "handled," given the big brush-off with the smallest amount of information. Ric's indulgent smiles and lack of any real cooperation made me wonder how Mike Quinn got through his days without punching something. Not only had my talk with the man cleared up absolutely nothing, it left me with more questions.

While Ric might see the details of his botanical breakthrough as his own private business, I didn't. Matt was about to publicly link us with Ric as his exclusive distributor. My ex might trust the man because of their lifelong friendship, but I was determined to find out who had attacked Ric, what "problems" were being resolved with his product, and why exactly my ex-husband was eager to shut down my snooping.

While Ric was dressing in Matt's room, I followed the only real lead he'd given me. Leaving the apartment, I descended the stairwell to the Village Blend's second floor, a genial space with a working fireplace, walls of exposed brick, and a bounty of overstuffed armchairs and sofas.

As an extension of the ground floor coffee bar, this floor was essentially a living room for customers, as well as a rentable space for small community gatherings. (We'd hosted everything from book clubs, singles mixers, and string quartet jam sessions, to theatrical script read-throughs, and "brag 'n' bitch" evenings for a group of professional illustrators.)

This floor also held my private office. With a battered wooden desk, utilitarian chair, files, and a coat stand where I hung my apron, the tiny windowless cell wasn't exactly Trump headquarters international. I didn't care. My real office was downstairs, anyway, behind the espresso machine with my baristas, waiting on the eclectic community I loved.

I sat at the desk and fired up my PC. Inside were Excel spreadsheets tracking inventory; daily, weekly, and monthly sales; and employee schedules. But I wasn't interested in any of that. To follow my lead, I logged onto the Internet, went to a search engine, and typed in the name "Ellie Lassiter."

Three seconds later, the screen filled with hundreds of search results, and I began combing through the listings. The first dozen or so were a bust—Ellie Lassiter wasn't a twelve year old *Mighty Marigolds* soccer player living in Indiana; a seventy-five year old nurse from New Zealand, traveling the world on a Norwegian cruise ship; or a twenty-two year old exotic dancer who made virtual house calls with her "easy-to-use Paypal account." I scrolled down more Lassiters—Ralph, Jonah, Lassiter Electronics in Kentucky, and Lassiter Footwear in Toronto, Canada.

Then I came to a blue hyperlink headlined "Curator's Corner." I hit the phrase. The screen dissolved and re-formed with photos and text . . .

> BBG is truly a living museum where plants come to life. Each of the distinct gardens within the larger Garden is carefully and artfully maintained by a BBG curator. The curator is responsible for the distinctive look and presentation of each plant collection, helping to enhance the natural beauty, horticultural significance, and educational experience of the overall Garden.

I surmised from the logo at the top of the page that BBG stood for Brooklyn Botanic Garden and this Curator's Corner page was just one part of the larger BBG Web site.

I scrolled down the page. It featured essays about the Garden's staff of managers, referred to as "curators" as part of the overriding metaphor of the Botanic Garden as a living museum. Smiling pictures of men and women were tucked in beside each essay, their CVs listing impressive credentials in horticulture, landscape design, and gardening seminars attended abroad. Then halfway down the list, I stopped dead . . .

"Ellie Lassiter," I murmured. "Gotcha."

The years were there in the photo—crow's feet and some added weight to her pale, oval face. I knew she would probably make the same judgment about me. Still, I could see the striking woman I remembered. Her glorious, hip-length strawberry blond hair was cut more practically now, into a short layered style. Her big hazel-green eyes weren't quite as big or bright anymore, and some of those adorable freckles had faded.

The sun seemed to be in her eyes, and she'd failed to smile. She looked severe and serious and a little bit sad, not the Ellie Shaw I remembered at all. The Ellie I'd known had laughed easily, smiled constantly, and loved fresh flowers, long velvet skirts, all things medieval, and my coffee. She'd lived in the Village back then and used to stop by the Blend every morning and evening for her fix, usually with a dog-eared paperback fantasy novel and an armload of college course work.

We'd continued our friendship after she'd finished her studies. But once she moved to Brooklyn, her visits to the Blend were less frequent. Then I moved to New Jersey, and our contact was reduced to a note written in a yearly Christmas card.

I remembered receiving an invitation to her wedding. She was marrying a corporate executive named Jerry Lassiter, at least fifteen years her senior. But I couldn't attend the ceremony for some reason, probably one of my part-time jobs. I'd sent her a gift, received a nice thank you note, and that was about the last time we'd communicated.

Now I clicked around the Botanic Garden Web site, looking for a contact phone number. When I called the administration offices, a woman connected me to another line. A young man assured me that Ellie was in today but was working on a special exhibit in the conservatory. Would I care to leave a message or call back later?

"Leave a message," I said, making an instant decision. "Please let Mrs. Lassiter know that Clare Cosi will be dropping in to say hello."

In less than ten minutes, I'd exchanged my T-shirt for a more presentable pale yellow V-neck sweater, had put a belt through the loops of my khaki pants, and was standing downstairs with my jacket on, my handbag slung over my shoulders, and my car keys dangling between two fingers.

The lunch rush hadn't begun yet. Only nine or ten customers occupied the tables and two were waiting at the coffee bar, so I approached Dante. He said he'd be happy to continue working, and I told Tucker to hold the java fort through lunch. Then I hiked to a garage near the river where I kept my old Honda (and the annual cost for my parking space was more than the car's blue book value).

I started her up (and she actually did start up, thank goodness). Then I exited the garage, heading east. After a few blocks snaking through the narrow Village side streets, I heard my name being called.

"Clare! Clare!"

It was Matt's mother.

Ten

MADAME Blanche Dreyfus Allegro Dubois had spotted me sitting at an intersection, waiting for a red light to go green. She strode up to the car and knocked on the passenger side window. I powered down the glass.

"Clare! I was just coming to speak with you," she said, somewhat breathlessly.

The Blend's elderly owner looked as elegant as ever in tweedy brown slacks and a burgundy wrap coat. Her hair, which had been dark brown in her youth, was rinsed a lovely silver, and she wore it down today in a simple pageboy.

"Where are you going?" she asked.

"The Botanic Garden."

She stared at me blankly, the clear blue eyes in her gently creased face appearing to be digesting this incomprehensible destination.

"The one in the Bronx?" she asked.

"Brooklyn."

She glanced up at the cerulean October sky, then down

at the stately old elms lining the cobblestone block. The sun was brilliant, the day warm, and the recent cold nights had begun painting the trees their distinctive golden yellow against black branches.

"You know," she said contemplatively, "it *is* a lovely day. And I've never been to the Brooklyn Garden. All right, I'm game."

"You're game?" I repeated in confusion.

She didn't explain. She simply climbed into the front seat beside me and slammed the door.

"Madame, I don't think—"

Beep! Beep!

A line of cars had stacked up behind me.

Madame pointed through the windshield. "The light's changed, dear."

Beeeeeep!

As my former mother-in-law strapped in, I gave the car juice and turned the corner. "Are you sure you want to go with me? I'm planning to meet up with an old friend . . ."

"I'll stay out of your way once we get there. Who are you meeting?"

"Ellie Shaw."

Madame tapped her chin in thought. "Ellie Shaw . . . Ellie Shaw . . . refresh my memory?"

"She was a loyal customer when I first managed the Blend for you. She was also madly in love with Federico Gostwick."

"Of course! I remember her. She was in the Blend day and night back then, and always so bubbly and happy. If memory serves, she had a gorgeous head of long, strawberry-blonde hair—"

"She's cut it. And she's married. She's Ellie Lassiter now."

"You and Matt went out with those two, didn't you? A lot of double dates with Ric and Ellie?"

"That's right."

"Federico must be one of Matt's oldest friends."

I nodded and considered blurting out what I'd just learned from Ric, but I knew the smuggled cutting alone wouldn't have overly concerned Madame. She was an honest businesswoman, but she was a canny one, too. During her decades of running our Manhattan business, she'd dealt with corrupt inspectors, mobbed-up garbage haulers, and underhanded rivals. The letter of the law was one thing, survival was another, and the woman wasn't going to blanch at a few sidesteps of regulations in sending a little ol' coffee tree cutting from one country to another. At the most, she'd be amused, and probably quote me the long history of coffee plant smuggling that I already knew.

Ric's mugging, his stolen keycard, and the possibility of attempted murder, however, were something else. But I still held my tongue. Ellie Shaw wasn't the only one who knew more than me about Federico Gostwick. Madame had known him for years, too, and I wanted her unbiased opinion.

"When you say Ric is one of Matt's oldest friends, you mean childhood, don't you?" I asked. "Years ago, Matt mentioned to me that he and Ric used to play together?"

"Oh, yes. Matt's father was good friends with Ric's father, and he often took Matt with him on trips to the Gostwick plantation on Costa Gravas. I went with them many times."

"What did you think of Ric's birthplace?"

Madame smiled. "Paradise."

"Really?"

"Oh, yes. You know, Matt's father was a true romantic. On our trips to Costa Gravas, he'd always arrange for Matt to stay with the Gostwicks for a day or two so he and I could share some time alone on the island." Leaning back against the car seat, she closed her eyes. "I can still see Antonio on that beach in his swim trunks, all that white sugar sand, the clear aquamarine bay stretching out behind him . . ." She sighed again. "Matt's father was such a handsome, passionate man . . . even after all these years, after marrying and losing Pierre, I still miss him."

"Of course you do."

"Sometimes my years with Antonio feel like a dream . . . but then I see my son, and I know they weren't." Madame opened her eyes. "Matt's the evidence, you see, Clare? The evidence of those years of love."

I shifted uncomfortably behind the steering wheel and cracked my window. Not only was the bright sun overheating the car, Madame's voice seemed irritatingly vested with meaning for me, but I wasn't catching what she was throwing, so I cleared my throat and politely posed my next question.

"I'm not really that familiar with Costa Gravas . . . if there were beaches on the island, then how flat was the land? Where did Ric's family grow coffee?"

"In the mountains, of course," she said. "The island had a range like Jamaica's, between four- and five-thousand feet—a splendid altitude for cultivating *arabica* . . ."

Madame was right, of course. *Arabica* coffee plants grew best at elevations between three and six thousand feet. "High-grown, high quality" was how some put it in the trade.

She closed her eyes again. "What a paradise that island was . . ."

By now, we were driving east on Houston (pronounced "How-stun" on pain of being corrected by snippy carpetbaggers eager to prove their New York savvy). And I'd changed my resistant attitude about Madame coming with me to Brooklyn. She was clearly going to be a help as far as info on Ric.

"About the Gostwick family," I said, "I was wondering if you could tell me something . . ."

Madame opened her eyes again. "What would you like to know?"

"If life on Costa Gravas was so wonderful, then why did Ric's family relocate to Brazil?"

Madame stared at me as if I'd just suggested we replace our thirty-five dollar-a-pound, single-origin Jamaica Blue Mountain with Folgers instant crystals.

"You don't know?"

"No."

"Matt didn't share that with you?"

"Matt and I were divorced then. The last thing I remember about Ric was his over-staying his education visa for Ellie, then returning to Costa Gravas anyway—and without proposing, which I also remember had absolutely devastated her."

Madame nodded. "Then you never heard the story."

"What story?"

"Ric's family didn't move out of Costa Gravas voluntarily. The government turned into a socialist dictatorship practically overnight, and all private farms and companies were seized."

"You mean like Cuba, in *Godfather II*?"

"I mean like Cuba *in reality*, dear. Federico's father had been an outspoken opponent of Victor Hernandez, who had close ties to Castro. The man's military swept over Costa Gravas. So the family fled to Brazil. It's a good thing too. Hernandez could have imprisoned Ric's father . . . or worse."

Now I felt like a geopolitical idiot.

I could only say, in defense of my ignorance, that I was overwhelmed those years with concerns closer to home (e.g. raising my daughter, keeping food on the table, paying New

Jersey Power and Lighting somewhere close to on time). Regardless of Costa Gravas' political history, however, I knew one thing—quality coffee no longer came off that little island.

Farming coffee was an art as exacting as any. Years ago, the trade journals had downgraded the quality of Costa Gravas cherries as well as their crop yields. I'd never researched why. I'd simply focused on other regions and coffee crops.

"Why exactly did Ric's family end up in Brazil?"

"A relative down there had some lands, and he gave them a section of it to farm."

"So that's why . . ." I murmured, turning south onto Broadway.

"What?" Madame asked. "That's why what?"

"That's why Ric buckled down . . . I mean, his botanical breakthrough came after his family lost their farm on Costa Gravas."

"What are you getting at?"

"I just couldn't reconcile a man who'd painstakingly create a new hybrid plant with the sort of carefree playboy Ric had been during his college years. You know that Brazilian term Matt uses?"

"A *carioca*?"

"That's the one."

Madame sighed. "Alas, my son's favorite foreign word."

"We're talking about Ric."

"Not just."

"What do you mean?"

"I mean, I want to talk to you about Matt. That's why I was coming to see you."

"Okay . . ." I said, curious at the suddenly hushed tone. "What did you want to talk about?"

"That woman."

"Excuse me?"

Thinking my ex-mother-in-law was speaking about a pedestrian, I glanced out the window. To our left was Little Italy, although lately it was hard to tell. Swanky Soho (to our right) had jumped the avenue, bringing its chic boutiques and trendy watering holes into the neighborhood of old school Italian restaurants and mirror-walled patisseries.

"Which woman?"

Madame saw me searching the crowded sidewalk and shook her head. "No, dear, not out there . . ."

"Where?"

"Right under your nose, that's where!"

"Right under my . . . ?"

"Breanne Summour."

By this time, my reaction to the woman was an autonomic response. At the sound of her name, my grip on the steering wheel tightened.

"What about her?" I asked levelly.

"I know Matt's been networking with her."

I laughed.

"What's so funny?" Madame sniffed. "That's the word he used."

"Networking?"

"Yes," said Madame. "I've seen their photos together in the tony magazines—you know, those charity party mug shots? I've met her a few times, too, and Matt continually tells me it's a casual thing, a collegial relationship."

"He's sleeping with her."

"Well, yes, of course."

I sighed. "You know your son better than anyone."

"What I know, Clare, is that Matt doesn't love this woman. Not even remotely."

I shrugged uneasily. "The *caricoa* strikes again. He's made it perfectly clear he doesn't need to love a woman to sleep with her."

"If all he was doing, or intended to do, was sleep with her, I wouldn't be so worried."

"Worried?" My ears pricked up. Had Madame heard something suspicious about the woman, something that might be linked to what was happening with Ric? "What worries you?"

"I think Matt may be getting serious about her."

"Oh, is that all . . ."

I tried not to laugh. *Matt* and *serious*—when it came to women, anyway—just didn't go together in the same sentence. To prove it, I considered telling her about the pass he'd just made at me the night before, but I held my tongue. Madame still entertained the ludicrous idea that I might one day remarry Matt. Why give her hope?

"I saw them together yesterday," Madame continued in a grave tone.

"Uh-huh."

"They were at Tiffany, Clare. They were looking at rings."

"Rings?" I repeated. My brain seized up for a second, but then I thought it through. "Breanne's quite the fashionista. She was probably just shopping for a new bauble—"

"They were diamond engagement rings. I kid you not."

Good lord. I managed to keep my foot from jamming on the brakes, but only barely. "Did you ask Matt about it?"

"No. I was with a friend and we were on our way out. But I tell you Matt and Breanne were very close together, very intimate."

"He is sleeping with her, Madame. I wouldn't think standing cheek to cheek in a jewelry store would be an issue."

"I want you to find out what's going on."

"Why?"

"I told you. My son doesn't love this woman. I can't have him marrying her."

"He married me."

"You're the only woman Matteo's ever loved, Clare. Don't you know that?"

"Frankly, no. His behavior during our marriage was unforgivable—the women, the drugs—"

"I can't defend him, and you know I've never tried. But that was a long time ago. He's been off the drugs for years now, he's working very hard, has wonderful ambitions for our business, and—"

"Please stop. We've hiked this hill already."

"But he still loves you. I know it. If he marries Breanne, there'll be no chance for you two to reconcile."

"We're not going to reconcile! I've told you before, we're business partners now, but that's all."

"True love shouldn't be ignored, Clare."

I took a deep breath. As gently as I could, I said, "Madame, listen to me. I love you. And I know how much you loved Matt's father. But Matt isn't his father. And I'm not you."

Madame fell silent after that. She leaned back in her seat and gazed out at the slow-moving traffic.

I could see by the crawling blocks that we were inching up on Joy's culinary school. I began to scan the sidewalks, a little desperate to score a glimpse of my daughter's bouncy ponytail. But then I remembered she was uptown these days, interning at Solange under that hot young chef, Tommy Keitel.

Given Madame's news about Matt, a feeling of empty-nest heartache stung me especially hard. I swatted it away. *You have a bigger problem to think about,* I reminded myself. *So think about that . . .*

Ellie Lassiter was my only lead on the mysteries surrounding Federico Gostwick and his magic beans. Once more, I considered discussing everything with Madame—the smuggled cutting, the mugging, the stolen keycard, the possibility of attempted murder. But when I glanced over at her again, the look in her eyes told me she was no longer in the present.

I wondered what she was seeing now; probably an image of her late husband, some memory from years ago, like my marriage to Matt, something long past.

I'll tell her about everything later, I decided, *after I speak with Ellie.* Then I juiced the car, swerved around two lumbering supply trucks, and moved with greater speed toward the Brooklyn Bridge.

Eleven

In person, Ellie Lassiter looked much the same as she had on her Web photo: the layered, shoulder-length strawberry blonde hair, the freckled, fair skinned oval face. She'd been so slender in college, the little bit of weight she'd gained over the last twenty years looked good, giving her attractive curves, even beneath the Botanic Garden's sexless green uniform of baggy slacks and zipper jacket.

"I almost forgot you went back to Cosi," she said as she shook my hand. Her voice was still softly feminine, but the big, joyful smile I remembered was now tight and reserved. "I'd known you as Clare Allegro for so many years . . ."

I shrugged. "That's all right. It's apparently hard for my mother-in-law to remember, too. But then she has a selective memory."

Ellie nodded. "My grandmother's like that. Terribly forgetful when the subject's irritating, but sharp as a pruning hook when she's got an agenda."

"Sounds like your granny and Matt's mother have been playing croquet together."

Madame might have made a barb of her own just then, if she'd been present, but she wasn't. She'd already obtained a map from the Botanic Garden's Visitor's Center and set off on a trek of discovery through the fifty-two acre sanctuary.

I envied her. The October day was bright and warm, the foliage around us displaying vibrant colors—deep russet and bronzed gold, brilliant yellow and blazing orange. We'd parked in the Washington Avenue lot, and then followed a paved pathway onto the grounds. The smells of the Garden hit me immediately: damp leaves, late season blossoms, freshly turned dirt. (Funny, how you can actually miss the smell of dirt when your entire range of outdoorsy experience consistently runs from Manhattan sidewalk to Manhattan asphalt.)

We strolled past an herb garden with hundreds of varieties, from medicinal and culinary to ornamental. I picked up scents of sage and rosemary as we walked. There was fresh mint and basil, along with some wild pungent fragrances I couldn't identify.

The Japanese Hill-and-Pond garden came next. A miniaturized landscape—Japanese maples dressed in bright vermillion and evergreen shrubs traditionally pruned into perfect cloud shapes—surrounded a manmade pool, alive with quacking ducks, turtles, koi, and elegant, slender-necked herons.

By then, Madame was hooked and so was I. But though I was dying to see (not to mention smell) the rest of the 10,000 plants from around the world, I had business. So while my former mother-in-law set out on a trek through the various little gardens within the larger one, I went to the administration building and set out on a quest for Ellie Shaw Lassiter.

Locating her wasn't difficult. The receptionist in the administration building simply directed me to the Steinhardt Conservatory, a collection of immense greenhouses no more than a stone's throw from the main plaza (not that I advocated throwing stones anywhere near those amazing glass buildings).

I found Ellie inside one of the warm, rather uncomfortably humid rooms of one structure. In the room next to us, I could see an amazing display of tiny, perfectly shaped trees. This was the Garden's Bonsai Museum, the oldest collection of dwarfed, potted trees in the country.

In Ellie's large, bright, transparent space, the display was much newer and closer to home—a collection of lush, green coffee plants in various stages of fruition. Some were flowering white, others were heavy with green, yellow, or red berries.

As I shrugged out of my jacket, I inhaled the wonderful, jasmine and bitter orange blossom scent of the white coffee flowers. It brought me back to one of the few business trips I'd taken with Matt—to the Kona district of Hawaii's Big Island. The buying trip had doubled as our honeymoon. Our hotel room's French doors opened to a view of the wild Pacific, and we'd made love so often during those two perfect weeks, I'd be hard pressed to guess a grand total.

"These coffee trees are beautiful," I said.

Ellie's reserved smile became warmer. "Thank you . . . although technically they're shrubs."

"Excuse me?"

"It's true, the *Coffea* plant is often called a 'tree' by people in the trade, but botanically it's classified as a shrub, more precisely as a perennial evergreen dicogtyledon."

"Right."

She smiled. "That just means it's a plant that's always green and has two seeds per fruit body."

She went on to explain that her month-long exhibit on the horticulture of coffee would officially open next week, in honor of the International Coffee Growers Exhibition. I could see she was proud of it.

"I'm just putting on the finishing touches . . . you see . . ."

Ellie took me to the center of the room where a diorama illustrated the origins of your average cuppa Joe. I was well acquainted with these basics, having written about the beverage for years. But most coffee drinkers downed pound after pound without considering the source.

Ellie's display nicely explained that coffee beans actually come from berries ("cherries" to those of us in the trade). These cherries are green in the early stages of growth. They then mature to yellow and red. They're ripe at dark crimson, which is when they yield the best coffee via the two seeds (beans) inside.

"The average *arabica* coffee plant takes about five years to mature and produce its first crop," Ellie said.

That I knew. "And of that crop, it will take an entire coffee 'tree,'" I added with air quotes, "to produce only one pound of coffee; i.e. about forty cups."

"Forty cups in one pound?" she said. "That I didn't know."

We both laughed, and I repeated how great her exhibit looked. Then I told her: "Actually, the reason I'm here, Ellie, is because of Ric. Matt and I are going into business with him—"

"I know. Ric's very happy. He and Matt told me all about it."

"Matt? You've been seeing Matt, too?"

"Yes, of course. We met many times over the summer.

I'm surprised he never mentioned it. I asked about you, and he said you were very busy in the Hamptons, helping a friend open a new restaurant?"

"Yes, I was."

"He assured me I'd be seeing you Friday," Ellie said. "So I was looking forward to catching up then—"

"Friday? You mean the Beekman Hotel? You'll be there for the big tasting and announcement?"

"Absolutely. Ric's counting on me. I'll be there to answer any questions the journalists may have about his hybrid's viability."

"You're his seal of approval then? Like *Good Housekeeping*'s endorsement of a really good floor cleaner."

Ellie's eyes narrowed slightly. "Something like that."

"He told me that you're helping him apply for a plant patent."

"A plant patent? No."

"No?"

I waited for Ellie to explain, but her attention had strayed to a small, middle-aged Asian man who'd wandered into the coffee plant room. He had short dark hair threaded with gray, a pale complexion, and slightly almond-shaped eyes. He wore loose silver-blue track pants and sneakers; and although it was a warm day, even warmer in the greenhouse, he'd kept his blue jacket on and zipped up to his chin.

I'd already removed mine.

"Excuse me, sir," Ellie called politely, "but you shouldn't be in here."

The Asian man didn't hear her, didn't understand, or was simply ignoring her. He continued around the room, looking at each of the plants.

"Is there a problem?" I whispered.

"The exhibit's not quite finished," she whispered in reply.

"So it's not yet open to the public. I'm surprised this gentleman didn't see the sign."

I raised an eyebrow. There was a single entrance to this room of the glasshouse, and the standing sign in front of that displayed a big red circle with a slash through it and the words: STOP! DO NOT ENTER. STAFF ONLY.

"I'm sure he saw it," I whispered to Ellie. "I'm also betting he ignored it. Big red stop signs are pretty universal. Maybe you should escort him out."

Ellie frowned. "Better not. I've seen him around the Garden recently. He's probably a new member—they pay annual dues to enjoy special privileges. It won't hurt him to take a quick look, as long as I stay to make sure he doesn't touch anything."

"Oh, okay . . ." I said.

We quietly watched the man after that. He carefully ignored eye contact with us as he worked his way around the room, studying the different varieties of coffee trees and the explanatory plaques beside each one.

"You were saying?" Ellie prompted, turning back to face me.

"Uh . . . yes," I said quietly. "I was wondering why Ric would mislead me. He told me that you were helping him file for a plant patent, but you said you weren't."

"No. Not a patent."

I shook my head, more distressed than ever. "I don't understand why Ric would lie to me."

"He didn't lie. He was simply using an incorrect term."

"I don't understand."

"His *arabica* hybrid can reproduce sexually, so I'm not applying for a *patent*."

"Are you joking?"

"Absolutely not. The Plant Patent Act of 1930 covers asexually reproduced plants. In other words, plants that replicate through means other than germinating seeds. Like vines, for example. Since Ric's hybrid reproduces through seeds, I'm helping him file for a plant variety protection certificate. It's an intellectual property protection, not a patent."

"But will it protect Ric's rights to the plant?"

"Yes, of course! The certificate will give him up to twenty years of exclusive control over his plant. If anyone attempts to breed and sell Ric's hybrid without licensing it from him, he has a right to file charges and sue them. It even prevents others from using it to produce a hybrid or different variety."

"Just in the United States?"

"Not just. He'll be protected all over the world."

Before I had to ask, she explained the Plant Variety Protection Act was really just the United States's effort to comply with the Union pour la Protection des Obtentions Végétales, an international treaty on plant breeders' rights. Every major country had signed on, including Brazil.

"So why didn't Ric file himself?" I asked. "Why didn't he work with the Brazilian authorities to protect his new plant?"

My question seemed to have rendered Ellie speechless. She stared at me, seemingly at a loss, and I couldn't tell if it was just the warmth of the greenhouse or something else, but a pronounced blush was spreading over her fair face.

"Ellie?" I whispered. "There's something you're not telling me . . . what is it?"

When she continued to hesitate, I took an educated guess—given that Ric hadn't even gotten the terminology right on the paperwork. "Ellie, are *you* the one who really produced this hybrid? Did *you* make the breakthrough?"

"Excuse me, Ms. Lassiter?"

I turned to find a young man staring at us. I hadn't heard

his footsteps, and I wondered how long he'd been standing there.

"What is it?" Ellie asked him.

"Your *Maragogype* just arrived via FedEx."

The young man wasn't much taller than my own five-two. He looked to be in his early twenties, had curly brown hair and a pale face with a bit of scruff on his chin and upper lip that I assumed were the beginnings of a goatee. I also assumed he was part of the staff since he was wearing the same spiffy green forest ranger ensemble that Ellie was sporting.

"Good," Ellie told him. "That's the last of them. Bring it in here, and I'll inspect it after lunch."

"You don't want to see it now?" the young man asked, his close-set brown eyes squinting slightly with disapproval.

"No, Norbert. I have a guest, as you see. We're going to have a bite to eat in the cafe."

"Oh, of course, Ms. Lassiter. If anyone deserves a break, you do. You work so hard." Now he was gushing. "Is there anything else I can do for you? Maybe your guest would like a complimentary Botanic Garden tote bag? How about it, Ms. . . . ?"

The question was pointedly leading. Norbert wanted to know my name. Before I could answer, I felt Ellie's hand on my back. She was gently pushing me toward the exit.

"Lovely thought," she called to Norbert. "Just drop it by our table later, okay?"

"Of course, Ms. Lassiter." He caught up to us, staying on our heels.

"And do me one last favor," she said, over her shoulder.

"Anything."

She lowered her voice. "There's a gentleman who wandered into my exhibit, and . . ."

As her voice trailed off, she turned to look for the

middle-aged Asian man. I turned too, but I could see the room was empty of human life. The man was gone.

"That's funny," I said, pointing. "Wasn't he just over there?"

Ellie looked puzzled. "I guess he slipped out. Forget it then, Norbert, just make sure you lock the door after you bring in my *marigo*."

"No problem. No problem at all. And I'm so sorry to have interrupted you."

"It's all right, Norbert."

TWELVE

"NORBERT'S your assistant, I take it?"

"That's right," Ellie replied as we walked toward the Garden's Terrace Café. "He's working here as an intern while he's finishing up his graduate degree."

"What's his field? Eddie Haskell Studies?"

Ellie's laugh was spontaneous and very loud in the quiet courtyard, its echo bouncing off the surrounding glass buildings. It sounded like the old carefree Ellie I'd known. But when a few dignified heads turned with curious looks, she quickly stifled herself.

I slipped my jacket back on as we walked across the courtyard's flat, gray interlocking stones. The Terrace Café was just ahead. We followed the delicious smell of grilling meat to an open kitchen housed under a glass pyramid. When we reached the cafe's counter, I could see the menu was a cut above the typical fast food fare. I ordered the Virginia ham and brie sandwich. Ellie went with the Cornish hen and brown rice. Then she surprised me by ordering a decaffeinated coffee.

"Decaf?" I said. The Ellie I remembered had been a caffeine queen. "You're kidding?"

Her response was a silent shrug.

We took our trays to the outdoor seating area, where a field of green canvas umbrellas sprouted above wire-meshed patio tables and chairs. Amid the tables were large ceramic urns containing plants as high as ten feet. Some displayed evergreen branches and bright red berries, others golden fall foliage. We chose a table on the fringes, away from the small crowd of Botanic Garden guests enjoying their lunch.

My sandwich was delicious—a crusty, fresh-baked baguette with sweet, smoky ham and buttery brie tucked inside. Still, my morning had been stressful, and after chewing and swallowing my first bite, I was desperate for a hit of caffeine. I frowned at the cup of large coffee I'd ordered, contemplating the age of the brew.

"The coffee here is actually pretty good," Ellie assured me. "Give it a shot."

"I have a better idea. I'll give it a test."

"A what?"

"A test. Watch. . . ." I took my small paper cup of cream and splashed a little into the coffee. "There it is. The bloom."

"What bloom?" Ellie asked, looking at the potted plants around us.

"Not out there," I said, and pointed to my cup. "In here. See how the cream blooms instantly to the top of my coffee?"

"Yes . . ."

"That means the coffee's fresh. When coffee's old, oils float to the top. That creates a kind of filmy barrier, so when you pour in the cream, the bloom doesn't come right to the top of the cup. It takes a few seconds longer to get there."

Ellie looked at me sideways. "You really do take coffee seriously, don't you?"

"Would a top sushi chef eat old fish? Would a master baker eat stale bread? Would an eminent butcher sink his teeth into—"

Ellie held up her hand. "I get it."

I pointed to her own cup and smiled. "And if decaf's your thing now, don't go to Italy. You may as well ask a Roman where to find the best topless bar in Vatican City as where to find a good decaffeinated espresso."

Though I'd been ribbing her in fun, Ellie didn't laugh. "I wish I could drink caffeinated again," she said. "But not long ago, I developed Graves' disease."

Oh, damn. "That's hyperthyroidism, isn't it?"

"Yes, and I'm afraid my doctor's made me swear off caffeine."

"I'm sorry, Ellie. You know, I was just kidding about Italy—"

"I know, Clare. And I do miss the old stuff . . ."

"Well, it's a good thing Ric made his breakthrough, huh? Just in time to give you a spectacular decaffeinated cup."

Ellie nodded as she sipped the Terrace Café decaf.

"Or . . . did Ric really make the breakthrough?" I quietly asked. "I'm sorry for bringing this up again, but was it really you who made the discovery? You never really answered me."

Ellie shook her head. "It wasn't me. It was Ric. You know, back in college, he even talked about creating a hybrid decaffeinated plant. He had all sorts of theories, but it wasn't until his family lost their lands that he committed himself to finishing his initial horticultural research."

"In Brazil?"

"Yes, he finished the work in his relative's nursery, but he actually began the research on Costa Gravas, using classical plant breeding techniques."

"Classical?"

"Right, as opposed to, say, DNA manipulation. Classical plant breeding's been around for thousands of years. Basically, it's controlled crossbreeding, where traits from one species or variety are introduced into the genetic background of another."

"Oh, crossbreeding!" I said. "Sure, I'm familiar with that. Coffee farmers have been doing it for centuries. Like that *Maragogype* your assistant, Norbert, mentioned. If memory serves, it's an *arabica* mutation that grows leaves and fruit much larger than the typical variety. Am I right?"

"That's right. It first appeared on a Brazilian plantation around the late Nineteenth Century."

She didn't have to quote me the rest of the history—that I knew, too. Farmers had planted *Coffea arabica Maragogype* like crazy during the Second World War. Because the *marigo* beans were twice the size of regular coffee beans, they produced a super-caffeinated cup of coffee utilized by soldiers and fighter pilots. Then the war ended, and the beans fell out of favor because the taste of the *marigo* was less than fabulous.

"The *Maragogype* is a great example of classical breeding," Ellie went on. "Here's another example: let's say you have a *Coffea* plant that's got a high fruit yield, but it's susceptible to rust disease. You can cross that with a *Coffea* plant that's resistant to the disease, even though it may have a low yield. The goal of the crossbreeding would be to create a *Coffea* plant resistant to rust disease that's also high-yielding."

"But you could also get a plant that's low-yielding and susceptible to disease."

"That's why it takes time and patience. With diligence, progeny from a successful cross can be crossed back with a parent to strengthen the desirable trait—that's back-crossing."

"So that's what Ric did?" I pressed.

"Yes. Ric crossbred and backcrossed different species of *Coffea* plants to produce his decaffeinated hybrid."

"And is it viable?"

"Oh, yes. It's hearty, resistant to disease, and high-yielding. I've been working with him for about a year now to help him properly document his work."

"I see."

"Look, I understand why you made the assumption you did. I know Ric doesn't come off as any sort of scientific genius. But he is gifted when it comes to living things. He grew up around coffee plants, and he's a naturalist at heart. Did you know when he was just a boy, he hiked almost every inch of his native island to see all the flora and fauna?"

"But he still needed your help to get his hybrid certified, right?"

"Ric never finished his degree because he's not very good at paperwork. If he wants legal protection for his hybrid, he needs to jump through a lot of documentation hoops—and, frankly, jumping through hoops is something I learned how to do well over the last ten years, and in more ways than one."

That was a loaded statement if ever I'd heard one, but I wanted to keep the focus on Ric. "So everything's legit?" I pressed. "Ric made an authentic breakthrough and you're helping him?"

"That's right. There's really nothing more to it."

"And yet . . . Ric seemed cagey with me when I asked why he didn't file for protection in Brazil. You already told me Brazil is part of the international treaty to protect plant breeders' rights, so what's the truth?"

"The truth is . . . Ric doesn't trust the officials in Brazil responsible for approving his protection certificate."

"He's worried about theft?"

"He's worried they'll charge *him* with theft."

"I don't follow."

"Brazil's government is very concerned about biopiracy."

I'd heard the term before. I just didn't see how it applied. "I'm not sure I understand . . ."

"Biopiracy is basically hijacking plants from their native country and patenting them for commercial exploitation in another country. In Brazil's case, plants have been taken out of the Amazon and brought to other countries for experimentation, cultivation, and marketing."

"But Ric's growing his hybrid in Brazil. He's not taking it out of the country."

"That's not the issue."

"Then what is?"

Ellie shifted uncomfortably. "Matt knows this already, and you're his partner, so I guess it's okay to tell you, just so you'll stop worrying."

"Tell me what?"

Ellie's voice dropped. "Ric discovered a plant growing wild on Costa Gravas—a naturally decaffeinated *Coffea stenophylla* plant."

"Not *arabica*?"

"No."

That surprised me. Notwithstanding my botanically inaccurate reference to the plant as a "tree," I was fairly familiar with the basic aspects of coffee as a cash crop. I knew there were many species of the plant, some decorative and some used by native cultures for stimulant value. But as far as commercial importance to farmers, there were only two players: *Coffea arabica* (referred to simply as *arabica* in the trade) and *Coffea canephora* (referred to as *robusta*).

Arabica, which covered about 80 percent of the world's coffee production, was the A-list star of the show. Grown at higher altitudes and considered high quality, *arabica* was the source for specialty coffees. *Robusta* was grown at lower altitudes and for years had been the source of cheaper blends and the basis for instant and canned coffees.

Within *arabica*, there were two "original" varieties, *Coffea arabica arabica* (or *typica*) and *Coffea arabica bourbon*, out of which many unique forms had emerged, either through deliberate breeding or accidental mutations in the fields. Two such spin-off hybrids popular with farmers were *Coffea arabica cattura* and *Coffea arabica catuai*, both of which grew much shorter than the original varieties, so they were easier to harvest. They were also more resistant to disease.

Coffea stenophylla, however, was new to me, and I asked Ellie to tell me more about it.

"Historically, *stenophylla* was considered to be better than *arabica*," she explained. "The plant was hardier, it had a higher fruit yield, and the final product had a better flavor."

"You're kidding? What happened then? Why aren't today's farmers planting that?"

"The English took it out of West Africa in the late 1800s and grew it in their colonies—"

"That would include Jamaica then? And Ric's old home—Costa Gravas?"

"Yes, exactly. But rust disease was a huge issue back then. It wiped out many of the plantations cultivating it. The farms had no time to recoup their losses fast, and *stenophylla* takes nine years to mature. Even though it produces a hardier plant with higher yields, it was abandoned in favor of the *arabicas*, which take only five to seven years to mature and bear fruit."

"Okay, I follow, but where does that fit in with Ric's breakthrough?"

"The key to Ric's hybrid decaffeinated plant is what he and I believe is a mutation from a surviving *stenophylla* plant. The plant itself wouldn't have been useful to a coffee farmer. It still took nine years to mature, its yield was low, and it produced a decaffeinated bean."

"I follow you. A decaf bean wouldn't have been an advantageous trait until lately, since decaf drinkers only recently became a larger percentage of the market."

"That's right. It wasn't worth a farmer investing time and effort into breeding a decaffeinated plant. But Ric never felt that way. When his family was driven off their estate, he smuggled this mutated *stenophylla*'s seeds and cuttings into Brazil. For years, he continued his experiments in crossbreeding using *Coffea arabica* plants, and finally he made his breakthrough."

"So you're saying the key to Ric's hybrid is a plant he smuggled out of Costa Gravas? And the authorities there might have an issue?"

"Not just there. Brazilian officials are pushing for world sanctions on biopiracy in their own rain forests. They'd look like hypocrites if they granted protection to Ric, since Costa Gravas might very well charge him with biopiracy once the word gets out."

"And that's why you're helping him file for protection outside of both countries?"

"Exactly. There won't be any issues here in the United States. Ric's horticultural work is real and visionary, and I can attest to its value and validity. He deserves the protection."

"You're his champion then?"

"Yes, I am."

I was about to ask Ellie another question when a startled look suddenly crossed her face. "Oh," she said. "Norbert, where did you come from?"

I turned to see Norbert standing near a potted plant, next to our table. Ellie and I had been conversing so intensely, we hadn't noticed his arrival.

"I'm sorry," he said, tilting his curly head. "I wasn't sure how to interrupt you without appearing rude, but I wanted to drop off that little parting gift for your friend." He held out a canvas tote bag with the words Brooklyn Botanic Garden embroidered on the side in forest green.

"Thank you." I took it from him. "It's very nice."

"Anything else, Ms. Lassiter?" Norbert asked, rolling forward onto his toes a bit. "Anything at all?"

Ellie's eyes met mine for a second and I could tell she was recalling my Eddie Haskell joke. I could also tell she was suppressing another laugh.

"No, Norbert. That's all. Why don't you take your lunch now, and I'll see you in an hour."

"Certainly, Ms. Lassiter. I'll see you later. And goodbye, Ms. . . ."

"Goodbye," I said quickly.

Norbert nodded, giving me a forced smile, then turned and departed. I watched him like a hawk until he was well out of earshot.

"Ellie, what's the story on your assistant?"

"What do you mean?"

"What's his last name?"

"Usher, why?"

"How long has he been working for you?"

Ellie looked to the sky, calculating. "About nine or ten months. He came on before this year's spring season." She sighed. "I know I'm a bit short and cold with him, but he's got a bit of a crush on me, and I'm trying to discourage it."

I raised an eyebrow. "How deep a crush?"

She waved her hand. "He asked me out a few times over the summer. Not directly, just dropping hints that I might like to go here or there with him—an outdoor movie in Bryant Park, a Sunday drive with him to Cape May."

"Doesn't he know you're married?"

"He knows. He also knows about Ric, unfortunately. You've seen how quiet he can be. He snuck up on us a few times out in the Garden. I thought we were well hidden, but he saw us . . . all we were doing was embracing, but . . ."

"But what exactly?"

Ellie shifted uncomfortably. "It's hard to explain, but when I'm with Ric . . . I'm a different person. He does something to me, Clare . . . he changes me . . ."

Oh, boy, did that sound familiar. "He's a drug?"

"Yes. He is."

"And you're addicted?"

"Yes. I am."

The years seemed to melt off Ellie when she talked about Ric. Her expression was animated, her complexion more vibrant, her hazel-green eyes bright.

My gaze fell to the gold wedding band on her finger, and I wondered how far things had gone with her old beau. She said they'd just embraced, but was that really all? Was it just a mutual admiration society? Or was it a full blown affair?

"You know, Ellie," I said, blatantly fishing, "I was always sorry that I missed your wedding. You had it here, didn't you?"

Ellie looked away—toward two reflecting pools standing in front of a beautiful glass structure that resembled London's famous Crystal Palace.

"Jerry and I took our vows on Daffodil Hill, in early

April—the optimum time to see the blooms. The Garden staff was there, and Jerry's entire lab came. We had our reception in the Palm House, and, of course, there was a *Times* listing. It was a perfect wedding."

The words painted a lovely memory, but Ellie's voice was a monotone. Her buoyant expression had gone blank.

"And how's the marriage?" I asked carefully. "Everything still perfect?"

"You're asking because of Ric?"

"You loved him so much years ago. You were devastated when he left without proposing. I remember how badly you cried."

"I cried so much because . . ." Ellie glanced down. She looked pained. "I was pregnant, Clare."

For a few seconds, I didn't move, and I questioned whether I'd heard her correctly. "You were pregnant?"

Ellie nodded.

"But you never said anything . . . not to me, and we were close back then. Or at least I thought we were."

"We were. I didn't tell *anyone*, not even Ric."

"Why not?"

"I didn't want Ric to stay in America and marry me just because of a baby. I wanted him to stay for me. I didn't want to quit college and end up like—"

Her run of words abruptly halted. She met my eyes, her expression somewhere between disdain and pity.

"End up like me?" I finished for her.

"I'm sorry, Clare. You have to understand . . . I was young at the time, and I had very little resources. I wanted to finish my degree, and I just couldn't do it alone with a baby. My family was in no position to help me financially. They barely had enough to cover their own debts, and they hated my coming to New York—"

She was talking very fast now, awkwardly trying to

make up for her insult. I patted her shoulder. "It's okay," I said, but she kept going.

"My family would have demanded I move back to West Virginia to have the baby, you see? And I'm sure I would have had to start working at some menial job to support my child—"

"Yes, I understand." *Like managing a coffeehouse?*

"And I just couldn't see myself doing that."

"No, no, of course not."

"The only future I could see was if Ric had decided to stay and marry me because he loved me . . . or asked me to go back to Costa Gravas with him. But he did neither."

"So you aborted your child?"

Ellie nodded. Now her eyes were wet. "It broke my heart, but I didn't see any other way."

"And did you ever tell Ric?"

Ellie nodded. "He was upset. He said I should have leveled with him back then. That he would have married me."

"Do you believe him?"

"It doesn't matter if I do or don't. I was afraid he'd end up resenting the child and me, or he'd end up cheating just like—"

Once again, she cut herself off. So I finished for her. "Just like Matt did to me."

Ellie closed her eyes. "I didn't mean to imply . . ."

Her voice trailed off, and once more I said, "It's okay. The truth is, I felt the same way you did. I just felt it after I married Matt. I found evidence of his cheating one morning, and I considered walking out, but I was afraid of raising Joy on my own . . . so I stayed."

"You're happy now though?"

"Yes. Maybe one day I'll finish my fine arts degree. Maybe not. My life's good. I love my work, and I love my daughter. I don't regret for one second what I gave up to have her. If you recall, Matt *asked* me to marry him. He didn't run off to another country like Ric . . . and because he asked, and I loved him, I gave the marriage a try."

"And now you've obviously forgiven Matt. You've gone into business with him."

"Yes, I have. And now *you're* Ric's champion."

Ellie looked away again. "I hadn't thought of it as the same thing."

"But it is. Time passes, and we forgive . . . don't we?"

Ellie smiled but very weakly. "Sure."

There was something about her smile that unsettled me. She was holding back again, and I wondered for a moment if Ellie was being totally honest . . . or playing me.

I hadn't seen her in so many years, and she'd changed so much it was hard talking with her. But in the last two minutes what hit me the hardest was finally realizing why we were no longer friends.

I understood what Ellie had done, and why she'd done it. And I wasn't about to judge her. But Ellie had judged me. That was clear to me now. She had no respect for me or my choices. Oh, she'd never stated it outright. Not ever. But somewhere along the line in those years past, she must have sent out the signals because I'd stopped caring whether we saw each other any more.

You'd think by now I would be a whiz at stumbling upon disturbing realities—like a pistol-whipped body in my back alley, for instance, or a homeless man's frozen corpse. But chancing upon the truth about an old friendship was no less disturbing. I did my best to cover my reaction, but it shook me up.

I began to wonder what kind of person Ellie Shaw had become and what she was capable of. Was it possible she hadn't forgiven Ric at all? Was she playing him now for some kind of latent revenge?

"Did you know that Ric was mugged behind the Village Blend?" I found myself asking, suddenly needing to see her reaction.

"What?" Ellie's weak smile disappeared.

"Last night. Someone pistol-whipped him from behind."

"Oh my goodness, Clare, why didn't you say something earlier? Does he know who did it?"

I shook my head. "He says it's no big deal. And he didn't see the man's face . . . of course it could have been a woman."

"What do you mean it could have been a woman? Women don't mug people on the street."

"Whoever this was used a prerecorded message of commands. The detective I consulted thinks it means Ric would have recognized the mugger's voice."

"You consulted a detective already?" Ellie asked. She seemed upset by this.

I nodded. "What do you think?"

"What do I think of what?"

"Do you know anyone who might want to harm Ric or steal his cutting?"

"What cutting? What are you talking about, Clare?"

"He smuggled a cutting into the country to show to the press and the trade this Friday at the Beekman. He mailed it to Matt initially for safekeeping, but he said he had to borrow it to show to you."

Ellie shook her head. "I don't know what you're talking about. He never showed me any cutting. He wouldn't have to. I'm well acquainted with his hybrid. I've been flying down to Brazil off and on for over a year now."

"You're sure you didn't need to see a cutting in the last few weeks?"

"I'm certain, Clare. I don't know why Ric would tell you—"

A series of electronic tones interrupted her. Taken together, I realized they were cell phone ringtones playing a familiar melody—the Sting song "Roxanne."

Ellie reached into her jacket pocket and pulled out her cell. "Excuse me," she said and opened her phone. "Hello?"

She listened for a moment. "Yes," she told the caller. "Yes . . . oh, okay. Right now then. Hold a minute."

"I'm sorry, Clare, but I have to take this call, and then I have to get right back to work. It was good seeing you." She held out her hand, and we shook. "I'm sure we'll talk again at the end of the week."

Before I could even bid her goodbye, she was turning to leave. I watched as she swiftly strode away toward the greenhouse that held her exhibit.

With a sigh, I rose from the patio table. Ellie had left her tray behind, a Cornish hen carcass on a half-eaten pile of brown rice. I bussed it to the garbage receptacle; then I bussed my own. I'd had more questions for her, but I let them go, mainly because my most pressing questions were for Ric.

"If Ellie didn't need to see the cutting, then why did he 'borrow' it from Matt?" I mumbled to myself as I left the Terrace Café. "And why in heaven's name did he lie about it to me?"

Thirteen

I didn't have to search long to regroup with Matt's mother. She was standing near the administration building between the two lotus-filled reflecting pools, gazing up at the Palm House where Ellie had held the reception for her perfect wedding.

"Ready to go, Madame?"

"You know, this little Crystal Palace would be an exquisite setting for the Theater League's next fundraiser."

"Think so?"

"It's wheelchair accessible, the restrooms are clean and convenient, and the people at the Visitor's Center told me the local caterers are quite good."

"Really . . ."

"You know, thanks to our donors, five thousand inner-city schoolchildren were able to experience live theater for the first time last year. And this year, we hope to double that amount."

"That's nice . . ."

She took a closer look at me. "Are you all right, Clare? Did you have a pleasant visit with your old friend?"

"No."

Madame's eyebrows arched. "Why not?"

"Because, from what I just learned, I think Matt may have put us in a precarious position."

"My goodness!" Madame's hand flew to cover her mouth. "Does your friend know that Breanne Summour person?"

Oh, for pity's sake. "No, Madame. Matt's love life is not what's putting us in a precarious position. His business deal is."

"Which business deal? You'll have to be more specific."

"The Gostwick Estate Decaf deal. There are a lot of issues that Matt's been keeping from me, and I think from you, too."

"Is that so? Then you'd better enlighten me. That boy's kept me in the dark so much, I swear chanterelles are growing out of my ears."

"Now that's a surreal image."

"Tell me the truth, Clare. Are you *investigating* something again? Because if you are—"

"I know. I know."

"I want in."

"That's what I figured."

I was about to spill everything, starting with the bizarre mugging with the prerecorded message, when I noticed an elderly couple strolling in our direction. "Come on," I grabbed Madame's elbow. "Let's go to the car. I don't think we should have this discussion in public . . ."

FIFTEEN minutes later, I was wrapping up the delightful tale of Ric's mugging, the smuggled hybrid cutting, the plant certification issues, and possible biopiracy charges. I was just getting to Ellie's secret pregnancy when I noticed the woman herself striding purposefully onto the parking lot's asphalt.

"Look," I said, pointing. "There's Ellie now."

Madame and I were sitting in my Honda. The doors were closed, the windows half open to keep the interior from getting too warm in the sun.

"What is she doing out here?" Madame asked. "Didn't you just say she had to go back to work?"

"Yes . . ."

We both fell silent as we watched her unlock a green paneled van and disappear inside.

"Perhaps she's retrieving something from that van," Madame speculated. "Or maybe she's going to drive somewhere for a meeting?"

"Maybe . . ." I expected the van to start up, but it never did. After about ten minutes, the van's door opened again, and Ellie emerged.

"She's changed!" Madame noted.

"Yes, I see . . ."

She'd dumped her forest ranger style uniform, replacing it with an outfit decidedly more feminine. Her loose slacks had been exchanged for a very short skirt; her boxy zipper jacket for a tight-fitting, cleavage-baring sweater. A dusty rose wrap was draped over her arm, and her manicured feet clicked across the parking lot on high-heeled sandals.

No longer the dignified Garden curator, Ellie was now Pretty in Pink.

Madame shook her head and murmured a series of regretful sounding tisk, tisk, tisks.

"What is it?" I asked.

"Strawberry blondes should never wear that color. What was she thinking?"

"I don't know, maybe that it worked for Molly Ringwald twenty years ago."

"Who?"

"Women pushing forty often have these jejune moments of fashion misjudgment, Madame. Take it from me, I know."

"But why?" Madame asked.

"Crow's feet, thickening thighs, those first threads of gray—"

"No, dear! Why did your friend change her clothes?"

"Oh, that? I have no idea."

I'd already assumed, since Ellie hadn't started up the van and driven away, that she was going to walk right back into the Garden. But she didn't.

Madame pointed. "It appears she's heading toward that Town Car."

A dark four-door sedan sat idling near the parking lot gate, a type of vehicle that car services used.

Although yellow cabs constantly prowled the Manhattan streets, they were practically nonexistent in New York's other four boroughs, so I wouldn't have thought Ellie's hiring a car service was particularly suspicious—except for the fact that Ellie already had her own set of wheels and wasn't using them.

Ellie approached the Town Car and climbed inside, but the sedan didn't take off right away. As it continued to idle, I noticed something else, or rather *someone* else. The Asian man, who'd barged into Ellie's exhibit, was now swiftly crossing the parking lot.

"That's funny," I murmured. "Where's *he* going in such a hurry?"

"Where's who—"

"Do you see that man?" I pointed to the middle-aged Asian man in the silver-blue track suit.

"Yes, I see him," Madame said.

We watched as the man climbed into a black SUV.

"What about him?" Madame pressed.

"I think it's a little coincidental that he's leaving at the exact same time as Ellie."

"Why? Who is he?"

"I don't know who he is," I said, "but he blatantly ignored a 'staff only' sign to inspect Ellie's Horticulture of Coffee exhibit while I was talking to her."

"Didn't she throw him out?"

"She politely asked him to leave. He ignored her. Or didn't understand her. Frankly, I thought he was playing possum, but Ellie was worried he might be a Garden member, and she didn't want to offend him, so she let him look around."

"Well, maybe he is a member, dear. Maybe it's just a coincidence that he's leaving at the same time she is."

"Let's find out."

The Asian man started up his SUV and pulled out of his parking space. As he drove it toward the parking lot exit, I started my own car and followed.

By now, Ellie's Town Car was taking off. The sedan turned left onto Washington Avenue. The Asian man's black SUV turned left, too. So that's what I did.

"Can you see Ellie's hired car?" Madame asked, her voice a little impatient.

"Not around that big SUV, I can't."

"Darn these ubiquitous all-terrain rollover hazards!" Madame wailed. "Monstrosities like this one have been crowding the New York streets for years now, and I can't for the life of me understand why—"

"A lot of people like the—"

"I've trekked Central America in my prime. I've visited high altitude farms in North Africa and Indonesia. I've ascended Machu Picchu. Those perilous, backwater, mud road topographies were what these four-wheel drive vehicles were invented for—not Park and Madison avenues!"

"Yes, I know, but—"

"What's the most challenging terrain these gas-guzzlers encounter? Tell me that? A slippery bridge surface followed by a pothole?!"

"Take it easy. We're just taking a little drive. No need to get stressed."

"But behind this man's big SUV, you can't even *see* Ellie's Town Car. And I believe you're following the wrong vehicle. I think you need to get around this man's and tail Ellie's hired car."

"Tell you what . . . if Ellie's driver turns one way and this man's SUV turns the other, then we'll go with Ellie, okay?"

"Will you even notice a turn like that?" Madame asked. "I thought the traffic was quite heavy on Flatbush Avenue coming in."

"Then why don't you keep your eyes open, too. Between us, we should be able to figure this out and not lose her."

With Madame so skeptical about the Asian man in the SUV, I decided that she was probably right. Any moment now, I expected him to peel off and head in a different direction than Ellie's car. But he never did. When Ellie's Town Car made a left, so did the black SUV.

Ahead of us now was the majestic Brooklyn Art Museum, rising like a beaux arts sentry over the congested traffic of Eastern Parkway. The Museum, designed by Stanford White, was part of a complex of nineteenth-century parks and gardens that included the Botanic Gardens we'd just left as well as nearby Prospect Park—a 500 acre area of land, sculpted into fields, woods, lakes, and trails by the landscape designers Olmsted and Vaux, the same ingenious pair who'd created Manhattan's world-renowned Central Park.

Eastern Parkway flowed us into Grand Army Plaza, a busy traffic circle dominated by the central branch building of Brooklyn's Public Library (one of the first libraries that allowed readers to browse). I remember one of my old professors calling the architecture a triumph of context. The smooth, towering facade was created to resemble an open book, with the spine on the Plaza and the building's two wings spreading like pages onto Eastern Parkway and Flatbush Avenue, two of the three spokes of Grand Army's wheel. Prospect Park West was the third spoke, but I didn't know which direction the vehicles in front of me were going to turn.

Sweat broke out on my palms as I followed the SUV around the whooshing spin-cycle of vehicles. While I was living in New Jersey, I'd driven every day. Now that I was a fulltime Manhattan resident again, my car sat in a garage while I mainly got around by subway, bus, or taxi, so I was pretty well out of practice putting pedal to the metal. On the other hand, I'd never liked traffic circles. I'd always end up going around and around, as if I were trapped on some out-of-control carousel, and I had to gather the nerve to jump off.

At the moment, I didn't have the luxury of going around more than once or I'd lose my quarry. Vans, trucks, buses, and cars were zooming by in lanes on my left and right. Signs announced the upcoming turnoffs, and it was difficult to keep my eye on the Town Car, the SUV, and the rest of the traffic.

"Madame!"

"Yes?"

"Make sure you watch for any sign of Ellie's Town Car

peeling off the circle and taking a turn, okay? My eyes are still on the SUV in front of us."

"Okay!"

"I'm anticipating a right onto Flatbush, by the way."

"Why?"

"That's the way we came in. It's a straight shot right up Flatbush to the Manhattan Bridge crossing, and I'm betting Ellie's destination is Manhattan. Here it comes . . ." I began to swerve the wheel, moving into the turning lane, and then—

Oh, crap . . . "They're not turning!"

"Stay in the circle! Stay in the circle!" Madame cried, her wrinkled hands practically lunging for the wheel.

I swerved back to my original lane and an immense, white SUV behind me blew his horn. I glanced in my rear view. The man driving was cursing at me, one hand on the wheel, another holding a cell phone to his ear, which was completely illegal and reckless, thank you very much!

"Someone should tell that guy 'hands free' is the law of the land now!" I cried.

"Eyes ahead! Don't try to turn before they do," Madame warned.

"Okay, okay! I was just anticipating—"

"Don't anticipate!"

The black SUV kept going. It was still following Ellie's Town Car. A few seconds later, Madame started shouting. "She's turning now! The Town Car's turning!"

"So is the SUV!" I shouted back.

Both vehicles had left the Plaza and were heading for Union Street.

"Union Street?" I murmured, continuing to trail the sports utility vehicle. "Now why does that sound familiar?"

We drove a few blocks, then a red light up ahead halted our progress for a few minutes.

"I'm not too familiar with this borough," Madame said, glancing at the rows of beautifully restored brownstones on both sides of us. "How often have you been here?"

"Quite a few times. Matt's been renting a storage warehouse not far from here."

"I remember coming to Brooklyn when Matt was very young," Madame's eyes took on that faraway look again. "Antonio took us to Coney Island. The park was a madhouse, of course, since we went on a sunny Saturday afternoon, Matt did so love the rides—"

My fingers tightened on the steering wheel. If Madame went down memory lane now, I'd lose Ellie for sure!

"Coney Island's *many miles* away," I pointedly interrupted. "It's on the south end of the borough, on the Atlantic, probably over forty-five minutes away from where we are now."

"And where are we now exactly?"

"Park Slope."

Brooklyn was home to at least ninety different neighborhoods and two hundred nationalities, many of whom had created ethnic enclaves (not unlike Manhattan's Chinatown or the nearly vanished Little Italy). Brooklyn's more recent immigrants—from the Caribbean, Middle East, and former Soviet Union—had brought cultural color to many of the borough's streets with native restaurants, festivals, and specialty groceries. In this upscale Brooklyn area, however, the overriding heritage appeared to be that of my own Village neighborhood: Transplanted Yuppie-Hipster ("Yupster" was the current pop-sociological term, Young Urban Professional Hipster). In fact, the area had so many relocated writers, editors, academics, and lawyers, Mike Quinn once joked to me that he'd blinked one day and realized Manhattan's Upper West Side had teleported half its residents to his borough.

The red light changed to green, and we moved forward. We were now crossing Seventh Avenue, the main shopping area for the North Slope (the northern end of Park Slope), which boasted the sort of bistros, restaurants, and boutiques typically seen in Manhattan's trendier neighborhoods.

"We're still close to the city," I mentioned for Madame, "certainly less than thirty minutes from the Manhattan crossings."

"Well, you know what they say these days about real estate," Madame noted, "anything within a half-hour commute to Manhattan, *is* Manhattan. I have an acquaintance in Brooklyn Heights, near the promenade—she tells me her brownstone's been valued as high as a Chelsea townhouse."

Brownstone . . . my memory kicked in, and I suddenly knew why Union Street sounded so familiar. It was Mike Quinn's old street address. I'd never visited him in Brooklyn, but one slow afternoon while I was doing schedules in my office, I took a break and regressed into teenage crush mode to find his home by satellite on the Web.

I knew he was melancholy over selling the place, which wasn't here in Park Slope, but two neighborhoods over in Carroll Gardens. Since his wife wanted the divorce, and they jointly owned the property, he was stuck. Apparently, the building was worth so much now (easily five times the value of their original purchase price fifteen years before), he couldn't afford to buy her out, but the good news was that he'd be getting a nice chunk of change from his share of the sale.

"Union is definitely a cross street," I told Madame, thinking back to that Web satellite map I'd consulted. "I'm sure we're heading West."

"Toward the East River?"

"Yes."

The black SUV was still rolling forward, right behind Ellie's Town Car. And I followed them for a few more minutes. We were now leaving the restored brownstones of Park Slope and entering the far less upscale neighborhood of Gowanus.

Madame pursed her lips as she took in the blighted area of rundown clapboard row houses tucked between dead factories and a network of abandoned shipyard waterways.

"Are those *canals*?" she said, gawking down one of the channels of water as we crossed the narrow Union Street bridge.

"You're kidding? You've never heard of the Gowanus canal debate?"

"Oh, yes, I've heard about that, but I didn't realize they were *actually* canals . . ."

Gowanus, with its maze of narrow waterways, once served as a working extension of the nearby shipyard. When the ports shut down, the heavy industry left, and this neighborhood of factories and warehouses became an urban eyesore. Then artists started moving in, taking over and transforming the large spaces. A former soap factory, for instance, had been converted into a site for a community arts organization.

In more recent years, the area was "upzoned" to allow for the construction of residential buildings. Now two new towers were standing, overlooking the once stinky canals (which had since been cleaned up). A Whole Foods store was about to open, and major developers were buzzing about turning the entire area into a "Little Venice," complete with the sort of Yupster restaurants and upscale rents we'd just left behind in the North Slope.

The debate right now was with residents who saw themselves being priced out of their homes. It was the same old song that had been sung so many times on Manhattan

Island. Low rent immigrant and industrial areas, plagued with cracked sidewalks, graffiti, and crime, became havens for struggling artists who turned them trendy, making them gold mines for developers, who boosted rents, squeezing longtime residents and poor artists out.

"Uh-oh," I mumbled.

"What?" Madame asked.

"This is the neighborhood where Matt's renting a warehouse. Do you think Ellie's on her way there for some reason?"

"For what reason?"

"I don't know . . . Matt's storing Ric's decaffeinated green beans right now. They're extremely valuable, and I have to tell you, at the moment, I don't trust Ellie . . ."

"They're not turning or stopping," Madame noted. "Where is Matt's warehouse exactly?"

"Just a few blocks away, I'm surprised he never took you to see it."

"What's to see? Bags of green coffee in a big building. I've seen them all my life, dear. Matt's handling all that now."

The buildings around us began to change again, from industrial to residential. The streets became cleaner, the graffiti disappeared, and well maintained brownstones now lined the blocks.

"We've entered Carroll Gardens," I informed Madame.

But my focus was momentarily off the vehicles we were following. Mike Quinn's brownstone was around here somewhere, and I was searching for a glimpse of it.

During my previous trips to Matt's warehouse, my ex-husband had been driving, and I wasn't about to sound like a teenager asking her father to "please drive by Mike's house. I want to see where he lives . . ." At the moment, Madame and I were still on Union. We passed the intersection with

Hoyt, then Smith (ten blocks down was the famous Smith and Ninth subway station, the highest elevated platform in New York's entire subway system). Suddenly, a woman in another SUV, a cherry red one, pulled out of her parking space, and jumped right in front of me, cutting me off.

I hit the brakes. "Damn!"

Now there were two SUVs between me and Ellie's car. Court Street was just ahead, and the line of traffic had stopped for a red light. I found it interesting that the Asian man in the black SUV was still following Ellie.

Coincidence? I wondered. Mike Quinn always said that in his line of work there were no coincidences.

The reminder of Mike and coincidences together had me back checking the street addresses. His old home had to be on this block. I peered down the row of connected brownstones, and noticed a FOR SALE sign in front of one of them. Like the others on this quiet, tree-lined street, the house was set back from the sidewalk, giving it a nice little front yard, delineated by a wrought iron garden gate.

I counted three floors and knew, on sight, that it was a valuable building. An owner could comfortably live on one or two floors and rent out the third. Buildings like this one, in this quiet, lovely neighborhood, a close commute to Manhattan, easily sold for one million dollars or more.

I tried to remember some of the funny things Mike had said about living here . . . how the area was named after the only Roman Catholic to sign the Declaration of Independence (Charles Carroll), but the area was more famous for a more modern Brooklyn native, Al Capone. The gangster had ended up in Chicago, but he'd begun his criminal career near here and was married at St. Mary's Star of the Sea church just around the corner.

I wondered in passing if Mike's wife and two kids had moved out yet, and I automatically scanned the street for any sign of them (Mike had shown me photos). But the narrow block was empty, save for a young woman with short dark hair and trendy glasses, talking on a cell phone as she pushed along a baby carriage. She was clearly one of the newer transplants to what had once been a neighborhood of working class Italian immigrants.

"Clare!" Madame suddenly cried.

I jumped in my seat. "What?"

"The light's changed! Look, the cars are turning onto Court."

I didn't have to ask what direction. It would have to be south, because down here Court was one way. I was about to make the turn when the tightly timed stoplight changed again. The woman in the cherry SUV in front of me hesitated on the yellow. She stopped, as if considering whether to go through it, then started up again, making the turn.

"Damn!"

The woman had left me stuck on a full blown red light, and traffic was starting to come through the intersection.

"Go through it," Madame demanded.

"I can't! There's no 'left on red' allowed in New York State. I don't think 'left on red' is allowed in *any* state!"

"Go through it anyway," Madame demanded. "This is an emergency."

"We don't know that."

"We'll lose both Ellie and the man in the black SUV following her—and you said someone is after Ric. You said they could have killed him the night he was mugged, and he looks so much like Matt that you're afraid someone might make a mistake. Am I wrong, dear?"

"No."

"Then do as I say. Put your foot on the gas, sneak out carefully into the intersection, and go through that red light, *tout de suite*!"

I did. Pretending I was simply entering another traffic circle, I waited for the oncoming flow of cars to lighten up just enough for me to nose out there, then I burned rubber, made a screeching turn and headed down the street. Within three blocks, I spotted that cherry red SUV.

"Where's the black SUV?!" I cried. "It should be in front of her!"

"It's up ahead. Look!" Madame replied.

"But there are two of them now!"

A pair of the same model black SUVs were rolling side by side down Court. Each of the large, boxy vehicles had a dark-haired man driving, and I couldn't tell which of them was the Asian man who'd been following Ellie.

"Oh, damn," I murmured. "Why didn't we get the license plate?!"

"Where's the Town Car?" Madame asked.

"I don't see it!" I cried.

Just then, the black SUV on the left, put on his left-turn signal. He was planning to turn soon, while the one on the right was obviously going to continue driving straight.

"Which way should I go?" I asked. "Should I turn with the guy on the left, or go straight with the guy on the right?!"

"I don't know, dear!"

The burst of siren nearly sent me through the car roof. I checked my rear view mirror. A half a block back, a police cruiser was threading through the heavy traffic. "You in the red vehicle," a loud voice suddenly boomed over a loudspeaker, "pull over."

Crap!

An NYPD traffic cop had obviously witnessed my little lapse in judgment back at the intersection of Union and Court.

"But officer," (I could say) *"right on red is legal on Long Island."*

"You're not on Long Island!" (The cop would probably bark.) *"And you made a left. License and registration, and get out of the car, we'll want to search the vehicle and give you a sobriety test."*

"Don't, Clare! Don't pull over!" Madame cried.

"Are you crazy?"

"I'm very serious. I bought a little something in the Garden."

"Excuse me?"

"There was this nice Jamaican man. He and I hit it off—you know, I've been to his native island many times—and he offered to sell me some clove cigarettes. But I suspect they might have a little something more than cloves in them."

"A little something more? What are you telling me? What something more?!"

"You know, something of that famous native crop from the man's island home."

"Coffee?"

"No."

"*Ganja*?"

Madame nodded.

"You made a *drug deal* at the Brooklyn Botanic Gardens!"

"I have the cigarettes in my bag, and I'll gladly throw them out the window, but you have to evade the police car well enough for me to get rid of them without those two nice-looking officers seeing me dispose of the evidence."

"For the love of . . . !"

The burst of siren was louder now and longer. "Lady in Red! Pull over!"

Clearly, the cop had a case of *agita*, and I wasn't helping. But I couldn't pull over if Madame was carrying marijuana. I had no idea how much she had, or how much was enough to land her in Rikers Island Correctional Facility for the night.

"Look, the Town Car!" Madame cried.

I'd sped up enough to catch sight of it near the end of Court Street. We were also out of Carroll Gardens by now and entering Red Hook, a neck of land that jutted out into Upper New York Bay. Years ago, Red Hook had been a bustling working class enclave for dock workers, then it fell on hard times.

A little over a decade ago it was discovered by artists, who were inspired by (as a visual artist put it to me one day in the Blend) "stunning harbor views clashing with urban decay." And now, the same old song was playing again: the area was on its way to gentrification, with waterfront development plans that included the largest Ikea in the world replacing a nineteenth-century dry dock.

The police siren wailed again, and I noticed in my mirror that cherry red SUV, driven by that lady who had stranded me back at the traffic light. She started pulling over, clearly misunderstanding that the cop was after me.

I took the opportunity to push the envelope—along with the gas pedal.

The cherry SUV moved between me and the police car to get to the side of the street, and I punched forward, just making the end of a yellow light at the bottom of Court. I didn't know where the black SUV was, but I saw Ellie's Town Car. It had swerved right, and was now heading for Hamilton Avenue and the Brooklyn Battery Tunnel Plaza.

"Of course! They're taking the tunnel!"

I always took one of the three bridges to and from Brooklyn, so I hadn't recognized this route to the tunnel.

"Looks like Ellie's going to Manhattan, after all," Madame noted, turning in her seat. "And it also looks like you shook that traffic cop."

"Yes, it seems I did," I said, checking my rear view, as well.

Thank goodness, I thought with relief. For once, it appeared I'd dodged the bullet. It also appeared I was wrong about the Asian man in the silver-blue track suit. He and his black SUV were now nowhere in sight.

Fourteen

"SHE'S still sitting in that Town Car," said Madame.

I nodded. "I think she's paying the driver."

We'd tailed Ellie's car from Brooklyn, racing through the Battery Tunnel, and up Manhattan's West Side Highway. After exiting on Canal, we drove north, snaked around some cross streets and came down Varick (the name for Seventh Avenue just south of the Village). Now we were sitting in my Honda, idling next to a curb in Soho. Ellie's hired car had parked in front of a hotel half a block away.

"There she goes," Madame said.

Showing a substantial amount of white leg, Ellie exited the parked Town Car. Her high-heeled sandals clicked their way into V. This chic Soho hotel was one my ex-husband had favored before his mother had offered him the rent free use of the duplex above the Blend.

"V's a lot like W on Union Square," Matt used to say, "only it's a different letter."

The V Hotel's front lobby was on the ground floor. Its

enormous plate glass windows easily allowed us to watch Ellie's movements. After striding to the front desk, she began a conversation with one of the clerks.

"Is she checking in, do you think?" Madame asked.

"I doubt it. She has no luggage with her, and why would she change clothes in her van before coming here?"

Ellie tossed her head of layered strawberry blond hair. Then she turned from the hotel counter, and moved into the large lobby. She settled herself into one of the many plush couches and crossed her long, bare legs. Her pink skirt was short enough to turn a passing gentleman's head.

"She must be waiting for someone," I said.

"I hear the V's Mediterranean Grill is quite good. I'll bet she's meeting someone for lunch."

"But she already ate an entire Cornish hen with me, back at the Garden's cafe."

Madame waved her hand. "Then she'll just order salad, or coffee and dessert. Eating two lunches for business reasons is not uncommon."

I glanced in my rear view mirror. Taxis were pulling up behind me, and a sign nearby warned that this lane was for V Hotel drop off and pick up only.

"If I stand here much longer, I could get a ticket," I said.

"Then you'd better park."

"But we don't want to lose sight of Ellie. You'd better get out and keep an eye on her."

"Yes, of course." With glee, Madame popped the door. "I'm on it!"

"Wait!" I cried.

"What?"

"Ellie hasn't seen you in years, but she might remember you, so be careful. Sneak in and hide behind something."

"Sneak in?" Madame frowned. "How?"

"I don't know. . . . Maybe—"

Madame patted my arm. "Don't worry, dear. Just park and join me—and be careful coming in yourself." She exited the car, then bent down. "Come to think of it, your friend will recognize you if she spots you coming in, so you'd better watch what I do . . ."

Madame shut the car door and walked behind the car toward the corner. She dug into the pocket of her burgundy wrap coat and fed coins to a *New York Times* vending machine. After retrieving a paper, she pretended to read it, keeping it to the side of her face as she passed V's picture windows.

At the hotel's front doors, she stopped and loitered for about a minute. When a group of trendy looking office workers ventured inside, Madame inserted herself among them. Holding the paper up again, to shield her face, she slipped into the front door, then quickly darted off to a far corner of the lobby and sat.

I shook my head, astonished. "Who needs Mike Hammer when you've got a nosey mother-in-law?"

I revved my Honda, pulled away from the curb, and circled the block twice. There was legal parking on the side streets, but all of the spots were taken—of course! I was just about to bite the bullet and start searching for an underground parking garage when I noticed an SUV (yes, another one, this time blue), pulling out of a legal space.

"Bingo!"

I parallel parked, cut the engine, locked the doors, then jogged to the corner. Mimicking Madame, I bought another *Times*, and snuck into V amid a newly arriving group of Yupsters. Shielding my face, I slunk across the lobby.

The large, high-ceilinged space was done in muted tones of buff and clay. Glass tables, slender black gooseneck floor lamps, and exotic, somewhat frightening-looking plants gave the entire decor a sleek, modern, rather disturbing feel.

"Did I miss anything?" I whispered, sinking into the corner couch's goose down cushions.

"No," Madame replied beside me. "She's just been reading magazines and checking her watch."

I didn't want to take any chances, so I kept the newspaper in front of my face. Peeking around the headlines, I could see that Ellie was sitting far away, with her Pretty in Pink back to us.

"Has she talked to anyone else besides the front desk clerk?" I asked.

"No," said Madame. "She tried to make a cell call, but it was so quick that I suspect she just left the other party a message."

We sat for a few more minutes, and I started glancing around the entire lobby. We weren't far from the Village, and I was a little worried about someone recognizing me.

I saw two young women talking in a corner, and an African-American man typing on his laptop. I didn't recognize any of them. One other man was sitting at the far end of the room in a large leather armchair. But he was holding his magazine so high, I couldn't see his face.

I tapped Madame's shoulder.

"What?" she whispered.

"Look over there. See that man in the corner, reading a magazine?"

Madame peeked around her newsprint. "Yes."

"Do you see what magazine it is?"

"*Girl* . . . It's hard to read the title from here. *Girl* . . . ?"

"*Girl Talk*. Joy used to subscribe to it when she was a teenager. It's filled with celebrity gossip—boy bands and young actresses, fashion, and sweet sixteen advice on dating."

"What's a grown man doing reading *Girl Talk*?"

"He's either in the young adult magazine business or

he's not reading it and just picked up the first magazine he saw on one of these lobby coffee tables."

"So?"

"So I need you to walk over there and get a look at the man."

"In heaven's name, why? Ellie might see me."

"I need you to risk it. I want to make sure that guy's not the middle-aged man we saw following Ellie."

"Oh, Clare, you're being paranoid. We lost that man before we entered the tunnel. The man over there isn't even dressed like the one we saw."

Madame was right about that. From this angle, I couldn't see more than the man's upper torso, but there was no sign of a silver-blue track suit. This man was wearing a tweedy brown sports jacket over a white T-shirt.

"I just think something's not right," I whispered. "Look! He's peeking around the magazine."

"I can't see his face very clearly," Madame said. "He's got that Mets cap pulled too low."

"Well, I can't walk up to him because, if he is that Asian guy, then he saw me talking to Ellie. But he didn't see you."

"All right," Madame said. "I'm going."

She rose slowly and took a leisurely spin of the room, moving around the perimeter. When she got to the man, she said a few words. He looked at his watch and, I assumed, told her the time. Then she moved casually back to me.

I was careful to keep the newspaper up. "What did you see?"

"It's him! You were right! It's the Asian man we saw in the Garden parking lot. He's wearing a tweedy sport jacket over a white T-shirt on top, but his pants are obviously the bottom half of that silver-blue track suit.

"He's followed Ellie here, I'm sure of it."

"But how? We lost him."

"He must have noticed that we were following him. So he shook our tail, then took up Ellie's scent again without our noticing. He's good."

"But who is he? And what does he want?"

"Look . . ." Madame whispered, "there's a dark-haired man walking up to Ellie, but I can't see his face!"

"Is that *Matt*?"

"Matt?"

"I recognize his clothes." The Italian made jacket was a beautiful peacock blue, and the gray slacks draped like fine silk curtains. "Breanne gave him those recently."

"They're very nice."

Ellie sneezed just then. Matt pulled out a monogrammed handkerchief and gallantly handed it to her. Then he took her hand, kissed it, and helped her rise from her seat.

When they embraced and locked lips, Madame and I stared in shock.

"Oh my goodness. What's my boy doing with that woman?"

"Wild guess? I'd say he's kissing her. Passionately kissing her."

But something wasn't right about the way he was kissing her. I knew how my ex-husband kissed, and the way he was holding Ellie just didn't seem right. A moment later, I realized why. As Matt turned with Ellie to walk out of the lobby, we finally saw his face.

"That's not Matt," Madame whispered. "It's Ric Gostwick."

Silently, we watched as they headed, not for the restaurant, but for the elevators to the bedrooms.

"I guess she's doing more than hugging him, after all," I murmured.

"What do you mean?"

"Ellie mentioned to me that her assistant, Norbert, caught her embracing Ric in the Garden. I pressed, but she implied it was just polite affection. She wouldn't admit that she was sleeping with Ric."

"Well, it certainly looks like she is."

"Unless tight sweaters and short skirts are some new requirement for discussing botany in hotel rooms, I'd say you're right."

I noticed the Asian man rising from his armchair. I tapped Madame and pointed. She silently nodded.

The man's magazine was gone. Keeping his head down, he moved carefully across the lobby, stopping as soon as he was within sight of the elevators.

"What's he doing?" Madame whispered.

"Nothing. He's just standing." I noticed him adjust his Mets cap again, and I squinted. "They make cameras now that are small enough to fit into hats, don't they? Do you think he's filming Ellie and Ric?"

Madame frowned. "I guess anything's possible, but I certainly can't tell. The man just looks as though he's loitering."

Ding!

One of the elevators arrived, and Ric and Ellie disappeared inside. Then the doors shut, and Mets Cap Man turned. A young blond woman in a dark business suit approached him. He spoke to her, as if he knew her. She nodded, said a few words, then she went directly to the armchair in the lobby that he'd just left.

"Come on," I rasped to Madame.

"Come where?"

"Where do you think? We're going to follow Secret Asian Man."

He left the hotel and walked south a few blocks. When he reached an underground parking garage, Madame and I hailed a cab.

"What about your car?" she asked.

"We're not that far from the Blend. I can walk down here, and pick it up later."

After a few minutes, a big, black SUV appeared in the garage's driveway and turned down the one way street. "Follow that SUV!" Madame commanded our cabbie.

"Yes, ma'am."

The black SUV headed east then north, traveling all the way up to Midtown. Madame barked orders to the cab driver, making sure he hung back. Judging from Secret Asian Man's ability to shake our tail in Brooklyn, then pick up Ellie's scent again—and without our noticing—we both agreed that he might get suspicious of a taxi hugging his bumper.

Traffic was heavy enough for us to blend into the sea of cars. Finally, the SUV pulled into a small parking lot, behind a clean concrete plaza near the United Nations.

"Dag Hammarskjöld Plaza," I murmured. "Okay, I've finally found a winner for the most obscure, hard to pronounce place name in New York City."

"Clare! I'm surprised at you. Don't you know who Dag Hammarskjöld is?"

"What do you mean *who?* Are you telling me Dag Hammarskjöld is a name?"

"He was the secretary general of the United Nations. He died in a plane crash in Africa in the 1960s. He also won the Nobel Peace Prize. In my time, every schoolchild knew his name."

"Well, I'm sorry to tell you, Madame, times have changed."

Madame sighed. "You don't have to tell me, dear. I notice every day—often several times a day. . . . So what do we do now?"

"We wait to see where he's going."

We sat in the cab until we saw Secret Asian Man again. He was leaving the parking lot on foot, heading up the block toward Second Avenue.

"You follow him," I quickly told Madame. "I'll pay the driver and catch up."

Five minutes later, I found Madame on the sidewalk, in front of a typical seventies-era Bauhaus office building—an avocado green box with pillars of faded aluminum, and all the charm of a thirty-year-old chamber pot.

"Where did he go?" I asked, worried she'd lost him.

"Tenth floor," she said with a smile. "And do you know who has an office on that floor besides a gynecologist and a marriage counselor?"

"Who?" I asked.

"A private investigator."

Fifteen

THE office wasn't large, about the size of a busy dental practice. The walls were a freshly painted off-white, the framed prints on the walls the sort of generic pastel landscape art designed to put one at ease, if not asleep.

"I'll be with you in a moment. Please have a seat."

The young African American receptionist with stylish jade eyeglasses and a beautiful head of long braids pointed us to a small waiting area before she turned her attention back to the receiver in her headset. "Yes . . . I understand," she murmured, "that's correct . . . would you mind spelling that for me?"

She appeared to be scribbling down an extensive phone message, and I was relieved to see that she was preoccupied. It gave Madame and me a chance to catch our breath and get our bearings.

Downstairs we'd already discussed strategy. The plan was simple. Madame would show the receptionist her set of keys and claim that she'd seen an Asian gentleman drop them when he'd parked his SUV near Dag Hammarskjöld plaza.

If the receptionist offered to take the keys, Madame would refuse to give them up, requesting a chance to speak to the man himself. When he appeared, she'd challenge him, recounting his movements and demand that he give up the name of the person who'd hired him to tail Ellie.

I didn't like the idea of direct confrontation, but I couldn't think of a better scheme at the moment, and my former mother-in-law felt confident she could make this work. Maybe she could. Madame was the sort of regal dame with whom most people were reluctant to argue. Secret Asian Man might be one of them.

Given the fact that he was a professional investigator, however, I was willing to bet we were in over our heads. My bookie dad probably would have given us 7 to 3 odds: the long-shot being our actually getting the information for which we came and the more likely scenario landing us unceremoniously on the sidewalk downstairs.

While the receptionist continued talking on the phone, Madame and I settled into the standard issue waiting-room furniture. Madame pawed through the magazines and brochures on the coffee table. I glanced around the room.

"Are you nervous?" I whispered.

"Not at all," Madame replied, opening one of the office's glossy brochures. "Just a little impatient." She dipped into her handbag and pulled out her reading glasses. "This is interesting . . ." she murmured a minute later.

"What?" I asked, my eyes still on the receptionist.

"This office is being run by a man named Anil Kapoor, but it's only one branch of a global company. Have a look . . ."

I took the brochure, and began to read:

> At Worldwide Private Investigations, Inc. (WPI), our licensed private investigators, forensic experts, and legal information specialists achieve results. With offices around the globe, we are especially equipped for international investigations, including missing persons, marital and child custody cases, property and copyright disputes, extradition and asset inquiries as well as a host of other investigations and security needs. At WPI, no case is too big, or too small. Whether you are an individual, a C-level executive, or a government official, you can rest assured that our confidentiality is paramount.
>
> Many of our agents are bilingual and are culturally, nationality, and gender diverse. All must clear a thorough background check prior to employment. In addition to military and law enforcement sectors, WPI recruits talent from private service industries such as accounting, computer information systems, and . . .

I flipped to another leaf of the brochure, where the company bragged about its protective services division, providing security and bodyguards for global corporations and diplomats. Their client list was extensive, and in very small print. I squinted as I scanned the list, pretending that I hadn't finally reached the age when I needed to borrow Madame's reading glasses . . .

> Ensor Pharmaceuticals, Gaylord Group, J.P. Madison Associates, Lamelle-Fressineau, Paratech Global, Snap Cola Enterprises, Komiyama Industries, Terra-Green International, XanTell Corporation . . .

My gaze returned to one of the company names. "Terra-Green . . ."

"What did you say, Clare?"

I pointed to the brochure. "TerraGreen International," I whispered, "they're a client of this office's protective services division, and Ellie's husband works for them."

Madame's eyebrows rose. "You're sure?"

I nodded. "About two or three years after Ellie and Ric broke up, she was still dropping by the Blend. I remember she'd gone through a stint interning at the TerraGreen labs on Long Island. That's how she first met her husband, Jerry Lassiter. He was an executive with the company."

"Did you say labs? What sort of company is this Terra-Green?"

"They make fertilizers and plant foods. Back then, I think Ellie was working on some sort of project to genetically engineer crops."

Madame frowned in thought for a moment. "Ellie was an intern and her husband was an executive when they first met? Is that what you said?"

"Yes."

"Then there must have been quite a few years between them."

"He's at least fifteen years her senior."

Madame sighed. "It seems we have a classic recipe here. Older, rich husband provides a young Ellie with security and stability, but years later, she begins yearning for the adventure and passion she lost. Enter old flame Ric . . ."

"But is Jerry Lassiter having his wife followed to document infidelity?" I whispered. "Or is there more to it?"

"What more could there be?"

"Ric was mugged last night. I doubt a professional investigator got involved with something like that."

"So you think Jerry Lassiter did the deed himself?"

"Or he hired someone to do it. Yes, that's what I think. What I can't do is prove it. I'm not even sure of his real motive."

"Real motive?"

"Don't you see? He could be after Ric's hybrid cutting . . . or he could be out to make it look like someone else is after it, so if harm comes to Ric the police will look for another suspect."

"Oh, yes. I see. If Jerry Lassiter is afraid of losing his wife to Ric, maybe his solution is to lose Ric first?"

"Exactly."

"Well, my dear, as far as proving it, we need to start right here with this agency. TerraGreen may be on its client list, but that doesn't prove Jerry Lassiter hired them to tail his wife."

"I know, and that's why we're going to dump your 'lost keys' approach."

"We are?"

"Yes."

"Then what are we going to do?"

"I think we should—"

The front door opened just then and I stopped talking. A well-dressed gentleman boldly strode up to the receptionist as if he owned the place. When I caught sight of his face, I realized he did.

Tapping Madame on the shoulder, I pointed to the section of the brochure that displayed the photo and bio of the man standing right in front of us.

> Anil Kapoor's twenty-five-year career spans work for the Drug Enforcement Administration, which led to his work in that agency's office in Marseille, France; Rabat, Morocco; and Brussels,

> Belgium, where he served as the technical advisor on U.S. drug intelligence and investigative matters. From there, he moved to the worldwide International Criminal Police Organization more commonly known as Interpol. There he worked for twelve years as the Director of the Criminal Intelligence Directorate, the number-two position in the organization, subordinate only to the secretary general.
>
> Now retired from his official work, he runs the New York branch of WPI. Located near the United Nations and the diplomatic office for which his office often consults, he has assembled a New York team with extensive experience in criminal investigations and intelligence collection from around the world.
>
> Mr. Kapoor's education and studies include: Princeton University, Bachelor of Arts degree in Sociology and Business; D.E.A. Executive Management and Financial Investigations; Harvard University, graduate course on National and Internal Security; USDA Graduate School Performance Audits.

An attractive man in his fifties, Kapoor looked much like his photo, with the exception of his jet-black hair, which now displayed noticeable strands of silver-gray. He had a full face, olive complexion, and East Indian features. Well under six feet, he had a paunchy physique, but he wore his clothes beautifully: a London tailored suit, a fine charcoal overcoat draped over his arm, a slim attaché case in his hand. Like Madame, he presented himself with a confident air of dignified elegance.

As he spoke to the receptionist, Madame leaned

toward me. "Clare," she whispered. "What do you want us to do?"

"Just go along with me," I whispered in reply. Then I silently pointed to the brochure and Anil Kapoor's bio. Madame began to read it over.

"Ladies?" the receptionist called after Mr. Kapoor left the waiting room and headed towards the agency's offices. "Do you have an appointment?"

"No, we don't." I rose from the couch and moved toward her desk. "This company was recommended to us . . . and we were in the neighborhood today, visiting friends at the French Embassy, so we thought we might just drop in and ask a few questions . . ."

I ran out of words, but Madame was ready—

"*Oui, oui* . . ." she said, summoning her old French accent. "We're a bit uncertain about the whole process, *comprenez-vous*? But of course if no one is available to talk to us about your company, we can call for an appointment, *une certaine autre heure, oui*? I believe there's another agency the deputy secretary recommended . . ." Madame made a show of looking through her Prada bag. She glanced at me. "Do you have that other agency's card, my dear, or do I?"

The receptionist quickly spoke up. "I'm sure you won't have to leave before seeing someone. Just give us another few minutes, and I'll ask if Mr. Kapoor's available. If not, I'm sure a member of his staff will answer all of your questions."

"*Merci*," Madame replied.

"Your names please?" the receptionist asked.

Five minutes later, the young woman was escorting us into a corner office. The decor in here was markedly different from the bland waiting room. Mahogany bookshelves lined the walls with leather-bound volumes. A thick Persian rug of sapphire, jade, and ruby covered a parquet floor, and the large room was dominated by a substantial desk of dense wood lacquered a shiny black.

Behind a sleek flat-panel computer monitor sat Anil Kapoor. He rose when we entered, his hand moving to smooth his pearl colored tie.

"May I present Madame Marie LaSalle and her daughter, Vanessa LaSalle," the receptionist announced.

"Madame, mademoiselle," Mr. Kapoor said. He extended his hand and we all politely shook. Then the receptionist backed out of the room and her boss gestured to the two mahogany chairs in front of his desk.

"What may I do for you today?" Mr. Kapoor asked, discreetly swiveling his whisper-thin computer monitor to the side.

"We have a few questions for you," I began. "We're looking to hire an investigator to help . . . with an investigation."

One of Mr. Kapoor's dark eyebrows rose very slightly. "What sort of investigation?"

"Well, the details are . . . they're very private. First we have some questions about your agency . . . you understand?"

Mr. Kapoor shifted in his chair, gave me a polite smile. "I'll answer any questions, if I can."

"You see, this is the first time we'd be using you, although a friend of ours recommended you to us."

"And who might that be?"

"He's an executive," I said, "with TerraGreen International."

"Oh? What division?"

"Division? I . . . I'm not sure . . ."

"What country then?" Mr. Kapoor asked.

"The U.S. He's based right here in Long Island."

"I see."

"Anyway," I said, "Jerry mentioned to us that he's very happy with the case you're working on now for him . . ."

Mr. Kapoor's forehead wrinkled. "Jerry?"

"Jerry Lassiter, of course. He did give me the right agency? You're investigating his wife, Ellie, aren't you?"

The man remained quiet for a long moment, his dark eyes studying me and then Madame. "I'd like to be helpful," he said, "but I'm not familiar with every case this agency handles. And, of course, it's not our policy to discuss any ongoing investigation. Now, tell me a bit about your needs. What sort of case do you have?" His eyes squinted a fraction. "If you really have one . . ."

"Of course we have one. It's . . . it's a case of . . ."

"It's a missing person's case," Madame levelly replied.

"I see," said Mr. Kapoor. "Man, woman, or child?"

"Man," said Madame.

"Age?" Mr. Kapoor asked.

"About thirty," Madame replied.

"And where was he last seen?"

Madame glanced out the window a moment. "The French Riviera."

"Can you be more specific?"

"The beaches of Nice. It's simply a question of finding the man again, you see?" Madame said. "After he shared himself for a few unforgettable months, he simply disappeared."

"Oh, yes. I think I see now." Mr. Kapoor nodded. "It's a love affair?"

"But of course," Madame replied.

Mr. Kapoor locked eyes with me. "And exactly how long did this missing man and your daughter have this love affair?"

"My daughter?" Madame repeated. "*Non, monsieur.* The love affair was mine!"

Mr. Kapoor didn't appear the sort of man to surprise easily, but his stoic expression cracked just then. His jaw slackened and his throat issued a grunt of incredulity.

"Yours, Madame?"

"*Oui!*"

He leaned forward. "Do you . . . have a photo?"

"I do . . ."

I tensed as Madame searched her bag. I had no idea what she was up to with this tale, but I was grateful she'd come up with something on a dime.

"Here you are," she said, handing Kapoor a snapshot from her wallet.

He gazed at it, then handed it back. "A very handsome man."

"*Oui*," said Madame with a quick glance at me. "His name is Antonio."

"And you'd like us to find him for you?" Kapoor asked.

Madame nodded.

Good luck with that, I thought. The late Antonio Allegro might very well have been on the beaches of Nice in his lifetime, but he'd been "missing" for a few decades.

"Well, Madame, I'm happy to inform you that we do have an office on the Riviera, and I'm sure we can accommodate this search. We can coordinate everything from here in the New York office. Would you like us to get started today? I'll assign a case officer . . ."

As Mr. Kapoor picked up the phone, I spoke up again. "I think we'll need to consider it for a few more days, won't we, Mother?"

Madame nodded. "*Oui* . . . you know, it is possible Antonio might still get in touch."

"Yes, of course," said Mr. Kapoor setting the phone down again.

"But, you know . . ." I said. "If Mother does decide to

use your agency, she needs to make sure we have the right one recommended to us. Jerry Lassiter is a client here, isn't he? You can confirm that much at least, can't you? You are investigating his wife?"

Mr. Kapoor pressed a button on his phone. "Ms. Cassel, if you please," he said into the intercom. Then he stood and glanced at his slim platinum watch. "I'm afraid I must apologize. I've forgotten about an agency meeting."

"But—"

He extended his hand. "Thank you for your interest in our agency. If you decide to pursue your case, please call Ms. Cassel for an appointment—" He gestured to his office door. The receptionist was standing there, waiting to escort us out.

Less than ten minutes later, we were back on the sidewalk.

Sixteen

On the cab ride back to the Blend, my cell phone rang. It was Matt. Apparently, his morning had gone much differently than mine.

"Clare, I had to call."

"Matt? What's wrong?!"

"This is the first time I've eaten at Joy's restaurant and the place is exceptional!"

"That's nice, but I have to tell you . . ."

"I'm just finishing my lunch of seared skate with baby root vegetables and sauce grenobloise. Our daughter prepared everything on my plate, and—"

"Matt, I need to . . ."

"—the skate just melted on my tongue! You know, I haven't had skate like that since—"

"Listen to me!" I finally shouted. "I have a lot to discuss with you and none of it involves Jacques Pépin's favorite fish!"

"Clare, why are you freaking?"

I quickly recounted my morning: interrogating Ric about the smuggled cutting; tracking down Ellie at the Botanic Garden; adding the word *biopiracy* to my vocab; seeing Ellie being spied on as she kissed Ric at the V Hotel; then tailing the man who'd tailed her to a private investigation office.

"Good god, Clare, have you lost your mind?"

"That's your response? Don't you understand that Ric is in danger? And Ellie may be, too, for all I know."

"Or all you *don't* know," Matt said. "You're not a professional investigator, and you're not a cop."

"I know, Matt, but I am—"

"I'll tell you what you are. You're a certifiable nosehound with an addiction to conspiracy theories."

"Well, if I am, then so's your mother."

"Back up. What are you saying about my mother?"

"She's been with me all morning, and she's right here in the cab with me now."

A long pause followed. "Clare," Matt said tightly, "I know Halloween's around the corner, but *please* tell me that you didn't drag my mother all over this town in some private eye masquerade."

"I didn't have to drag her."

"For the love of . . ." He cursed. "Are you telling me that you're taking my elderly mother on some ridiculous Nancy Drew joyride—"

"It's not ridiculous—"

Madame tapped my shoulder. "What's he saying, Clare?"

"He's going on about how we're ridiculous."

"Give me that phone," she snapped.

I handed over the cell. Matt was still ranting on the other end about how we were on a wild goose chase.

"Young man," Madame barked into the cell, "this is your mother—"

I raised an eyebrow at "young man," but then realized just how young a son in his forties was to a woman pushing eighty.

"Look here, Matteo, Clare and I were not just chasing feathered foie gras. We've uncovered some rather significant information. So stop spouting off, and for once in your life, listen to your wife!"

"Ex-wife," I corrected as Madame handed the phone back to me.

"Okay, *what*?" Matt said. I could practically hear him pouting through the audio signal.

"Here's what. You need to warn your friend Ric what's happening with this private investigation business. I've already called Ellie—twice. But I'm only getting voicemail, and she hasn't returned my calls. I don't have Ric's cell phone number, so I tried calling his room at the V Hotel, but they said Federico Gostwick isn't registered there, and—"

"He's not registered there because I booked the room for him under my name, just to be on the safe side."

"Well, that's exactly what I'm talking about, Matt! You see the need to protect your friend, right? That's all I'm doing, and I'm telling you he's not safe. A private eye was on Ellie's tail, so now he knows where your friend is staying, which means whoever hired the P.I. also knows where he's staying. I think that mugging last night was someone—possibly Ellie's husband—attempting to steal the cutting or harm Ric."

"Okay, okay. Calm down. I understand what you're worried about, and I'll talk to Ric about everything."

"Promise?"

"Yes, I promise. But you have to promise something, too."

"What?"

"I need you to chill. Stop interrogating Ric and following

people he knows. This is important, Clare. I don't want Ric spooked."

"I'm only doing it to help him—"

"He's a private man, and he's not going to appreciate your butting into his business. And we need his business, Clare. We can't afford for this deal to fail."

"What do you mean by that? The Blend is doing fine."

"We're in trouble, Clare . . ." He paused. "Okay, I'm in trouble."

"The cutting? Someone figured out it was smuggled into the country?"

"Forget the cutting. It's far worse than that."

I heard him take a breath. "The kiosks are in trouble. Financial trouble. For the last few months, I've been transferring funds from the profitable kiosks to the unprofitable ones, to shore them up. Keep them going until I can remedy the situation—and the kiosk expansions are partially leveraged against the Village Blend and its townhouse."

It took me a minute to catch up with Matt, but I still couldn't believe what he was saying. "I don't understand. I saw the kiosks' early numbers. They looked great."

"The first wave of startups did well. Interest was initially high. But the new kiosks, mostly the ones in California, are in trouble."

"Why?"

"A lot of the patrons of the high-end shops in those areas have a problem with caffeine. We tested processed decafs as a possible alternative, but a lot of them weren't happy with the quality. Ric's hybrid would be a high-profile splash, the kind of new product that's sure to reel in those premium customers."

"No wonder you've been so eager to make this thing with Ric work."

"That's why Friday night is so important. These decaffeinated beans, my exclusive deal with Ric . . . they're the life preserver for almost half of the Blend kiosks. It's a new revenue stream, as well as a way to promote the kiosks that are about to go under."

"Oh, god . . ."

"Clare, I need you onboard now more than ever. I need your support in making this launch a success. Do I have it?"

I touched my fingers to my forehead, where a migraine was about to set up shop. I knew how hard it was for Matt to confess this. He'd been trying to strike out on his own, to make his mark and probably prove to me, to Joy, to his mother that he could make up for lost time.

"Okay," I said. "You have my support."

"Then you'll suspend this . . . this investigation of yours, at least until after the launch of the Gostwick Decaf on Friday?"

I sighed. "All right. On one condition."

"What?"

"That nothing bad happens—to Ric or anyone else we know."

"We're not in an Alfred Hitchcock movie, Clare. I'm sure everyone is safe and sound."

"Well, I'm not so sure. And, just so you know, I plan to keep calling Ellie until I reach her. I want her to know what I uncovered today—that she's being followed by a private investigator or a team of them. And I still want you to talk to Ric. Tell him Ellie's husband probably knows about their affair. Ric needs to keep his eyes open and watch his back—and so do you for that matter."

"I will, Clare. I'll tell him, and I'll be careful."

"And one more thing . . . since you happen to be at

Solange, would you mind checking out this hot young chef Joy is working for?"

"Tommy Keitel? What do you mean check him out?" Matt asked. "I'm already eating here, and the food's outstanding."

"I'm not interested in his cooking. I want to know what sort of person he's like. He's Joy's new boyfriend, isn't he?"

"Yes, but—"

"Then just make up some stupid excuse to barge into the kitchen. I told you, Joy has yet to bring the young man around the Blend."

"But that's Joy's business. We'll meet Keitel when she wants us to. She won't like my invading her—"

"Just do it, Matt. Please."

"Sorry. That I can't promise."

"But—"

"Tell you what," Matt said. "Before I leave, I'll suggest to Joy that she bring Keitel with her to our launch tasting on Friday. Then you can 'check him out' yourself. Okay?"

"Okay."

"Now will you please just go back to the Blend. Make yourself a nice *doppio* espresso. I'm sure once you have a little caffeine in your veins, you'll see the world in a whole new light."

I did as Matt suggested. After dropping Madame off at her apartment building and leaving a third voicemail message for Ellie, I went back to my coffeehouse, downed a double espresso, and tried to focus on Friday. There was certainly plenty to do for the Beekman Hotel party, and I began to do it.

Seventeen

TWO nights later, the last thing I expected to see was a body plunging from the twenty-sixth floor balcony of a New York City landmark. But that's exactly how the "fun" ended for me that evening—not to mention the person who'd splashed onto the concrete right in front of my eyes.

Yes, I said "splash."

Drop a water balloon on the sidewalk from twenty-plus floors, and you'll get a pretty good approximation of what I'd heard, since I actually didn't see the impact.

Mike Quinn told me that because people have bones and aren't just a bag of fluid, they don't explode so much as compress into something still recognizably human . . . but I'm getting ahead of myself . . .

THINGS started out well enough the night of the Gostwick Estate Reserve Decaf launch party at the Beekman. My baristas for the evening, Tucker, Esther, Gardner, and

Dante, had all arrived at the hotel on time. They'd even dressed appropriately.

Matt had suggested long sleeve white shirts, black slacks, black shoes, and our blue Village Blend aprons. Only Dante had violated the dress code by wearing bright red Keds. I let his artistic statement pass without comment. He was a great barista, I was short staffed, and I never believed in stifling creative expression—even if it was just a pair of shoes.

The Beekman Tower Hotel was located on Forty-ninth Street and First Avenue, which was the extreme East Side of Manhattan, close to the river, and next door to the United Nations plaza. Built in 1928, the Beekman was one of the city's true art deco masterpieces, the fawn brown stone giving it a distinctive facade amid the gray steel of the city's more modern skyscrapers.

The Upper East Side address was in one of the city's most exclusive neighborhoods, and because the Beekman was literally steps away from the UN, it hosted more than its share of foreign dignitaries along with upscale leisure travelers.

Two small elevators delivered us to the Top of the Tower, the hotel's penthouse restaurant. The event space was elegantly appointed with a polished floor of forest green tile and walls of muted sandstone. A dark wood bar was located to the right, a grand piano to the left, but the dominating feature was the panoramic view. Burgundy curtains had been pulled back to reveal Midtown Manhattan's glimmering lights beyond soaring panes of thick glass. A narrow, open-air balcony, accessed from the side of the room, jutted out just below the tall windows, allowing guests a bracing breath of fresh air.

As soon as we arrived, my baristas began unpacking the fragile French presses and the two hundred Village Blend coffee cups—not the usual paper but porcelain, which we specifically used when catering. I checked in with the kitchen manager, one floor below, then visited the ladies' room, and when I returned to the Top of the Tower event space, I found my staff embroiled in another caf versus decaf discussion.

"I know why we're here tonight, but this whole anti-caffeine movement offends me," Esther grumbled. "Creative artists have thrived on the stuff for centuries."

"Word," said Gardner.

"I know an artist who actually paints with coffee," Dante noted. He folded and unfolded his arms, as if he were itching to roll up his long sleeves and show off his tattoos. "But I'd say artists and coffee have gone together for a long time. Take Café Central . . ."

"What's that?" Tucker asked. "More competition for the Blend?"

Dante laughed. "Café Central was the hangout for painters in turn-of-the-century Austria."

I smiled, remembering my art history classes. "Klimt hung out there, right?"

"That's right, Ms. Cosi," Dante said.

It made sense that Dante admired Gustav Klimt. The artist created works on surfaces beyond traditional canvas. He'd also been a founding member of the Vienna Secession, a group of late nineteenth century artists who were primarily interested in exploring the possibilities of art outside the confines of academic tradition. "To every age its art and to art its freedom" was their motto.

"Lev Bronstein hung out at Café Central, too," Dante added.

"Lev who?" Tucker asked.

Dante shifted back and forth on his red Keds. "He's better known as Leon Trotsky."

"Oh, Trotsky!" Tucker cried, nodding, then began to

sing: "Don't turn around . . . the Kommissar's in town . . . *and drinking lattes*!"

I burst out laughing.

Esther, Gardner, and Dante just stared. Apparently, they were too young to remember "Der Kommissar."

"It's old New Wave," I tried to explain. "A pop eighties send-up of cold war communism—"

Tucker waved his hand. "Don't even try, Clare."

Good god, I thought. *Did I actually use the phrase "old" New Wave?*

Folding his arms, Tucker leaned his lanky form against the bar. "Well, artists and political revolutionaries aren't the only caffeine addicts. Did you know when David Lynch is directing a film, he downs bottomless pots of coffee and gallons of double chocolate milkshakes to maintain a constant caffeine buzz?"

"And did you know Honoré de Balzac drank forty cups a day?" Esther noted. After a rather long pause in the conversation, she felt the need to add: "Balzac was a nineteenth-century French writer."

Tucker rolled his eyes. "You may not remember 'Der Kommissar,' Esther, but we know who Balzac is. . . . Now are you sure you know who David Lynch is? Or do Hollywood movies offend your literary sensibilities?"

Esther narrowed her eyes as she adjusted her black glasses. "Actually, Lynch is an acceptable postmodern filmmaker. His short films are particularly effective."

Tucker threw up his hands. "Well, I'm sure he'll be glad to hear *you* approve."

Gardner stroked his goatee. "Lynch also uses coffee as an image system. You can see it in *Twin Peaks* and especially *Mulholland Drive*."

Esther, Tucker, Dante, and even I stared for a moment in dumbfounded silence.

We were used to hearing Gardner discuss music theory or bebop versus West Coast jazz, but we'd never heard him wax philosophical about "image systems" in film before.

"What gives?" Tucker asked, raising an eyebrow.

Gardner shrugged. "My new girlfriend works at the Museum of the Moving Image, and she likes Lynch. Anyway, she's right. If you watch his movies, you'll see the guy's seriously into coffee."

"I wish my new boyfriend were as well connected as your new girlfriend," Tucker said with a sigh. "If she hears about any new TV series in pre-production over at Astoria Studios let me know, okay? Off-Broadway's good for the artistic soul, but I need a paycheck like my last one."

I cleared my throat and gestured in the direction of the two elevators, where a group of men and women were waving their invitations.

"Speaking of paychecks," I told my staff, "it's time we earned ours."

The space filled steadily after that. I acted as the hostess, greeting each new elevator full of people as it arrived. Matt should have been doing this, but although he'd arrived looking gorgeous in a sharply tailored black dinner jacket, he was now talking constantly on his cell phone.

Tonight's guests were culled from a list that included trade magazine writers and food critics from many nations, all of them looking for a brand new angle or a breakout product while they covered the International Coffee Growers Exhibition. These men wore jackets and ties, the women tailored business suits.

Convention attendees and members of international coffee cartels were far more affluent, and generally arrived in evening clothes, their escorts or obscenely young trophy wives resplendent in shimmering gowns—an indication they had more elegant parties to attend after the tasting ended.

Local chefs had been invited as well. I spotted celebrity chef Robbie Gray. His famous restaurant, Anatomy, featured delicacies made of organ bits. Basically, the man had become famous serving animal parts most American housewives wouldn't be caught dead feeding to anything but the garbage disposal, but his three-star rating was no joke, and if he liked what he tasted tonight, the Blend could land a lucrative contract to provide him with our micro-roasted Gostwick Estate Reserve Decaf.

To keep Robbie and the rest of the arriving guests in a jovial mood, we began to serve brie, a variety of wines, and Italian sesame cookies—delicate nibbles that wouldn't hijack anyone's taste buds. Before the actual tasting of the Gostwick Decaf, we would serve glasses of sparkling water so guests could clear their palate.

After about twenty minutes of greeting guests, I was becoming annoyed. I was supposed to be *helping* Matt and Ric throw this press tasting, not running the show solo. But Matt continued to keep his ear glued to his phone. Finally, as I moved to greet yet another batch of arrivals, Ric stepped up to take over. With a nod, I returned to the bar.

A few minutes later, I noticed Matt's mother exiting the elevator. Madame's escort this evening was her longtime beau, Gary McTavish. The good doctor looked quite dashing in a dark suit and Scottish plaid waistcoat. Madame was dressed stylishly, as well, in a charcoal cocktail dress trimmed in silver, her necklace and earrings simple delicate twists of platinum. Instead of her usual relaxed, confident self, however, she appeared agitated.

Ric was busy with a small crowd, and Matt was still doing some sort of business. He'd failed to greet her with even a wave, his ear still plastered to that damn cell phone. I quickly moved from behind the bar to welcome the senior pair. To my surprise, the usually friendly Dr. McTavish barely acknowledged my presence with a nod.

"Some wine?" he tightly asked Madame.

"Perhaps later," she replied.

McTavish raised a gray-white eyebrow. "Another pleasure postponed?" he tossed off before heading for the bar.

The two were obviously fighting about something. "What's the good doctor peeved about?" I whispered.

"Never mind," said Madame. "Tell me what's happening with your friend, Ellie. Has she called you back yet?"

I shook my head. "I've left messages for two days now. She hasn't returned one call."

"Did your messages include the fact that you think her husband is having her followed?"

"Yes. At first, I didn't want to drop a bombshell like that on a voicemail message, but I had no choice. I felt she needed to know . . ."

"I agree. From what we witnessed at the hotel, Ellie and Ric aren't fooling anyone, and we don't know what sort of man her husband really is."

"I'm worried about her."

"Do you think her husband would turn violent?"

"That's the problem. I need to speak with Ellie to find out more. And after that, I plan on speaking with Ric, too. Matt doesn't want me to upset him, and I'll be as polite as I can, but I'd honestly like to know what Ric's intentions are towards Ellie. He's either planning to leave her again. Or . . ."

"Or what?"

"He's making plans for their future together."

"What do you mean plans? Plans of marriage?"

"Maybe."

Madame groaned. "If that's true, there must be something in the air."

"What do you mean?"

She shook her head. "Gary asked me to marry him. That's why he's in a foul mood."

"But that's wonderful news. Why would he be in a—*wait*, what did you tell him? Did you turn him down?"

"I'm thinking it over."

"You've been dating the man for more than a year. He's an intelligent, accomplished, respected oncologist with the sex appeal of Sean Connery. He's got a romantic Scottish lilt and actually looks good in a ceremonial kilt—what's to think about?"

"You don't understand. Gary's giving up his position at the hospital in a few months. He wants to move to an exclusive community in Albuquerque. Can you believe it?"

"I hear New Mexico's beautiful."

"It's the desert. What will I do with myself? Listen to coyotes bay all night? Head out to the chuck wagon in the morning to rustle up chicken fried steak?"

I began to laugh, and then realized Madame wasn't joking. "Okay, I'll bite. Why Albuquerque?"

"Gary has some friends who've retired there and say they love it. He wants to take up golf and the community has a golf course."

"And you don't want to golf?"

"I see no point in spending hours hitting a tiny white ball with a stick."

"I'm sure he has other plans for his retirement."

"He wants to try camping, too."

"That sounds interesting."

"It sounds dreadful."

"But what about all those trips to the bush you took with Matt's father? You loved those adventures."

"I trekked the wilderness—*in my youth.* I have no desire to sleep among cacti on a cold desert rock at this age.

I want to die from dancing the Argentine tango, Clare, not a rattlesnake bite."

"Oh, come on. You know there's plenty of culture in a city the size of Albuquerque. Art galleries, concerts, even Broadway shows—"

"But not the original casts. The only show out of New York that doesn't use a touring company is the Big Apple Circus."

"So what are you going to do?"

"I don't know yet." She began rubbing her temples. "I was ambushed. The man didn't even have the decency to hint at what was coming, so I told him I had to think it over."

I tipped a glance at the bar. The good doctor was knocking back his wine rather quickly. "I can see how well that went over."

She pulled me closer and lowered her voice. "To be perfectly honest, I think it's unwise to settle down so soon. I'd really like to start playing the field."

Playing the field at eighty? I thought. Coming from anyone else, I might have doubled over with laughter, but the woman just had a summer fling in the Hamptons with an elderly artist. She wasn't kidding.

Madame's gaze shifted to Matt. "Has my son had that phone surgically grafted to his ear?"

I shrugged. "I'm sure it's important business."

"So he's not talking to *that woman*."

"No. She's already here." I gestured to Breanne Summour. She was standing alone, near the enormous windows, gazing out at the view, the crystal stem of a wine glass pinched in her French-tipped fingers.

Gary McTavish returned; each hand held a glass—one a German Riesling and the other a California Pinot Noir. "Are you sure you wouldn't care to indulge?" he asked Madame, offering her either.

Madame shook her head. Gary downed the Pinot Noir in a single gulp and started sipping the Riesling.

Madame exhaled in disgust.

"I've got to go," I chirped uneasily, relieved to be escaping the immediate vicinity of the not-so-happy couple.

I circulated for a few minutes and noticed Dante Silva was the only barista who didn't seem to be busy. He stood with a tray of empty glasses in his hand, watching a new group of people arrive on one of the elevators.

"Dante?"

He jerked, startled. The glasses clinked together on the tray and he reached out with one hand to steady them. "Sorry, Ms. Cosi—"

"Why are you so jumpy?"

Dante shrugged. "Just nerves, I guess."

I studied his expression. Dante seemed as uneasy as Madame. "Did somebody ask to marry *you*?"

"What?"

"Forget it. Could you grab another tray of brie and sesame cookies from the kitchen, and make another round?"

Dante did a bobblehead impression. "Will do."

I relieved him of his burden and carried the spent glasses to the bar. Tucker was standing behind it, opening bottles of sparkling water and pouring them into crystal tumblers.

Ric Gostwick approached me from across the room. He glanced at his watch. "Have you seen Ellie?" he whispered.

"I haven't, and I'm looking for her, too. Hasn't she been staying with you at the V Hotel?"

Ric frowned. "No, of course not. She's married."

"Yes, but . . . didn't Matt talk to you? About the private investigator . . ."

Ric turned his frown into a smile, but his eyes narrowed and his body appeared to tense. He touched my arm and leaned closer. "Matt spoke to me, Clare, but I'd appreciate it if you'd drop all of that tonight. This isn't the time or place . . . and, just so you know, Ellie and I are affectionate. We hug and kiss . . . but we're not sleeping together." He held my eyes, shook his handsome dark head. "The day you saw us, she merely came to the hotel to update me on our work; but, of course, I can see how you might have misunderstood."

It was my turn to tense. Misunderstanding was one thing, but Ric was trying to sell me on the idea that two plus two equaled five. "It's just that Ellie never returned my calls," I said carefully, "and I wanted to make sure she got my messages."

"She got them, Clare. I saw her a short time ago."

"You did? Where?"

Ric looked away. He shrugged. "Just on the street. She was in Manhattan already, but she had some errands to run before coming to our tasting."

"What sort of errands? What part of Manhattan?"

Ric didn't answer, not directly. Instead, he checked his watch again. "She should have been here by now. I tried calling her mobile phone, but her voicemail answered. I can't imagine what's keeping her."

"Well, I did spot her assistant, Norbert," I said. "He arrived about ten minutes ago. Maybe you can ask him if he knows where she is?"

Ric made a face at the mention of Norbert's name. He scanned the room, rubbed his closely-shaved chin. "Let's just hold off the tasting, give her another fifteen minutes."

"Of course."

Ric gently squeezed my upper arm. "Thank you, Clare. I'm very lucky to have your help tonight. Would you mind very much asking your staff to open more bottles of wine? And maybe serve more of those delightful little cookies. I'll—"

"*Darling*, there you are . . ."

A woman's voice interrupted us, the word "darling" stretched out in an accent that sounded something like Marlene Dietrich's, without the Old World charm.

The moment he heard it, Ric's tense expression morphed. He smoothly removed his hand from my arm. Like an actor slipping into the role of his career, he transformed his entire demeanor from anxious host to easygoing charmer.

"Ah, Monika, my love . . ."

I studied the arriving woman. I'd never seen her before. She was fashion-model tall with high cheekbones, full lips, and narrow, catlike eyes of ice blue. Her golden hair was elegantly styled into a neat chignon and her milky complexion wouldn't have needed much airbrushing for a magazine cover. But she was a bit too heavy and a decade too old to be a working model now. Hands on hips, she cocked her head and offered Ric a coy half-smile.

"Federico," she sang, glancing briefly at me with undisguised disdain. "What are you up to? Flirting with *the help*?"

I was a business partner here, not "the help." Unfortunately, Ric didn't bother correcting the woman. Instead, he turned his back on me, took one of the woman's hands in his and placed it to his lips—just as I'd seen him do with Ellie two days ago.

"I wasn't sure you were coming," he said.

"What do you mean? How could I miss tonight?" She looped her arm around his bicep.

"May I get you some wine?" Ric asked.

The woman tightened her grip, pulling his body closer. "And let you out of my sight? Never."

They toddled off like Siamese twins, moving across the crowded room. I might have dismissed the woman as an old friend or past lover, but the way she was pawing him up, it certainly looked as though the relationship hadn't been left in the past.

I returned to the bar and spoke to my staff, asking them to make another round or two with the wine. Then I sought out Madame again.

"Do you see that woman?" I whispered. "The one with Ric? Do you know her?"

"That's Monika Van Doorn," Madame informed me. "I knew her late father quite well."

"And he is?"

"Joren Riij."

"Sorry, should I know that name?"

"Joren was the founder and CEO of Dutch Coffee International, a distributor based in Amsterdam."

"You said 'was.' Did he retire?"

"He passed away about a year ago, left the controlling interest in his company to his only child—that woman you pointed out, Mrs. Van Doorn. She's the daughter of his second wife, Rachel . . . or was it his third? You know, I'm not sure who her mother—"

"So Monika Van Doorn *distributes* coffee?"

"Oh, yes. Dutch International is a major distributor in the Central European and Eastern European markets. They haven't had as much success in the European Union." Madame leaned close to my ear. "Inferior beans," she whispered. "For years, they've sacrificed quality for a higher profit margin. And their buyer has a less than brilliant palate."

Madame and I continued to watch Monika. Now she was whispering in Ric's ear, and when she finished, the tip of her pink tongue flicked out to touch his earlobe.

"You referred to her as 'Mrs.,'" I whispered. "Is she married or divorced?"

"She's married," Madame replied, arching an eyebrow,

"but she certainly doesn't behave that way, does she?" Squinting a little, she searched the room. "That's her husband, over there: Neils Van Doorn. He's the handsome blond chatting with that young woman."

I followed Madame's gaze to an attractive man with Nordic features and light blond hair hanging down rakishly past the collar of his Egyptian cotton shirt. He had a lean build, a striking smile, and his clothes screamed fashion house. The tailored suit of dark bronze with that Japanese silk print tie probably cost more than the Blend took in on an average day. Tucker would have pegged him "*GQ* Man," for sure.

Neils didn't appear to mind his wife's aggressive flirtation with Ric. Either that, or he was so busy showering attention on the lovely young reporter from Taiwan that he hadn't noticed.

"So the Van Doorns are here for the coffee exhibition?" I asked Madame.

"Yes, of course. You know, I was a friend of Monika's father for so many years, I'm still on Dutch International's guest list for their big costume party tomorrow night. The Village will be a madhouse, of course."

"Oh, right . . . Halloween . . ."

I'd been so busy, I'd almost forgotten the date, but Madame was right. Thousands of people would be pouring into Greenwich Village on October 31st for the annual Halloween Parade. If you were a resident, you either joined in the fun or got out of Dodge because there was no escaping the wall-to-wall throng of costumed revelers.

"If it were any other ICGE party, I'd skip it," said Madame. "But there are a few old friends of Joren I'm hoping to see there."

"Getting back to what you said about the buyer . . . that he has an inferior palate—"

"No, no. I said their problem was inferior *beans* and a buyer who has a *less than brilliant* palate. He's competent, of course, but nowhere near as sharp as you and Matt."

"Is Monika's husband over there . . . Neils? Is he their buyer?"

Madame laughed. "Neils has nothing to do with our industry. Or any industry, as far as I know."

"He's a playboy?"

"I believe he raced cars once and skied in the Olympics two decades ago." Madame shrugged. "Joren was dismissive of his son-in-law. He referred to him once as Monika's toy. The pair of them live on Aruba. It's Dutch controlled, as you know, although too dry and flat to grow coffee. I understand they enjoy the Caribbean lifestyle, and when they grow bored of the beach and casinos, they either come to New York or fly to Rio."

"But what is she doing here at this party?" I asked. "This event is supposed to be for international press or potential Blend clients, not other coffee distributors. Did you invite her, Madame?"

"Me? Good heavens, no." She lowered her voice. "The truth is, I enjoyed the company of her father. He was a real gentleman, but Monika . . . how shall I put it? When the woman's not acting like a total snob, she's talking like a total—"

Madame was about to continue when we were interrupted by an explosion of activity near the elevators. We both heard a loud shout over the noise in the room.

"You can leave on your own, or I'll gladly *throw* you *out* of this building myself!"

The voice belonged to Matt, and he sounded furious.

Eighteen

"I better see what's wrong," I told Madame.

I tried to cross the room, but it was slow going. The guests were packing the place by now, and I was too short to see over most of them.

"Did you hear me?!" Matt shouted.

"Get your hands off me," another man loudly replied, the accent sounding Spanish. "Or I swear to you . . . !"

"Are you threatening me?!" Matt again.

I still couldn't see anything as I continued to squeeze through the mob. "Excuse me! Pardon me!"

Finally, I broke through the human wall. I saw my ex-husband facing off with a man half his age. The stranger had a thick moustache, curly black hair that just touched his ears, and an athletic build that rivaled Matt's. I didn't recognize the stranger, and apparently someone behind me didn't, either, because I heard a woman ask, "Who is that?"

"That's Carlos Hernandez," another woman replied.

"Who?" I turned to find two young women, one a

brunette, the other a redhead, both dressed in business suits. They looked like members of the invited press. "Does one of you know that man?" I asked them.

"Not personally," the brunette replied. "His picture was in 'Page Six' last week. Carlos Hernandez is the nephew of Victor Hernandez. You know, the socialist dictator of Costa Gravas?"

"Yes, I've heard of him," I assured her. "So why was his picture in the paper? I didn't see the *Post* last week."

"He's here as part of a UN delegation. He joined in a coalition with the new socialist governments in Venezuela and Bolivia to pass a resolution opposed by the United States, but the paper was more interested in covering his extracurricular activities."

"His what?"

"He's here on his government's dime, but he spent two hundred thousand dollars celebrating the resolution's passage in a New York City strip club."

Matt's voice was still loud and angry. And Carlos Hernandez was still refusing to leave. He tried to step around Matt, but my ex moved quickly to block the man. Hernandez muttered something under his breath. I couldn't hear the words, but Matteo did and he became even angrier.

"You've got nerve showing up here!" Matt's face was flushed, the tendons quivering on his tanned neck. "You and your uncle are nothing but glorified thugs! You stole the Gostwicks' plantation—land that family's farmed for generations! You took it away by force, without a penny of remuneration!"

Oh, this is peachy, I thought. My ex was about to cause an international incident within spitting distance of the UN.

I looked around for some help. Only then did I notice Tucker standing right beside me. I pleaded with my eyes for him to step in and end the stalemate, but Tuck didn't get the message. He just kept staring at the bickering men with fascinated glee.

"Amazing, isn't it?" he said. "A pair of fiery Latins in designer suits. It looks like an outtake from *Scarface*!"

"No, Tuck," I mumbled. "It looks like we've got Der *real* Kommissar in town."

Madame appeared just then. She was moving toward Matt from one direction. Breanne was closing in from another. The two women's eyes met and they both stopped dead in their tracks, just short of their goal.

I guess that leaves little old me.

If I didn't step in, Matt was going to flatten this guy—unless Hernandez flattened Matt first. Either way, it was a lose-lose situation for my ex because Hernandez would certainly have diplomatic immunity. That realization spurred me forward. If nobody else was going to stop this, then I would!

I launched myself out of the crowd—only to be jostled aside as Federico Gostwick pushed by me.

"Back away, Matteo," Ric warned, stepping up to face Hernandez.

"Oh, god," I whispered, and held my breath. A silence fell over the room. Everyone in the know wondered what Ric Gostwick would do to the nephew of the man who'd exiled his family and destroyed their legacy.

"Let me handle this, my friend," Ric told Matt. His tone actually sounded calm and reasonable.

The tendons in Matt's neck continued to twitch, but he didn't move. A tense moment passed. Finally, Matt stepped away.

I expected him to stick around, but he didn't. Pushing past Hernandez, he stormed towards the stairwell door, which I knew would take him directly down one flight to the restaurant's kitchen.

"First, let me apologize for my friend's reaction," Ric said to Hernandez. "Matteo has only my best interests at heart."

Ric scanned the faces in the room. When he spoke again, his voice was loud enough for everyone to hear. "Let me also say that *everyone* is welcome to this tasting—" He turned back to Hernandez. "Most especially a representative of the nation that was once my home, and a land I still love. In fact, Mr. Hernandez might actually benefit from witnessing the progress free men achieve when they are permitted to keep the results of their labor."

A smattering of applause greeted Ric's words. He nodded, accepting the support. Then he placed his hand on Carlos Hernandez's shoulder. "Please enjoy the tasting."

As Ric personally led Hernandez into the restaurant, I found Gardner Evans. "Do me a huge favor, Gardner?"

"What's that, Clare?"

I took his tray from him and pointed to the grand piano at the side of the room. "Play something."

"Sure . . . Anything in particular?"

"Upbeat."

He smiled. "I've got just the tune for this crowd."

Gardner sat down and began playing jazz riffs on the song "Java Jive."

The tension was finally broken, and the room's buzz of conversations resumed. A few minutes later, Ric found me. "Help me out, love," he whispered, pulling me close. "Ellie hasn't arrived yet and we can't wait any longer. Find Matt. Tell him I'll need his help during the presentation."

"All right."

Ric released me, and I moved through the crowd, making a beeline for the door to the stairs. I found Matt in the stairwell, on the damned cell phone again. I folded my arms and waited for the conversation to end. I could tell

Matt wanted privacy, but I refused to budge. After listening for a moment, he interrupted the speaker.

"Look, I have to go. I'll call you back in twenty minutes." Obviously still boiling with anger, he closed the phone and glared at me.

Hands on hips, I glared back. "Matt, for heaven's sake, what's gotten into you?"

"Not now, Clare," he snapped. Matt tried to brush past me, but this time I was the person doing the blocking.

"Oh, no," I said. "You're not going anywhere until you tell me what's wrong. This is your big night, yet you've been on the phone since you arrived. You hardly said hello to your mother, and you haven't lifted a finger to help with this party. And then you instigate an international incident with a relative of a Latin American dictator? It's crazy. Irrational."

"Clare, I—"

"Do you want to get us all in trouble?"

"I'm brokering a big deal, Clare. The timing is bad, but it can't be helped."

"You're brokering coffee *now*?"

Matt shrugged and looked away. "Not everyone is in the same time zone."

"I don't believe you," I said. "But I don't have time to figure out what you've really been up to. You're needed upstairs. Ellie Lassiter is a no-show, and Ric wants your help to begin the presentation."

Without another word, Matt climbed the steps. I watched his broad back rise then disappear through the heavy, metal door. With a sigh, I collapsed against the cold stone wall and massaged my throbbing head.

A young sous chef from the room service staff appeared in the hallway. Noticing my distress, she asked if I wanted something to drink.

"I could use an aspirin," I replied.

"No problem. Come on in."

I followed the girl into the crowded kitchen. We kept to the edges of the busy room, away from the ovens and grills.

"Here," she said, shaking two pills into my palm. Then she poured me a cool glass of a syrupy golden beverage to take with the medicine. "Apricot nectar," she explained.

She wasn't much older than Joy, and she projected that same kind of sweetness I saw in my daughter, despite her pierced tongue and scarlet hair under a mesh net.

She pointed to the apricot drink. "My grandmother swears by the stuff."

I knocked back the pills and the nectar, which actually did make me feel a little better. I thanked the girl and headed back upstairs, arriving just in time to help Tucker close the burgundy curtains that framed the plate glass windows. Ric wanted to block the stunning view of midtown skyscrapers so his audience would focus solely on his presentation.

As Tucker and I brought the curtains together, I glanced outside. Rain showers were moving in over the city, and dark clouds were forming all around us. The omen wasn't lost on me.

Between Ellie abandoning Ric at the last minute and Matt causing a scene with a visiting dignitary, I had a dreadful premonition that the gathering clouds would bring more than one storm before the night was done.

Nineteen

"I'M sure everyone here knows that the market for decaffeinated coffee has exploded in the past few decades. One in five coffee consumers prefer it at least some of the time . . ."

While Ric spoke, I oversaw the preparation of the French presses at the bar. The Gostwick Estate beans had been burred in the kitchen to spare the guests any unpleasant noise. Now my baristas were pouring steaming water over the grounds, sending the aroma of the rich, earthy decaffeinated beans through the crowd.

"The decaffeination process was started in Germany over a century ago," Ric continued. "Though effective, it is far from a perfect method."

Ric was a natural salesman. He moved around the room with ease, holding the attention of a jaded audience, most of whom had heard more than their share of presentations and sales pitches.

"Refinements and new techniques have been made, but

all of these technological processes—Swiss Water, Royal Select, the solvent method, or pressurized gas—rob the bean of its freshness and complexity, its pleasing gusto." He stopped and grinned. "At my family's estate in Brazil, I think we've discovered a better way."

Matt stepped forward, holding the cutting. The sprig had been planted in a mocha-colored ceramic pot filled with topsoil. It seemed like such a small thing, yet it had the potential to transform the coffee industry, not to mention put processing plants in Switzerland and Mexico out of business.

"As you can see from this cutting, the hybrid I developed is not a typical *arabica*. I used another variety of the genus *Coffea*, crossbreeding and backcrossing with *arabicas* to create a wholly new, naturally decaffeinated variety of *Coffea* plant."

Men and women stepped forward to examine the cutting. "I don't have to tell you what this breakthrough will mean. Without the intervening technological process, decaffeinated coffee will reach the market more quickly. For the consumer, that means decaffeinated coffee that is fresher, cheaper, and far superior to the products currently available."

While Ric spoke, my staff pressed the coffee and began to pour it into the Village Blend cups.

"With approximately a two percent caffeine content—which is less than the amount of caffeine in average decaffeinated *arabica*, and far lower than decaffeinated *robusta* products—this hybrid bean already has been certified as a caffeine-free product."

Thanks to Tucker's able choreography, my baristas moved with theatrical precision, fanning out into the crowd with their trays of cups, just as Ric's sales pitch ended. "As for the taste? Please savor it now and judge for yourself."

The audience members accepted their samples, and I soon heard ohs, ahs, and a growing buzz of excitement. I wasn't surprised. Ric had a superior product and most of the people in this room were discerning enough to appreciate it.

Matt placed the cutting on a table in the center of the room. Ric stepped up to stand right next to it and spoke again. "The sample is here. Please feel free to take photos. I'll be here with it, to answer any questions you may have."

And make damn sure it doesn't disappear, I thought, especially since it didn't take long for the first round of cups to disappear. With each new round, people seemed more impressed. I could tell by the astonished expression on the faces of many that Ric Gostwick's hybrid was a genuine hit.

Since this wasn't a traditional cuptasting (i.e. the noisy slurping of pure, steeped coffee grinds, which were then spit out), we made sugar and cream available at the bar. Few guests used either.

While the participants enjoyed their second or third cup, I sent Gardner back to the piano, then grabbed Esther to help me pass out the prepared press kits. They included photos and a history of the Gostwick Estate in Brazil, photographs of an actual shrub, the cultivated fields, rows of mature plants, along with close-ups of the cutting, the cherries, and contact information. I'd seen the package earlier and thought Ric and Matt had done a thorough job.

"I know you all want to sample more after you leave here," Ric said. "The good news is—you can. The first batch of my hybrid bean has already been shipped. You can sample it at the Village Blend here in New York City, and any Village Blend kiosk in the United States, Europe, or Canada. A new world of decaffeination is coming to the premium market in the next few weeks."

A smattering of applause greeted the news. I returned to the bar to continue helping with the coffee service. Tucker had transferred a third round of French pressed brew to insulated carafes, and I moved around the room with Esther, refilling cups.

Along the way, I spied Joy. She looked lovely tonight with her hair smoothed into a grown-up French twist. Her makeup was a little heavier than usual, and the décolleté on her aquamarine dress was way too daring for my comfort level, but I said nothing. Why? Because I decided to at least try following Matt's advice and start treating Joy like a grown up. If she chose to wear a plunging, borderline indiscreet neckline, that was her business, and I would keep my mouth shut about it.

I was delighted that she'd come at all. And I wondered where Chef Tommy Keitel was. She'd told Matt that he was coming, but I didn't see anyone close to her age around her, and I feared the new wunderkind chef had bowed out on my daughter at the last minute.

With the press kits distributed, and Ric handling the questions while watching the cutting, everything seemed to be under control. Except Matteo, who was back to romancing his cell phone. I couldn't believe it, but I spotted him in a secluded, corner booth with the thing pressed to his ear as he scribbled notes on a tiny pad.

Too busy and weary to argue with him again, I returned to the bar to refill an empty carafe, and found Dante Silva standing behind Tucker.

"Dante," I said, "shouldn't you be serving?"

The young man ran his hand over his shaved scalp, like he was combing back hair that wasn't there. "I can't go out there, Ms. Cosi. He'll see me."

"Who'll see you?"

"That guy, over there," Dante said, suddenly looking trapped, hunted, desperate—a little like Java when I put the little fur ball in a cage for a trip to the vet. "He works for the *Times*. Last week I met him at a gallery show. He said really great things about my work in the past. I . . . I kind of left him with the impression I was more successful than I am—"

"You don't want him to know you're working as a barista?"

Dante shook his head. "Can't I work here behind the bar? Or help with something downstairs in the kitchen?"

I sighed and looked at Tucker. "I hate to pull Gardner off the piano. The crowd's responding well to him."

Tucker grabbed a tray. "I'm going!" he sang.

Dante exhaled with relief. "Thanks Ms. Cosi—"

"Dante, once and for all, will you please call me Clare? And you better not stay up here if you don't want to be seen by that *Arts* reporter. Just go down to the kitchen and start packing up the grinders, okay?"

"Sure, Ms. . . . Clare . . . thanks."

Dante disappeared and I felt a tap on my shoulder. It was Joy! She gave me a hug and a peck on the cheek.

"Looks like this new decaffeinated thing is a hit," she gushed.

I nodded, my gaze drifting to a young man lurking behind my daughter. Tall and rather shy, he was handsome and seemed very sweet. Standing next to him was an older man, maybe early fifties. He was attractive in a different way. With arresting blue eyes, a jutting chin, and salt-and-pepper hair, the man radiated confidence. He was casually dressed in an open sport shirt that revealed wiry muscles, a silver chain, and curling chest hair.

"Mom, I want you to meet a friend of mine," Joy announced breathlessly.

I self-consciously wiped my damp hands on my apron, ready for a handshake from the young man at Joy's side.

"This is Chef Tommy Keitel."

I looked at the young man. He looked away. Then a strong hand wrapped around mine, pumped my arm.

"Wonderful to meet you, Ms. Cosi," said the fiftysomething man.

Still clutching his hand, I blinked in surprise. Chef Tommy Keitel, my daughter's new flame, had enough years on him to be her father's older brother. Still smiling, his left hand covered mine.

That's when I saw it—the wedding band. I'd been able to avoid my daughter's plunging neckline, but I *could not* tear my eyes away from the gold circling the third finger of Tommy Keitel's left hand. My gaze shifted to the shy young man at Joy's side. He shuffled his feet, smiled tentatively, and looked away again.

Joy followed my confused stare. Noticed the young man. "Oh, god, how rude I've been. This is Vinny. He works at Tommy's restaurant, too."

Chef Keitel's hands released mine. I smiled wanly, extended it to the young man.

"Vincent Buccelli, ma'am . . . I mean, Ms. Cosi." His words were halting, and his eyes were downcast, but his handshake was firm.

"I tasted that coffee you're shilling," Chef Keitel announced with a superior smirk. "Good stuff. I like coffee, don't love it, mind you. My thing's wine, but I couldn't tell the coffee was decaffeinated, and I think I have the palate to tell. Of course, you did use a French press. That's sort of like cheating, right? Christ, I bet tinned coffee would taste good if you made it with a French press."

When he ran out of gas (and I'm being kind), I watched Chef Keitel wrap his arm around my daughter's young waist, pull her against his aging body. My reaction was similar to the one I had watching a snake devour a bunny rabbit on *Animal Planet*.

"Of course, caffeine has its uses. You don't always want to sleep, right?" He looked at my daughter and winked. "Sometimes you want to stay up all night long."

I decided that Chef Keitel's lewd innuendo was reason enough to kill him right then and there, and I had to restrain myself from tightening that silver chain around his throat until he turned the color of a Japanese eggplant. Instead, I put my hands together and forced a smile.

"May I speak to you for a minute, Joy? It's about your father . . ."

I shifted my gaze to Chef Keitel. "So nice to have met you."

I maintained my rigid grin throughout the exchange, but I felt the time bomb ticking inside me. I walked behind the bar, not sure if Joy would follow. I think she hesitated, but I refused to turn around and look. Then I heard Chef Keitel cry out. He'd spotted Robbie Gray, and the two chefs loudly greeted one another. Locked in animated conversation, they wandered away. Vinny Buccelli lingered for a moment, then followed his boss.

Joy appeared at my side. "What about daddy?" she asked.

"Your friend, Chef Keitel—"

"Tommy?"

I nodded. "Didn't you notice, Joy, that he's *older* than your *father*."

I expected an angry outburst—a none-too-gentle suggestion to mind my own business, though not put quite so tactfully. But Joy surprised me. She just rolled her eyes and shook her head.

"I knew you were going to do this," Joy said in a voice that was dead calm.

"Do what?"

"This. Make a scene. Humiliate yourself."

"I'm humiliating myself? I'm not the lovely, charming, sweet young girl who's dating an octogenarian."

Joy's lips curled into a superior smirk—an expression that unsettlingly resembled Chef Keitel's. "Oh, mother. Now you're being ridiculous."

Hands on hips, I stepped closer. "You're young, Joy," I quietly told her. "You haven't accomplished much, so you're using a smug, superior attitude as a way of elevating yourself. That's fine. That's what young people do. But don't make the mistake of thinking you know it all. You have a lot to learn, and I just don't want to see you learn it the hard way."

Joy stared into the distance. Since the moment I'd brought up her boyfriend's inappropriate age, she'd refused to look me in the eye. That gave me hope that somewhere deep inside, Joy knew she was headed down the wrong path.

"I've heard this before," she declared in a bored voice. Then she sighed theatrically. "I'm leaving."

I held her shoulder. "He's married, Joy. He's wearing a wedding band. That means he has a wife—and, I assume, a family."

"What do you know about anything, mom? When you were my age, you were married, too. Now you're not. What does that tell you? That things change, that's what."

"You're making a mistake."

"No I'm not." She shook off my hand. "I'm leaving."

"Excuse me." The voice belonged to Esther Best. I turned to face my barista. She appeared uncomfortable about stumbling upon a mother-daughter spat.

Who wouldn't? I thought.

"Sorry, boss," she said. "We're about out of coffee again, and nobody looks like they're leaving anytime soon.

Should I go downstairs and grind more beans? I would have asked Ric, but I don't see him."

I glanced around the room. Esther was right. I didn't see Ric by the cutting. Matt either.

"Take the cutting down to Dante in the kitchen," I told Esther. "Tell him to keep an eye on it, and ask him to grind more beans, but only enough for one more go round."

Esther nodded. I turned to face my daughter again, but Joy was gone.

I tore off my apron and dashed for the elevator. I made it in time to see Joy enter the car and the doors close. I slammed my finger against the button and the doors opened again. Joy frowned when she saw me.

"Joy—"

"Don't talk to me."

"But—"

"If we're going to fight, let's do it in the street," she hissed.

There were six other people in the elevator, casting curious glances at us. I gritted my teeth, willing to wait until we got outside—but not a moment longer.

When we reached the lobby level, Joy slipped through the art deco elevator doors before they even opened all the way. I raced to catch up. The Beekman Hotel's lobby was small, and we were across it and out the front door in seconds. Still Joy kept walking, her heels clicking on the wet sidewalk.

I shivered, wishing I'd brought my coat. The threatening downpour had not yet arrived. Instead, there was a misty precipitation that seemed to hover in the air, turning flesh clammy and clothes damp. The street was busy with Saturday night traffic. Headlights gleamed like halos in the haze as they raced uptown. A Gala tour bus rumbled out of the UN plaza. But the sidewalk was deserted save for a couple coming out of a brightly lit liquor store and a few teenagers across First Avenue, slamming their skateboards on a makeshift jump along the dark sidesteps of Trump World Tower.

"Joy, wait," I pleaded, running after her.

She stopped dead and whirled to face me.

"Joy, please understand. I only have your best interests—"

"Blah, blah, blah." She folded her arms. "I've heard this speech before. Try something original."

"Okay. I know this guy makes you feel special. I know that because I know his type—"

"Right. You've exchanged, like, ten words with Tommy, but you already know he's a 'type'?"

"Listen, Joy. You're special. Special to me. Special to your father. But not to this guy. He's an operator."

"You're wrong," she said. "Tommy *does* think I'm special. He's teaching me all sorts of new things—"

In the kitchen or the bedroom? I nearly shot back.

"He's an amazing man," Joy went on. "It's you who can't face reality. You don't want to let me grow up. Well, you're going to have to face it. I am grown up. I'm gone."

She turned to walk away. I grabbed her arm.

"What tales does Tommy tell you?" I asked her. "That his marriage is in trouble? That he's going to divorce real soon." I used air quotes on the *real soon* part. "Does he tell you his wife doesn't understand him?"

"It's my life, Mom. Let me live it. What do you care if I mess up. How does that affect you?"

"Oh, Joy," I said, looking for strength from the heavens. "How can I make you understand—"

That's when I saw the free-falling body, the black silhouette blotting out the lights of the Beekman Tower like an instant eclipse.

I grabbed my daughter, dragged her backwards with

me, up against the building. She squirmed in alarm. "Mom! What are you—"

The body hit the sidewalk with a sickening sound, like an overripe watermelon splattering on a slab of concrete. Joy turned her head, saw the blood, and screamed. I hugged her closer, shut my eyes, and bit down on my own lip so I wouldn't. Someone in a passing car cried out. I heard the squeal of tires on wet pavement, then footsteps. A hand clutched my arm.

"Are you okay, lady?"

I opened one eye. A black teenager in a denim jacket with the words FREN Z CLUB emblazoned on its pocket stared at me with wide eyes. He had a red bandanna covering his head, a skateboard under his arm.

"I think so," I stammered. Then I looked at my daughter. Her head was still tucked into my shoulder.

"Damn, that dude just fell out of the sky!" the kid cried. He stared at the corpse.

I could see the victim was male. He'd landed on his side and his head was turned, so I couldn't see his face. The dead man wore a black dinner jacket, similar to the one Matt was wearing. I stopped breathing. He had hair like Matt's, too, thick and black.

Joy slowly pulled away from me. Tears stained her cheeks. Her face was ghostly white. She saw the corpse and began to tremble.

"Mom . . . *who* is it?" she whispered in a little girl's voice.

The teen crouched over the victim. "Dude's dead, man." His skateboarding friends rushed up to join him.

"Dang, Z! Did you see that?!"

"That's messed up!"

I heard other voices.

"Call 911! Get an ambulance here!"

A gray-haired gentleman rushed toward us, Burberry raincoat billowing in the wind. He'd come from the direction of the United Nations building. I held Joy by her shoulders, fixed her with my eyes.

"Stay right here."

I waited until she nodded in response, then I approached the body. It seemed to take forever to walk those few steps. I circled around, moving into the street. Traffic was at a standstill, so I didn't have to watch for cars.

Finally I saw the dead man's broken face. I recognized him. It wasn't my ex-husband, thank god. The corpse was Carlos Hernandez of the Costa Gravas delegation to the United Nations—the man my ex-husband had threatened to *throw out* of the building a little over an hour ago, in front of one hundred and fifty witnesses.

Twenty

In New York City, a dead man on the sidewalk always attracts a crowd, and one was forming now. Corpses attract sirens, too. I heard them wail in the distance.

Tearing my gaze away from the body, I hurried back to my daughter. Joy was hugging herself, shivering. I put my arm around her.

"Who is it?" Joy asked, her voice trembling. "It's not . . . Dad—"

"No, no, honey. It's no one you know."

More people arrived. Soon it would be New York's Finest, and the questions would begin. I took Joy's arm.

"Come on."

She resisted. "Where are we going?"

"Back upstairs, to the Top of the Tower. We're going to find your father."

Joy surrendered and I took the lead. We reentered the lobby, dodging a bellboy and the desk clerk; both were scrambling to join the mob outside. One of the elevator's doors opened. The car was filled with faces I recognized from the party. They appeared serenely decaffeinated, all of them calmly chatting among themselves.

It was clear they hadn't yet noticed Carlos Hernandez's swan dive, and I wondered if the mood would be the same upstairs. If it was, I knew it wouldn't be for much longer.

When we arrived at the Top of the Tower, the restaurant was less crowded, but far from empty. Ric was chatting with a reporter from the *London Times*. Monika Van Doorn, who'd been glued to Ric's side since she'd arrived, was now nowhere in sight. Had she left? I looked around for my ex, but I didn't see him. The booth where he'd been making calls was empty except for a few scraps of paper.

I noticed the heavy burgundy curtains were still drawn, blocking the view of the outside balcony. I crossed to the side of the room and stepped through a doorway. Misty rain beaded the veiled window behind me, and the winds were more tempestuous this far above the street. It was also very dark because the clouds had grown even thicker. My eyes needed a moment to adjust to the gloom. When they did, I paced the length of the narrow balcony.

I saw no evidence of a struggle, no blood or broken glass, no sign that anything violent had happened at all. I gripped the stone railing and leaned over the edge. Fighting a wave of vertigo, I spied the body directly below.

Presuming Carlos Hernandez fell straight down—and I didn't see any ledges for him to strike or flagpoles to bounce off of—then he went over the side right where I was standing. That made me feel queasy, but I continued surveying the scene.

Three police cars and an ambulance had arrived by now. Men in blue cleared the sidewalk, redirected traffic, and cordoned off the area with yellow tape. While I watched, an unmarked police car with a magnetic bubble light on its roof double-parked next to a squad car. Two plain-clothed detectives stepped out. I knew it wouldn't be long before they arrived at the Top of the Tower.

For a minute, I considered the possibility that Matt actually was responsible for what happened. If Carlos Hernandez had decided to confront Matt while they were alone out here, well . . . that would have been a mistake for Carlos. Tonight, Matt was as harried as I'd ever seen him. On top of that, I knew my ex could throw a punch because I'd seen him do it.

Did he kill Carlos Hernandez, perhaps accidentally, in a fit of fury, and then flee? It didn't seem possible, yet I was sure there were many dead spouses who'd never imagined the person they shared their life with was capable of violence.

Just then, I felt a hand on my shoulder.

"Ahh!" I cried, jumping and turning.

"Mom, it's me," Joy said. "Calm down."

"I'm calm. I'm calm. Just don't sneak up on me like that again," I said. "Did you find your father yet?"

Joy shook her head. "I didn't see him. But what's with Grandma tonight? She's in a *mood*."

"Forget your grandmother for now. We've got to find your father fast. The police will be here any minute. We've got to establish an alibi."

"What?" Joy blinked. "Did you say *alibi*?"

"Before you arrived, your father threatened the man lying on the sidewalk down there."

"Threatened how?"

"Your dad announced, quite loudly, that he wanted to throw the man out of the building."

Joy glanced at the street below. "C'mon, Mom. You can't think Dad had anything to do with that?"

"It doesn't matter what I think. It matters what the police think. Let's go."

Joy in tow, I reentered the building. No one in the room even glanced my way. They hadn't noticed me go out, or come back in. It was easy to see how they might have missed Carlos Hernandez's fatal swan dive. Whatever happened on that balcony had been masked by the heavy curtains.

But if the victim had screamed, wouldn't someone have heard it? The noise in the room was relatively loud—laughter, boisterous conversations, and Gardner's lively jazz piano. Still . . . I couldn't see how a loud scream would not have been heard by someone.

Could Hernandez have jumped on his own? I wondered. Committed suicide for some reason? Or was he dead or unconscious before he went over the edge?

I massaged my temples to keep my headache at bay. It wasn't working.

"You go that way, I'll go this way," I told Joy. "If you find Matt, bring him to me."

I circled the room, scanning the faces in the crowd. I found Madame at a table with Dr. McTavish.

"Have you seen Matt?"

"Joy asked me the same question," Madame replied. "What's he done now?"

"Never mind."

"Gonna make a bundle, Blanche," Dr. McTavish muttered, draining a wine glass. That's when I noticed the empty bottle on the table. He'd obviously snatched it off someone's tray earlier in the evening when we were serving alcohol.

"That son of yours will be able to retire before he's fifty. Move someplace where the weather's always nice. Golf all day. Soak up the rays. Here's to fun in the sun." He put the glass to his lips before he realized it was empty.

My jaw dropped. The good doctor was sloshed.

Madame rolled her eyes. "Put the glass down, Gary, and

Clare will get you a cup of black coffee. A very large cup. *With* caffeine . . ."

"I'll see what I can do," I replied.

Madame faced her date. "And after that, you'd better call a car. I feel a headache coming on . . ."

Before the moment became a scene, I moved along.

I spied Breanne, sitting on a loveseat beside Roman Brio, the flamboyantly acerbic food writer for *New York Scene* magazine. A heavyset man with a broad, round face and large bright eyes, his features resembled the young Orson Welles—the *Citizen Kane* filmmaker years. His formidable girth, however, had more in common with the older Welles, the one selling "no wine before its time" during situation comedy network breaks.

"Excuse me, Breanne, I'm sorry to interrupt. But do you happen to know where Matt is right now?"

"Haven't a clue," she replied, without bothering to look at me. "Perhaps he's in the kitchen. I'm sure *you* know how to find the kitchen."

As rude as she was, Breanne did have a point. I did know how to find the kitchen, and it was possible Matt was there, so I headed for the stairs—but I didn't get there, at least not right away. As I moved by the elevators, the doors opened and a friend walked out—Detective Mike Quinn, flanked by a pair of uniformed officers young enough to be one week out of the police academy.

I stared in surprise at Quinn. *What in the world is Mike doing here?* I'd expected the police to show, but Quinn was part of the Sixth Precinct's detective squad, which handled Greenwich Village. This area of town wasn't even close to his beat. Even so, I was relieved to see his familiar face.

Quinn didn't appear to share my feelings. His frown actually deepened when he spotted me.

"Mike," I said, walking up to him, "I'm so glad to see you."

"In another minute, I'm not so sure you will be."

"What do you mean?"

"I'm here to take your ex-husband in for questioning."

I was all set for this, ready to jump to Matt's defense in the case of Carlos Hernandez. But the next words out of Quinn's mouth left me speechless.

"I'm sorry to inform you, Clare, that Matteo Allegro is a person of interest in the murder of Ellie Lassiter."

"The murder of . . . ?" I stepped back, stared for a silent, confused moment. "Ellie Lassiter? I don't understand . . . you're saying that Ellie was . . ."

"Murdered. That's right."

"How?"

"She was found in a guest room at the V Hotel. The room was registered in the name of your ex-husband. There was also physical evidence that placed him at the scene of the crime."

"Physical evidence?" I repeated as my mind raced. *What does that mean? Blood? Saliva? Semen?* "What kind of physical evidence?"

Quinn ignored my question. "Is Matt here, Clare?"

"Yes. I think so . . ." I blinked. "Somewhere."

The news of Ellie's murder threw me completely. I was still in shock as Mike glanced around the still crowded room.

"Do you know anything about the body on the sidewalk?" he asked. "We saw the activity on our way in."

"His name is Carlos Hernandez," I said. "He was here, at our party."

Just then, a group of people moved around us to board the elevator.

"Stop them," Quinn said to the rookies in blue. "Secure

the area. Don't let anyone leave. Call down by radio. Tell the detectives from Midtown East to get up here, they're going to want to question everyone."

While Quinn spelled out procedures to his young officers, I slipped through the door to the stairs and down to the kitchen. Rushing through the short corridor, I nearly stumbled into Matt, who was walking out.

"Where were you?" I demanded.

"Right here. I haven't had real caffeine all day. Now I've got a withdrawal migraine. I needed aspirin."

I saw a paper cup of apricot nectar in his hand. Apparently he'd visited the restaurant's pierced sister of mercy, too.

"Where were you before you came down here?"

Matt shrugged, clearly annoyed. "Sitting in the booth upstairs. I was on the phone."

"Matt, something's happened—"

A shout interrupted me. "I saw her go down there, Detective Quinn."

I looked up the staircase, saw one of Quinn's rookies staring down through the door. "Ms. Cosi?" he called. "Detective Quinn would like to speak with you—and your ex-husband, if that's him."

"Quinn?" Matt griped. "What does that flatfoot want?"

I shushed him. A moment later, Quinn ambled down the stairs with the young officer in tow.

Matt greeted him with a smirk. "Well, well, what do you know, it's one of Clare's favorite customers. What brings you here, Quinn? A sudden interest in decaf?"

"Thanks for *finding* him, Clare," Quinn said, his tone dryly implying I'd been *warning* him instead. "You can go now."

Matt stared at Quinn. His smirk was gone. "What's this about?"

"Mr. Allegro," Quinn said, "where were you between four o'clock and eight o'clock tonight?"

"Don't you want to know where I was before I came down here? *She* did."

Shut up Matt, I wanted to scream.

"Just answer the question," Quinn said.

"I was right here at the hotel."

"This hotel. The Beekman Tower Hotel?"

"What the hell is this about?" Matt demanded.

"Ellie's dead, Matt," I said. "Quinn says she was murdered."

I saw the shock on Matt's face.

"I said you can *go*, Clare." Quinn didn't look at me. Instead he met the eyes of the young man in uniform.

The patrolman touched my arm. "Ma'am, come with me, please," he said quietly. "Let's go upstairs."

I didn't know what else to do, so I let myself be led back to the restaurant.

At the top of the stairs, it was pandemonium. Two more detectives had arrived. One was issuing orders. He was tall, with receding blond hair, round wire-rimmed glasses, and an exceedingly neat appearance.

"Who's this?" he said when he saw the young officer escorting me.

"This is Ms. Cosi," he replied. "Detective Quinn asked me to bring her upstairs."

"Quinn . . . Quinn . . . Why can't I place that name?" He tucked a thumb into the vest pocket of his three-piece suit.

"Lieutenant Michael Quinn," said the young officer. "He's from the Sixth, sir. He's here about another matter."

The tall detective scowled. "He needs to talk to me."

The detective then ordered the policeman I was with to start corralling the potential witnesses to Carlos Hernandez's drop. He and his men were going to start questioning them. The policeman took off and so did I. I hurried over to the booth I'd seen Matt using when he'd made those final calls.

The slips of paper I noticed earlier were still there, and I snatched them up. There were numbers scrawled on the page. Big numbers, little numbers, no dollar signs. I tucked the paper in my pocket just as a new officer approached.

"Ma'am, I need you to come with me. We have to ask everyone at this event a few questions . . ."

I nodded. A few minutes later, I saw Quinn again. After speaking with the nattily dressed detective from Midtown East, he and two uniformed officers escorted both Matt and Ric Gostwick to the elevators.

Twenty-One

It was very late when I found myself standing on the corner of Forty-ninth Street and First Avenue. In the darkness I could see the long trail of traffic lights, running up to Harlem. They looked like a surreal runway, marking the path north with colorful points of illumination. First they glowed green, like newborn coffee berries; then they turned yellow, the color of caution, of not quite ready. Finally, they went red. All the way uptown, I could see the color of ripeness, maturity, fruit ready to be picked, sold, and roasted for someone else's morning delight.

Red was also the color of blood, and I remembered the blood on the sidewalk. I looked for it on the shadowy pavement. But the dark stain was gone, washed away, I presumed, by the storm. When I looked up again, a strange, dense mist was sweeping toward me. Like those earlier clouds that enveloped the Beekman Tower, it encircled my body, blotting out everything.

"Mommy?"

The voice came to me, sweet and young. It was Joy's voice, from years ago. Had I imagined it?

"Mommy, I'm here."

I felt the smallness of her hand as it gripped my shoulder. I turned quickly, but no one was there. "Joy?!" I called, rubbing my arms. Alone on the street, I shivered, aware the damp night had grown colder.

"I'm up here, Mom!"

Joy's voice again, but she wasn't close anymore. She sounded older, angrier, much farther away. "I'm falling!" She was high above me now. I could hear her voice, near the Top of the Tower, beyond the fog.

"I'm falling, Mom!"

Frantically, I searched the misty ceiling. But there was no sign of her. No movement, no colorful points of light to guide my way north to her.

"Mom!"

"I'll catch you, Joy!" I promised, running up and down the block, my arms outstretched. "I'll catch you!"

I slammed into something—a solid wall. As I reeled backward, a woman stepped out in front of me, right out of the mist. She stood and stared.

"It's me, Clare."

"Ellie?"

It was Ellie Lassiter, but not the Ellie I'd met at the Botanic Garden. It was the Ellie I'd known years ago, when we'd been friends, with her long strawberry blond hair lifting on a breeze, her freckled smile wide. It was Ellie when she'd been young and happy . . . and alive.

"Catch him, Clare," she urged me. "Please, catch him."

I heard a vehicle racing up the avenue. I turned to see a pair of headlights cutting through the mist. The pale, weak beams grew stronger, then came the vehicle itself, a black

SUV. It passed through the fog like a phantom, coming into view, then vanishing again.

I turned back to the sidewalk. Ellie was gone.

I opened my eyes.

A toy piano was playing "Edelweiss." Still fuzzy from the dream, it took me a few seconds to realize I wasn't listening to a child tapping out my favorite tune from *The Sound of Music*, but the ringtone of my cell phone.

I pulled it from the pocket of my black slacks, flipped it open. "Hello?"

"Clare, it's me."

"Where are you?"

"Out front. Let me in."

It was more of a command than a request, but I wasn't going to stand on ceremony with Mike Quinn at two in the morning.

"Okay. Give me a minute."

The lights were off downstairs because the Village Blend was closed. I'd been working in my second floor office when I grew chilly, lit a fire in the hearth, and dozed off on an overstuffed armchair. The dream I'd had was disturbing, but Mike was here and I focused on that.

Rising from the armchair, I groaned, my back stiff from the twisted way I'd been napping. Rubbing the tendons in my neck, I descended the customer staircase, a spiral of wrought iron that led right down to the first floor coffee bar.

Matt and Ric were still in police custody, and I'd had no idea what to do, other than wait for Quinn to get in touch. Breanne had run off to call one of her attorney friends, and I'd thanked her for any way she could help.

As for me, once the Midtown detectives finished questioning my staff, I returned with them to the Blend. Because of the launch party, we'd closed the coffeehouse for the night, but I still had to properly stow the French presses, cups, and the unused roasted beans. I was behind on paperwork, too, and the next day was Saturday, one of our busiest. I knew the morning would be here all too soon.

"Are you okay?"

Quinn's first words. I was glad they were personal.

"Yes," I said. "Just a little stiff."

"It's freezing tonight, don't let in the cold."

He looked weary but still alert. His blue eyes were sharp, though the dark smudges under them told me he hadn't slept in a long time. His sandy brown hair was tossed by the wind, and his jawline was rough with stubble.

We headed upstairs, back to the second floor, where my fire was still burning. Quinn declined coffee, said he needed to power nap and get up early. The investigation was in high gear, but before heading back to his East Village flat, he wanted to check in with me, see how I was, and ask me a few questions.

Of course, I thought, *I'm part of your case now. Well, that's okay, because I have a few questions for you, too.*

"What's going on with Matt?" I asked as he shed his trench coat and threw it over a chair. "Where is he? Why are you charging him with Ellie's murder?"

"Slow down, Clare. Nobody's charging Matt with murder." He settled into the overstuffed sofa, across from the hearth. "We're actually done questioning him at the Sixth, but Midtown wanted him for questioning in the Hernandez murder."

"The man was murdered then? For sure?" I paced back and forth, in front of the fire.

"The autopsy results aren't in yet, but there's evidence

the man's clothes were torn before he went over the balcony. It looks like he struggled with someone before taking the plunge."

"And your colleagues in Midtown think Matt did it?"

"They know he was angry at Hernandez and threatened him physically. It doesn't look good, but they're going to need more than that to get the DA to charge him. They also know Ric Gostwick had a motive, although no one at the party remembers seeing him go out on the balcony."

"What about Ellie? What happened to her, Mike?"

He held my eyes a moment, then looked away, into the flames. "I shouldn't discuss the details . . ."

"Please. You know I was her friend."

"I know."

"And you know you can trust me . . . don't you?"

Mike rubbed his eyes for a long, silent minute. "She was found naked," he said quietly, "although it looked like she'd had a bath towel around her and had just finished showering. No sexual assault. The physical evidence leads us to believe that she'd made love with someone in the room's bed, showered, and then was attacked. She struggled—there are signs of it on her body. We've got blood and tissue under her fingernails. We've got a contusion at the base of her skull, and hairs and bits of blood on the edge of a heavy chest of drawers where it appears she struck her head."

"Oh, god."

"That's enough—"

"No! Please, keep going, Mike . . . How did you find her body . . . you know, when you first came into the room? Was it near the chest of drawers where you found the bits of blood and hair?"

"No . . . we found her . . . I'm sorry, Clare, we found her hanging by an electrical cord from the shower curtain rod."

"What?"

"The killer tried to make it look like she'd hung herself. He did a piss poor job of it, too. We didn't need an autopsy to see that hanging wasn't the cause of death, that the scene had been clumsily manipulated."

"You said *he*. Are you sure it was a man?"

"The injuries, the way the body was hung. If it wasn't a man, it was a pretty strong woman."

I thought of Monika Van Doorn . . . the woman looked tall and strong, all right. And she'd arrived well after Ric. Could she have gone to Ric's room, looking for him, found Ellie, and flown into a rage? I told Quinn as much. He pulled out his detective's notebook and jotted down her name for follow up. I mentioned Norbert Usher, too, Ellie's slightly creepy Eddie Haskell-esque assistant.

"Norbert was at the Beekman event, too. I remember seeing him there."

He scribbled the name.

"And while that notebook's out," I continued. "I have something else to tell you."

"Shoot," he said. His eyes found mine. "Not literally."

"Don't even *try* to make this easier."

"Tell me."

I gave him the condensed tale of what I'd discovered earlier in the week—how I'd talked to Ellie at the Botanic Garden, followed her to the V Hotel, saw her meeting Rick, but also saw a man tailing her.

Mike sat up straighter. "Where did you follow him?"

"An agency near the United Nations. They're called Worldwide Private Investigations, and I spoke to a Mr. Anil Kapoor."

"Spell it all for me . . ."

Mike wrote everything down. "This is a solid lead, Clare. I'll phone my partner. We'll go there first thing in the morning."

"I want to go with you. Mr. Kapoor will remember me. He'll probably be more willing to talk once he sees I'm your witness."

"Okay."

"And one more thing. Have you looked at Ellie's husband as a suspect?"

"We always do in cases like this, as a matter of course, but Jerry Lassiter has an alibi."

"Well, look hard at that alibi—and any associates Lassiter might have hired to hurt his wife—because Worldwide Private Investigations lists TerraGreen International as a client."

"TerraGreen?" Mike flipped through his notebook. "That's the company where Lassiter's a VP."

"That's right . . . so how *could you* pick up Matt?" I heard myself snapping. I couldn't help it. I was extremely tired, it was very late, and my feelings toward Quinn had been a mixed bag for a long time. "Do you really believe he had anything to do with something so awful?"

"Let's leave my assessment of your ex's character out of this, okay?" His tone was strained now, too, and a little defensive. "I had enough circumstantial evidence to grill him, and you know it. The hotel room was registered in his name, and his clothes were there. We even found his monogrammed handkerchief."

"Ric borrowed those clothes!"

"We know. We know the whole story now, Matt gave us every detail. It was Ric's room, and Ric was having an affair with Ellie."

"So Matt's off your 'persons of interest' list?"

"We won't get DNA results for a while, but we already have a blood type on the tissue under her fingernails. It's not Matt's type."

"What about Ric?"

"It's not Ric's, either. He's the same type as Matt. Neither man appeared to have been the person Ellie Lassiter struggled with before she died."

"So Ric and Matt are both off the hook?" I pressed.

"For Ellie," Mike said. "But not for Hernandez. Midtown's making the call on charging someone for that . . . it could be Matt or Ric . . . or neither."

"Oh, god . . ."

"You'll know soon, Clare. They won't hold those guys long. They can't. Habeas corpus, you know? And they won't dare make a charge until they know the DA can make it stick in court. Just hang in there."

I sighed, rubbed my neck, which was still sore.

"Come here," Mike said quietly. "Sit down, try to relax."

I sat next to him. He put one strong hand on my neck, used his fingers to gently loosen the muscles.

"Oh, Mike . . . that feels good . . ."

The warmth of the fire felt good, too, and the warmth of Mike's strong leg against mine. I closed my eyes. My hand lightly settled on top of his thigh. The moment I touched him, I heard his sharp breath. I opened my eyes. This wasn't a dream. Mike was really here. He was bending toward me, his mouth covering mine. The kiss was sweet and hungry and a little desperate for both of us.

I wasn't the one to break off first.

Mike stared into the glowing hearth, put his arm around me, tucked me close against him. "Let's take it slow," he said.

"I like the sound of *let's* . . . you know, you and me . . . plural."

Mike laughed. "I like the sound of it, too, Clare. But I want it to be right between us . . . long and slow and beautiful, not here . . . not like this."

"You mean not with two unsolved murders on the table and my ex-husband in custody?"

"Yeah . . ." He exhaled. "You know my personal life's been in flux. God . . ." He cursed softly. "Why mince words? It's been a hell of a mess for a long time. I never wanted to bring you into my mess. I didn't think it was fair. And now I'm living like a college kid again, out of my old home, into this spare apartment . . ."

I smiled. "How spare?"

"Nothing I want you to see."

"Come on, how bad could it be? A mattress on the floor? A bare lightbulb."

"Close, Cosi. Very close."

"Well, you could always ask me to help you decorate the place. I'm not bad at it, you know?"

"I don't want you to be my interior decorator, Clare. I want you . . ." His voice trailed off. "I just want you."

"I want you, too, Mike."

"And it'll be right between us soon . . . I promise."

I couldn't argue with him. This guy was a romantic. That was okay. So was I.

We closed our eyes then. We were both exhausted, and in a few minutes, we dozed off. When I woke again, about twenty minutes later, Mike was sleeping soundly, and I realized the Blend's second floor couch was about to become a temporary bed for another lost soul.

I rose, letting his body fall gently into a reclined position. I removed his shoes, went to my office, and looked for the thick wool throw I kept there. Back at the fireplace, I covered Mike's lanky form, kissed his cheek. Then I wished him sweet dreams and climbed the back stairs to find my own bed.

Twenty-Two

BLEARY eyed, I stumbled down the stairs at ten minutes to six to greet the baker's truck. I didn't even have time to brew a pot of the Village Breakfast Blend before I heard the delivery bell ring. I unlocked the door and held it open.

"Howya doin', Ms. Cosi," announced Joey, the delivery driver.

I inhaled the warm batches of muffins, croissants, bagels, and mini coffee cakes, and wondered what Quinn would like with his Breakfast Blend. I couldn't ask him yet. When I came down to open the shop, he was still snoring on the couch.

I started the coffee, and was putting the pastries in the case when the bell above the door jingled. I peeked over the counter in confusion. We weren't open yet, and I thought I'd relocked the door after Joey left.

When I glanced up, I saw Matt standing in the doorway, fumbling to get his keys out of the lock. Shoulders hunched, eyes bloodshot and weary, he seemed to have aged five years since the night before.

"Hey," he said, noticing me behind the counter. Matt's ever-present masculine bravado was gone. He seemed baffled and defeated.

"Coffee's almost ready," I replied, setting two cups on the counter.

Matt shook his head. "I need sleep. Not coffee."

"No. You need to tell me what's going on."

He exhaled heavily, sat on a stool behind the coffee bar, and leaned his elbows on the marble countertop. The Breakfast Blend was finished and I poured. He took a sip, then two. Finally he swallowed a large gulp and set the half-empty cup on the counter.

I topped off his mug.

"I get it," he said as I poured. "You're trying to keep me caffeinated, so you can grill me."

I smiled. He did, too. But I figured I had a limited amount of time before Matt crashed and burned, so I cut to the chase.

"What happened, Matt?"

He took another gulp. "Ellie's dead."

"I know . . ."

I let him tell me some of the things I already knew from talking to Quinn. Finally I interrupted, "How's Ric taking Ellie's death?"

"I only got to talk to Ric for a few minutes, but from what I can see he's taking it pretty hard." Matt rubbed his face with both hands. His flesh looked pale and clammy from lack of sleep. "Ric admitted to me that he and Ellie had made love Friday afternoon, to celebrate the rollout at the Beekman. I think he's still in shock."

"Do you think Ric was telling the truth?"

"About Ellie? Yes."

"So the police let you go . . ."

"For now . . . Quinn believed me about Ellie. Or, at least, he pretended to. I told him what I knew about her relationships. And after your boyfriend was done with me, I thought I was free to go." Matt sighed in disgust. "Man, was I wrong. Instead of being released, I was handed off to some blueblood flatfoot, if you can believe it, a detective named Fletcher Endicott. What a piece of work. I've decided the only thing worse than a street cop with an attitude is an Ivy League cop with an attitude."

I remembered seeing the nattily-dressed detective in charge at the Beekman, the one with the glasses and the three-piece banker's suit, though at the time I didn't know his name. I was interrogated by his partner, a Detective Fox. He seemed fixated on the time of Hernandez's death, kept trying to pinpoint the minute. I felt terrible for not knowing, but the moment a body lands on the sidewalk right in front of you, checking your watch is not the first thing that occurs to you.

"Endicott hauled me all the way up to Midtown East, so he could 'interrogate me on his own turf' as he put it, and I spent the rest of the wee hours denying I threw Hernandez off the balcony. Then they kicked me out."

"So in the end, Detective Endicott let you go, too?"

"Believe me, he didn't want to. I'm sure he's looking for more evidence to officially charge me. Apparently, they're going with Hernandez's broken wristwatch as the time of death, and the girl in the Beekman's kitchen was helping me find some aspirin around that time—so, for now, it looks like I might have an alibi. But I've been warned not to leave the country, so clearly I'm still on their 'persons of interest' list."

I wasn't surprised. "You did threaten the man publicly."

Matt didn't argue. He took another noisy gulp, draining

his cup. "Detective Endicott's still looking at Ric, too. I'm pretty sure they're checking over his business visa and paperwork."

It was the perfect segue, and I took it. "You said Ric was being honest about Ellie. You also hinted that there was something he *wasn't* being honest about. Fill me in on that . . ."

"I heard things. Maybe it's nothing," Matt replied.

I could tell he was hedging. "Please, Matt. You have to be straight with me now. That's the only way I can help."

Matt looked down, sighed heavily. Finally he nodded.

"There's a guy I know. Roger Mbele, a West African coffee broker. Last month I ran into him at Kennedy Airport and we got to talking. He already knew about Ric's hybrid coffee plant and congratulated me on the exclusive deal. Then, yesterday afternoon, he calls me out of the blue to tell me that Dutch International just cancelled its order for three hundred bags of his green beans. Roger was stuck holding the bags—so to speak—and he wasn't happy."

"I don't understand. Why did he call you?"

"Roger wanted to know why his deal collapsed, so he called the buyer at Dutch International's corporate headquarters in Amsterdam. The buyer told Roger that the company would normally purchase his beans for decaf processing, but they didn't need Roger's green beans any longer because they'd just made a deal to sell beans that were already *botanically* decaffeinated, and they were expecting their first shipment in the next few weeks. That's when he called me."

"Is it possible that someone else came up with a similar product and beat Ric to the market?"

Matt stared down at his empty cup. "I think it might be worse than that."

I didn't get much sleep the night before. Maybe that was

the reason, but I didn't make the connection until Matt mentioned her name.

"Monika Van Doorn was with Ric at—"

"That woman!" I cried. "I saw her at the party, pawing up Ric!"

Matt nodded. "Now that her father's passed away, she's the head of Dutch International. That's the first thing I thought of after I got Roger's call."

"So you think Ric made a deal with her?" I asked. "I thought the Village Blend had an exclusive distribution deal for the initial rollout?"

"So did I."

"Is that what all those cell phone calls were about at the tasting last night? You think Ric is cheating you?"

"Not me, Clare. I have the hybrid beans in my warehouse. Enough to last six to eight months. Ric told me I had practically his entire harvest and I believed him. I still do . . ." Matt's voice trailed off.

"So what were all those calls about last night? All those numbers you scribbled on pieces of paper?"

"I called a couple of growers, asked for some up to date numbers on Brazilian yields. Then I did a little calculating."

I was anxious to hear Matt's conclusions. I knew that coffee yields varied wildly among countries and regions. Factors like soil, weather, and irrigation techniques had as much influence on the quality and quantity of coffee as they had on wine grapes. And yield per acre on *robusta* farms was generally twice that of farms that produced *arabica* (one reason, but not the only reason, why *arabica* beans were generally pricier).

"You know that Brazil is the number one producer of coffee in the world, right?" Matt said.

"Right."

"The country averages around twenty million bags a year."

I nodded. "At about one hundred pounds per bag."

"One hundred and thirty-two," Matt noted, "but there are problems in Brazil. For one thing, it's the only high-volume coffee-producing nation subject to frost. And Brazilian estates have some of the lowest yields. In Hawaii they get over two thousand pounds of clean coffee per acre. In Brazil that average is less than nine hundred pounds per acre—which is up substantially from the four hundred pounds in the sixties, but not even close to equaling Hawaii's output."

Matt took out a pen and started writing on a napkin.

"The Gostwick Estate is fifty acres, but not all of their trees are mature. At best Ric is harvesting forty thousand pounds of clean hybrid coffee, probably less. So if he's selling Dutch International three hundred bags, at one hundred thirty-two pounds a bag, that equals nearly twenty tons—Ric's entire harvest and then some."

Matt looked up from his scribbles. "These numbers don't add up, Clare. Either Ric's got another estate somewhere, which is possible but highly unlikely, or—"

I closed my eyes. "He's perpetrating a fraud on Dutch International."

Matt rose and began to pace. "Do you know what that means? I'm in partnership with Ric Gostwick. My reputation and the reputation of the Blend will be ruined along with him if word gets out."

"What do we do, Matt? I'm in this with you, you know?"

He stopped pacing. "I know . . . and I have to tell you, Clare, I'm grateful you are." He squinted. "Not that you're in trouble, too, but that you're here for me . . . here for me to talk to about all this, I mean . . . it's a lot to deal with, and I'm . . ." He moved closer, sat down and took my hand. "I'd never tell anyone this but you," he whispered, "but I . . . I'm scared."

"It's okay, Matt." I squeezed his hand. "I'm here for you."

"I know, and I—"

His words were interrupted by the sound of a man clearing his throat. Matt fell silent, turned abruptly to find Mike Quinn standing at the base of the wrought iron steps. The detective's suit was rumpled from sleep, jacket slung over his shoulder, tie hanging loose.

"What are you doing here?" Matt stood, his expression furious. "Are you here to take me in again? Why did you come back?"

"What do you mean back?" Quinn replied, glancing momentarily at me. "I never left."

Matt glared at me in disbelief. I waited for the explosion, but when he opened his mouth to speak, no words came out.

"He fell asleep on the couch, Matt," I hastily explained. "Mike came here last night to tell me what was going on. He was so exhausted he passed out. That's all."

"He passed out on the couch? You expect me to believe that? Well, I don't, Clare!"

"Matt, please calm—"

"How could you do it?" he went on, clearly strung out beyond reason. "I'm getting a sleep deprivation third degree, and you're . . . you're *entertaining* the man who put me there—"

"That's enough, Allegro!" Mike finally roared. "Sit down and shut up!"

Matt blinked, opened his mouth, then shut it again. With an exhausted exhale, he collapsed on a stool.

"Why can't I control him like that?" I muttered.

"Listen to me, Allegro," said Quinn. "I personally don't believe you killed Ellie Lassiter *or* Carlos Hernandez. But others don't share my opinion. That means I'm one of the few friends you've got, and you better take advantage of that fact, as soon as possible."

"Yeah? How?" Matt replied. "What exactly are you saying?"

"I'm saying we should all work together to clear this mess up—for all of our sakes."

Matt stewed silently for a minute. Finally, he said, "What do you propose?"

"For starters, I'm meeting my partner uptown, at the WPI agency office."

Matt squinted. "What agency office?"

"Worldwide Private Investigations," I said.

"They're the private eyes that Clare uncovered," Quinn explained.

I nodded. "They're the ones who've been following Ellie Lassiter. Don't you remember my telling you, Matt?"

"Oh, god." Matt held his head. "I do remember. It seems like ages ago."

"I think Ellie's ex-husband hired them," I said. "Frankly, I think he's involved in her murder. He either killed her himself, or hired someone to do it for him, maybe the same someone who mugged Ric two nights ago."

Matt processed the information. "I'm going with you, Quinn."

"No you're not. I'm the one going with him," I said. "One look at me and the head of the agency won't be able to deny anything. I sat right there in his office two days ago, asking about Ellie."

"And if he does deny it. We'll get a warrant," Mike assured me.

"You're staying here," I told Matt. "There's more important things to be done, and only you can do them."

"What things?" Matt's tone was belligerent, but I couldn't blame him. The man hadn't exactly been partying all night.

"I want you to call every coffee broker you know. Try to find out if Ric is buying beans."

Comprehension dawned on Matt's exhausted face. "I understand where you're going. Okay, I'm on it."

As Matt poured himself another mug of coffee, I grabbed my jacket. His "I'm on it" echoed through my head, and before I headed out the door with Mike, I almost told Matt that he was finally beginning to sound like his mother. But then I bit my tongue.

As Matt began talking on his cell in a rough approximation of French, I decided that if anything could put Matt in a fouler mood than he was now, it was pointing out to him that he'd finally climbed aboard my Nancy Drew train.

Twenty-Three

When I returned to the Blend, a throbbing sonic wall smacked me in the face at the front door. Someone had replaced the subtle sounds of Gardner's smooth jazz program with the sort of thumping electro-synth fusion found in Euro-urban clubs. Not only was the music inappropriate, the volume was pumped to the limit. I approached Tucker at the espresso machine.

"What's this stuff coming out of the speakers?"

Tucker directed his eyes to the ceiling, then rolled them. "There's a man in the house."

"Matt?"

Tuck nodded. "He's taken over the upstairs lounge. I'm sending up an espresso shot every twenty minutes, and he's getting more manic. The music started about half an hour ago. Thank god it's not too busy. I think some of our regular customers would complain."

"Oh, for pity's sake . . . you don't have to wait for a

customer. I'm complaining. Right now. Put Gardner's CD back on."

"But Matt told me—"

"I'll handle Matt."

With two espressos in hand, I climbed the stairs. I found Matt slumped in an armchair, surrounded by a half dozen espresso cups. His shoes were off, and a fire roared in the hearth. His laptop computer was open on the table. Matt nodded when I entered, ended his call to someone on the Commodities Exchange.

"You're recovering nicely," I said.

Matt frowned. "So, did you and the flatfoot get the goods on Jerry Lassiter?"

I handed Matt the cup. With jittery hands, he added a large amount of sugar before he swallowed the demitasse in a single gulp.

"What are you doing?" I asked. "You never add sugar."

"I do when I need to stay awake. Now tell me what happened."

"Well . . . Mike was in rare form. By the time he was finished talking, Mr. Kapoor was only too happy to cooperate with the NYPD. The bad news is that Jerry Lassiter didn't employ the detectives. It was Carlos Hernandez."

Matt sat up. "Hernandez? Why?"

"Apparently, Hernandez hired the agency to dig up evidence of biopiracy for a possible lawsuit against Ric and the Gostwick Estate."

Matt rubbed his eyes. "Then it must have been Hernandez who had Ellie killed. She was helping Ric file for the legal protection of his hybrid. That has to be what happened."

"Mike thinks so, too. They're going to look for a blood type and DNA match with the crime scene evidence. But . . ."

"But what?"

"But what if Hernandez didn't kill Ellie?"

"Come on, Clare. It's the only scenario that makes sense."

"Not so fast," I said—an admittedly useless thing to say to someone as wired as Matt. "Isn't the whole point of a civil lawsuit to be awarded monetary damages? Why would Hernandez want to mess up the progress of getting the hybrid to market? Wouldn't it make more sense to let the decaffeinated plant be a success, then sue for a share of it? And if Hernandez killed Ellie, then who killed Hernandez?"

The questions hung there for a moment. When I decided I'd given Matt enough time to come to the same conclusion I had, I answered my own question.

"Could Ric have done it? Did he somehow find out about Ellie's murder, and then take revenge on the man who killed her?"

Matt shook his head. "Ric's a lover, not a fighter. In all the years I've known him, I never saw him raise a hand to anyone. Not even guys who tried to provoke him. He always used his wits and charm to get out of a bad situation."

My memories of Ric validated Matt's claim. After all, the man hadn't exactly held his own against the mugger who'd attacked him a few nights ago, though by his own account Ric was taken by surprise and from behind.

"Look," Matt said. "Hernandez had a lot of enemies. I know about this guy, and he's a real piece of work. Brawling at New York nightclubs. Hanging out with known drug dealers. Gambling debts. Running out on restaurant and nightclub bills. A guy like that can make a lot of enemies."

"Then why did he come to the Beekman alone?" I said. "Why wouldn't a man like that have a bodyguard with him?"

"I don't know, Clare, but if you ask me, Hernandez had it coming."

"Don't talk like that! You'll get arrested for suspicion again."

"Even if I had wanted to kill Hernandez, I would have had to get in line—a long one."

"I suppose it's possible somebody with a grudge finished Hernandez off," I said. "But I'd like to know the connection . . ."

Matt had no reply. He was staring at a graph on his laptop screen. "I made a few connections of my own."

"Good news or bad?"

Matt's grim expression said it all. "Ric's buying beans. Colombian beans. A good quality Bogotá. Only I know this little fact, but Ric was going for the taste and complexity of Bogotá beans when he developed his hybrid."

He paused. "It gets worse. Ric contracted a Mexican firm to decaffeinate the beans he bought. I just talked to a fellow in Chicago who confirmed that a Royal Select Company processing facility in Mexico will take a delivery of Ric's Bogotá in a couple of days."

"The cutting!" I realized. "Now it makes sense!"

"What?"

"Remember the little hybrid cutting you helped Ric smuggle into the country?"

"Yes?"

"Well, Ric lied to me. He said he borrowed it from you to show to Ellie. But Ellie assured me that she never saw it. Ric must have borrowed that cutting to show to Monika Van Doorn and her people at Dutch International. I'm sure everyone was impressed, and Dutch International signed the contract. Now Ric is going to deliver beans. Only they're not going to be from his hybrid decaf plants—"

"They're going to be Mexican water-processed decaffeinated Bogotá packed in Gostwick Estate Reserve Decaf bags," Matt said, finishing my thought.

I nodded. "It's the Kona scandal all over again. Only this time you and I are right in the middle of it."

"But you didn't do anything wrong," Matt assured me. "It's all my fault. I helped Ric smuggle the cutting, and I'm an accessory to fraud. Not you."

"I'm in this with you, Matt. Both of our reputations are on the line, not to mention the reputation of this coffeehouse. It's ugly what Ric is doing, but we have to face it. The Village Blend is about to become a party to fraud."

Matt stood. "It isn't fraud if it's exposed. I'm going to pay a visit to Monika Van Doorn. I'm going to tell her what I know, and what I suspect. After that, it's between her and Ric."

"But you don't even know where the woman is staying."

"Yes I do. Mother's invited to the Dutch International Halloween party tonight. The RSVP contact is a number at the Waldorf=Astoria. So I called the hotel and checked with the desk clerk. The Van Doorns have been staying in a suite for over a month."

I rose to join my ex-husband. "Let's go."

OUTSIDE the weather was blustery; the storm from the night before hadn't completely dissipated. Periods of menacing clouds were followed by flashes of blue skies. After I instructed Tucker to call in barista help, Matt and I flagged a cab on Hudson and rode uptown.

The old, original Waldorf=Astoria was located where the Empire State Building now stands. The current structure is a forty-seven story art deco landmark on Park Avenue. The grand hotel has been a temporary home for kings, princes, and the über-wealthy. I was reminded of that fact when we exited the cab on Forty-ninth Street and saw the commemorative plaque affixed to the wall. (Former President Herbert Hoover and retired U.S. General Douglas MacArthur had both lived in Waldorf suites.)

Matt paid the fare while I stepped into the crowd. I glanced up at the MetLife Building looming in the background. Then I glanced at the hotel's majestic entrance and stopped short.

Matt joined me on the sidewalk. "Let's go."

"Wait," I cried, dragging him off to the side.

Matt resisted, so I pulled harder. "Clare, what's the matter with you?"

"That man, coming out of the hotel," I whispered, trying not to point. "That's Neils Van Doorn, Monika's husband."

He followed my gaze. "No way, honey. Look at the way he's dressed. Van Doorn always looks as if he just posed for a "Fashions of the *Times*" layout. That guy's either a recent immigrant or a style-challenged tourist."

Matt was certainly right about the clothes. Neils wore a lime green polyester track suit and matching jacket over an orange sweatshirt. The shiny material was decorated with shoelace trim in chocolate brown. Not even the discount chains would be caught dead selling clothes that tasteless. Neils Van Doorn was wearing the kind of cheap stuff hanging on racks outside outlet stores on Fourteenth Street, right down to the no-name twenty-dollar sneakers on his size twelve feet.

"That's him!" I insisted, seizing Matt's hand and tugging him back to the middle of the sidewalk again. "He's waiting at the light. Look at his face when he turns . . . There."

Matt nodded. "You're right. I don't get the clothes, though. Maybe that's his Halloween costume. Superior Dutchman dresses as typical American hip-hop mook."

"Too subtle for an elitist's Halloween costume," I replied, still dragging Matt by the hand. "Men like Van Doorn dress up as Julius Caesar or Napoléon Bonaparte. I think he's wearing a disguise."

Matt touched his forehead. "So now we're going to follow him, right?"

"From a distance. We don't want to spook him."

"Don't you need a license to do detective work in this state?" Matt shot back. "I have an idea. Why don't you follow him, and I'll go talk to his wife."

"No!" I cried, dragging my ex-husband across the street. "There's plenty of time to corner Monika later. Anyway, I'm too nervous to follow Van Doorn alone. In that disguise, who knows what kind of dive or dump he's heading for."

Matt rolled his eyes. "Clare. This is gentrified Manhattan in the twenty-first century. There are very few dives or dumps left."

Twenty-Four

"There's no way I'm going in there." Matt folded his arms over his chest and stood his ground.

"I don't want you to go in *now*," I said. "Wait until after Van Doorn leaves. Otherwise he'll see you."

But Matt shook his head. "Not now. Not ever," he replied.

Here we go again.

My ex would—and did—travel through the most primitive underbelly of the Third World in search of specialty coffee beans. But a few years back, during another crisis, he'd refused to enter the men's room in a gay bar that we had staked out. Now he refused to enter an admittedly seedy pawnshop on Manhattan's West Side.

We'd followed Neils Van Doorn on a long trek to this disreputable looking shop on the ground floor of a decrepit warehouse, a half block away from the Hudson River.

"What do you think he's doing in there?" I asked.

"Why don't you go in and find out," Matt replied. "Van

Doorn doesn't even know who you are. You might pull it off."

"Maybe I will," I declared.

From the recessed service door we'd ducked into, Matt watched with disbelief as I approached the pawnshop's front window. I paused, perusing the array of stuff on the other side of the grimy glass.

While pretending to examine the old microwave ovens, cheap stereo systems, and kitsch jewelry from the 1960s, '70s, and '80s, I watched Neil Van Doorn inside the shop. He spoke with a three-hundred-pound bald man sitting on a tall stool behind steel bars. Neils slipped the watch off his left wrist, handed it up to the fat man, who examined it closely. I moved to the next window, still pretending to shop. I found myself gazing at old military gear—web belts, rusty helmets, bayonets, a compass, and an old, olive green box with U.S. ARMY stenciled on its side in bold white letters.

It started to drizzle and I pulled my collar up. Meanwhile Neils and the fat man haggled. Finally the man behind the bars opened the cash register and counted out money, slipped the bills through a hole in the bars. I hurried back to Matt.

"I think he's pawning his watch," I said incredulously.

"That's ridiculous," Matt replied. "The Van Doorns are rich. He's been living at the Waldorf=Astoria for over a month. Do you realize what that costs?"

"I know what I saw. Anyway, his wife has all the money. Maybe she has him on a tight leash—wait, he's coming out."

I ducked into the doorway with Matt, but we were on the same side of the street. If Neils walked in our direction, there was no way he would miss seeing us. Fortunately, he paused under the shelter of the doorway.

He reached into his jacket, pulled a New York Yankee

cap out of his pocket, and slipped it over his head to protect himself from the rain. Then he stepped onto the sidewalk and moved toward us.

Remembering the cap I saw on the night Ric was mugged, I was about to say something, when Matt's hands closed around my waist. He turned me completely around and pushed my spine against the door. Then he pressed his heavy form against me, bent low and covered my mouth with his before I could say a word.

With Matt's back turned to Van Doorn, and our faces pressed together, there was no way the man would recognize either of us. Through eyelashes dampened by the light rain, I watched Neils Van Doorn pass us by without a second glance.

I gently pushed Matt's chest. He kept kissing me. "Matt," I murmured against his gently moving lips—and pushed *harder*.

"Sorry," Matt mumbled sheepishly as he finally broke off. "I saw it in a Hitchcock movie once, thought it was a nice ploy."

"Well, the last time I checked, I wasn't Ingrid Bergman, not even close. And you aren't Cary Grant, either."

"It was a nice kiss, though." His eyebrow arched. "Don't you think?"

I had no time to be annoyed. I'd recognized that Yankee cap, and I told Matt about the night Ric was mugged. The attacker had knocked me down, too, and dropped the headgear. I told Matt about catching a glimpse of it.

"Come on, Clare. There are a lot of Yankee caps in New York City. Probably a million." But even as he said it, I could tell Matt was wavering.

"It's too much of a coincidence," I insisted.

He gazed up the block, in the direction Neils had disappeared. "Maybe."

"What should we do now?" I asked.

Matt frowned, glanced over his shoulder. "I guess I'm going inside that damn pawnshop."

AS I followed Matt through the door, a buzzer went off beside my ear. Loud and piercing, the sound startled me. I heard the fat man behind the caged counter chuckle at my reaction.

Inside the pawnshop, the air was warm and close. A radiator hissed somewhere nearby, and the place smelled of mildew and old paper. With each step we took, the warped hardwood floor bumped hollowly.

The shop itself had a strange layout. There was merchandise in the window, but nothing at all in the front of the store, not even shelves. Instead, all the items were piled onto aluminum racks on the other side of the cage. The items were identified by cardboard tickets attached with strings. Prices were scrawled with black magic marker on the tags. The prices seemed absurdly low, but how did one gauge the value of a used and dented microwave oven, anyway?

The wall on the right of the room was the building's original exposed brick—highly desirable in a SoHo or NoHo loft. Oddly, the wall on the opposite side of the room was covered floor-to-ceiling by sheets of plywood painted a faded and dirty white.

There was a large square hole cut into the wood close to the ornamental tin ceiling. I would have thought it was some kind of ductwork for the heating system, but Matt warned me before we came in here to be careful—there could be a man with a loaded gun watching us through that hole right now.

"Need any help?" asked the fat man behind the cage.

He was either smiling or sneering, I couldn't tell which.

But as Matt approached the steel bars, I could see the man sizing up my ex. From Matt's wardrobe (he still wore the formalwear from the Beekman party) the clerk could guess Matt wasn't from the neighborhood.

Matt smiled through the bars at the fat man, who stared with close-set eyes over a pug nose.

"I believe a man came in here a few minutes ago," Matt began. "Blond guy. Track suit. Sneakers. Yankee cap . . ."

The fat man nodded, bored.

"So you know him?" Matt asked.

"He's been in and out for the past couple of days," the fat man replied, regarding Matt with rising interest. "Why do you want to know? Are you a cop or something?"

I sensed no hostility in the man's response, only wariness.

"Nothing like that," Matt said quickly. "Van Doorn is a friend of mine, that's all."

"That's his name? Von Doom?"

"Van Doorn," Matt corrected. "Didn't you know?"

The clerk shook his bald head. "We don't ask for names around here. Not his. Not yours. We respect our customer's privacy."

"I see. Very commendable," Matt said, humoring the man. "I appreciate your discretion in this matter, as well. You see, Van Doorn is a friend of mine. Lately I've become concerned. He seems to have fallen in with a bad crowd. He's been gambling, and I'm rather afraid Mr. Van Doorn might have accrued some debt with a local gangster."

The fat man snorted. "Do tell."

"If you could answer a few questions, I would be very appreciative." While Matt spoke, he laid a fifty-dollar bill on the counter. The fat man's meaty hand slammed down on the bill like he was swatting a fly. When he lifted his hand again the money was gone.

"What sort of business does my friend do here?"

"Look around, pal," the fat man replied. "This here is a pawnshop, and he ain't been buying."

"So he's pawning things? Valuable items?"

The man behind the counter shrugged. "A cigarette case. A money clip. Cufflinks. A couple of rings. The other day he brought in an Omega watch. Today he brought in a Rolex. Took three hundred bucks for it."

Matt pursed his lips. "And you say Van Doorn's been doing this for a week."

"Maybe longer," the big man said, showing a bit of sympathy for the first time. "Folks get in trouble—"

"I know. And they have to sell their lives away, piecemeal." Matt cleared his throat. "Roughly how much money have you paid Mr. Van Doorn for these items?"

The fat man scrunched up his face. "Hard to say, buddy. He didn't always take money. Sometimes he traded his stuff for other merchandise."

I was surprised and baffled. In this sea of junk, I could find nothing Neils Van Doorn would need or want. But Matt didn't miss a beat.

"I see you have a collection of military items in the window," he said. "Did my friend trade his jewelry for something like that? A knife, perhaps? Or something more lethal?"

The question dangled in the close air. The fat man studied Matt for a moment. My ex-husband slipped his hand into his pocket and produced another fifty dollar bill. Slowly, he slid it across the counter. But this time, when the fat man's hand came down on it, Matt didn't let go.

"What did Van Doorn buy from you?" he asked in a firm voice.

The fat man leaned close, until he was eye to eye with Matt. When he spoke, it was in a whisper. "Listen, buddy, I don't want no trouble and neither do you." The fat man's eyes drifted up to the hole in the wall. "Let's just say your friend took something a little more dangerous than a bayonet and leave it at that."

"Are you saying he bought a firearm?"

The fat man yanked the bill out of Matt's hand, leaned back. "You said your friend was in trouble, right? That he got in deep with the wrong guys, right?"

"That's right," Matt said with a nod.

"Then take my advice. Instead of buying his stuff back, just give him the money you were going to spend. Tell Von Doom to pay off the guys carrying his marker, and throw that .38 he's packing in the East River."

"Then you did sell him a gun," Matt pressed.

The fat man spread his arms wide and grinned. "Gun? Who said anything about a gun? You sure didn't hear it from me."

The man sat back in his stool, peered down his nose at Matt.

"Now beat it. You and that nervous-looking babe over there. I don't want no trouble."

Matt grabbed my hand and practically dragged me out of the pawnshop. In the street, the wind was blowing off the Hudson River, but the misty drizzle had ceased. We walked almost two blocks before Matt spoke.

"Call Quinn. Tell him what we found out."

I pulled out my cell, speed dialed his precinct number. To my surprise, I got through to him. While we headed east, back to Midtown, I filled Mike in on what we'd learned. I told him about my suspicions, about the hat Van Doorn was wearing, and how the man who mugged Ric that night was wearing the same kind of cap.

"It's a nice theory, Clare, but there are several holes in it," Mike told me.

"Holes? What holes?"

"For starters, this Neils Van Doorn has no connection to Ellie. As far as I can see, he never even met Mrs. Lassiter. And anyway, Ellie wasn't shot."

"Then why did he buy a gun?"

"Maybe he didn't," Quinn replied. "Matt was feeding cash to the guy at the pawnshop. He was probably telling tales to keep the payoff flowing. If the only proof you have is the word of that pawnshop scumbag, you really don't have much at all."

"But owning an unlicensed handgun in New York City is illegal, right?" I argued. "There's no way it could be licensed. The pawnshop clerk didn't even know Van Doorn's name!"

I could hear Quinn's sigh over the cell phone. "I'll look into it," he said.

"How about putting a tail on Van Doorn," I suggested.

"We don't have the manpower to chase everyone we think might have an illegal handgun."

I didn't know what to say to that, and I was beginning to think maybe I was on the wrong trail again.

"I'll look into it, Clare," Quinn finally said. "That's all I can promise."

I thanked him and closed the phone. When I looked up, I noticed Matt was on his own call. He spoke for a minute, and then hung up, frowning.

"I just spoke to Monika Van Doorn's personal assistant. Mrs. Van Doorn is unavailable. She's making preparations for tonight's Dutch International Halloween party."

"Great. How are we going to talk to her about Ric's decaf scheme?"

"Come on . . ."

Matt bolted for the corner of Eighth Avenue, where he frantically tried to wave down a cab.

"Where to now?" I asked.

"We're going to see my mother. She's been invited to Monika's big party tonight. We're going with her. We'll crash it if necessary."

"But, Matt, it's a costume party! Do you know what the population of this burg is? Every masquerade shop is certainly cleaned out by now. Where are we going to find costumes in New York City *on* Halloween?"

Twenty-Five

"SORRY, ma'am. We can't be going any farther. There's craziness ahead."

I could hear exasperation behind the limo driver's Caribbean lilt. His Lincoln Town Car was completely surrounded by the mob of people. There was no going forward, or turning back.

"I tried to tell you two," Matt said. "Traffic's blocked by the parade. We're lucky we got this close to Sixth Avenue."

Madame sighed. "Very well, we shall walk from here."

Matt climbed out of the Town Car. Adjusting his Zorro hat over his black mask, he circled the car and opened the door. Madame lifted her hand. With a dramatic flourish, Matt tossed the ebony cape over his shoulder, pushed back his plastic sword, and took his mother's hand. Madame's elaborate red and white gown rustled as she exited the car.

"Welcome to the Halloween parade, Your Majesty," Matt said with a deep bow.

The Queen of Hearts curtsied, eliciting a smattering of applause from the spectators, many of whom were also in costume.

Madame's outfit was suitably outrageous. Her faux Elizabethan dress, with a large scarlet heart bodice, ballooned when she stepped onto the sidewalk, and the crowd parted to give her room to pass. She wore a tasteful tiara in her upswept silver hair and long red opera gloves on her arms. A heart shaped mask with a sequin-covered handle completed her disguise.

When we'd arrived at her penthouse apartment earlier in the day, Matt and I found Madame assembling her costume. We explained our situation, and our desire to crash the party, and Madame declared she had the perfect costumes for both of us.

"Matteo shall wear the costume with which he dazzled the ladies back in his early twenties. You remember that year?" she asked Matt. "Both you and Ric went to the Dutch International party dressed as Zorro. You made the ladies swoon, and confused them, too. They never knew who they were kissing!"

"I can't believe you still have that outfit," Matt replied.

"You forget how much of an impression the pair of you made. The company's trade magazine, the *Dutch International Journal,* even published your pictures and a lengthy caption."

Matt winced. "My fifteen minutes of fame."

Madame produced the costume, sealed in Mylar like the bulk of her vintage fashion and accessories. After some adjusting for size and hasty pressing, Zorro walked the wild frontier once again.

Thankfully, my costume proved to be much simpler. Madame raided her closet for vintage fashion from the Swinging Sixties, and once again I was to play that iconic

First Lady, Jackie O, as I had when we were investigating a stock scheme a year ago. This time I was playing her in a simple yet stunning Cristóbal Balenciaga black dress in silk gazar (according to Madame).

"Cristóbal is not nearly as well remembered as Christian Dior, but I so adored his look," Madame said. "He never achieved true immortality because Balenciaga was a perfectionist who closed down his house of design in 1968 rather than see it compromised in a fashion era he did not respect."

I'd slipped into the impeccably cut black dress that ended at the knee, and stood before the full-length mirror. The dress featured the popular "sixties silhouette," but the seven-eighths sleeve that widened into a bell gave the garment an ephemeral, fairy-like air.

"That type of sleeve also flatters women of a certain age," Madame observed. "Balenciaga was a sycophant to the imperfect body. His clothing always looked elegant, even on women whose bodies did not fit the popular standards of beauty—not that it matters to you, Clare. You are as beautiful as you were in your twenties. Isn't that right, Matteo?"

Matt, who was struggling with his sash, nodded. "In my opinion, she's more beautiful."

Oh, lord. I thought. *Madame really does want to be the Queen of Hearts.*

Now, while the Queen strolled toward the Village sidewalk, Matt opened the door for me. I draped a vintage Balenciaga lace veil over my straight black wig, then slipped on the oversized Jackie O sunglasses. Wobbling on four inch heels, I stepped onto Eleventh Street.

The time was only seven forty, but the sun had set over an hour before and the Greenwich Village Halloween Parade was in full swing. The mile-long parade was the largest event of its kind in the world. Costumes weren't the only attraction. Dancers, artists, musicians, and even circus performers strutted their stuff beside floats, live bands, and street theater troupes.

Though we were only about a block away from Sixth Avenue, I couldn't see the parade beyond the crowd on the sidewalk, but I could hear the blaring music—everything from swing to rock and roll to traditional Tibetan chants. And I could make out the tops of large animal puppets bobbing up and down over the heads of the massive, costumed crowd.

The puppets didn't surprise me. It was a puppeteer who'd started the whole thing back in 1973—Ralph Lee had staged a wandering neighborhood puppet show to entertain the children of his friends and neighbors in the Village. A few hundred people attended that first event. Within eight years the simple street show had expanded into a parade and pageant that attracted over 100,000 participants. These days we were seeing as many as two million attendees, which didn't even include total spectators since almost one hundred million people watched the parade on television worldwide.

While Madame boldly pushed through the mob, I followed, and we made our way down the block to the edge of Sixth Avenue. We'd already waded through zombies, ghosts, ghouls, superheroes, politicians, and bugs (spiders, flies, and a pair of New York cockroaches), as well as inanimate objects (chairs, couches, tables, iPods, a pizza box, and a can of Campbell's soup—no doubt a homage to Andy Warhol).

Matt joined us at the curb. The Dutch International party was at a chic new eatery on Mulry Square. We were on Eleventh, and the square wasn't far—but to get there we had to cross the crazily crowded Sixth Avenue parade route.

"I guess we'll wait for a break in the march," Matt said uncertainly.

I was about to reply when I heard an electronic voice. It was robotic, like a computer's . . . and I whirled around in time to see an elderly Asian man with a box full of round plastic disks decorated with creepy creature faces.

"Robot voice, five dollar," he said, speaking into the plastic disk.

The man's voice came out the other end of the electronic device sounding like a combination of Darth Vader and Stephen Hawking.

I tapped his arm. "How does that work?" I asked.

"Robot voice, five dollar," he replied, obviously not understanding.

I gestured to the object, and the man finally nodded. He showed me a button, pressed it. Then he put the disk to his lips and spoke into it. This time no sound emerged. He held out the disk, pressed the button again.

"Robot voice, five dollar . . . Robot voice, five dollar . . ." came out of the tiny speaker.

"So it records, too . . ." I murmured. *Just like the prerecorded message Ric said he'd heard the night he was mugged. . . .*

The man pressed a second button and the machine amplified and distorted the recording. Impressed, I fumbled for my wallet. I intended to show this device to Mike Quinn, and play it for Ric, just to see his reaction.

"I'll take two," I said, handing the man a ten. He gave me two disks, one blue and one red. I slipped them into my purse and faced Madame, who was huffing impatiently.

"We'll never get across if we wait," she declared, stepping off the curb.

Matt's head was turned—a beach-bunny float carrying a

dozen young women wearing nothing but the skimpiest bikinis imaginable had caught his eye—and I tugged his arm.

"Will you control your mother!" I cried.

"Too late," Matt said. Madame was already blocking the parade. Her son shrugged and followed her into the street.

Boldly, Madame strode into the path of the marching mob. I rushed to catch up, and block anyone who might knock the frail woman to the ground. But a long chorus line of garishly clad transvestites stopped dead in their tracks to allow Madame to pass.

"After you, Your Grace," Carmen Miranda called, adjusting a headpiece made of waxed fruit.

"Jackie O, that dress is *so* divine," Tina Turner called in a voice much deeper than any recording of the Acid Queen I'd ever heard.

Jayne Mansfield whipped a white feather boa around her closely shaved throat. "Well, I never," he/she snorted.

"You don't really love Jack!" a gold lamé-clad Marilyn Monroe called in a silky voice. "Set the President free so I can have him!"

A man in Yankee pinstripes waved a plastic bat at Marilyn. "I told you to stay away from those Irish boys. They'll be the death of you," the Joe DiMaggio look-alike complained.

We passed Elizabeth Taylor, Joan Crawford, Bette Davis, and Divine. (A drag queen imitating a drag queen. Too surreal.) Finally we arrived at the opposite side of Sixth Avenue. The crowd on the sidewalk parted for Madame, and we were on our way to Mulry Square.

The Dutch International party was being held at Han Yip's Rice Shop, an upscale restaurant designed to resemble a downscale Chinese joint. The tables were green Formica, the floors covered with matching linoleum. Han Yip's menu was displayed on a huge backlit sign over the kitchen counter. Instead of showing faded photographs of chicken chow mein and pork fried rice, there were striking photographs of pan-Asian fusion delicacies beautifully presented on bone white porcelain plates, with no price less than thirty dollars.

While we waited in a short line to be admitted, Madame touched her son's arm. "I know you're angry and anxious, but I don't want you to make a scene."

Matt had taken a short nap, but he'd never recovered from his caffeine and sugar high. In fact, since he'd arrived at his mother's penthouse, he'd continued to feed his habit. Now his nerves were more jangled than ever. The veins protruded from his neck as I adjusted his black mask.

"She's right, you know," I cautioned. "You've got to cool that hot Latin blood, Zorro."

Finally we reached the door. Madame's invitation was for her and a guest—in this case her son. But she introduced me as her "amanuensis" and the man at the door let us right through.

"Why didn't you just tell him I'm your personal assistant?" I whispered.

Madame chuckled. "Did you see the look on that young man's face? Amanuensis! He probably thinks you're some sort of personal physician. There's no way he'd keep you out, for fear of my dropping dead and spoiling the fun."

The restaurant consisted of two floors connected by a wide, red carpeted staircase. The main floor was quite spacious, with the kitchen in the back. Upstairs was mostly balcony, with ornate golden railings in the shape of twisting Chinese dragons. On both the upper and lower level, two of the four walls were lined with picture windows fronted by simple fiberglass and Formica booths. Between upstairs and downstairs, there were three open bars and five buffet tables. An efficient waitstaff was also circulating among the guests with trays laden with spring rolls, wontons, spicy hot shrimp, and tiny egg rolls.

Munching away, I scanned the room for any sign of our hostess. I didn't see Monika, but I did spy her husband. I half expected to see Neils Van Doorn in his American mook disguise. Instead, he opted for a pirate of the Caribbean look—red greatcoat, knee length black leather boots, a three cornered hat and an eye patch to complete the effect.

I faced Madame again, saw a look of determination on her face. I followed her gaze to the bar, where an elderly gentleman in a Roman centurion costume stood alone, nursing a glass of wine.

"Excuse me, dear. I see someone I know."

I watched her cross the crowded room and greet the man. Although she held her mask over her face, the man recognized Madame at once. Apparently, the Queen of Hearts had already started stealing one. But then I remembered Dr. McTavish and knew she'd soon be breaking one, too, if she hadn't already.

I turned away from the animated couple, scanned the room for Matt. I spied the Zorro costume across the room at one of the open bars. Matt's back was turned to me, and he plucked a glass off the counter—some kind of cocktail.

Dammit, Matt, don't start drinking. The man hadn't slept in over twenty-four hours, and I thought he wanted to keep his wits about him (what little were left anyway) to speak candidly with Monika Van Doorn.

I pushed my way through the crowd, searching for any sign of our hostess. When I reached Matt, I touched his shoulder. The man in the Zorro costume turned, and I blinked in surprise. Hat askew, mask pulled up to his forehead, Ric Gostwick offered me a crooked grin.

Twenty-Six

"YOU'RE looking lovely tonight, Clare," Ric said. He leaned against the bar and his arm nearly slipped off the countertop. Some of his drink sloshed over the edge of the glass. He didn't seem to notice.

I pulled my sunglasses off and tucked them into my purse. "How are you doing?"

Ric shrugged.

"I'm sorry about Ellie," I told him.

"So am I." Ric's liquid brown eyes looked haunted. He drained his glass, reached for another.

"Matt told me you were interrogated by the police about her murder?"

Ric's frown turned into a sneer of contempt. "They detained me for hours, even though they had no proof that I did anything wrong. And even when they let me go, they strongly hinted I was still their 'person of interest' in Ellie's death, and told me I shouldn't leave town. Apparently, I'm off the hook for Carlos Hernandez . . . they're still looking at Matt for that one . . . No evidence, but if your police are anything like the ones that now operate where I used to live, they'll trump it up soon enough . . ."

"Ric, I'm sorry about everything that happened. I—"

"The detectives asked me a thousand questions. I answered them all with a simple question of my own. Why would I kill Ellie? Why? She was my lifeline. I needed her—"

"And yet you're also wooing our hostess, Monika Van Doorn—*Mrs*. Van Doorn."

Ric's crooked smile returned, and this time he directed his contempt at me. "Little Sister Clare . . . did you actually use the word *woo* in a conversation?" He threw back his head and laughed. "You're such a prude. Presuming to judge how an adult like me conducts his life, as if it's any business of yours. No wonder Matt . . ."

His voice trailed off, but he didn't need to complete the sentence for me to understand where he was going.

"No wonder Matt cheated on me? Is that what you were going to say?"

"You don't understand. Monika is just business. Ellie was . . . something else."

"That 'something else' doesn't include the word *love,* I noticed."

"It's beyond your understanding—"

"You mean you don't think I'm sophisticated enough to understand your motives, your actions? What you're trying to accomplish? You're probably right, Ric. But if I don't understand, others might not get it, either. Like Jerry Lassiter, Ellie's husband, who might still love his wife, the woman you were sleeping with. Like Neils Van Doorn—"

Ric snickered into his drink. "Don't worry about Neils. He's been the perfect host. Now *there's* a civilized man. My relationship with his wife doesn't bother him in the least! The man even brought me my first drink, we shared a toast with my second. He's a real man of the world, that one . . . demonstrable savoir-faire . . ."

"Is that what you call it?"

"Yes, he had this costume for me, you know? I showed up here, and didn't have one, but Neils . . . good man . . . he presented me with a package and *voila*! Inside was my Zorro . . . but . . . where is our lovely hostess?" Ric said loudly. "I really ought to give her a kiss. You know, when Monika and I first met? It was at a party like this. I was Zorro and I kissed her, and she never forgot me. Besides . . . if I don't find her, I may have to spend the night alone, and I wouldn't want to do *that* . . . my old hotel room . . . it's a crime scene now . . ."

Ric was beginning to attract attention. He lurched forward, bumping into a woman dressed as Cleopatra. I reached out to steady him and he pulled away; I was nearly jerked off my too-high heels. Ric caught me in his arms, held me close—a little too close. When I looked up, he moved to kiss me. I turned my head and felt Ric's sour breath on me as he nuzzled my throat. I laughed it off, as if his mauling was some sort of amusing prank. Gently but firmly, I pushed him away.

"I really don't believe you hurt Ellie, Ric. At first, I thought it might have been her husband, and then maybe Carlos Hernandez, but—"

"I hope Hernandez had something to do with Ellie's murder," Ric said.

"Why?"

"Because . . ." Ric's eyes glazed a bit. "Because then I've avenged her."

I blinked a moment, trying to comprehend the implications of what Ric had just said. I remembered the robot voice toy in my bag. I had planned to show it to a sober

Ric, asking if it sounded like the voice he'd heard the night of the mugging. Now I fumbled with my bag, curled my fingers around one of the robot voice discs. But I didn't pull it out. Instead, I simply pressed record.

"What did you say about Hernandez?"

Ric's expression darkened. "I said I hope the son of a bitch did have something to do with Ellie's death, because if he did, then she's avenged—"

"You're talking about cosmic justice?" I asked.

"Real justice, Clare. You like to talk about morality, but look at the world we live in. Hernandez's family and that gangster government of theirs, they stole my country, they took my family's land. We went into exile, started over. But even here in America they hound me . . . I tried to be gracious, accept the inevitable, the way things are. Then that bastard Carlos followed me out to the balcony, demanding more."

Ric's eyes met mine. For a moment I was afraid he'd realized what he'd been saying and pull back. But Ric didn't care—or he was so eaten up by it all, he had to tell someone.

"He tried to extort money from me, Clare. That's why he came without a bodyguard. He wanted no witnesses from his entourage and that was his mistake."

"His mistake?"

"The bastard wanted to be cut in. Hernandez knew there were no real legal means for his country to easily take my hybrid, so he threatened me. Unless I quietly paid half the profits on my new hybrid's earnings to him personally, he would see that the rights to my plant were tied up in international courts for decades. That was his leverage. By the time my plant was free again, other inventors would surely beat me to the marketplace. But I refused to give in to his blackmail. I spat in his face, and he attacked me. I couldn't take his abuse anymore, so I . . . I dealt with the problem. I finally fought back. I punched him hard, and he went over the balcony."

Near the end of his tirade, Ric's voice seemed to fade. Suddenly pale, he swayed on his feet.

"I'm going to the men's room . . ." he said in Spanish, and he stumbled off toward a doorway near the bar. I almost followed, but decided to check the robot voice recording instead. There was a three minute memory limit, but I'd gotten the entire confession on the digital recording. Even if the evidence wasn't admissible in court, if the detective in charge of the Hernandez murder heard the recording, they would let Matt off the hook for good.

I had to find Matt and tell him. I turned to begin my search when I noticed Monika Van Doorn finally making her grand entrance. Dressed as a regal Marie Antoinette, she descended the carpeted staircase on ribboned pumps. Bedecked in an elaborate, pearl-trimmed gown, Monika's expression was haughty under a towering, white powdered wig. In one raised hand she fluttered an ornate oriental fan. It was quite an entrance, and many of the guests applauded as she reached the bottom of the stairs.

I continued searching for Matt. Finally I saw Zorro emerge from the crowd, pushing his way toward Marie Antoinette. For a moment I thought it was Ric, since he'd been dressed as Zorro, too. But this man's stride was steady—too steady for someone who had been so drunk only a few moments before.

"So Matt's making his move," I whispered, silently wishing him luck. I knew what happened in the next few minutes might very well determine the future of the Village Blend. From my angle, I could only see Matt's broad back under his flowing Zorro cape. I wondered how he was going to broach the subject of the fraudulent beans. He must have started out friendly, because Monika turned and greeted him with a smile. That's when I saw the gun.

Zorro's hand pulled the weapon out from under his cape. Three cracks came in quick succession. Monika was thrown backwards, hitting the steps with the first shot. The second and third bullets struck her sprawled body. She must have died quickly because she didn't even raise her arms in defense.

As the echo of the shots faded, Zorro spun around and fired another shot into the ceiling. The screams of the crowd were deafening. Everyone (including yours truly) dived for the floor.

Zorro raced across the cowering mass of bodies, heading right for a door near the bar. I realized it was the same doorway that Ric had stumbled through in his Zorro costume a few minutes before!

But the gun-toting Zorro didn't make it. Another Zorro, swathed in black, dived from the second floor balcony, and landed right on top of the shooter. Both men tumbled to the ground. Tables spilled over and partygoers scattered while the two men wrestled on the linoleum.

I scrambled to my feet and raced to the middle of the restaurant, or tried to. I was fighting against a sea of costumed guests, all of them moving in the opposite direction. Finally I got a good look at the two Zorros struggling on the floor. One clutched a .38, the other held the first one's arm and was trying to shake the weapon from his grip.

The gun boomed again, shattering a picture window to my right. The glass crashed to the floor and someone cried out. On the sidewalk outside the restaurant, people shouted and screamed.

Suddenly, the armed Zorro broke free. Using his gun, he pistol-whipped the other Zorro, who clawed at the mask of his armed opponent. The mask was ripped away, and his identity finally exposed.

Neils Van Doorn waved his gun at the partygoers. "Stay back!" he cried as he made his way to the shattered ground floor window. Leveling his gun at the restaurant crowd, Van Doorn backed out through the broken frame. He was seconds away from escaping into the chaos of the Village Halloween Parade crowd.

He never even noticed Detective Mike Quinn coming up behind him—not until Mike's seasoned grip took hold of the Dutchman's wrist and twisted it behind his back. Neils howled and doubled over. The .38 tumbled to the sidewalk.

"You're under arrest for murder," Mike said.

At that moment two uniformed officers arrived to help Mike cuff the man. Sirens wailed nearby. Behind me, I heard a familiar groan and rushed to Matt's side. He sat up, yanked the mask off his face with his left hand. His eye was swollen and a welt marred his cheek from the pistol-whipping he'd received.

"Your face!" I cried.

"It's my arm that's wrecked. I would have beaten the guy if I hadn't broken it when I did my swan dive." Matt clutched his right arm with his left, hugged it close to his body. "Some swashbuckler I turned out to be. I couldn't even save Monika's life. But I thought . . . if Neils was gunning for anyone, it would have been Ric."

Suddenly Matt tried to rise. "I still have to talk to Ric. Where is he?"

"He's probably unconscious in the bathroom." I told Matt about the talk I'd had with his old friend, and the recording I'd made. "Ric was drunker than I'd ever seen him, and I'm guessing Neils slipped him some kind of a Mickey. Grain alcohol in his cocktail, or maybe a nice date-rape drug. Either way, Ric was loopy and way too chatty. Then he got sick and ran to the men's room—"

I pointed to the doorway next to the bar. "That doorway is exactly where Neils was going. I'm guessing he was going to plant the gun on Ric, make it look like Zorro Gostwick killed his wife. Then Neils would slip back into the chaos of the party, wearing his pirate gear and looking innocent."

Beads of sweat dewed Matt's upper lip. The shock was wearing off, and the pain setting in. "What about Ellie?" he asked.

"I'll bet it was Neils again, looking for Ric's cutting. Neils was already pawning his expensive things, so Monika must have cut him off financially. He was probably desperate to make his own fortune. Stealing and selling that cutting to Carlos Hernandez or someone like him would have gotten it for him. But when Neils broke into Ric's hotel room, looking for the cutting, Ellie was there. You yourself told me that Ellie and Ric had made love that afternoon—"

"I see where you're going," Matt said. "When Neils kept failing at getting his hands on the cutting, he resorted to securing a fortune the old fashioned way—by murdering his rich, cheating wife and inheriting everything before she could dump him."

"Exactly."

Mike Quinn appeared a moment later. "You were right, Clare," he told me.

I met his blue eyes. "I thought you said you didn't have the resources to follow Neils Van Doorn?"

"We don't. But I decided to follow Van Doorn during my off-duty hours. See what the guy was up to. I figured you had something on him, so . . ."

I blinked, genuinely flattered. I was about to tell him so, too, but he was glancing in another direction, toward the staircase. "I only regret I couldn't prevent the murder of Mrs. Van Doorn," he said. "Her doorman wouldn't let me into her party. I had no costume or invitation. The sidewalk outside was the best I could do."

While we spoke, more uniformed police officers arrived. I saw two of them escorting a stumbling Zorro out of the men's room.

"Hey, Mike! Look what we found. Another Zorro!"

"That's Ric Gostwick," I told Mike. "But before you cut him loose I think you'd better listen to this . . ." I pulled out the robot voice toy and handed it over.

"You're not kidding?" Mike asked, looking at the cheap plastic recorder.

"I wish I were . . ." I glanced at Ric. On many levels, my heart went out to him. "But in this country, we don't exact justice at the top of twenty-sixth floor balconies. And as trying as Matt can be, I'd really like his name *off* that Midtown detective's 'persons of interest' list."

Mike nodded. "I think you missed your calling, Cosi."

"Is that right?"

"With your nerve, you should have been a cop, a thief, or a demolitions expert."

"Well, I'm too moral to become a thief, I'm too old to get into the police academy, and I've got more interest in working with flavor profiles than plastique. Guess it'll have to stay a hobby."

"Case by case, then?"

With everything that had happened, it felt wrong to smile, but a part of me was glad I'd finally done something right.

"Yeah, Mike," I said. "Like I tell my Blend trainees. 'One customer at a time.' "

Epilogue

"WHAT'S that?" I asked Mike Quinn a week later.

It was early evening, a slow night, and Mike walked into my coffeehouse, ordering up his regular, as usual. When I put the double-tall latte on the counter, however, he pulled out an unusual looking piece of paper and dangled it right in front of my nose.

"This is a BOLO, Cosi. And it's got your name on it, and your license plate number."

"*What* is it?"

"A 'be on the lookout'—for your red Honda."

"It's not a traffic summons?"

"Someone driving your car went through a dead stop red light in Brooklyn last week, sped recklessly down Court Street, refused to pull over, and evaded a police chase. So, *please* tell me that your car was stolen."

"It wasn't."

"You're guilty of all this?"

"I can explain."

Mike reached behind him, pulled out his handcuffs, and slapped them down on the coffee bar. "These would be going around your wrists if I hadn't seen this issued last week and claimed it for follow up."

"You're burying the violation?"

"You're lucky you live in my precinct. I'll talk to the Brooklyn officer who's charging you, get him to reduce it to a traffic ticket. But I'm warning you right now, you're going to owe me."

"Well, I could give you free lattes for a month, but I don't know, Mike . . ." I picked up the handcuffs. "It seems to me I could do a whole lot worse than having you use these on me."

Mike smiled—a rare occurrence. "I told you, Cosi. You owe me. But the cuffs are Stage Five."

"And where are we?"

He plucked the cuffs from my hands and put them back on his belt. "Stage One."

"Which is?"

"Dinner and a movie."

My eyes widened. It was the first real date he'd ever proposed. "When?"

"How about every Saturday night for the foreseeable future?"

I laughed. "What if there are no good movies playing?"

The detective took a long, satisfying sip of his latte. "I think we'll come up with something else to occupy our time. Don't you?"

"Oh, sure, let's see . . ." I scratched my head. "There's Yahtzee, Scrabble, Crazy 8s . . ."

Mike glanced around the coffee bar. "So where's Zorro?"

"Uptown. His girlfriend's taken him in. Since his arm's in a cast, she's having a high time playing nursemaid. Believe me, he's living like a prince. I actually think they're getting serious . . . and speaking of serious. Any word yet from the district attorney's office?"

Mike nodded. "No plea deal. Van Doorn's lawyered up pretty well, and he doesn't want to admit his guilt, so he's going all the way to trial. But old Neils is going to have a rough time of it. We've got DNA evidence nailing him to Ellie's murder, a security camera showing him leaving the V Hotel near the time of death, not to mention all those witnesses to the Halloween shooting of his wife. There's more than enough for a conviction on something . . . Gostwick, as you know, was another story."

"I know . . ."

In the end, Ric wasn't a stone-cold sociopath. He may have been a serial cheater, but he didn't really want to see his oldest friend sent up for a murder he didn't commit. When the police played him my recording, Ric officially confessed. The DA worked out a manslaughter charge of eight years, and he would likely get out in four or less for good behavior.

As for his magic beans, they were contractually in the possession of the Village Blend. If I let Matt's kiosks have them all, which I intended to, the Gostwick Estate Reserve Decaf would easily last the year. We'd have a good chance of turning those floundering kiosks around . . . and, in the meantime, Matt already found a horticultural consultant for Ric's family, to help them keep the hybrid crops producing—Norbert Usher.

Ellie's young assistant at the Botanic Garden was quite eager and knowledgeable, as it turned out, and he'd learned plenty from working with Ellie and Ric over the last eight months. The Gostwick family was only too happy to have him come down to Brazil and work in their nursery and on their farm.

The Dutch International contract for those fake Gostwick

Estate decaffeinated beans was voided, and Matt was going to see what he could do to help Ric's family expand legitimately, albeit slowly.

Ric admitted that his fraud scheme with the late Monika Van Doorn's company was a way for him to purchase more land and quickly expand his crops. He'd been a little too eager to restore his family's fortune to what it once had been . . . but all of that was behind us now.

As for my baristas, things were working out well for them, too, although not for me. Gardner had gotten so many solo piano gigs from his single appearance at the Beekman that I was now super short-staffed, and working 24/7 while still looking for good trainee baristas.

Meanwhile, Dante was very close to getting a second gallery show, Esther was after me to hold a Poetry Slam night at the Blend, and Tucker was auditioning for an Off-Off-Broadway revival of *The Importance of Being Earnest in the Twenty-First Century* . . . or, at least, that was the production's working title.

Joy and I were back on civil terms. We agreed to call a truce in our battle over Tommy Keitel. I told Joy (again) that I loved her, and I didn't want to see her hurt. She reiterated her intention to continue her relationship with fiftysomething Tommy, although she did at least acknowledge my worries, and (in what I saw as an encouraging sign of growing maturity) said she was glad to know I'd be there to catch her *if* she ever fell. And we'd left it at that.

All in all, it had been a rather trying week, and I figured I'd earned a coffee break. Reaching toward the burr grinder, my hand shifted to the one with the green tape. A decaffeinated espresso actually sounded like a nice, calming alternative for the night.

I took a seat beside Mike at the bar. "So are you about

ready to accept some help furnishing that apartment of yours?"

"Yeah . . . that would be nice. The mattress on the floor currently has all the charm of Sing-Sing solitary."

"I'll tell you what else would be nice."

"What?"

I turned on my stool, reached my hands around his waist, grabbed the cuffs again. "Jumping forward on a few of your 'stages' . . ."

"Oh, no, Cosi. You're on my watch now . . ." He pulled my wrists away from his belt, repositioning them around his neck. "And I'm a procedures kind of guy. I don't skip stages. That's what I tell my rookies, you know?"

I arched an eyebrow at that. "First things first?"

"Or second," he whispered. Then his smiling lips covered mine; and although they kept moving, they finally stopped talking.

Recipes & Tips From the Village Blend

Visit Cleo Coyle's virtual Village Blend
at www.CoffeehouseMystery.com
for more coffee tips, trivia, and recipes.

Buzzkill

While coffee is my business, everyone has their threshold for caffeine consumption. If you're worried about ingesting too much, try replacing one or more of your regular daily cups of coffee with decaf. Or try ordering a cup that's half decaf and half regular. Remember a demitasse of espresso has less caffeine than a regular cup of your typical Colombian morning brew, and be aware of what foods and beverages have caffeine besides your favorite cuppa Joe. Here's a short list . . .

Starbucks House Blend (16 oz.)	223 mgs.*
Dunkin' Donuts House Blend (16 oz.)	174 mgs.*
7-Eleven House Blend (16 oz.)	141 mgs.*
Espresso (2 oz.)	50–100 mgs.
Caffeinated soda (12 oz. can)	38–45 mgs.
Tea (6 oz./3-minute steep)	40–50 mgs.
Dark chocolate (1 oz.)	20 mgs.
Milk chocolate (1 oz.)	6 mgs.
Chocolate milk (6 oz.)	4 mgs.

Coffee Milk

Coffee Milk is a seventy-year-old tradition in Rhode Island, and the official state drink. Our barista Dante Silva explained to me that it's very much like a glass of chocolate milk, except the syrup used is coffee flavored instead of chocolate flavored. The origins of the drink is believed to be with the Italian immigrants who settled in the region. At the Village Blend, many of our customers order it made with steamed milk, much like a hot cocoa.

---

*Source: *Wall Street Journal,* April 13, 2004

2 tablespoons of sweetened coffee syrup (regular or decaf)
8 ounce glass of milk

Mix together and enjoy cold or warmed.

Homemade Coffee Syrup

If you wish to make your own coffee syrup, there's the traditional way and a modern method. I would recommend the newer recipe, but if you're adventurous and have a percolator on your stove, give old school a go.

COFFEE SYRUP THE MODERN WAY

Step 1 – Make super-strength coffee by brewing coffee (regular or decaf) at a ratio of 1 cup—yes *cup*—of ground coffee to 16 ounces cold water.
Step 2 – In a medium saucepan, combine 1 cup of sugar with 1 cup of super-strength coffee.
Step 3 – Bring to a boil, stirring constantly to dissolve sugar.
Step 4 – Lower heat and simmer for about three minutes, stirring often.
Step 5 – Let cool and refrigerate. This method will yield one cup of thick syrup.

Coffee syrup can be stored in the refrigerator, in a tightly sealed container, for up to one month.

COFFEE SYRUP THE TRADITIONAL WAY

Step 1 – Percolate one pot of coffee (regular or decaf), then discard the grounds.
Step 2 – Add fresh grounds (regular or decaf), percolate again, using the coffee as liquid instead of fresh water.
Step 3 – Do this three times.
Step 4 – Measure the finished coffee mixture. (The amount may vary.) Combine sugar and coffee in a medium saucepan at a ratio of 1 cup of sugar for every 2 cups of coffee. Heat until boiling and sugar is dissolved, stirring constantly.

Italian Sesame Cookies

This sophisticated cookie has just a slightly sweet flavor. When you want your beverage to be the star—be it coffee, tea, or wine—this is a nice, subtle accompaniment whether before or after dinner, and it pairs beautifully with most cheeses.

This recipe makes about 18 cookies.

½ cup butter
¼ cup sugar
¼ cup brown sugar
2 eggs
2 teaspoons vanilla
2 cups flour

2 teaspoons baking powder
¼ teaspoon salt
Milk
1 cup sesame seeds

Mix flour, baking powder, and salt in a bowl and set aside. In a separate bowl, cream the butter, white sugar, and brown sugar, then add the eggs and vanilla and blend well with an electric mixer. Gradually add the dry ingredients to the wet ingredients, blending into a rough dough. Turn out the dough onto a floured flat surface and knead 1 to 2 minutes until the dough is smooth.

Now you can begin to break off small pieces of dough and shape them with your hands into small logs about 2 inches long and 1 inch thick. Dip the logs in milk and roll in sesame seeds. Place the cookies on the cookie sheet at least 2 inches apart. Use a non-stick pan or try parchment paper, otherwise make sure your pan is well greased so the cookies won't stick. Bake in a 350° F. oven for 20 minutes.

Optional: For a richer, sweeter variation, try dipping half of this small cookie in melted milk or dark chocolate. Let cool before serving.

Carne Con Café "Matt's Ragout"

Matt was actually a pretty good cook during our marriage. Those rare times he was home more than two days together, he taught me that coffee could be used as a meat tenderizer or as a marinade. In this dish, it acts as an earthy flavor enhancer. This recipe is actually a variation of a traditional Mayan dish from El Salvador that Matteo enjoyed. He recreated it for me in our kitchen one afternoon.

This recipe makes about eight servings.

2 to 4 tablespoons vegetable or corn oil (cover bottom of pan)
2½ to 3 pounds beef chuck, cubed
3 cups diced sweet onion
1 cup sliced red bell peppers
1 cup poblano chile peppers
1 cup chopped ripe tomatoes
6 garlic cloves, crushed
2½ cups strong coffee
6 oz. tomato sauce
8 small carrots, halved
¼ cup tomato catsup (optional)
salt and pepper to taste

Heat the oil and brown the meat over moderate heat, turning often. Add the onions, peppers, garlic, tomatoes, tomato sauce. Mix and bring to a boil, add the coffee and catsup (optional). Cover the pan and continue to cook over a low heat until meat is tender—approximately two hours. Stir often. Peel and halve the carrots and add to the pot in the last twenty to thirty minutes, cook until carrots are tender. The resulting sauce will be thick and bright and quite savory. It can be served as a stew with crusty bread or ladled over rice. You might even try it tossed with rigatoni or penne.

No Biggee Coffee Cake

Here's a simple recipe for a quick, delicious coffee cake, from one of my old "In the Kitchen with Clare" columns . . .

3/4 cup sugar
1/4 cup butter (1/2 stick)
1 egg, beaten
1/2 cup milk
1-1/2 cup flour (sifted)
2 teaspoons baking powder
1/2 teaspoon salt

STREUSEL INGREDIENTS

5 tablespoons butter
1 cup brown sugar
4 tablespoons flour
2 teaspoons cinnamon

Make the cake batter: Cream the sugar and butter together. Add the egg and milk, and mix with an electric mixer until blended. Dump in the sifted flour, baking powder, and salt. Mix together until a smooth batter forms, but be careful not to overmix.

Now make the streusel filling and topping: Melt the butter over low heat in a saucepan. Add the flour, brown sugar, and cinnamon. Mix well, but don't worry if the mixture is lumpy.

Assemble your coffee cake: Grease an 8×8 square pan, pour half the cake batter. Note that the batter will be a little doughy. Use a rubber spatula to spread batter into pan corners. Spoon half your streusel filling over the batter. Now cover the filling with the remaining cake batter and top with the rest of your streusel. Bake at 375° F. for 25 to 30 minutes. Cool and cut into squares.

PB and Nutella Sandwich

Peanut butter
*Nutella**
2 slices of bread

In this sandwich, the jelly in your PB&J is replaced with Nutella. What is Nutella? It's a wonderful hazelnut chocolate spread that originated in Italy, where the hazelnut is king. Most major American grocery stores now carry it. Look for the jar in the peanut butter aisle. And speaking of peanut butter, if you actually need the recipe, here it is:

Spread peanut butter on one slice of bread. Spread Nutella on the other. Put the slices together and enjoy. (Hey, didn't somebody once say peanut butter and chocolate go well together?)

I also enjoy Nutella on crackers, bread, and fruit slices, especially bananas.

---

*Helpful hint: never refrigerate Nutella, even after opening. Treat it like peanut butter and keep it in your kitchen cabinet or pantry.

Clare's Cappuccino Muffins

The sour cream is the secret to making these muffins taste rich and delicious. Pair them in the morning with your favorite Breakfast Blend, a medium roast Columbian blend, or a cappuccino.

This recipe makes 12 big muffins.

2 cups sifted flour
1 tablespoon baking powder
1 teaspoon baking soda
½ cup unsweetened cocoa powder
2 tablespoons darkly roasted ground coffee beans
½ teaspoon salt
½ cup semi-sweet chocolate chips
1 cup finely chopped hazelnut or almonds
1 teaspoon orange zest minced
½ cup (1 stick) butter softened
½ cup sugar
½ cup brown sugar
1 cup sour cream
¾ cup whole milk
2 eggs
¼ cup espresso or double strength drip coffee (cooled)
Paper muffin cup liners

Preheat oven to 375° F. Sift flour and mix with the dry ingredients including the cocoa, chocolate chips, nuts, and orange zest. Set aside. Using an electric mixer, mix together the butter, sugars, sour cream, milk, eggs, and coffee. Fold in dry ingredients with a spoon, just until moistened and smooth (don't over mix). Place paper liners in 12 muffin cups and bake approximately 20 to 25 minutes, until a knife inserted in muffin comes out clean.

SWEET FROTHY TOP

2 cups powdered sugar
1 teaspoon vanilla extract
2 tablespoons milk
½ stick butter

After the muffins have cooled, whip ½ stick butter with an electric mixer. Add powdered sugar, vanilla, and milk. Mix together until well blended into a smooth icing. Lightly smooth glaze on top of cappuccino muffins.

Don't Miss the Next
Coffeehouse Mystery

FRENCH PRESSED

Chef Tommy Keitel runs Solange, one of New York's hottest French restaurants, and Clare Cosi's daughter, Joy, has become his favorite intern—in more ways than one. When Tommy's competitive kitchen literally turns cutthroat, Clare worries her daughter may be in real danger. Resolved to spy on Joy's workplace, Clare makes a deal to micro-roast and French press exclusive blends for Tommy, a man she wouldn't mind seeing roasted and pressed himself. Then Tommy ends up dead, and it's Joy who lands in hot water with the NYPD. To clear her daughter of the crime, Clare knows she must catch the real killer, which is why she's determined to solve this Coffeehouse Mystery, even if it leads to a bitter end.